Prince(ss)
A fair(l)y (odd) tale

Sara Gravatt-Wimsatt

Jenn and Alyse-thank you so much for being my test readers. I appreciate all the time and effort you put into reading my story and giving me feedback to help make it the best work it could be.

Jamie-thank you for not only being my test reader, but also my cheerleader and a great source of support. I truly appreciate your passion for my story and the way you've helped me to believe in its value.

Joe-thank you so much for helping to bring my characters to life. You were able to create something marvelous in a short amount of time, and you were flexible and responsive to my feedback. You made my cover magical!

Augustine Jayne, my wife, my editor, my biggest fan-I love you so much, and could not have finished this novel without your feedback and support. I truly appreciate you-all the love and support you give to me, and how you make my world beautiful every day.

LGBTQ+ fantasy fans who've spent their lives reading fantasy novels and wishing there could be more (any?) people like themselves in their favorite stories-I see you. I understand you. This story is for you.

This is the story of Julian Stoneshire, the prince of a land whose name has been lost to the years. It is also the story of Liliana Almwick, aged twenty-six, a noblewoman living in that same kingdom. In this tale one of them will become a princess—but, it isn't the person you might expect it to be.

And what do I mean by saying that, you might ask? Well, I suppose you'll just have to read the story and find out for yourself.

1.

Prince Julian had just turned twenty-five, and he was not happy about it.

It was not the age itself that bothered him, really, but rather the fact that his parents expected him to wed at that age, and he was sorely opposed to marrying while still so young and handsome. Julian had delicate features, shoulder-length brown hair, and large hazel eyes ringed by thick lashes, and he was slender in build and free of the abhorrent thick hair on face, limb, and trunk that most men were plagued with. He wished he was a bit taller but apart from this quite liked his appearance—and many women did as well.

That was one reason why he had dreaded the coming of twenty-five—he was not ready to marry and to, consequently, stop gallivanting from one girl to another. His life was a series of pleasant clandestine meetings: a tryst with a chambermaid in a rarely used castle bedchamber; an encounter in the kitchen with the baker's daughter; a stolen moment with a flower-seller in the palace gardens. In all there were half a dozen women with whom he regularly shared enjoyable kisses and caresses (and, occasionally, more indecent acts), and he was not yet willing to give up all this entertainment.

The other reason why he had feared the coming of his twenty-fifth year was because he knew he would have to choose his mate from among the daughters of the wealthy landowners in his kingdom and, frankly, did not feel there was much stock to choose from. Many of the women were physically lovely and many were clever or talented, but, unfortunately, beauty and intelligence seemed to rarely coexist in a single person. When Julian dallied with a maid or flower-seller, he did not have to worry about conversing with them and so could choose whoever caught his fancy— but a wife? He would surely have to speak with her, and he hated the thought of spending the rest of his life with someone possessing a radiant face and a head full of foolishness.

He had at times considered flinging himself from a palace tower on the final day of his twenty-fourth year so that he might avoid having to make the dreaded decision, but he unfortunately enjoyed living too much to do away with himself. So now it was his twenty-fifth birthday, and he knew that he would have to spend the afternoon meeting eligible maidens in hopes of finding one he could stomach enough to marry.

Julian rose from bed, sighing, and went to his closet to choose an outfit for the day. He viewed the assortment of garments shelved within and briefly considered picking something drab to wear—for perhaps then all the maidens would pass him over and he could wait another week, month, or year before having to select a mate? He knew his thoughts were unreasonable, though, for, when he checked himself in the mirror, he found that his skin still glowed, his eyes still sparkled, and he was just far too extraordinary to be ignored. He resignedly chose a royal purple tunic and black velvet breeches and put them on, then, glumly acknowledging that he was still beautiful, he headed out of his chamber and down the stairs to his matrimonial doom.

Liliana Almwick had also risen from bed sighing that morning, for she knew the day had come when she must go to the palace to compete for Prince Stoneshire's hand.

Liliana's mother, the Lady Satiana Almwick, had always

been fiercely supportive of her daughter, but was recommending that she participate in the farce because the family's neighbor, Lord Gruntheon, was slowly encroaching upon their lands. The Lady was hoping that, should an allegiance form between the prince and Liliana, Gruntheon would stop his invasions, but she had no expectations of success and was not pressing her daughter to do anything more than attend the event.

Despite knowing this, Liliana still dreaded the day for many reasons, the first being that she hated having to compete with other women for a man as if he were a piece of meat and they were slavering beasts trying to satiate themselves; it felt discomfiting and degrading. Another was that, despite her being able to acknowledge to herself that she was attractive in some ways—her thick copper-colored hair, soft blue eyes, striking facial features, and voluptuous figure had gotten her enough unwanted attention over the years—she was also aware that she did not really look the part of a princess.

Liliana was as tall as many men, and was broad-shouldered, well-muscled, and more comfortable with a sword than with a hand fan. Her father and elder siblings, a brother and sister, had died in a carriage accident when she was very young, so from an early age she had assisted her mother with both traditionally feminine and typically masculine duties. Twenty-odd years of this had left her strong and work-hardened, not at all what she believed others thought a future queen should be like. The fact that she had poor eyesight and wore spectacles, which she kept secured with a chain for fear of losing them, further cemented this in her mind, and, though she understood she was being irrational, she worried she might be laughed out of the castle for attempting to create a union with the prince.

The greatest reason why Liliana was not looking forward to the day, though, was that, simply put, she did not think she would be able to love the prince even if he did ask her to marry him, and she was a person who could not abide the thought of marrying for any reason other than for love. She knew her parents had loved each other passionately, and she hoped to have a similar love of her own one day—and doubted anything of the kind would develop between herself and Prince Julian.

It was not that she did not feel attraction toward the prince—out of all the men in the kingdom he was the prettiest, and, when she was being fully honest with herself, she had to admit that she did not find most men attractive—but he seemed to lack in personality what he possessed in physical beauty. He was haughty, put on superior airs, and consistently treated others poorly. His dalliances with the palace staff were known far and wide, and Liliana could not help blanching in distaste when she thought of how women seemed so expendable to him.

She knew, though, that, if a marital alliance was forged, it would likely preserve her family's lands...so she reluctantly put on her finest gown and bravest face, then she joined Lady Almwick in their carriage and they set off for the palace.

***

After a long and sumptuous breakfast filled with Julian's complaints that he was too young to settle down and should put off marriage for at least another ten years—all of which fell on the unhearing ears of his parents, who had foreseen his grumbling and had stuffed them with beeswax—he begrudgingly agreed to meet with the ladies seeking his hand. Removing the wax, the king thanked Julian for his cooperation and reminded him that it was important for him to marry not only to carry on the royal lineage but to also acquire realty for the family, as the properties of those who married into it were counted as "royal lands."

The queen, unplugging her own ears, added that she was eager to have a grandchild to fawn over and so hoped Julian would find a suitable wife and quickly begin having children. This reminded him that he certainly did not want to wed a woman like her, as it seemed her most positive quality was the lovely face that he had been fortunate enough to inherit from her. He certainly did not desire a wife who was overly reliant upon him—not for any charitable reason, really, but mostly because he hoped to still have considerable freedom (especially of the carnal variety) after he married.

His parents led him down the corridor connecting the dining room to the great hall, and, when the large double doors were thrown open, he found himself faced with a room full of women. To his horror, he estimated that there were at least fifty there vying for his affections; to his greater horror, he felt that he already knew most of them and that they were a group of boors and bores. He recognized Rosemary Redmount, a pretty golden-haired girl who behaved like a ten-year-old and had the most infuriating childlike voice; Paulette Ourviere, who was good with horses and could hold meaningful conversations but had a mustache thicker than his after he had not shaven for a week; Annielle Grouse, whose figure had ventured beyond pleasingly plump into "at constant risk of toppling over due to ankle strain" territory. He expelled a disappointed groan, for the lot was even worse than he had expected.

He scanned the hall, dismayed eyes lighting upon each woman, until he noticed one that he could not place sitting in a far corner of the room. She seemed almost as reluctant to be a part of the proceedings as he was, for, while all the other women were scrambling for his attention, she appeared hesitant to interact with him. This intrigued him, so he looked her over, trying to get her measure.

She was about his age and had a distinctively attractive face framed by waves of copper-colored hair, and her figure, clad in a green gown, curved in an appealing manner. Her eyes really drew his gaze, though; an extraordinary shade of blue, they sparkled with an intelligence and willfulness that was clearly visible through her thick spectacles...and also clearly conveyed her uneasiness. Julian found himself feeling oddly pleased that the woman seemed so unnerved by the ordeal, and he decided that he might find more entertainment at the party than he had expected to by perhaps unnerving her further.

The women were lined up so the prince might speak with each of them, and the fiery-haired stranger positioned herself near the end of the line, seemingly in hopes of avoiding a conversation with him. This irked Julian, and he was tempted to start at the end just to confound her, but, after some consideration, he decided to follow convention and began at the front of it. Rosemary, as shrill and insistent as usual, was waiting for him there. "Greetings, my Lord!" she trilled. "I hope this pleasant day finds you well."

"I was well," he responded coldly, "until your grating voice echoed through my ears. You have no chance with me, Rosemary. You are dismissed."

As expected, the girl burst into tears, and she was ushered away by her equally annoying mother, who cast Julian a withering look as she steered her daughter out of the room. The other women responded to this scene either by glancing around uneasily or smiling at their increased chances of winning him—except for the copper-head, who wrinkled her nose in disdain. Julian felt a thrill of excitement course through him. *Oh, she wants to be offended, does she? Well then, I'm sure I can manage to properly offend her.*

The next few girls were unmemorable and were

dismissed with little fanfare, but then came Paulette, who stuck her hand out confidently. "It's a pleasure to see you, my Lord. I trust you've been well?"

Julian shook the proffered hand, then said loudly, "Paulette, you've always been enjoyable to speak with, and we've had many good times riding together, but kissing you would be like kissing one of the pages due to the caterpillar above your upper lip. You are dismissed." The color drained from Paulette's face, and Julian could see her struggling to hold back tears as she stiffly left the room.

He peered at the red-haired woman and, finding that she was trying to suppress a look of outrage, felt pleased with himself. It was obvious she thought he was awful, and, frankly, he enjoyed seeing her reactions and wondered how she might next respond. He would find out soon enough, for Annielle succeeded Pauline in line; her pale face shone with sweat, her forehead creased in worry, her limbs trembled. Julian pitied her, for it was clear that the shy girl's piggish, gold-hungry father had forced her to come to the event, but this did not stop him from saying, "Annielle, it's so nice to see you! I am always glad to look upon you, for, whenever I do, I'm reminded of the lovely cows we keep in the royal barn. However, as I am not seeking to marry one of them, you are dismissed."

As Annielle shuffled away, face red with shame, tears streaming down her cheeks, Julian heard a horrified yelp. Glancing at the end of the line, he was delighted to find that the high-and-mighty copper-head openly wore a look of disgust. He knew it was time to strike, and so he sauntered over to the woman, stopping directly in front of her. "It seems the things I've been saying have displeased you. Tell me, who are you?"

Startled at being singled out, the stranger, relaxing her expression, said, "My Lord, I am Liliana Almwick, daughter of Satiana Almwick, a landowner in this kingdom. I have come today to seek your hand in marriage."

"If that's so, then why do you seem so disenchanted whenever I speak?"

"To be honest, my Lord, I wasn't expecting you to be so cruel to the disfavored ladies. If I had known you would treat them in this manner I wouldn't have come today, for I am only attracted to men who behave honorably toward women."

Several attendees gasped, and Julian, stepping closer to Liliana, sized up her appearance. He noted that, for a woman, she was exceedingly tall—a few inches taller than himself—and was strong and well-muscled, and so he decided to remark on this in hopes of provoking a reaction. "Hmm. As you seem to be a giantess, shouldn't you be in a forest felling trees with your bare hands rather than attempting to win the heart of a dashing prince?"

Many of the women tittered, and Julian awaited Liliana's response, hoping she would grow ashamed or tearful like the other women had. To his surprise, she stood resolute and retorted, "I have heard it said that short men often feel deficient, and so make hurtful comments to make themselves feel bigger. I can now say that I've found proof that this is indeed the truth."

As the words left her lips, she immediately blanched, and her mother, who had been warily watching the interaction from the side of the room, moaned, for she knew this level of impertinence might result in her daughter's imprisonment. Julian, however, was not upset, for he had never had a woman speak to him in this manner before and it was, frankly, more than a little exciting. This Liliana did not appear to be wife material due to her towering stature and obvious contempt for him...but, the more distaste she showed for him, the more attracted he was to her. He was, after all, a man accustomed to getting what he wanted, and he always desired what he could not have.

Moving in close to her, he whispered, "You've made it

clear that you're not terribly fond of me, and I, frankly, do not think you're marriageable...but I've never had a woman say such things to me and, to be honest, I'm finding my interest aroused by the thought of dallying with someone who so obviously dislikes me. What would you say to our parting ways now and, once this event is over, meeting in a private location to see if that dislike translates into different passions flaring between us?"

He leaned back to find her face stonier than ever, and she hissed, "I would say that I wouldn't give you another minute of my time, even if you paid me."

She stalked toward the door, her mother following behind her, but, before she could leave, Julian called after her, "I was actually going to suggest payment! It's such a shame you're not interested." As usual, he could not resist getting in the last word.

2.

Liliana held her tongue while still inside the palace, but, once she and her mother had mounted their carriage, she exploded. "What a disgusting, uncouth pig!" she cried, pounding a fist on her seat. "He has the audacity to be so barbarous to those women, who did nothing to deserve such treatment, and then, upon noticing my distaste for his behavior, tries first to cut me down then to transmute my anger into carnal passion? I love and respect you, Mother, but I knew I shouldn't have vied for his hand. I would never have gone through with it had I not known how desperately you'd hoped the union would save us from Gruntheon. I had a feeling a man so full of himself would have no idea how to be kind or courteous."

She spent almost the entirety of their drive home ranting about the prince's behavior—his history of dallying with women and casting them aside once he tired of them, his dishonorable interactions with the castle help, his cruel treatment of ladies he deemed unattractive—before leaning back and letting out a deep sigh. "He's had affairs with so many women that it's only predictable he should be unaware of how they truly feel, and I doubt he would care even if he was told. What a foolish waste of time."

Lady Almwick, who had patiently listened to Liliana's tirade, spoke once her daughter had finished, a smirk playing upon her lips. "It's too bad he's such a prat, for he's quite pleasing to look at, isn't he?" Liliana bolted upright in her seat, sputtering, face crimson, and, though her mother assured her she was merely baiting her, she asserted that it was a shame a man so beautiful should seemingly have an ugly soul. The pair lapsed into silence, and the Lady appeared deep in thought, though what about Liliana had not the slightest clue.

Soon a broad grin graced Satiana Almwick's face and her eyes sparkled with mischievous glee—and this made Liliana nervous, for, whenever her mother's eyes twinkled like that, she was generally plotting an escapade that was likely to not only get her into trouble but to also drag her daughter into it. "He really has no idea what it's like to be a woman," the Lady said. "Perhaps...we can teach him what it's like. Perhaps it's something he needs to be taught." She took her eyes off the road for a moment to look at Liliana, who was staring at her apprehensively. "I've always been skilled at...certain arts. Maybe it's time for me to once more use my talents for a greater purpose."

Liliana was equal measures thrilled and terrified by her mother's words, for she knew which "arts" the Lady spoke of. During her younger years, Satiana Almwick had been renowned as a sorceress who used magic to benefit others, but, since the passing of her husband and children, she had all but given it up—she always said that, if she could not use it to restore the lives of her beloveds, then what good was it? She had, to her daughter's knowledge, breached her promise to abstain from magic use only a handful of times during the many years since the accident, and her deciding to do so now made Liliana very uneasy. She wondered, *What, exactly, does my mother have in mind?*

Upon their arrival home, after securing the horses Lady Almwick rushed into the house, gown billowing behind her, and Liliana hastily followed her as she ran through the entry hall, up the winding staircase, and into the area they used as a study. She ran to a bookshelf, grabbed a large book bound in cracked leather, and flipped through its pages while her daughter watched uncertainly. All of a sudden, her face lit up. "Here it is, just the thing I was looking for: The Spell of Transmutation."

Liliana trembled when she heard this, for she knew the Spell of Transmutation, when properly executed, had the power to transform a man into a woman or woman into a man and to keep them that way until the one who cast it broke it; it did not change much about a person, did not make the tall short or the bulky thin, merely changed their sex. It seemed her mother truly did mean to teach the prince a lesson, likely the most serious one he had ever been taught. She found herself wondering if she should try to convince the Lady otherwise—surely no one deserved to have their gender abruptly altered for no clear reason, no matter how much of a swine they might be?—but then she remembered how the Grouse girl's face had crumpled into tears when the prince insulted her and her pity for him quickly dissipated.

Lady Almwick had Liliana fetch six black candles and, while she did this, burned a strange-smelling powder in a glass bowl containing the wax figure of a man. Once the Lady had been given the candles, she set each in a candlestick and placed them into a hexagon around the vessel. The women sat next to the bowl and waited for night to fall, then the Lady lit each candle, filling the room with a soft glow. She resumed her place next to Liliana, took her by the hand, and recited the words of the spell:

Oh, Mother of Us All, Mother of Night,
I beg you that my will be done.
Please grant to me a simple wish,
Create me daughter from a son.
Take manly limbs and make them soft,
Take his deep voice and make it sweet.

I beseech you, make this person
Change in form from head to feet.
Let this be so, and let it stay
This way until I call again
And ask for you to lift this curse
And let him walk once more as man.
I beseech thee, hear my plea,
Please transform Prince Julian.

After finishing the incantation, Lady Almwick blew the candles out one by one until the room was shrouded in darkness. She told Liliana, "Close your eyes, and think about Prince Julian. Create an image of him in your mind and send it to the Mother Goddess so that she may grant our request." Liliana shut her eyes, focused inward, and recalled the prince as he had been earlier that day—how handsome he had appeared, and how ugly he had acted. Anger once more burned in her brain, and she sent the vision of him out of her mind and into the unknown, hopefully into the realm of the Mother Goddess.

She opened her eyes to find that her mother had lit one of the candles and was holding it over the glass bowl. When Liliana looked into the vessel, she saw the masculine figure had changed into a feminine one. "I believe the spell has worked," said the Lady, "and we shall find out for certain soon enough."

"W-what? Whatever do you mean, Mother?"

"Although the physical change alone will move Prince Julian toward learning his lesson, he will also need guidance to find the right path. We will make sure he faces the trials he needs to, so that he really understands the challenges women face. He will learn how strong we can be—how strong *he* can be as one of us—and will then hopefully acknowledge our worth. We must also make sure he accomplishes what he needs to, as we do not want him to suffer unduly. Once he has completed the task, I can restore him to his male form."

"I think...I know who might best help us to ensure he receives the assistance he requires," she finished with a wink, and Liliana found herself completely in thrall to her mother in spite of her reservations, willing to help her enact whatever plan she had in mind, for she had a feeling that, no matter her role in it, the exploit would be the greatest she had ever known.

***

Prince Julian had retired to bed early that evening, for he was exhausted from his day of interacting with swooning maidens. After he had driven away the haughty copper-head the remainder of the proceedings had been uneventful, and he was grateful when the festivities ended so he could retire to his bedchamber to think.

While pondering the circumstances of the day, he grew aware of but was loath to admit that the only person he had felt any spark of attraction toward had been the curmudgeon, Liliana Almwick, and that this was likely just the result of incompatible passions flaring. As he had suspected, he would unfortunately have to choose for his bride a woman palatable enough to have a few children with but who would not mind if he continued his dalliances so long as she was Queen. He believed he might settle for Falina Sedgwick, an icy fair-haired beauty whose motivations to wed him were far from noble but who would likely ignore any infidelities so long as she had coins to count.

Try as he might, though, he could not keep Liliana Almwick from popping into his mind. He found that, in some small way, he regretted how their interaction had gone—how he had outraged her into leaving the palace and, as a result, had destroyed his chances of getting to know the one person who was both pleasant to look at and seemed to have a mind more than equal to his own. Julian was a stranger to feeling remorse and it irritated and confused him, so he decided that he would slumber his way through his emotions in hopes of waking the next morning with a clear idea of who his future wife should be, but even while attempting to rest he could not escape the red-haired creature. He lay in bed staring at the ceiling, envisioning her disapproving scowl, and wondered why he could not shake her from his thoughts. His body felt strange, unusually tired and heavy, and he tingled all over. The sensation, though disconcerting, was not unpleasant, and he soon drifted off to sleep.

In the depths of his dreams he found her once more, but, on this occasion, she looked kindly upon him and put her arm through his. Together they walked through a beautiful garden, and, when they sat down by a fountain, she lifted his hand and clasped it to her. Julian was so delighted by this that it took him several seconds to register that the hand she was holding seemed more feminine than his own. His eyes traveled up his arm, which was encased in a sleeve of lace, until they reached the point where limb met chest—then he let out a startled gasp, for he found himself staring down at a female figure clothed in a fine gown.

He understood that he was no longer in his own body, that he was in the unfamiliar body of a woman, and a shriek erupted from his lips in a voice no longer his own, a high musical voice rendered terrible by the note of fear in it. The dream-Liliana gaped at him, brow wrinkling in concern, as he rose from his seat and dashed away from her. He ran forward blindly, tripped on his dress, and fell, hitting his head on the garden's stony ground. Everything faded to black and he was consumed by terror...then he found himself in his own room, in his own bed, throwing off his covers.

Relief washed over him as he realized that it was early

morning and that he was in his bedchamber; it had all just been a harrowing nightmare. Feeling comforted, he glanced down at his body, bathed in the light of the rising sun, and, after a moment of disbelief, understood that his chest was just as ample as it had been during his dream.

Julian felt the urge to scream but covered his mouth to keep from doing so, as the last thing he wanted to do was draw attention to himself. Screwing up his courage, he walked over to the mirror on his bedchamber wall. Up until that day he had considered it a friend, for it had always shown him his handsome princely self, but now, as he approached it, he felt a strong desire to smash it to pieces, for it clearly displayed how his form had changed while he had slept.

Clothed in the nightshirt and soft breeches he had worn to bed was a girl he would likely have been attracted to had he not known she was his own reflection. She was comparable to the man he had been in many ways—she had shoulder-length brown hair, large hazel eyes ringed with thick lashes, and a pretty mouth that was currently forming a scowl—but was, of course, quite different in others; she had two prominent mounds upon her chest, and the breeches she was wearing appeared...*loose*. Feeling a sense of dread, he took hold of them, pulled them from his body, and looked down. This time he did scream, for he understood that the part of his body that had made some of his affairs so enjoyable had thoroughly disappeared.

He heard a knock at his bedchamber door; it was his manservant George, voice heavy with concern. "My Lord, are you well? I heard an awful scream—it woke me from sleep—and I worried you might be in trouble. Are you ill, my Lord? Speak to me, sir!"

Knowing his voice would likely be higher than usual, Julian lowered it and grumbled, "I'm fine, George. I just had a bit of a nightmare. Don't worry about me, go back to your room."

"You sound strange, my Lord—are you sure you're all right? I can get help if you need me to. I could even get your parents if you'd like, sir—"

"No!" barked Julian. "It was just a bad dream. Respect my wishes and return to bed."

George mumbled in assent and stumbled back to his room. Once Julian was sure he had gone, he tumbled onto his bed and lay there, hot tears burning his eyes as he tried to figure out what had happened and what he could do about it.

He at last concluded that he must tell his parents what had occurred, as they might be able to help find a solution to his problem. Rousing his courage, he knocked on the wall separating his bedchamber from George's, and, when the manservant sleepily returned to his doorway, said, "George, would you wake my parents? I have something of import to tell them." Assuming his master's message had something to do with his having chosen a bride, George ran off to wake the king and queen. Julian climbed into his bed and covered himself so that only the top of his head was visible, and, filled with true concern for the first time in his life, waited for his parents to come to him.

Julian had begun to nod off when he heard his father's sharp knock at his door. He rasped, "Enter!" and his parents barged into the room, faces gleaming with hopeful expectation.

They grew crestfallen when they spied him huddled in bed, and King Stoneshire roared, "Trying to hide so we cannot marry you off, eh? I'm afraid that isn't going to work, my boy. Playing sick isn't going to get you out of making your decision, so you might as well get out of bed and let us know who it is you've picked."

Julian, voice muffled, responded, "If only my wanting to avoid choosing a wife was my reason for hiding, Father. I'm afraid circumstances are direr than that."

The queen grew ashen. "Oh no! My son, what's happened to you? Are you ill? Whatever can we do to help?"

"To be honest, Mother, I don't think there's anything you—or anyone else, for that matter—*can* do," said Julian, "because I'm not sure how I...got this way." He gulped. "I'd best not delay things. Mother, Father, I woke this morning to find...well, have a look for yourselves." He dropped the sheet, revealing his changed form, and his father turned red and sputtered while his mother paled and uttered a shriek.

After a few minutes they composed themselves and, shaking, sat down on Julian's bed. The queen was first to speak, her voice barely a whisper, "My child, what's happened to you? You look like you, but a *girl* you. You're not my son anymore, you're...my daughter!"

She burst into tears, and the king placed a comforting arm around her shoulders. "My child," he addressed Julian, voice cracking, "I cannot help but think that this has something to do with the way you behaved yesterday. There were many doting parents at that event, and you were quite cruel to some of their daughters. One might have gone to a sorcerer to have a curse placed on you. I knew we should have warned you not to act in such an unruly manner."

Julian sat up in bed. "What's done is done, Father. The important thing is that I must find a way to regain my previous form. I cannot stay like this; I shall be the spectacle of the kingdom! Father, what can I do? Please, help me!"

The king gazed off into the distance, then cleared his throat and said, "I think, my child, that you will need assistance that neither your mother nor I can give you. What you need is a guide, one well-versed in the magical arts, who will be able to aid you by either preparing the cure for your condition or by identifying the acts you must perform to break the curse."

"Acts?" asked Julian, blanching.

"Yes, acts. Oftentimes spells require the completion of certain tasks to be broken. You may be lucky and find someone who can help you make a potion to fix things, or you may be not-so-lucky and may need to accomplish feats to return to your male form. Regardless, you're not improving your lot by staying here, so you must leave as soon as possible to find the help you require."

King Stoneshire asked his wife if she might fetch some worn clothing she could bear to part with, and, once she had left the room, turned to Julian. "I will say this whilst your mother is gone, for it would likely upset her to hear it. There is a tavern down in the town, the Red Rooster, where many rough men congregate. Some would kill for money or sport, and some would thieve from right under your nose, but many are adventurers and mercenaries and would help you to discover the cure you seek so long as they're paid satisfactorily."

He took a drawstring pouch from his jacket and placed it in Julian's hand. "There are twenty gold pieces in this bag. Offer ten to the person you feel can best assist you and save the rest for when you need them. Choose wisely before you offer the money, or you may end up having someone take it off your hands without your receiving any gain. Question the person regarding his knowledge of magic and the breaking of spells to ensure he knows what needs to be done. Make sure he doesn't know who you truly are and merely knows what sort of trouble you're in, as it's important that your state be kept secret to preserve your dignity. Once you are certain you've found someone able to help you, make sure you do exactly as he says so the curse might be broken. I believe in you, my child, and know you are capable of doing this."

The king pulled Julian into a firm hug, and his eyes once

again welled up. "I will succeed and return to you, Father, I promise."

The queen interrupted their embrace at that moment, for she rushed into the room with a pile of clothing and tossed it on the bed. Julian rummaged through the garments and chose a simple blue woolen dress to wear, layered a cloak with a hood over it, and put woolen stockings on underneath it. He then tried several pairs of ladies' boots, and chose ones made of brown leather that fortunately lacked heels. He washed and dressed in his bath chamber, then stuffed the remaining clothing, along with some food, a vessel of water, and a jeweled dagger he had inherited from his grandmother, into a sack. He placed the coin purse into a cloak pocket, and, once he had done this, felt he was finally ready to leave the home he had scarce ventured out of for the past twenty-five years.

His parents walked him to the palace's front doorway, where the king told him, "Remember, go directly to the Red Rooster, and heed the warnings I have given you."

"Yes, Father, I will," he said. "I love you both, and I'm sorry I've gotten myself into this mess. From now on I'll be more careful regarding what I say and to whom I say it." He embraced his parents, then pushed open one of the massive double doors and crossed the threshold into the sunlight.

As he made his way down the hill to the town, he acknowledged to himself that, although he was afraid, he was also a bit excited. He was making his way into the world for the first time, and, since he believed he could find his cure and hoped to prove himself as brave along the way, this made things a bit easier to bear. He even started to whistle as he walked along, and he was so focused on the road ahead that he did not once take his eyes off it. If he had looked to his right, though, he would have noticed a strangely familiar young man lurking in the shadow of a building just outside the palace gates—and that, as he passed the man, he began following him, keeping pace with yet staying some distance from him, as he made his way to the Red Rooster.

3.

Falsa, the town surrounding the palace, was a maze of winding streets crowded with men, women, and children who all peered curiously at Julian. At one point he stopped to ask a maternal-looking woman washing clothing in front of her home how he might get to the Red Rooster, and she replied in concerned tones, "A pretty young lady like yerself should take care going to that place, for there are men there who would take advantage of ye. Must ye go? Perhaps ye might take food or drink elsewhere?"

Julian lied that he would be meeting his father at the place and so the woman relaxed and gave him directions, but her words provided him a new source of worry, for he had not considered that, since he was now an attractive woman, some men might try to foist themselves on him. Nevertheless, he proceeded to the tavern, for he knew that finding the appropriate guide therein might be the only way to break his curse.

Upon entering the town square Julian caught sight of the tavern, a large building that bore a wooden sign decorated with its namesake fowl. He felt his stomach knot, but, steeling himself, he approached the Red Rooster's doorway. A large man stood before the door, and he cast an appraising glance at Julian, who tried his best to smile confidently. He told the doorkeeper that his brother was within, and, when the doorman shrugged his shoulders and bade him enter, Julian hurried inside before the fellow could change his mind.

The tavern was packed with people; most were men ranging from around his age to his father's, but there were a few barmaids and "common women" trying to acquire clients scattered about the room. When Julian entered there was a noticeable lull in conversation as all eyes turned to him, and he noticed that, disconcertingly, many of those staring were men who seemed to have indecent intentions if their expressions served as any indication. He hastily approached the least-crowded portion of the bar and, waving over the barman, asked, "Where would I find adventurers and mercenaries who might assist me with a quest?"

The gentleman, who was fat and jovial with drooping jowls and kindly eyes, informed him that the men he sought would be located near the rear of the tavern, and would be recognizable due to their large travel packs and the maps they often pored over. Julian thanked him, then turned and made his way to the back of the room. Sitting at a large table, flagons in hand, were five men who matched the description the barman had given, for each had a sizable pack and they were all peering at a large map spread over the table.

They were an odd assortment of characters. One man looked to be about his age and was tall and thin with cropped brown hair, another appeared slightly younger and was short and stout, one would have seemed grandfatherly if not for the scar that traversed his face from temple to chin, and another was tremendously plump with a balding pate and tiny chin-beard. The man at the center of the table, who looked to be about his father's age and was tall and broad with black hair and a black beard, appeared to be leader of the bunch. "Excuse me, gentlemen," said Julian as he timidly approached them. "I wonder if any of you might be able to help me."

"Oh, don't worry, I'll help you," chortled the youngest man, grinning lecherously, but a withering look from the bearded man silenced him.

"Please forgive him, young lady," said Black-beard. "We rarely meet women as fair as you, so he has likely been momentarily startled into forgetting how to behave properly." Short-and-stout nodded vigorously, and Black-beard introduced himself and the other men as each in turn nodded in greeting. "I am Jack Crowninshield, the fool is James Deerborn, our tall friend is Fritz Applethorn, the large fellow is Thaddeus Oakbriar, and the old man is Joseph Branchstone. You're searching for assistance—may I ask what kind you require?"

Julian hesitated, then leaned in toward the table. "I need to have a curse lifted. I'm seeking a guide that will aid me by either teaching me the incantation that will break the spell or by leading me through the trials I must complete to undo it."

He stepped back from the table and waited for the men to respond. He did not have to wait long, for Masters Deerborn, Applethorn, and Oakbriar started laughing riotously, and Jack Crowninshield sneered, "You dare to waste our time with foolish requests? Get ye to bedlam, you must be mad if you believe we'll assist someone claiming they've been cursed."

Only the old man, Joseph Branchstone, remained silent, and the others soon noticed this and encouraged him to speak. "I would not laugh about these matters if I were you," he murmured, "nor would I be so certain that they're hogwash. When I was younger, there were many great men and women who practiced sorcery; some would heal the sick, others would harm using their magic, and still others would raise the dead from their graves. These people aren't well-known nowadays, but it's likely some still walk among us. It's not unreasonable to think that one might have

24

cursed this young lady if they felt hurt or slighted."

"Nonsense," said Jack Crowninshield, "those stories are naught but rumors and superstition. They are relics of a bygone age, existing more in fantasy than reality."

"I wouldn't be so sure of that if I were you," a voice rang out. The band of men lifted their heads to stare at the speaker, and Julian, turning, came face-to-face with the person who had followed him from the palace gates. The man looked to be about his age, and had red tresses tied back with a leather lace and a matching ginger mustache. He was tall, appeared strong yet graceful, and was robed in a motley array of garments: a dashing black hat with a feather, a flowing purple shirt overlaid with a leather vest, a black waistcoat, black wool breeches, and shiny leather boots. He carried a large pack over one shoulder, as if prepared for a long journey, and had wise eyes that sparkled behind the thick spectacles he wore. There was something familiar about him, but Julian had a hard time placing it. He had to admit that this clever stranger made him feel slightly awed due to the confidence with which he spoke.

"The old man is right," said the new arrival, his tone genial. "Those who use magic, and who might wish to harm this woman, still exist to this day." He stepped closer to Julian and whispered, "I know who you are, and I can help you." When Julian, mouth gaping, asked how he had gained this knowledge, the mysterious stranger replied, "I have my ways."

The mercenaries, stunned by the interloper's intrusion, said nary a word when he took Julian by the elbow and whisked him away toward the building's exit. Julian did not know why, but he instinctively felt that he could trust this man, and so he let himself be led out of the tavern and into what appeared to be an adventure.

Once they had left the Red Rooster, the stranger pulled

Julian into a deserted alleyway. He started to protest, but the man said, "Do not be afraid, I mean you no harm. I just wanted to go somewhere private so that I could explain to you how I know what I know."

Julian relaxed, and the stranger continued, "I am Lord Landon Almwick, son of Lady Satiana Almwick and twin brother of Liliana Almwick—but you can just call me Landon. I trust you know my mother and sister, for they certainly know you, Prince Julian Stoneshire—or, should I say, 'Princess Juliane,' as that's now a more fitting name for you. In fact, you should probably start referring to yourself as 'Juliane', so people don't figure out you're the prince transformed."

The newly christened Juliane, who now understood why the man's face seemed familiar, sputtered, "B-but how...I don't...I..."

"I was sent to help you by my mother and sister, as it's partly their fault you're in this state." When Juliane grew outraged, Landon added, "Now, don't get upset with them, for the part they played was unintentional."

Juliane's indignation dulled to confusion, and Landon explained, "They arrived home in a terrible mood after attending your party yesterday, as they were disgusted by your actions. They shared their opinion of you with some friends later that day, and, as it turns out, there's a woman in their circle who's a powerful sorceress and who does not take it lightly when men are unfairly callous and cruel toward women. When she heard about both your behavior at the party and your history of careless affairs she determined she would teach you a lesson, and so she cast the Spell of Transmutation on you—that, in case you were wondering, is a spell that changes one's gender. Liliana and Mother felt sorry for you and pleaded with her to undo the spell, but she explained that you must complete a quest before it can be broken. They sent me to accompany you on said quest, as they've told me what you need to accomplish to end the curse."

"Well then, please let me know what I must do to regain my previous form!"

"I don't believe you'd be so eager to hear of the cure if you knew what I know, but I shall tell you it regardless. You must find a prince and get him to fall in love with you, and, once you've succeeded, must cut off a lock of his hair and burn it to ash. I will then bring you to the enchantress responsible for the curse, who will use the ashes to turn you back into your princely self. It's a vast undertaking, but I'm afraid it's the only option."

Juliane leaned against the wall, dejected, then slumped to the ground with a sigh. "How am I ever supposed to improve my lot, then? I'm the only prince in this land and cannot fall in love with myself—and, even if I could, I'm not truly a prince right now."

Landon smirked at him. "Liliana was right. You really are full of yourself."

Juliane lifted his head sharply, hurt and annoyance commingling on his features, then pushed himself up the wall until he was almost face-to-face with Landon. "What do you mean by saying that?"

"I mean that you're by no means the only prince in the world, but it appears that you believe you are, and that is a pretty arrogant way of thinking. I have done my research, and you're in luck. The kingdom east of your family's, the Darklands, happens to have a royal family, and one of its members happens to be a prince. His name is Arthur, and he is the sole child of the reigning king, Korben Darkwood; in fact, the two are the only remaining members of their family, as Arthur's mother died while giving birth to him and the king's parents are deceased. Their kingdom is only about a week's walk from here. If we travel there and you succeed in ensnaring the prince, you will soon have your lock of hair and the cure that comes with it—although, who knows, perhaps you shall fall in love with him, marry him, and live out the rest of your days as a princess-turned-queen?"

"I most certainly will not! How dare you suggest that?" cried Juliane, face reddening. "I want to be a man again. I would never want to live my life as a woman, that would be awful."

"And why would it be?" snapped Landon. "There's nothing wrong with being a woman, and your believing there is got you into this mess." He pointed at Juliane. "You, my friend, need to start appreciating everyone around you, and you especially need to stop treating women like lesser beings. Hopefully going through all this teaches you a lesson, but, if you remain thickheaded even after the trials you'll undoubtedly face during our journey, you will more than likely be on the receiving end of another curse at some point. Do not assume all women are simple, or you may attract the attention of more than one sorceress in your lifetime."

Juliane's face grew despondent, and Landon took pity on him. "Come," he said gently, "we must be on our way, for we need to find shelter by nightfall. We have many miles to go before crossing the border to the Darklands."

He took Juliane by the hand, and the duo headed down the town's main thoroughfare toward its gates. Juliane—who had begun to think of himself as such to ensure he did not muff things up when asked his name—once more found his thoughts wandering to Liliana Almwick, for he again regretted the way he had behaved on the day they had met. Although some of this regret certainly resulted from his plight, some of it came from the knowledge that, if Liliana had sent Landon to help him, then she must care about his well-being in some way. He understood that, had he acted civilly during the party, he might have gotten to know her, and would not have ended up needing to accompany her brother on a quest that would be difficult at best and futile or fatal at worst.

Tears formed in his eyes, but he wiped them away with the back of his free hand, for it was no use crying about what had already passed. His only hope was that Prince Arthur was not nearly as much of a vain fool as he had been, so that he might complete his mission successfully. Perhaps, along the way, he could prove himself to Landon, and then Liliana might later give him a chance to make a better impression?

He would have dwelt on this further, but they had reached the town gates and passed through them, and he felt it wise not to let himself be too distracted; he was venturing beyond the walls of a place he had never before left on foot, heading to a land he had never been to in a body he was not accustomed to, and so he knew that he needed to stay vigilant. As he and his guide continued down the road, leaving the familiar town behind them, he glanced back at it and wondered if he would ever again step through its gates.

4.

The road heading away from Falsa seemed to wind ever onward, passing mainly through field and forest but occasionally through a small village. Landon let go of Juliane's hand once they had left the town, and they walked side by side in silence until Juliane could bear it no longer. He began asking his guide questions about himself, and, though Landon at first seemed hesitant to answer, he let down his guard a bit with each reply and soon the two were chatting like old friends.

Juliane learned much about Lord Almwick—how he had trained with a blade and could wield it with skill, how his mother had created herbal remedies to help the sick when she was younger, how he had devoured every book in his home by the time he was ten years old—and also revealed things about himself he had been loath ever to tell another: that he enjoyed baking pies, that he wrote poetry, that he had once owned a dog named Scamp whose passing had left him distraught for a week. He found himself feeling exceedingly comfortable with Landon, and he began to hope they might remain friends after the quest had ended.

He scarcely noticed when his feet started to grow sore from all the travel, but, after many hours, they began throbbing with pain—as a prince, he was not used to walking such distances—and he let his guide know he needed rest. Landon was understanding and, when they arrived in the next village, suggested they head to a nearby tavern for a meal before journeying onward.

The decision regarding where to eat was made for them, as they discovered that the town had only one such establishment, a hovel with a faded sign that declared it "The Golden Duck." Upon entering the tavern they discovered that they were its only patrons, and the barman, a sour-looking old gentleman, brightened only when Juliane removed a gold coin from his pouch; though Landon had refused to take any money for his assistance, he had allowed that it would be best if Juliane paid for their food and lodgings. The travelers requested two tankards of ale, two pasties, and two plates of bread, cheese, and boiled eggs. Once the food was before them, Juliane gobbled his greedily—he had not noticed how hungry he had grown—while Landon munched his in a contemplative fashion.

Midway through the meal, two men broad as barns entered the building and, after placing an order at the bar, sat at the table nearest the travelers. This seemed intentional, for they would not stop staring at Juliane, which made him very uncomfortable. After the barman had delivered their food, they noisily ate it but continued to regularly glance over at him. Once they had finished their meal, they rose from their seats and, to his horror, approached him.

The smaller of the two, who had shrewd piggish eyes and a roguish countenance, reached their intended target first. "Well, well, what 'ave we 'ere? We ain't used to seeing so pretty a face in our village, are we, Brom?"

The larger man nodded his head enthusiastically. "No, we ain't, Merek."

Merek bent over the table and, putting his elbow on it, rested his head on his hand so that he was almost face-to-face with Juliane. "What's your name, my darling?" he asked, grinning.

Juliane replied insolently, "I'm not your darling, and my name is none of your concern."

31

Merek's smile wavered a little, but he leaned toward Juliane and placed a hand on his arm. "Don't fret, poppet, I'll take good care of you. You're such a fair thing, how about I buy you some pretties and then you show me a nice time?"

Juliane grew indignant at this remark, but, as the man was so large, he was unsure of how to respond to his overtures; he looked to Landon in the hopes he might come to his aid, but, as the lord was watching the scene with an amused look upon his face, he seemed unlikely to intervene. He decided to handle the matter himself and so, slapping away Merek's hand, he shrieked, "I cannot be plied with gifts; how dare you suggest that? Royal blood flows through my veins! I have no interest in you, so begone."

Merek's face smoldered in anger. "Royal blood? Who are you, the Queen o' Rubbish? Whoever you are, you ain't too good for Merek." The man grabbed Juliane's arm and pulled him forward until he could feel hot, rancid breath upon his face. "Come on, love, give us a kiss."

"Leave her alone," Landon's voice sounded, gentle but firm. (*And none too soon*, thought Juliane.)

"Or what?" asked Merek. "What'll you do, fancy man, serenade me to death—"

His words were unexpectedly curtailed as he found a sword at his throat, blade pressed into the meaty part where chin met neck. "I said, leave her alone," repeated Landon, more forcefully this time.

Merek released Juliane's arm, and he seemed to be leaving to join Brom, who had taken one look at the weapon and retreated to the doorway, when suddenly he lunged at the lord. Landon was much quicker than the larger man, though, and sidestepped the blow easily. He took his sword and, with a single sweep of the blade, cut through all the buttons on Merek's coat, which flapped open, revealing the stained shirt underneath. Wearing an expression of commingled anger, fear, and shame, Merek cried, "Fie to ye both!" then stalked out of the tavern, his friend trailing behind him.

Juliane turned to Landon. "You might have helped sooner! That brute almost kissed me."

"I know, but it was so entertaining to watch. You should have seen the look on your face! Terribly diverting." Before Juliane could offer an outraged reply, the lord continued, "Don't get upset. I knew exactly what I was doing and wouldn't have let anything happen to you. I merely believe that it's important that you understand the struggles women go through, and you must experience some of them in order to. It's only through the development of this sort of understanding that you'll learn to appreciate women and will avoid getting yourself into future trouble." Juliane, unsure of how to respond, placed his head in his hands, and he waited for what seemed like ages while Landon finished his meal.

When they were on the road once more, Juliane asked him, "Why are you such a staunch defender of women? Most men are just as rude and careless" —Landon raised an eyebrow, and he corrected himself— "fine, almost as rude and careless as I am—was—when it comes to them. Why aren't you like us?"

"I think it's because my twin, Liliana, is a woman, and so I've walked through life beside her and have witnessed how she and I are treated differently due to our genders. For example, my sister's as skilled with a blade as I am—we learned to fight together—but, are there opportunities for her to regularly use her skills? No, there are not; there are no tournaments for women, women are discouraged from fighting in battles, women with such abilities are told they should be more feminine. The only time my sister ever gets to use a sword is when she's practicing with me, and that, my friend, is unfair. In fact, women's whole lot is unfair. They're expected to put up with boorish behavior and remain kind, and to help men obtain power without desiring any of their own. I see the injustice in this and so try to help by lending my voice to the chorus of those that deserve to be heard but are often not."

Juliane had never considered this. He bowed his head and, as he walked along, recalled all the women he had dallied with. He realized that he had never considered what they might do when they were not entertaining him, or what their hopes and dreams might be. Feeling ashamed, he muttered to himself, "I've never taken the time to muse upon what women might really want and how they might truly feel. I must seem like such an ass."

He caught Landon smirking at him, and, though there was haughtiness in the man's smile, there was surely sympathy in his eyes. Juliane straightened, cheeks burning, and stared ahead of himself, not daring to look at his companion for fear the other might be peering at him, waiting for him to turn so that he could make him acknowledge his past errors. He was not yet ready to do this, and so the two proceeded without speaking for the next few hours, an awkward hush hanging between them like a curtain.

***

Evening fell, and Landon broke the silence. "We must find shelter presently, for it will soon be dark and we do not want to be caught overnight in the woods." He stopped, reached into his pocket, and removed a roll of parchment. It seemed to be a map, and he unfurled it and then pored over it while Juliane peeked over his shoulder. "This is where Falsa is located," he said, pointing to a spot on the west side of the map featuring a cluster of buildings, then he traced the road leading from this picture with his finger until he came to a spot slightly to the left of it. "This is where my mother's lands are, on the outskirts of the city."

He moved his finger back eastward, tracing the road through countless small villages and forests. "Here!" he said at last. "This is the town where we ran into those ruffians earlier today. If I know how to read a map—and I most certainly do—we should be nearing...this place." He pointed to a spot marked "Wareston." "If we walk quickly, we should get there in no time."

"Can you show me where the other prince's palace is?" asked Juliane.

The lord slid his finger to the far right of the map. "It's over here, off the edge of this map, for it only shows the lands your family rules. Once we cross the border into the Darklands we shall be on our own, and can only hope that, if we follow the main road, it will take us where we need to go." He rolled up the parchment and, placing it back in his pocket, continued along the road, Juliane trailing behind him.

After a brief walk the pair arrived in Wareston as predicted, and they were pleased to find it a larger and more welcoming place than the village they had dined in earlier that day. Walking along the main thoroughfare, they came upon a cozy-looking inn signed "The Homely Cottage" and decided to stop there for the evening. Before they entered, Landon told Juliane, "For tonight you and I are wife and husband, for many establishments might not allow an unmarried couple to share a room and, as it behooves us to use your gold sparingly, we must procure one together."

Juliane begrudgingly acquiesced, then they opened the door and stepped into the inn, where they were met by a cheerful older woman who wore her gray hair in a bun atop her head. "Hail, my dears," she greeted them. "Will ye be wantin' a room?"

"Good evening, dear lady. I am Lord Landon Almwick, and this is my wife, Juliane. We are seeking a comfortable chamber to spend the night in, as we have journeyed far and still have far to go. We are traveling to a neighboring kingdom to meet with its king."

The woman's mouth fell open. "Yer nobility, and will be visitin' a king? Well then, I'm honored to have ye stay at my establishment." She stuck her right hand out and firmly shook each of theirs. "I am Rose Crestshorn, owner of this inn, and I will give ye my best room."

She led them down a hallway to an ornate door and opened it to reveal a beautiful bedchamber furnished with a large bed, folding screen, and chest of drawers. "You have our gratitude," said Landon. "Would two gold coins cover the cost?"

"Oh, that's more than enough for one night!" exclaimed Rose, so Juliane handed over the promised sum. Beaming, their hostess said, "Seein' as ye have been kind enough to grace my business with yer presence and to compensate me so heartily, I will ask ye to take a meal with me before ye settle in for the night." As both were hungry from the day's travel they gladly accepted, and they were led by Rose into a comfortable sitting area featuring a table with four chairs and a hearth with a roaring fire. "I was just about to have m'self some smoked pig, and have more than enough to share," Rose told them. "I have bread, spinach, carrots, cheese, and ale as well. We shall have a feast!"

The travelers were fulsome with their appreciation, and they sat down with Rose and eagerly tucked into the meal. There was so much food that the three ate until they were nearly sick, and afterward they moved their seats in front of the fire, where they talked—or, more accurately, Rose mostly talked while Landon and Juliane mostly listened, for she admitted that the inn rarely received guests she could hold conversations with, as most were merchants peddling wares town to town or men transporting goods. She shared her adventures from her younger years with them at length-for she had traveled quite a bit with her husband Wilbur, a rug merchant-until Juliane impulsively asked, "But, Rose, where is your husband now?"

The innkeeper abruptly fell silent, face downcast. Landon, glaring at Juliane, stammered apologies, but Rose interrupted, "It's all right, dear, one of you was bound to get curious and ask. I've never really shared my story with anyone, but I might as well tell it whilst I have the courage to." She gazed at the fire a moment, then said, "As I've mentioned, my husband bought and sold the most beautiful rugs in the world; he went all over to get 'em, and even kings and queens would buy 'em. Wilbur would also weave his own rugs at times, and, though I might have been partial, I believed these were most beautiful of all. We used the money from his sales to open this inn, and I enjoyed runnin' it whilst Wilbur did his business."

"One day my Wilbur had a message delivered to him by a representative from the king of a neighboring land, the Darklands—I think he is called 'Darkwood'." Upon hearing the name Juliane moved to say something, but the lord stilled him with a stern look, and he was able to restrain himself as Rose continued, "The king was seekin' a very special carpet. It was rumored that he was—well, is, really, for he's still alive as far as I know—a powerful sorcerer, and that he was wantin' it for some sort of ritual. Wilbur didn't believe in sorcery, so he set about findin' the carpet for the king. After weavin' what he thought was the right one—for he couldn't find it, no matter how he searched—he left to deliver it."

She paused, her eyes filled with tears, and, when she spoke again, her voice came out a whisper. "Wilbur never came home. It's been three years since last I saw him." She pulled out a handkerchief and dabbed her eyes. "It's rumored that Korben Darkwood is a cruel ruler. I'm afraid my husband didn't bring him what he wanted, and so he...did somethin' to him."

She finished speaking and, letting out a sob, sat staring at the fire, tears streaming down her cheeks. Landon said,

"I'm sorry we've opened old wounds, Rose. I hope we haven't caused you too much pain."

Rose sniffled and smiled weakly. "Don't fret about me, dear. I needed to share that, and I needed to have myself a good cry about it too. To be honest, I've never told anyone my story, and it feels good to. Thank ye for listenin'." She rose slowly from her chair and informed her guests that, as it was getting late, she needed to get some rest. They walked her to her bedchamber and, after making sure she was ensconced safely within, headed to their own.

Upon entering they took turns washing behind the folding screen, for both were filthy from the day's travel. After Juliane had finished, he changed into a clean chemise and climbed into the bed, and he thanked the heavens that it was large enough that both travelers could sleep in it without being awkwardly close to one another. Landon had taken the second turn, and he emerged from behind the screen clad in bedclothes not unlike the ones Juliane had been wearing that morning. He had removed his hat and was combing his long red tresses, and he grinned sheepishly when he noticed Juliane watching him. "I must do this, for if not it tangles so."

Juliane gazed at Landon's striking features and intense blue eyes, and it crossed his mind that, since he was stuck in a woman's body, he might as well try using it—perhaps the handsome lord could make him sigh the way he himself had made countless maidens?—but he immediately pushed the thought from his mind, ashamed at having entertained it, for he had never before found a man attractive. Attributing the notion to the machinations of his fiendish new female form, he turned over and attempted to sleep, though he remained well aware of Landon's body as it slipped beneath the covers next to him. Soon the lord was breathing quietly and steadily, and Juliane was able to relax and float off into slumber.

Juliane awoke with an urge to relieve himself several hours later, and, after he had found the chamber pot and used it, shuffled back to the bed. As he crossed the room, he noticed a bright moonbeam casting its glow on Landon, who at that moment groaned and shifted in his sleep. He noticed that the lord's nightshirt had pulled to one side, partially revealing the area it had kept covered, and, as something about the view struck him as odd, he tiptoed over to the bed to investigate. Peering down at his companion, he determined that something was indeed amiss, for the rise of a breast, clearly discernible in the moonlight, stuck out of the gap in Landon's shirtfront. Perplexed, Juliane took a closer look, and verified that the remainder of that breast, as well as the entirety of another, were hidden beneath the lord's garment.

He was at first confused as to how Landon could have such a sizable bosom, but then abruptly realized who his companion might be. He reached toward the lord's face and, very gently, pulled on his ginger mustache. It peeled back a bit, revealing itself as false, and Juliane understood that he had been duped. His guide was no brother of Liliana Almwick—*he was Liliana herself*!

Juliane felt many things, foremost among them anger, for he was uncertain as to why Liliana had lied about her identity and was unsure if she even intended to help him with his plight—knowing the way he had made her feel, she might be leading him on an overlong hunt for the cure or, worse, leading him away from it. He felt the strong urge to wake her and demand an explanation, but he resisted, for he knew that in doing so he might accidentally disturb Rose. He instead pulled the nightshirt up so that it covered her, then lay in bed seething, pondering how he might call her bluff. It was only after he discovered the answer that he sought that he was able to fall asleep once more.

5.

The next morning the travelers woke early, quickly dressed and repacked their things, and left the room to find Rose preparing them breakfast. She had also packed them a bag of food and, when they expressed their gratitude, replied, "It's the least I can do after ye listened to my story. I feel that, now that I've told ye about Wilbur, he's more likely to return to me."

Juliane, who could no longer bear to hide the truth from her, blurted, "I must tell you, Rose—Landon and I are on our way to Korben Darkwood now. He's the king we plan on seeing." Rose's eyes widened, "Landon" gaped, and Juliane, feeling pleased with himself, said, "If we know what Wilbur looks like, we can search for him whilst we're in the Darklands. We can encourage him to return to you if he is well, and, if he's in danger, can try to help him escape it. Do you have a picture of him?" Rose nodded eagerly, then ran to her room to fetch it.

"Landon" frowned at Juliane. "I fear we're setting the poor woman up for heartbreak. Even if her husband is alive, it may not be possible for us to ensure he is returned to her intact."

Juliane replied smugly, "Well, it doesn't hurt to try, and I think we should."

Rose soon entered the room, carrying something. "This is it, one of the few I have of him, drawn right before he left." She handed Juliane a small image of a kind-looking rotund man with thinning gray hair and a gray mustache. "Please take it, and I pray ye find my Wilbur." The travelers promised they would do their best, and, after some affectionate farewells, they were off on their journey once more.

As they walked together "Landon" chattered amiably about a variety of topics, but Juliane was not really listening, for he was still secretly seething. He knew that "Landon" was a mask Liliana lurked beneath, and he was waiting for the perfect opportunity to challenge her act. "Landon," sensing something was awry, gradually stilled his prattle and began whistling uneasily. They entered a thick growth of forest, and, once they had not encountered anyone for many miles, Juliane determined that it was time to make his move. Complaining that his feet ached and that he needed a rest, he found a suitable clearing and, sitting upon a large stone, took off his shoes and rubbed his soles. "Landon" sat down next to him, removed a pear from the bag Rose had given them, and began eating it.

Juliane at first pretended to be deep in thought, then abruptly broke the stillness. "You know, Landon, I've had many strange experiences since getting this new body, and I've noticed a most peculiar change in my attractions." He turned to "Landon," who had stopped munching the fruit and was staring at him with cautious curiosity. "I had never before desired a man, and I find that I most certainly desire you."

"Landon" flushed crimson and stammered, and Juliane, enjoying making the impostor uncomfortable, decided to kiss the pretender to see how she would react. Throwing his arms around her, he closed his eyes and pulled her mouth to his. He was pleasantly surprised by how good the kiss felt. "Landon" had soft lips and, unexpectedly, did not immediately try to break away; Juliane could feel her hands moving along his back, and, though they were not

41

quite stroking him, they were certainly not clawing or striking at him either.

Just as he was really beginning to enjoy himself, "Landon" recoiled and, hair mussed and mouth gasping, stumbled away from him. Juliane, only somewhat feigning disappointment, said, "Why do you flee from me, my handsome lord? Do I not feel pleasing in your arms and upon your lips?"

"Landon" approached him warily, then sat back down next to him. "Juliane, I must ask you to cease your kisses and caresses, for you know not whom you're lavishing affection upon. I haven't been honest with you, and it's time for me to make a confession: I'm not who you believe me to be."

Juliane felt anger flare up inside him, for this person had misguided him and he would not allow her to steal the glory of his revelation. He screeched triumphantly, "You needn't tell me who you really are, for I already know, LILIANA ALMWICK!"

He shot out a hand and ripped the false mustache from her face, and she threw her palm over her mouth and whimpered. Juliane jumped from his seat, tossed the mustache upon the ground, and began dancing a spirited jig upon it. Recovered from her pain and shock, Liliana shrieked, in a voice that was, satisfyingly, undeniably her own, "What are you doing?"

"I'm destroying your tool of trickery!" Juliane proclaimed gleefully, trampling the item until it was barely recognizable.

"You fool!" cried Liliana. "Do you know what you've done? I had planned on revealing my identity to you later on in our journey, once you had gotten used to traveling with me, as I knew I couldn't keep up my ruse for long—I even packed other clothing in preparation for this—but I planned on continuing to present as male whenever we entered a town. I will now no longer be able to do so effectively. Do you know how much more unwanted attention we shall get whilst traveling as two women rather than as a married couple?" She sank back onto the rock. "You have just made our already difficult journey substantially harder."

Hearing this, Juliane stopped his dancing. He was a little ashamed of how he had impulsively ruined her disguise, but this feeling was tempered by his still-smoldering indignation, so he stomped over to her and leaned over her, glaring. "Well, if you didn't want me to be cross with you, you should have been honest with me in the first place!"

Liliana sat up, eyes blazing. "Oh, really? Tell me, oh spoiled one, would you have listened if I had been? Would you have followed me to obtain the cure for your ailment? No, you wouldn't have. I knew I'd have to present as male initially for you to take me seriously, so I pretended to be my own brother. That got you to attend to me and follow me, and you even tried to understand how women might feel and how they might struggle—but, only because you were hearing about their feelings and struggles from a man. In saying that you'd have listened to me even if you had known who I truly was, you're being just as dishonest as I was in telling you I was my own twin."

Juliane, contemplating her words, felt his anger dwindle. He hated to admit it, but she was right; if she had told him she knew a way of fixing his problem while presenting as her usual self, he would likely have brushed her off to search for a man that he felt could help or, worse yet, would have propositioned her. As "Landon" she had cut a formidable figure, and he had followed her without hesitation because he had perceived "Landon" as a more competent version of Liliana simply due to his maleness. He approached the rock, sat down next to her, and softly said, "You're right."

She stared at him, astonished. "Am I mistaken, or did

you just acknowledge that my judgment of you, regarding this matter, was correct?"

"I've said it once, I won't say it again," he muttered defensively. "You can think you've heard whatever you'd like."

She raised her eyebrows and clucked her tongue. "Oh, Juliane, you were so close to being endearing for a moment, but then you had to speak and ruin the illusion."

He made a face at her, then his eyes narrowed suspiciously. "Now that you're being honest with me, it's time you explain what's really happened to me. I am guessing 'Landon's' story wasn't the whole truth?"

Liliana bit her lip, then took a deep breath and said, "After you were so dreadful at the party, I had very negative feelings toward you, and thought you were a beast. My mother agreed with me, and, well—she's a powerful sorceress, so she cast the Spell of Transmutation on you. She was hoping you might be kinder to women after you walked in their footsteps." Juliane was growing red-faced, so she hastily continued, "I was telling the truth about the cure. You must make a prince fall in love with you, then must remove a lock of his hair, burn it, and bring her the ashes so she can paint you with them. Only then will you regain your—my mother's words—'true form'."

Juliane balled his hands into fists and roared, "That foul woman! How dare she place a curse on me! I shall see to it that she rots in our dungeon once I've had her cure me."

Liliana's face grew stony, and she got up and started to walk back in the direction they had come from. "Wait, where are you going?" Juliane called after her.

"Home," she replied, "to warn my mother that you mean to come for her. She was the one who asked me to help you on your journey, to ensure you learned your lesson but didn't suffer unduly. If you're planning to harm the only person I have ever truly loved, then I cannot assist you further. Farewell."

44

She continued to stride forward but heard footsteps behind her, and then Juliane was standing before her. "Please don't go," he begged. "I won't harm your mother, I swear. I spoke out of anger. I need you, Liliana. I don't know where I'm going, I don't know how to defend myself. If I'm being honest, I would likely become lost and perish without your guidance." Tears filled his eyes. "I don't really have any skills, because I've never been taught any. I've had everything done for me my entire life, and now...I am useless."

Liliana was seized with pity for him, and said gently, "I won't leave you. I just need you to think about the things you say before you say them. I can help you, but you must be willing to be helped—and, if you're viewing my mother as an enemy, you're also viewing me as one, as my feelings were what incited her to curse you. Please, work with me, and hopefully we'll get you back to your old self—but perhaps a wiser, kinder version of that self."

Juliane wiped his eyes with the back of his hand. "I'll work with you, Liliana, and will become better, I promise. In fact, I think I'm beginning to change already. I'm so full of feelings..." He leaned toward her and she understood that he meant to kiss her again, so she stepped aside as he lunged at her, and he stumbled forward and landed on the ground.

He looked up and found her frowning down at him. "You will not use my caring nature to take advantage of or obtain affection from me. That is something that might work well with most women, but I shouldn't be mistaken for most women."

She turned and stalked off along the path, and Juliane, mumbling, "It was worth a try," got up and trotted along after her. "By the way," he said, brushing himself off as he caught up to her, "if your mother could turn me into a woman, why couldn't she just make you a man for the journey? If she'd done that, I might never have recognized you."

Liliana, staring straight ahead, curtly responded, "Because it's not that simple." Acknowledging that she was likely still annoyed with him due to his lecherous behavior, Juliane shrugged his shoulders and fell into step alongside her.

The day wore on, and the pair trudged along until their feet could barely carry them; the path had become jagged with rocks, they had eaten much of what Rose had given them, and the vessels they had filled in Wareston were almost emptied. Finally, Juliane could bear it no longer, and he fell onto a shady patch of grass next to the path. "I cannot walk any more, I feel as though my legs will fall off!"

Liliana, agreeing that they had traveled quite far, sat down next to him and pulled her map out. Moving her finger along the path, she came to a town marked "Thrallwood." "If we don't spend too much time resting, we shall make it here by nightfall."

"Where are we now?" asked Juliane. She showed him their location, a point on the path quite far from Wareston but still some distance from Thrallwood, and he said, "But, how do you know this?"

"I can estimate where we are using this." She pointed at the bottom corner of the map, where a certain distance was marked as "one mile." "I know that I walk about three miles in an hour, so, in the six hours we have been walking, we should have covered about eighteen miles. That puts us about where I pointed to on the map, which is six miles from Thrallwood—so, it should take us around two hours more to get there."

"How can you tell what the time is now, though?"

"By looking at the sun and its position, and by checking this," she said, removing a small sundial from her pack. "It should be late afternoon right now."

Juliane exclaimed, "I cannot believe you know this! You

really are clever." Liliana eyed him warily, and he said, "Don't worry, I'm not trying to get another kiss from you. I'm actually astounded by all the things you know that I don't." He leaned back against a tree, sighing. "You can use a sword and read a map, and you know about lands other than our own. I barely know anything. My schooling was in reading, writing, and arithmetic, but I never learned about magic; I was taught how to care for myself—how to wash, groom, and clothe myself—but never how to *take care of* myself—how to fight with fist or blade, how to read a map or sundial, how to cook or clean for myself or grow my own food. I'm not of much use to you, and I'm aware of that."

A small smile crept across Liliana's face. "I never thought I would hear the haughty Prince Julian speak this way. Your humility is refreshing." She laid a hand on his shoulder. "I know you haven't gotten to do or see much, because being a prince has kept you 'locked away.' I think your parents feared harm coming to you, and so didn't really let you try many things or interact much with others."

He found himself nodding in agreement, surprised at how she seemed to understand what his life had been like. As if she had read his mind, she continued, "My mother was the same way with me for a while. When I was small, my father, brother, and sister died in a carriage accident. It broke my mother's heart, and she wouldn't let me out of her sight for a long time because she was so afraid of losing me also. There came a time, though, when she recognized that she had to let me live my life without worrying about the harm that might befall me, because, to grow up, I needed a chance to make my own mistakes." She was quiet a moment, then added, "I don't think you've really gotten a chance to grow up yet. Perhaps this journey is what you need to finally become a man...um, woman...an adult...you know what I mean!"

Juliane started to giggle, and Liliana could not help but

join him. Before long the sound of their laughter echoed off the trees, and they flung themselves onto the grass, letting it cradle them. The day was blissful, perfectly warm with a slight breeze, and they started to drowse in the late afternoon sun. Liliana, knowing that they could not allow themselves to nap long if they meant to reach Thrallwood by nightfall, tried rousing herself, but Juliane suggested that she relax and let him keep watch a while. "After a bit I will wake you, and then you can keep watch over me and wake me early enough that we can make it to Thrallwood before dark."

As Liliana was very tired, she hesitantly agreed to this plan and allowed herself to fall asleep. Juliane, leaning against a tree, busied himself with counting items to stay awake, for he figured he would not sleep if he counted the leaves above him. However, he did not notice that his eyes were becoming heavier and that he was seeing less with each number he counted, and before long he, too, had dozed off.

6.

Liliana woke to find the sky darkening, and, checking her sundial, confirmed her suspicion that night would soon be falling. Startled by the time and wondering why she had slumbered so long, she sat up and discovered that, despite his vowing to keep watch, Juliane had also fallen asleep. "The damn fool," she hissed, then she leaned over him and yelled, "Wake up!"

He mumbled in his sleep, and she shook him until he opened one eye and muttered, "What?" Quickly recognizing his mistake, he gathered his pack and stood. "I'm so sorry, Liliana, I didn't mean to slumber! I was keeping myself busy, but—"

"Stop making excuses, we have no time for them. There's less than an hour until the sun sets, and we are in a *bad* place to be traveling through after dark."

Grabbing her bag, she stalked away down the path, and he trotted along after her, yelling, "Wait for me!" He reached her, but found he was growing winded from trying to keep up. "Liliana, I cannot stay at this pace," he moaned. "Please slow down."

Slowing slightly, she snapped, "Maybe I should just let you fall behind, to teach you a lesson about keeping your promises!" He wondered why she was so insistent on their making it to Thrallwood before dark, and, though afraid of her answer, asked anyway.

Glaring at him out of the corner of her eye, she explained, "It's rumored that the forest surrounding Thrallwood's western entrance is occupied by three sisters. I don't know why, but they're much feared by those who live in and travel to and from Thrallwood. The stories vary, and it seems people are afraid to say much, but what's certain is that many have disappeared in that stretch of wood. It is said that, if one makes it to Thrallwood before nightfall, one can avoid the Sisters altogether. If not, one must make haste to get through the town's west gate, which displays a large charm to ward off evil, before the Sisters can discover those who walk their woods at night."

Juliane gulped, looking slightly ill, and Liliana said, "Don't get sick on me now, you'll just waste more time, and we are in danger. If we hurry, it should take us only one-and-a-half hours to get to Thrallwood, and we'll be in the forest only a short while after sunset. Hopefully we can make it to town without attracting any attention." They walked faster than Juliane ever had before, but he managed to keep up with Liliana despite his legs aching considerably. There was something about the notion of "the Sisters" that terrified him, although he was not sure why, and this gave him the strength to move faster than he had ever dreamed he could.

They had covered substantial ground by the time it grew dark, and, when Liliana stopped to light a small lantern she pulled from her bag, she took the opportunity to check her map. "We're in luck. We're only a short distance from Thrallwood now. If we keep moving at the pace we've been going, we shall reach it shortly."

"That's wonderful news!" cried Juliane.

Liliana stared at him in horror and hissed, "What are you doing? You need to keep your voice down. We'll only get through this unscathed if we're cautious, so I need for you to be less impulsive. Agreed?"

"Agreed," he whispered sulkily, and they resumed their hasty journey.

After they had walked a few minutes more they saw a light ahead, and Juliane said, "Look at that! It seems we've reached the town earlier than expected!"

"I wouldn't count on that," replied Liliana, face creased with worry. "There's no way we could have covered that much ground so swiftly."

The travelers tiptoed toward the glow and, as they neared it, discovered that it issued from a lantern that hung from what appeared to be a traveling wagon. A woman with thick black hair topped with a headscarf and wearing a flowing blouse and skirt sat upon its steps, warming her hands before a fire. Juliane was relieved to see her. "It seems she's just another traveler. Perhaps we should ask her for a ride into town?"

"I don't think that's a good idea," Liliana said uneasily, for, though the woman seemed safe enough from a distance, there was something unsettling about her. "Let's walk past her and only speak to her if she addresses us."

Juliane agreed, and so they walked toward the woman, then passed to the right of her. They thought they might continue onward without interacting with her, but suddenly a voice called out, "Where are you young ladies off to that you must travel so late in these woods?" They turned to find that the stranger had risen from the steps and was beckoning them to draw nearer, but neither wished to approach her, for, though it could have been a trick of the light, both had received the unpleasant impression that, when she had spoken, her lips had not moved.

When she noticed their hesitation, she said (via a clearly open mouth), "Are you afraid of me? You shouldn't be—I'm just a traveler crossing these woods later than expected. Why are you so skittish?" She paused a moment. "Ohhhh, I think I know why. You're afraid of the Sisters, aren't you?"

51

"Well, yes, we are," replied Juliane. "We've heard enough of them to cause us alarm."

The woman laughed. "The stories about the Sisters are tales told by grandmothers to keep children from wandering into the woods at night. Girls your age shouldn't believe in fables! Why don't you join me by the fire?"

"I'm sorry, but we cannot," said Liliana. "We have an engagement in Thrallwood and must arrive there as quickly as possible. Please take care of yourself in the woods."

The travelers started off toward the town but were once more halted by the stranger. "I lied," she shouted. "The Sisters really do exist, and I'm also scared of them. I was hoping that, if I told you they didn't, you would feel brave enough to stay with me. Won't you join me in my wagon? I can hitch my horse to it, and we can ride into town."

Liliana could not see a horse anywhere, and it crossed her mind that the woman might be trying to save herself from the Sisters through using others as a distraction. "We really must be going," she said firmly.

"That's too bad, for I was going to tell you a secret about the Sisters."

Juliane took a tentative step forward. "If it's something that might help us reach Thrallwood safely, then, please, tell us. Once we get there, we'll send someone to fetch you."

"Well," began the woman, "they *are* sisters, but there aren't really three of them—at least, not in the traditional sense. I guess you could say they aren't separate...entities. Something terrible happened to them when they were younger, so now one of them looks like a regular woman, but the others...well, they're more like *parts* of their sister."

"That's awful!" Juliane exclaimed.

"You're right," the lady agreed, "but that's not even the worst part. The two grotesque sisters, embittered by their lot, have grown to hate humankind, and, due to this, seek to destroy any person they come across. Their sister longs to stop them but is unable to, for the others have control over parts of the whole she does not. Whenever the one tries to make friends the others invariably take over, and, well, I suppose you can guess what happens after that." She clucked her tongue. "Such a shame, really."

Liliana had experienced a sense of mounting dread as the woman's tale had progressed; she had, without noticing, grabbed Juliane's hand, and the pair had started backing up toward Thrallwood. As the stranger finished her story, she finally found her voice and asked, "But...how are you privy to this information?"

The woman smiled sadly while seconds that seemed like ages passed, and Liliana's blood turned to ice when she said, "We unfortunately have firsthand experience in the matter"—*for her voice had come from beneath her clothing*. A chorus of laughter exploded from the stranger's stomach and the back of her head, and her face crumpled into a mask of self-loathing as she mouthed one word: "Run."

Paralyzed by fear, the travelers watched as the woman's head twisted upon her neck with a sickening crack, and, once the back of it was visible, she removed her headscarf and parted her thick black tresses to reveal a face that was decidedly *upside down*. It resembled her other one but, when it opened its eyes, they were completely black. "Surprise!" chortled the demonic face, revealing a mouth full of jagged teeth.

Juliane grabbed Liliana's arm and tried pulling her in the direction of Thrallwood, but she had taken her pack off and was rummaging through it. "What are you doing?" he shrieked, and, when she did not respond, he spun back around to find the woman had further changed. She had turned and now faced away from the travelers, and she fell backward toward them, catching herself with her hands as she neared the ground, arching her back to contort herself into a spider-like shape. The upside-down head was now right side up, bouncing close to the ground and grinning its sharp-toothed grin at Juliane, and he screamed, for an even more terrifying head had emerged from beneath her blouse and now sat atop her body. This abomination was almost all mouth, with large razor-like teeth and an enormous tongue that stretched like a vine from its gaping maw.

The Sisters—for that was quite clearly what this creature was—advanced toward them, its faces cackling with inhuman delight. Juliane was debating whether to run and be taken down some distance away or to challenge the beast and give his companion some time to escape, when a triumphant Liliana pulled something from her bag and threw it at the Sisters. As it landed in front of the creature it produced a flash of light and a cloud of smoke, and, once it had cleared, Juliane was amazed to find that the monster had frozen on the spot. "A gift from my mother—you can thank her later," shouted Liliana. "It will only hold the thing a short while, so run to Thrallwood as fast as you can!" She grabbed her pack and, flinging it over her shoulder, sprinted in the direction of the town. Juliane followed her, lungs burning, running harder than he had ever run before.

Soon the entrance to Thrallwood, its storied charm gleaming, came into view, and Liliana cried, "Look, Juliane, the town! We're saved!" They heard a screech from behind them, and, peering over their shoulders, found that, to their horror, the Sisters had regained the ability to move and was now charging toward them. They barreled toward the gate, and Liliana, arriving first, hastily threw her weight against it until it opened enough for her to squeeze through. Juliane remained a few paces away from it, the Sisters mere steps behind him. "Come on!" screamed Liliana, pulling the gate wide. "They're nearing you!"

Filled with terror, Juliane gathered the remainder of his strength and, with a mighty lunge, flew to the gate and through it, crashing into Liliana. They landed in the dirt, and the Sisters, halting a few paces from the charm, released a shriek of anger, then resignedly turned and trudged back into the wood. The travelers sprawled panting on the ground, dazed and fully amazed, still scarcely believing that they had been able to best the hideous creature.

7.

Juliane was first to catch his breath, and crowed, "We did it, Liliana! We've bested the Sisters! No one else has, and we have!"

Once the color had returned to her cheeks, Liliana said, "If not for my mother's gift we would be as dead as the rest of them. We should remember that before congratulating ourselves too heartily."

He rolled his eyes, then asked, "What did you toss at that thing?"

"A charm my mother gave me in case we ran into something like that. She traveled these lands often when younger, and so knows the dangers they hold and wanted to ensure we had protection."

Juliane's face lit up with curiosity. "What else did she give you?"

"That is for me to know and for you to hopefully never find out," said Liliana. "Since you aren't competent in magic use, it would be irresponsible of me to show you what she's given me without cause." Juliane at first pouted about this, then begrudgingly conceded she had a point and pressed the matter no further.

The travelers soon noticed they were no longer alone, for a crowd had gathered behind them. The townsfolk of Thrallwood initially said nothing, brave enough only to gape at the strangers, but presently a short, portly man broke rank and shuffled over to them. "A pleasure to meet you, my dears!" he said, grasping each's hand. "My name is Neville Wrathscalder, and I'm the mayor of Thrallwood. We all bore witness to your escape from the Sisters and are honored to have such fine warriors grace our town, for you must be warriors indeed to have thwarted it. Please, tell us how you managed to accomplish this feat."

Juliane, feeling haughtily proud of their escape, considered telling the man of how they had used magic to freeze the beast, but, when he noticed Liliana sending stern warnings with her eyes, realized that it might not be wise to reveal they were carrying charms and spells. "We were fortunate to have...a good plan and substantial knowledge of the creatures in these parts," he told the man, and, though Wrathscalder seemed disappointed with this response, he nevertheless invited the travelers to stay in his home that night, promising them both a hearty meal and a warm bath.

He was not lying on either count, for his supper table was bedecked with fine foods and his wife had filled a large tub with heated water. She encouraged the travelers to carry it into another room to have a wash, opining, "As you're both ladies, it won't be a problem for you to bathe together." When they entered the chamber and put the washtub down, Liliana warned Juliane, "If you try making a frolic of this, I will stick your head in the filthy water and hold it there." She stripped down and, turning her back to him, hopped into the tub and scrubbed herself vigorously; when he entered it, he carefully positioned himself to keep from rubbing against her, something he would have enjoyed but that would have resulted in his being assaulted and so was best avoided.

Once they had finished their wash, they dressed themselves in the garments Mistress Wrathscalder had left for them, for their clothing had been taken for cleaning and was drying on a length of cord in the Wrathscalders' yard. Juliane had been given a gown of green satin and, once he had put it on, could not stop preening in the mirror. Liliana, groaning at his vanity, pulled on her own dress, and had to admit the purple satin gown was deliciously soft and undeniably suited her. That such obviously costly things had been gifted to complete strangers set off warning bells in her head, but, as she was tired and hungry, she did not pay much heed to her worries, and instead pulled Juliane away from his self-admiration and toward the meal that awaited them.

When they joined Master and Mistress Wrathscalder at the supper table, they found themselves seated across from two men they had not seen upon their arrival into town who were introduced as the Wrathscalders' sons, Ignus and Horace. Ignus, a tall, heavyset man who appeared about twenty-seven, had hardly any hair on his head and an excess of it on his face and body. His vapid stare and clumsy mannerisms made Liliana think he should have been called "Ignorance" rather than his given name, and she giggled to herself as she watched him first fumble with his fork and then use his fist to shove a piece of mutton in his mouth.

Horace, the younger and slighter of the brothers, seemed more alert than Ignus but had long black hair that appeared unwashed and a tiny mustache that, along with his perpetually lascivious facial expression, made him resemble a rat. Liliana had a hard time believing that persons as jolly as Master and Mistress Wrathscalder could produce such offspring, but she reminded herself that sometimes rotten fruit falls from healthy-looking trees and tried to enjoy the admittedly delicious meal despite Horace's constant leering.

Master Wrathscalder regaled the diners with stories from his many years as mayor of Thrallwood, sometimes spraying bits of food from his mouth as he guffawed at one of his not-so-clever jokes. As the party wrapped up the meal the topic of conversation turned to the visitors—who they were, where they were from, why they were traveling— and Liliana reported that their names were Lily and Julia Crestshorn, sisters from Wareston, and that they were on an errand to Hawthorn (the next town over, which she fortunately recalled from her map) to fetch fabric for their mother; Juliane, recognizing that she was making them out to be Rose's daughters, nodded at everything she said.

The Wrathscalders seemed to believe her story, but this unfortunately resulted in Master Wrathscalder asking which shop they needed to visit so that he might have someone fetch the items for them on the morrow. As Liliana stammered, trying to think of a suitable response, he continued, "After all, then you'll be able to stay in town to prepare for the festivities."

Liliana felt her stomach tighten, and she croaked, "What festivities?"

"Why, the celebration we shall have tomorrow when you marry our sons," said Master Wrathscalder, eyes gleaming.

Juliane, who had been nibbling on a piece of bread, nearly choked on it, and he coughed and spluttered as a shocked Liliana asked, "What are you talking about?"

"You're the only people who've managed to get past the Sisters, so you must be brave, and at least one of you must be bright" —he cast a glance at the still-hacking Juliane to indicate which traveler he felt the adjective did not describe— "and, frankly, there are no maidens in Wareston fit to marry our boys. Therefore, you shall have the honor of becoming their wives, and our daughters!"

He and Mistress Wrathscalder got up from the table and rushed from the room to begin preparations, leaving a horrified Liliana and a now-only-mildly-wheezing Juliane to stare at their unexpected betrotheds. Ignus, looking up from his plate for the first time since the meal's beginning, beamed at Juliane, who grimaced at the several shards of meat stuck in his teeth. "I'm goin' to marry you, cus you're pretty and you don't talk much. I don't like too many words, they make my 'ead 'urt." Juliane's eyes bulged and he emitted a tiny squeak, but Ignus did not seem to notice this, for he had returned to shoveling food in his mouth.

Horace was, unfortunately, more loquacious than his brother. "I get to marry you, because you're the clever one in your family and I'm the clever one in mine," he said to Liliana, then he lowered his voice. "Also, I really like redheads. Tell me, is *all* of your hair red?"

Liliana, understanding what he was asking, blushed crimson and told him, "You, sir, aren't going to find out."

Horace, proving he was not quite as sharp as he considered himself to be, replied, "Ah, yes, I see, won't tell me, eh? Have to save it for later, we don't want to ruin the discovery."

He gave her a wink that made her blood boil, but, before she had an opportunity to chastise him, Mistress Wrathscalder bustled back into the room. "Come on girls, time for bed!" she said. "You've got to rest, for you'll want to look your best for your weddings tomorrow." Juliane started to protest, but Mistress Wrathscalder offered misguided assurances that all would be fine. "I'm taking care of all the arrangements, so there's nothing to fret about. I know how a girl wants to feel like a princess on her wedding day." Feeling indignant, he almost claimed that he *was* a princess and so did not need anything in particular to feel like one, but, as Liliana had ceased objecting, he decided it would be wiser to remain silent.

They followed their hostess out of the dining area and down a hallway to a large oak door, which she unlocked and opened to reveal a room containing a bed, coffer, and bedside table. "You two shall be quite cozy in here tonight, and, when you wake tomorrow, you'll be getting married!" she squealed, then she left the room, slamming the door behind her.

The travelers stood still and held their breath, for they worried she would lock the door behind her, and they sighed in relief when they did not hear the bolt turn. "Oh, that is fortunate," said Juliane. "It's a good thing none of these Wrathscalders are terribly bright, otherwise they might have locked us in here." He flopped down next to Liliana, who had seated herself on the bed. "Now, how are we going to get out of this mess?"

"Though I'm loath to be using so much of my mother's magic so early on in our journey," she replied, "I believe I have something to help us escape this predicament." She rummaged through her bag and, uttering an "ah ha," removed a small packet from it. "Here it is, the Pulvis Lapsus Memoriae."

Juliane reached for it. "What does that mean?"

"It means 'Powder of Memory Loss'," said Liliana, holding it out of his grasp. "Don't touch it. You don't know how to use it."

"Well, then at least tell me how *you're* going to use it."

"When the powder is sprinkled on someone and accompanied by the appropriate words, it causes them to forget things," Liliana explained. "If you put just a tiny bit on someone, it will make them lose a few hours; if you sprinkle a lot on them, they will lose full days. If you pour an entire packet on them" —she made a sweeping motion across her forehead— "their whole life will be gone."

"That's amazing!"

"Yes, and it's also obviously quite dangerous," she continued sternly, "for we run the risk of losing our own memories should we spill some on ourselves whilst reciting the incantation. It also tends to make whomever it lands on fall deeply asleep for minutes to hours depending on their constitution, so our accidentally touching it could stop us from getting out of here. That's why it's important that you leave its use to me. This is the reason I was so upset when you stomped on my mustache," she reminded him

61

pointedly. "They wouldn't be trying to wed us to their sons if they thought I was your husband."

"I know, I know," Juliane said testily. "I won't touch your powder, I promise."

Liliana took the packet and placed it on the coffer. "We should try to rest now. We must make sure to rise just before dawn, when all the Wrathscalders are still abed, to sprinkle a bit of powder on each. Then they won't remember us when they awaken, and those two brutes will not come after us to reclaim us as their betrotheds." She pulled the bedclothes down and got into bed, and Juliane followed suit. "Hopefully we do not oversleep; we must risk it, though, for we need our strength for tomorrow. Goodnight, Juliane." He responded in kind and, exhausted from their trying day, the pair soon drifted off to slumber.

***

Juliane was awakened hours later by a knock at the bedchamber door, and, after another sounded, he got out of bed to investigate. "Who is it, and what do you want?" he whispered through the keyhole.

He was displeased to receive the answer, "It's Horace. I was hoping to speak with your sister."

"It's late and she is asleep. Can it not wait until the morrow?"

"It really cannot," said Horace, and, hearing the lecherous note in the man's voice, Juliane understood, with a sickening feeling, that the dolt had mistaken Liliana's declaration at the dinner table for an invitation to their room to discover "all her hair's color" for himself.

Knowing that the door was not locked and so Horace could enter at any moment should he choose to, Juliane asked him to wait a moment, then considered what to do. Glancing around frantically, his eyes lit on the packet of memory loss powder, and an idea popped into his head. He knew Liliana had not wanted him to touch it, but these were desperate times, and he felt certain she would not mind his using some to get them out of the mess Horace's visit was likely to otherwise become.

Remembering her warning about the effects of touching it, he scrambled for some gloves to wear and found some in his pack. After putting them on, he grasped the packet and, very carefully, poured a tiny amount of powder into his left palm and clenched his fist around it. He placed the packet back on the coffer, then walked to the door to put his plan into action.

Opening it, he found Horace standing in the hallway in his bed clothing, wearing the same unsettling leer he had worn throughout dinner. "Hail, my lovely," he said. "Have you woken your sister for me?"

Juliane forced an alluring smile onto his face and, in the sultriest voice he could manage, said, "I was actually hoping that she could continue sleeping, and that you and I could have a chat instead. I know you prefer redheads, but I was hoping that someone with my hair color might be capable of rousing your interest."

He beckoned Horace to enter, and the man needed no further prompting. His grin spread from ear to ear as he came into the room, softly closing the door behind him. "Sure, we can talk," he whispered. "You're just as pretty as your sister, and you seem more accommodating than her, if you don't mind my saying so."

Juliane inwardly recoiled at the man's oily, charmless manner, but continued his feigned seduction. "Horace, I don't like men like your brother," he pouted. "They may be strong, but they're not smart. I need a man who can excite me...intellectually."

He moved toward the bed and, sitting down, requested that Horace join him. The man quickly did so and, taking liberties, threw his arm around Juliane. "I think we might be able to change our marital arrangements," he said, "provided you can show me you're more interested in me than your sister is."

The weaselly fellow pulled Juliane into an embrace, and he felt the bristly mustache nuzzle against his neck. Doing his best to keep from pulling away, for Horace's caresses were repulsive, Juliane stroked the man's back with one hand and lifted the other over his head. Horace was fortunately so focused on being amorous that he did not notice this happening—but, all of a sudden, he lifted his face and kissed Juliane full on the mouth. Disgusted, he dropped the contents of his fist on the man. Horace's grip on him slackened immediately, and, as Juliane moved away from the lecher, he fell backward onto the bed, fast asleep.

Juliane experienced a strange mix of emotions regarding his victory, for, while he was revolted that he had needed to kiss Horace to subdue him, he was delighted that he had been able to so easily charm the man despite his minimal experience in exercising feminine wiles. Overshadowing both feelings, though, was pride that he had been able to defeat the awful fellow through a plan of his own creation and with no assistance from Liliana. He mused upon his success until it dawned on him that he was wasting time, for it was uncertain when Horace might recover from the powder's effects. He reached over and shook Liliana, who, stirring from sleep, groaned, "Is it dawn already?" She rolled over and, finding Horace on the bed, jumped out of it. "Juliane, what happened? Why is Horace here?" she asked shakily.

"There's no time for me to fully explain right now— suffice it to say that I used a bit of memory loss powder to put him to sleep so we could get out of here safely. I used gloves, so please don't be cross," said Juliane, fearing he had upset her.

To his relief, she seemed more concerned than angry.

"But there's still enough left to make the other Wrathscalders forget us, right?"

"Yes, the packet's still mostly full."

"Good! Then on to the incantation. He's already been doused, so I just need to say the words." Putting her hands together, Liliana chanted, "Let memory fade, in sleep be lost." Having completed the task, she asked Juliane to grab his bag so that they could leave once they had finished enchanting the other family members. He did this, then took off the gloves he was wearing and gave them to her to use; thanking him, she made sure they were free of Pulvis before pulling them on. Slinging her bag onto her shoulder, she grabbed the packet and rushed out of the bedroom, and Juliane hastily followed her. The sun had just started to peek over the horizon when they cautiously crept into Ignus's room and found him snoring atop a pile of soiled linens. Liliana swiftly sprinkled some powder onto him and recited the incantation, then they hurried on to the parents' bedchamber to place them under the spell.

The land was bathed in a soft orange glow as the travelers silently exited the Wrathscalders' home after having first filched some food from their larder, and they made sure to remove their slightly damp clothing from the line before leaving the yard. As they walked toward the town's east border, Liliana peered at Juliane curiously. "I think we might now have the time to discuss what happened whilst I slept. How did Horace get into our bedchamber, and how were you able to subdue him?"

"Well, he came to the room looking for you, and he, erm...apparently wanted to discover for himself whether all your hair is red or not." Liliana groaned, and he went on. "But, knowing how men like him think—as, well, I used to be one—I made him believe I was interested in him and, when he was, uh, distracted, I poured some powder on his head."

He noticed Liliana had halted and turned to find her

gaping at him. "And how did you manage to 'distract' him?" she asked.

"I'm not proud of it, but I let him kiss me." Liliana's eyes bulged, and he hastily continued, "I didn't want to, but it was the only way to dust him. Don't worry, though, it was much more enjoyable to kiss you, even when you had the mustache on. Your false one was much nicer than his real one."

Uncertain as to why he had added this last bit, he uneasily awaited her reaction. "You didn't have to do that," she said softly. "I could have dealt with him. It was sweet of you to think of me like that. Thank you, Juliane."

She impulsively embraced him, then, red-faced, mumbled a curt, "I suppose it's time to get going, then." The pair marched toward the east gate and hastily exited through it, for they were eager to bid farewell to the thoroughly unpleasant town of Thrallwood.

8.

The road just outside the town was well-trodden and easy to follow, but, after walking a while, the travelers reached a place where it branched off in three directions. Liliana pulled her map from her pack and, after consulting it at length, showed it to Juliane. "I'm not sure which way it would be best to take." She pointed at the topmost path. "This one heads to Hawthorn, where I'd claimed we were on our way to last night. It would get us to our destination quickly, but a part of me fears that one of the Wrathscalders might not have completely lost their memory, and, if so, it would be the first place they'd search for us."

Juliane recalled Horace's repulsive kiss and suppressed a shudder. "Then it may be wise for us to avoid it."

Liliana moved her finger to the lowest path. "This one goes to the town of Lavinia, which is rumored to be lovely, but curves so substantially southward that it would add a day or two to our travel time. And this," she said, pointing to the middle road, which appeared to traverse a wooded area, "is the most direct route. Based on the distance, it would likely take us about two days to cross the forest, and we would end up where the three paths meet near Silvan, the town on the other side. However, it is the most perilous option. My mother traveled these lands extensively, but never took that path. In fact, few have gone through that wood, and many who've entered it have disappeared, so it is unclear what dangers lurk therein."

She closed the map and placed it in her pack. "I think we should take the path to Lavinia. Though it may take us longer to get to Silvan, we're more assured of arriving there safely."

Juliane was surprised. "But why should we take the long way when there's a shortcut? We have enough food from the Wrathscalders to hold us over for three days and could surely reach Silvan by nightfall tomorrow. Why don't we chance it?"

"Because we've already been attacked by a creature that I will have nightmares about for the rest of my life, and I don't wish to run into something even more dreadful. There are no monsters in and around Lavinia."

"True, but there are men, and, frankly, I think we've been having—and may still have—less luck with them than with monsters."

Liliana bit her lip thoughtfully, then admitted, "You're right. Since you've destroyed my disguise our prospects for safe travel among men have dropped considerably, as they aren't nearly as respectful to unmarried women as they are to those they perceive as 'belonging' to other men." She sunk to the ground, face downcast. "Why must they behave so awfully?"

Juliane, feeling momentarily indignant, considered snarling a suitably antagonistic response but then thought better of it. He squatted next to her and said, "I'm sorry, I don't know why. I guess we've just always been allowed to, and so we've gotten used to it."

Liliana lifted her head sharply. "Oh, Juliane, I don't mean to imply you're like that, I—" She stopped to correct herself. "I mean, you certainly *were* like that, but I don't think you are anymore. I believe your having to live as a woman is changing you, and I'd forgotten that what I say about men might hurt you because I'd forgotten that...you aren't a woman. I'm sorry if that makes you feel uncomfortable."

He contemplated her remark and determined he was not upset by it, which led to the revelation that this was because he was getting used to living as a woman. "I'm not uncomfortable, really, just confused by how I feel— because, surprisingly, I'm all right with masquerading as a girl. I think I was very bad at understanding women before I was cursed, even though I spent a lot of time with them. I can now admit that I didn't treat them very well, and I don't think I would have been able to do that had I not been turned into one...so, I suppose something good has come of my plight."

Liliana grinned. "Juliane, that's wonderful! It seems my mother's curse has worked the exact change in you that she hoped it would. By the time we've cured you, you'll be a completely new person!"

She rose from the ground and reached down to help him up, but the reminder that Lady Almwick had caused his predicament made anger flare within him, and he refused her assistance. "I had forgotten your mother was the source of my worries. Suddenly I'm no longer feeling as charitable as I was just a moment ago." He stood on his own, then stomped away toward the middle path of the crossroads.

"Juliane, wait! We hadn't yet decided if that path is best to take!" Liliana called after him. Catching up with him, she grasped him by the arm. "I'm sorry I've upset you; I was just being honest. I didn't mean—"

He turned his head to gaze coolly at her. "I have just discovered that I am decidedly *not* all right with being a girl, and so have determined that we will take this road so that we may reach the Darklands as soon as possible. You can choose to travel it with me, you can go to Lavinia on your own, or you can even return home to your dreadful mother, I care not. I am focused only on finding my cure and regaining my rightful form."

He tramped forward, leaving Liliana behind muttering under her breath, "And I thought we had made some progress. What a stubborn goat." She reluctantly followed him down the path, and they soon disappeared into the forest.

They walked for what felt like hours, though it was difficult to tell just how much time had passed, for the wood's vegetation grew so thickly that it was as dark during the day as it might be at night. Juliane had also vowed not to speak to Liliana for as long as he could manage, for the recollection that she was in a way responsible for his plight had made him sullen; once she understood he was ignoring her she followed suit, and the silence made minutes feel like eternities.

Determined not to let him bother her, Liliana instead focused her attention on their surroundings, and noted, with apprehension, that the plants they passed as they walked along were not of a kind she had ever seen before. Strange tendrils of bluish-gray vines clung to the trees populating the forest, and plants similar to ferns but of a purplish-red color grew copiously alongside the path. There were also plants that seemed livelier than they should—dark purple flowers resembling hands that seemed to grasp at them, and patches of grass that wriggled with a conscious life force. Liliana was certain to avoid them, but Juliane was oblivious and at one point stepped squarely upon one. "Ugh!" he cried. "That grassy spot moved under my boot!"

"Ah ha! Just as I've suspected," declared Liliana, glad to have a way of breaking the silence but dismayed that her suspicions regarding the forest appeared correct. Juliane stared at her, perplexed, as she pulled a worn-looking book from her pack. "My mother gave me this. It's the knowledge she'd obtained about extraordinary creatures during her years of studies; she took up researching beasts

70

of legend after my father passed. It also contains spells she determined might be of use to us." She vigorously thumbed through the volume until she found what she was seeking. "As I'd guessed, we seem to be in a faerie wood, and that, my friend, is bad news indeed."

She held the book out to Juliane, who, glancing at the page she was pointing at, read the heading, "Signs of a Faerie Wood." Below this were pictures of some of the unusual plants they had seen during their travels: the ugly blue-gray vines, the oddly colored fern-like plants, the purple grasping-hand flowers. Unconcerned, he said, "So, what's the trouble? I thought fairies were nice and did things like grant wishes."

Liliana was outraged. "Have you only read children's stories? Haven't you ever studied intellectual tomes on the behavior of fairies?" Finding all the answer she needed in his confused expression, she continued vehemently, "Some fairies are lovely, but others are horrifying. Haven't you ever heard of a Water-horse? They look like beautiful horses and may even present themselves as attractive humans, but they're malicious spirits related to fairies, and they eat people. They lurk near lakes and other bodies of water, and, if you sit on one, its skin will hold you to it. It will then plunge into the water with you stuck to its back, hold you under until you drown, and feast upon your tasty flesh." She waited for Juliane to respond, and, when her lecture was met with a roar of laughter, crossly asked, "What's so amusing?"

"You are. Do you actually think that some fairies—the tiny things with wings that fly about and sing songs in nursery tales—eat people? That sounds ridiculous. Frankly, I don't believe any of this 'faerie wood' nonsense, and I'm not sure why you, as clever as you are, accept any of it as truth."

Pleased with himself, he turned from her and headed off down the path, but he heard her call after him, "If I'm wrong and this isn't a faerie wood, then tell me—how many roads lay before you?"

Confused, he replied, "Why, only one..." then stopped mid-sentence, for the path that had moments before seemed a solid, continuous line now branched off in half a dozen directions. "Six, there are six paths. How are we ever going to figure out which is the right one to take?"

"*We* don't have to," said Liliana. "*I* see only one."

Juliane meekly asked, "Then why do I see so many?"

"Because you stepped on a stray sod."

"A what?"

"A stray sod. They're patches of grass enchanted by fairies. I made sure not to step on any, but you walked on one—it was the thing you felt move under your boot. Once you tread on one, you're doomed to wander the faerie wood aimlessly until daybreak the following morning—or, you can turn your coat inside out to end the enchantment."

"Turn my coat inside out? How absurd," sneered Juliane, though with less bravado than he had previously shown. Seeing that she was not going to be baited into an argument, he continued, "Besides, I'm not wearing a coat. I have only a cloak, and it's in my pack."

"Then I suppose you'll have to take off your dress and reverse it. That will likely have the same effect."

When he understood she was being serious, Juliane reddened and roared, "I will not remove my dress and put it on inside out! You just want me to do that so you can have a laugh at my expense, and I won't give you that satisfaction."

"Well, I guess I'll just continue on, then, and you can follow behind me. I'm sure you'll be fine on your own." Liliana proceeded along the path, and, as she passed in front of him, an odd thing happened—she began to blink in and out of his vision; one second she was there, the next she was not, and, when she was visible, it was unclear which of the six roads she was walking on.

"Wait!" cried Juliane.

Liliana, solidifying as she halted, turned to face him. "Yes, what is it, Juliane? I thought you were managing just fine without me."

"I'm not," he begrudgingly admitted. "Do you really think that, if I turn my dress inside out, I will be able to see the path rightly again?"

"I'd be willing to bet on it."

Grumbling, Juliane unlaced the bodice of his dress, then pulled it off to reveal a frumpish chemise. "What a charming undergarment!" shouted Liliana, barely suppressing a giggle.

"You're not supposed to look at it!" he bellowed, and, face burning, he hastily reversed the dress and put it back on. "Do I have to wear it like this for the rest of the time we're in the wood?" he asked.

"No, the spell should be broken now, so you should be fine wearing it the proper way again—that is, as long as you don't step on any more stray sods."

Juliane grew more at ease once he had confirmed that the six strange paths had indeed reunited, and, after putting his dress back on properly, he rushed to join Liliana, as he did not want to be too far from her if the wood was as treacherous as she claimed it to be. Liliana, for her part, mused that he had looked quite endearing in his undergarment—though she would never have admitted this to anyone—and she was pleased that he behaved civilly toward her from that point forward. Both made sure to keep a close watch on their surroundings as they traveled along, alerting each other to any unusual patches of grass, as the idea of getting lost in the menacing wood did not much appeal to either of them.

***

The pair traveled many miles, and the day faded to a

night so dark that Liliana had to construct a torch, as she had unfortunately dropped her lantern during their escape from the Sisters, so that they might make their way through the thick wood. Nighttime in the forest made the landscape seem even more perilous, and they had to move carefully to avoid stepping on or brushing against anything that might bring them undesirable consequences. Juliane grew increasingly worried that something horrible was lurking in the dreadful forest, and he followed Liliana so closely that she at times scolded him for stepping on her heels—though not too harshly, for she, too, was afraid despite her brave exterior.

They eventually came to a fork in the road, and Juliane made sure to ask Liliana if she saw it as he did, for he had earlier learned that things in the wood were not always as they seemed. She assured him that the road did split before them, but, fortunately, there were signs posted at the intersection. The one pointing to the right-hand path was marked "S," while the left-hand one featured a picture of a house and the letter "R." "It seems the left path leads to someone's home, whilst the right likely leads to Silvan," said Liliana. "Should we continue onward toward the town, or chance begging a stranger for shelter overnight?"

Juliane much preferred the notion of sleeping in a bed— even if it was in the home of someone unknown and potentially dangerous—over that of spending the night huddled on a hard patch of forest floor while the things that lurked all around closed in on them, and he was about to say so when he noticed the two were no longer alone. Standing to one side of the right-hand path, teeth bared, was a dog the size of a small bull. It was covered in shaggy dark green fur and had a long tail plaited into a thick braid, and it emitted a soft green glow as it stepped into the middle of the road, barring the travelers from passing.

"Oh, no," said Liliana, face contorted with fright, as she backed away from the animal.

"Oh no, indeed." Juliane rushed up behind her and clung tightly to her shoulders. "A beast like that could tear us apart in an instant. Maybe it won't come after us if we move away from it slowly."

"I'm not worried about it harming us bodily," said Liliana. "In fact, that's the least terrible thing it could do to us."

"What?" yelped Juliane. "Whatever do you mean?"

"It's a faerie dog, a hound of hell, and is said to perform two tasks. The first is to bring maidens to fairy mounds so that they might provide milk-nursing to fairy young—"

"But we don't have any milk to give," he interrupted. "How would we..."

His voice trailed off and he blanched, and Liliana said wryly, "See, I told you that being torn apart would be more desirable than the other fates. But that's not even the worst one."

"Then what *is* the worst one?" asked Juliane, voice choked with terror.

"Faerie dogs serve as collectors of souls and are rumored to howl thrice whilst hunting for them. The first howl serves as a warning to take shelter in a place where you can no longer hear its call. The second serves as a signal that the third is nigh. The third—well, it's said to provoke such fright in those who hear it that they die on the spot. Then the faerie dogs take their souls and deliver them to their fairy masters and mistresses, so they may do their bidding until the end of time."

Juliane, struggling to hold back a scream, managed to wheeze, "What should we do?"

"We run to the house down the left path and beg to be let in. The person who lives there must have protections in place against the creatures of this forest, or else they wouldn't have survived here."

"But what if they didn't survive? What if the house is empty?" asked Juliane, despite not really wanting to know the answer.

"Then we're doomed," replied Liliana, face pale, "but at least we'll have tried our best to avoid our fate. Run after me on the count of three. One...two...three!" She sped off down the left-hand path, Juliane following closely behind her. The faerie dog uttered a bloodcurdling howl, and, fearing that it would come after them—or worse yet, howl twice more before they reached safety—they dropped the torch and dashed headlong into the darkness.

Juliane soon fell panting onto the path, and Liliana turned and raced back to him. "Leave me here," he said. "I'm slower than you are. Perhaps the dog will take me and spare you."

"No!" she cried. "We can both make it. I promised I'd help you reach the Darklands, and I do not intend to let you perish here. We flee together, we fight together, and perhaps we die together." She lifted him to his feet and, placing her arm around his shoulders, pulled him along as they tried to escape the terrible beast that they sensed closing in on them.

Just when they felt they could go no further they spied a soft glow in the near distance, and, as they drew closer to it, saw that it came from a candle burning in the window of a small cottage. They rushed toward the building, stumbled up its short flight of stairs, and feverishly pounded upon its door, for they heard, off in the distance but not far enough for their liking, the unmistakable second howl of the faerie dog.

They were about to run down the steps to seek another way into the home when the door swung open, a flood of light poured from the doorway, and a voice cried, "Come inside, quickly!" Not needing to be given the order twice, the travelers scrambled into the cottage and, overcome with relief and overwhelmed by terror, promptly collapsed onto the floor.

9

Liliana regained consciousness to find that she had been draped in a quilt and was lying before a great stone fireplace in a comfortable chamber featuring white walls decorated with a green leaf pattern. When she lifted her head to look around, she discovered a large oak table covered with delicious-looking dishes in the center of the room behind her. It was surrounded by four stout chairs, and Juliane was perched on the rightmost one. He was stuffing his face and, as she lifted herself to a seated position, he crowed, "Liliana, you're awake! Guess what? There's pie!" then continued shoveling food in his mouth.

As he was too distracted to speak with her further, she turned her attention to the person next to him, for occupying the seat at the head of the table was the most beautiful woman Liliana had ever seen. She wore a floor-length gown of green silk embroidered with a leaf pattern, and a circlet of gold with a large emerald at its center adorned her head. She had golden hair, pale skin, rosy cheeks, large green eyes that sparkled, a dainty nose, and a beguiling mouth that was curved into a benevolent smile. "Hail to you!" the voice issuing from between the perfect lips greeted her in a mellifluous trill. "It's so wonderful that you've come out of your faint to join us. I rarely receive visitors, so having two at once is thrilling."

The stranger reached out an arm terminating in a

delicate hand and beckoned for Liliana to join them at the table, so she seated herself in the left-hand chair, next to their mysterious hostess. "I am pleased you appear to be all right," said the woman. "I worried I might not have opened the door in time to save you from the beast following you. I'm afraid not everyone who has come through this forest has been fortunate enough to find me before running into one of the numerous creatures that dwell within. Many are quite dangerous and may rob one of one's life or sanity. This is a faerie wood, after all, and isn't safe to wander about at night."

Liliana mouthed "I told you so" to Juliane, then politely but solemnly addressed their hostess. "Miss, we are undoubtedly grateful for your intervention, but, as we are strangers to this land, we know naught of you. Would you mind telling us who you are and how you've come to live in such a dangerous place?"

The extraordinary woman giggled. "Your companion was speaking the truth when she described you as very forthright! My dear, I will gladly share who I am and how I came to dwell here if you will indulge me by eating whilst I do. Juliane has already explained that you are traveling to the Darklands and has told me that you've walked all day and have eaten very little, so please do enjoy some food whilst I tell my story."

Liliana was uncertain whether she should eat what the woman had provided, as it was unclear whether she could be trusted, but it looked delectable and she *was* dreadfully hungry, so she decided to try one of the golden-crusted pies on the tray nearest her. It was, to her surprise and delight, one of the most delicious things she had ever tasted, and, begrudgingly admitting that the food likely would not kill her, she filled a plate with fruit, pies, and cheese.

The woman laughed as if she could read Liliana's thoughts, then began her tale. "My name is Rhoswen Briarleaf, and I am one of the fair folk." Liliana stopped chewing and stared at her warily, and she hastily reassured her guests, "I know that your experiences with others of my ilk have been unpleasant thus far, but you needn't fear me, for I am a fairy of light and live in this forest to combat the evil that dwells herein."

Liliana relaxed a little, and Rhoswen continued, "This wood was a very dark place before my coming here, and many were lost as they traveled through it. Some grew confused due to the stray sods and wandered aimlessly until they died of starvation, whilst others were hunted and taken by the faerie dogs. Some were said to have been lured into lakes or rivers by a Water-horse, but I'm not sure if this is true, for I have never seen one. And, of course, there are many other nasty creatures haunting these woods."

"So, I decided to come build my home here. I made it cozy and welcoming, so that weary travelers could find rest within rather than risk sleeping in the woods; Silvan is but a day's walk from here, so, if one spends the night with me, one need only travel during daylight. As a fairy I know how to keep the darker forces of the wood at bay, and this house has protections built into its walls that keep those inside safe. In this way, I have helped several travelers." She sighed. "I so rarely receive guests nowadays, though, for most are too frightened of the wood ever to enter it. I'm often quite lonely, which is why I'm so happy to have not just one, but two guests—and two maidens at that! Why, I cannot recall the last time I've met a woman crossing these woods. It is such a treat to have you come stay with me. I'm most willing to provide any assistance you might require."

"Quite a lucky spot we've gotten ourselves into!" said Juliane, beaming at the fairy. "We can stay here tonight and continue on to Silvan in the morning. Rhoswen is so kind, isn't she?"

Liliana felt a slight twinge as he gazed at Rhoswen, but, as it was unthinkable that she would experience jealousy regarding his attentiveness toward the fairy, she attributed this prick of emotion to her unease regarding their hostess and surroundings. Something did not seem right—their finding a safe place to stay filled with glorious food and a charming and hospitable landlady in the middle of this wood filled with dark magic seemed too good to be true. However, as she knew she tended to be overly wary and that this had served to her detriment at times, she decided that, though she would remain alert, she would give Rhoswen a chance to prove herself trustworthy before assuming otherwise.

The travelers nibbled the fine food while Rhoswen amused them with tales of her countless years of life—for, though she seemed near to them in age, she confessed to being much older—for many hours, until the fire in the hearth dwindled to cinders. Noticing her guests yawning, the fairy said, "I guess it's time for you to be off to bed. As an immortal I do not require rest, and I forget how you humans tire! Come, let me show you to your rooms."

"Rooms?" asked a surprised Liliana, for she had been sure that, in a house of this size, the travelers would be sharing a bedchamber.

"Yes, rooms. Since I have no need for sleep, I will give one of you my bedroom, whilst the other can sleep in the room I keep for guests. As the beds are small, this will provide you with the greatest comfort. Juliane, you seem the type to enjoy luxury, so you may have my bed."

"Oh, thank you!" he cried, and he got up to follow the fairy, who had risen from her chair and had started down the hallway leading from the main room. Liliana was seized with the unwelcome notion that Rhoswen was purposely separating the travelers, and she determined that, though she would go to her room as instructed, she would take extra precautions to keep herself safe once ensconced within.

She trailed the others down the passage, which featured

three doorways, one on each side and one at its end.
Rhoswen reached into a hidden pocket in her gown and
removed a ring of keys. She used one to open the right-
hand door, and revealed a room painted in soothing blue
tones with a washstand, night table, and canopied bed.
"Liliana, you may sleep here tonight. I hope you have
pleasant dreams," Rhoswen said, and she kissed Liliana's
cheek, leaving behind the scent of roses. This gave Liliana a
momentary thrill that swiftly turned into a chill, for she
had sensed hunger in that kiss. She watched the fairy lead
Juliane down the passage, usher him into a larger green
bedchamber, and kiss him as well, and she shivered when,
afterward, the fairy smirked suggestively over her shoulder
at her—as if to say, *And wouldn't you like another?*

She hurried into her room, closed the door, and turned
the key that had been left in the lock, then she stripped to
her chemise, washed herself, and took the still-damp items
from the Wrathscalders' line out of her pack. She hung
them to dry on the canopy, and she was about to climb into
bed when she heard a rustling outside her door. "Who's
there?" she called out timidly.

"It is I, Rhoswen. Could you come to the door to speak?
I do not wish to disturb Juliane, as she seems to have
already fallen asleep."

Liliana crept to the doorway and, ducking near the
keyhole, whispered, "Yes, Rhoswen? What do you want?"

"I've come to ask you that same question!" Rhoswen
said, giggling. "I wanted to know if there's anything I might
get for you to make your stay more comfortable."

"I'm not in need of anything, but thank you," Liliana
replied.

She turned from the door and started to move toward
the bed when the fairy stayed her. "Are you quite sure?"
Rhoswen's tone at first puzzled Liliana, but her heart sank
as she realized she detected a lustful note in the fairy's
voice. "I was wondering if you would like it if I joined you

in your room for a while, just for a chat."

Liliana felt a flutter of fear, for the fact that the fairy had separated the travelers and now seemed to be trying to seduce one of them did not belie her having pure intentions. Struggling to keep her voice calm, she responded, "I'm sorry, but I'm terribly tired. Perhaps we could talk tomorrow instead?" She then fled to the bed, where she huddled under the bedclothes.

There was a soft sigh outside the door, and she heard Rhoswen say, "Goodnight, clever Liliana." The fairy moved away from the door, and soon the only trace of her that remained was the strong scent of roses.

Liliana remained curled up under the blankets, afraid Rhoswen might return with some means of entering the room. She relaxed when she did not, and unexpectedly found herself floating off to sleep, something she had been sure she would be incapable of doing after the discomfiting interaction. She experienced a passing worry that Rhoswen might try the same approach with Juliane, and, as she floated off, prayed he had locked his door before retiring to bed.

Juliane, encased in comfortable covers, rested peacefully; after having been escorted to her bedroom by his hostess, he had barely removed his gown before he was overcome by exhaustion and tumbled into the bed. Inhaling the scent of roses Rhoswen had left behind, he told himself, *How strange life is! I feared for my very soul mere hours ago, and now I'm lying safe and cozy in the sumptuous bed of a real live fairy. Liliana and I are so lucky to have reached her before the faerie dog got us.* Having recalled Liliana, his thoughts drifted to her, for he regretted being shuffled off to bed before he had gotten a chance to speak with her. He had left the chamber door unlocked on the off chance she might come to visit him, and, dwelling on this pleasant possibility, he swiftly dropped off to sleep.

He was woken, what seemed mere minutes later, by a movement in the room. His eyes popped open, and he stiffened as it crossed his mind that one of the wood's many fiendish creatures might have come to pay him a visit, but he was relieved when a female silhouette passed through the moonlight filtering into the room. The figure climbed wordlessly into bed with him, and he whispered, "Liliana, have you come to see me? I am glad you did, for I had gotten used to our sharing a bed. It was a bit lonely and frightening without you."

He was about to say more when, to his surprise, she threw her arms around his neck. "Liliana, what's going on?" he asked, at first confused, then, exhilarated, he cried, "Oh, Liliana, you must have finally decided that, whilst we're on this journey, we should enjoy each other's company! I had been hoping you would..." He trailed off abruptly, for he had noticed that the person embracing him smelled strongly of roses, much like... "Rhoswen?" he yelped, pulling away from her. "What are you doing here?"

The woman sat up, and, relighting the candle on the bedside table, revealed herself to indeed be his hostess. She was clothed in a filmy green garment that accentuated her every curve, and Juliane gulped, for he found himself powerfully attracted to her. "Well met, Juliane," she purred. "I know you thought that I was Liliana, but you don't mind that it's me, do you?"

He shook his head. "N-no, of course not, I just—"

"It's fine," she interrupted. "I agree she's lovely, but, when I kissed her cheek before bed, I received the impression that, although she would very much like for it to occur, she hasn't yet been with a woman—at least, not in the way in which you, and I, have." His eyes widened, and she grinned. "Yes, Juliane, when I kissed your cheek, I discovered that you're a woman who greatly enjoys the company other women, and that you hoped Liliana might one day give in to your temptations. Well, I was wondering if instead *I* might tempt *you*."

He nodded enthusiastically, and she leaned forward, pressing her mouth to his. He eagerly returned the kiss, and, when their lips parted, said, in the most alluringly feminine manner he could muster, "Oh, yes, please tempt me, Rhoswen."

"Only if you promise to stay with me and be my lover awhile. I have been so lonely, and I need someone to care for my needs. Can you vow to do this for me?"

Believing that she meant to keep him for a month at most—as it usually took him about that long to tire of a dalliance—he thought things over for half a second before determining that circumstances such as these justified delaying his transformation a few weeks more. "Yes, Rhoswen, I promise I will care for your needs for as long as you require me to."

A delighted Rhoswen covered him in kisses, and he was so pleased that he did not notice that, oddly enough, she had kept her boots on in bed. At one point Liliana's disapproving face flashed through his mind, and he fleetingly wondered if he might have made a mistake in promising Rhoswen his allegiance for an unspecified period of time—but then the fairy reminded him that there were many wonderful things about his new body that he had not yet discovered, and all his thoughts disappeared.

10.

The following morning Liliana woke in Rhoswen's guest room feeling well-rested, and she noted that she had slept deeply for the first time since they had set off on the journey. This concerned her, for she had a hard time attributing her sound slumber to exhaustion and instead suspected it had resulted from an enchantment. She remembered the sigh that had accompanied Rhoswen's leaving her doorway and wondered if the fairy had done something to render her unconscious, for she recalled a powerful scent of roses, stronger than the usual fragrance that surrounded the fairy, filling her nostrils before she drifted into oblivion.

She was seized with a dreadful thought: perhaps Rhoswen had put her to sleep because she had intended to do something to Juliane and did not want her to interfere? Worried, she dressed herself and then left the room to investigate. She noticed that the door to Rhoswen's bedchamber stood partially open, so she tiptoed down the hallway and, reaching it, opened it as noiselessly as she could.

Peeking through the doorway, she was taken aback by what she saw. Rhoswen and Juliane slumbered in the bed entwined in each other's arms, and it was clear from their mussed hair, the rumpled bed covers, and the satisfied smile upon the fairy's face that they had not done much sleeping the night before. Cheeks burning, Liliana backed out of the room. She felt angry and disappointed, and she considered leaving the fairy's house to return home—after all, Juliane could surely ask Rhoswen for the assistance he required.

Once she had taken some time to cool off, though, she still felt unsettled. Thinking things over, she determined that this unease was not the result of finding out that Juliane, whom she had considered to be making slow but steady progress, was still throwing himself at any maiden who batted lashes at him; rather, something about his appearance had unnerved her. She peered into the room once more and confirmed that he did indeed look strange— while Rhoswen seemed radiant and restored, he seemed pallid and weary.

A very unpleasant thought crossed her mind regarding who—or more accurately, *what*—their hostess might be, and she decided to explore the home for evidence confirming her suspicions. After closing the door softly, she headed into the sitting room, where she found Rhoswen's glorious silk gown tossed upon a chair. Remembering that the fairy had kept a keyring in her dress, she silently prayed that it would be there and was pleased to discover that it was. Once she had acquired it, though, she experienced fresh apprehension, for she had to admit to herself why she needed it: she planned on entering the room Rhoswen had not shown them the night before.

She crept down the hallway to the left-hand door, gingerly tried keys until she found the one that unlocked it, then slowly pulled the door open and peered into the room. She was, in that moment, thankful for her strong constitution, for, if she had been a weaker soul, she might have fainted. As it was, she had to bite her hand to keep from screaming, for leaning against the chamber's rear wall were five hideous things that had once been people.

It was at first hard to determine what they were, for they resembled hides left to cure in the sun, but it grew dreadfully clear that they were human corpses once she had taken a closer look at them. Four of the bodies were men's—they varied in hair color and skin tone and it was difficult to determine their ages due to their desiccated state—but the fifth was that of a woman who might have been pretty once, but whose features had become horribly sunken and distorted.

Choking back a cry of fright, Liliana retreated into the passage, closing the door to the obscene room behind her. She leaned against a wall until she had composed herself, then flew into her room, grabbed her pack, and took out the book her mother had given her. She flipped through it until she came to a section on dark fairies, then scanned the page until she found the passage she had been seeking; though she blanched at what she read there, she knew the time had come to bring to light what had been so skillfully kept in darkness.

Carrying the book at her side, she marched down the hallway to the fairy's bedchamber. Opening the door cautiously, she slipped inside the room and crept to the foot of the bed. Lifting the bedclothes covering Rhoswen's legs, she steeled herself and pulled off one of the large furred boots the fairy was wearing. What she discovered beneath it confirmed her fears, and she cried out at the top of her voice, "Juliane!"

Feeling groggy and out of sorts, Juliane came out of his stupor to find Liliana standing at the foot of the bed. He was at first ashamed and remorseful, for he was certain she was upset about how carelessly he had gone to bed with Rhoswen, but then he noticed that her expression was one of alarm rather than outrage. "What's wrong, Liliana?" he asked, worried, and he hopped out of the bed to see what she was staring at. Underneath the blanket, where the fairy's foot should have been, was a horse's hoof crowned with silky white fur.

"You fool!" she shrieked as he staggered backward. "Do

you have any idea what you've done?"

Rhoswen had woken, but, rather than halt the dramatic interaction, chose to lay back on the pillow and watch. "Do let her know, dear," she mischievously goaded Liliana.

Grabbing Juliane by the shoulders, Liliana screeched, "You've become the lover of a fairy mistress!"

"What?" he squawked. "What exactly are you saying?"

"I am saying that you've dallied with a dark faerie seductress known as a fairy mistress, as that is most certainly what that thing in the bed is."

Rhoswen, taking offense at having been called a "thing," decided it was time to insert herself into the conversation. "She's right, you know." Juliane gaped at her, mingled confusion and fear spreading over his face. "I am indeed a fairy mistress. What does that mean, you may ask? Well, let's see—it obviously means that I have hooves rather than feet, and that I'm incredibly beguiling."

"It also means," interjected Liliana, "that you are a being who stays alive and eternally young by stealing the life-forces of others, and that those who vow to be your lovers are gradually drained until they become dead, brittle husks like the five abominations you keep in your locked room!" She heard a soft thud to the side of her, and she turned to discover that Juliane had swooned and had fallen to the floor.

Rhoswen clapped her hands. "Oh, Liliana, you are as intelligent as you are beautiful!" She surveyed the insensible Juliane and clucked her tongue. "It's just too bad you weren't able to impart your knowledge to her before she pledged herself to me."

Liliana stormed over to where the fairy reclined and, leaning over her, screamed, "I was supposed to look after her and make sure she got what she needed! I cannot let her be sucked dry by you." She picked up the candlestick from the table near the bed. "I could kill you for this."

Rhoswen was unconcerned. "Oh, Liliana, you're likely just as aware as I am that you cannot kill my kind. We merely go on, living off the energies of others, fading away only if we cannot feed. Your friend is mine until the end of her days, which are currently quite numbered—that is, unless you're willing to make a bargain."

Liliana took a step backward, replacing the candlestick. "What did you say?"

"You know perfectly well what I just said," teased Rhoswen. "It's obvious you're educated regarding faerie folk, so you must know that the only way one can be released from servitude to the likes of me is through their being replaced with another. Frankly, I wanted you in the first place, for you're stronger and wiser than your companion—and, of course, your being a virgin makes you an even tastier meal."

Liliana gasped. "How do you know I'm a—"

"I gleaned it when I kissed your cheek last night," said the fairy. "I haven't had a virgin in such a long time—and a female one, of your caliber?" She licked her lips. "You, my dear, are a delicacy. I only snared your friend because she was easier prey." She moved toward the edge of the bed and grabbed Liliana's arm. "Be mine, Liliana," she cooed. "The remainder of your life may be brief, but, oh, the glories you'll experience during it! I'm known to be quite the muse to humans in my thrall. Think of the sonnets you'll write, the works you shall create! You'll die the sort of death all artists dream of."

Liliana jerked her arm from the fairy's grasp. "I've never considered myself an artist, so I believe I'll pass."

Rhoswen pouted, then, noticing that Juliane was stirring, said, "Well, I guess I'll just have to consume your friend, then. It's too bad, though. I'll tell you a secret: when I came to her room to tempt her, she at first believed that I was you and was elated at the possibility. I also sense that you're attracted to her but for some reason choose to deny it. It's such a shame that nothing will ever come of these hidden desires."

Blushing, Liliana looked down at Juliane, who had come out of his daze; he sat up, and, when he heard what Rhoswen had said, reddened until he resembled a fully ripened apple. Liliana refused to address the fairy's insinuations, and instead asked, "What if I was to find a replacement for her? Someone who longs for the fate you can provide, who would willingly sacrifice their life for a taste of magic?"

Rhoswen pondered her words a moment, then said, "Fine. I will allow you to find a suitable substitute. I shall give you two days to do this, for it takes hours to reach Silvan from here and you're unlikely to find anyone in these woods. Search for someone who desires to belong to me, body and soul. If you find them, bring them here. Once they're delivered to me, I shall release your friend." Having been given this permission, Liliana rushed to her room and quickly packed her belongings, pulled on her stockings and shoes, and grabbed her bag.

When she returned to bid Juliane farewell, he threw his arms around her and, gazing up at her, apologized for getting them into such a mess. Fear and regret twisted his face, and, momentarily forgetting that his poorly managed desires had caused their troubles, she pitied him and reached down to return his embrace. "I hate to insert myself into such a touching scene," Rhoswen interrupted, "but, Liliana, may I make an entreaty of you before you go?"

Liliana straightened and peered at her warily. "What is it, Rhoswen?"

"Could you, well, try to bring me someone a little less 'experienced' than Juliane? You see, those who've had many affairs tend to taste...staler than others. If you could do that, I would greatly appreciate it."

Despite the dire circumstances, Liliana could barely

suppress a giggle as Juliane's expression grew indignant. "I'll see what I can manage," she promised, then she ran out of the house before the fairy could change her mind.

Rhoswen sighed as she watched her go. "It's too bad she didn't offer herself in your stead. She's just so...fresh." She looked down at Juliane, who sat glowering on the floor. "Why don't you come to bed? You're mine until she replaces you, and I want to enjoy you."

"I thought I was too stale for your tastes," he remarked huffily.

"Oh, darling, don't be cross about that! Remember, what you lack in flavor you make up for in skill," she said with a wink, and this admittedly softened him. Figuring that there were worse ways to go than being dallied to death, he climbed onto the bed and determined to make the most of his servitude until Liliana returned.

***

Once she had left Rhoswen's, Liliana followed the path she and Juliane had run down in terror the night before back to the crossroads. As she tramped along, she wondered whether the faerie dog had been as great a risk as it had seemed to be or if it had merely been working in concert with Rhoswen, but she supposed it did not matter regardless. Grumbling to herself about Juliane's inability to keep his hands off any attractive woman within arm's length of him and the inevitable problems this caused, she came to the fork, then headed down the right-hand path toward Silvan.

After walking for hours and finding no sign of the forest's end, she grew concerned that she might not make it out of the wood before nightfall; additionally, her water supply was dangerously low, as she had forgotten to replenish it in her rush to leave Rhoswen's that morning. She suddenly experienced a stroke of good luck, though, for the thick woods opened into a clearing and she beheld a large lake before her. Thrilled, she left the path and crossed the grass to the water. After determining that it seemed clean, she gulped great mouthfuls of it until her thirst was quenched, then filled her drinking vessel to the brim.

She was rising from the lakeside when, to her surprise, she heard hoof beats. Glancing up, she discovered the most regal-looking horse she had ever seen galloping toward her. It was powerfully built with a silky white coat, its mane and tail were coal-black, and it wore no saddle, only a bit-less bridle of fine leather. As it neared her, it slowed its pace and then shyly approached her, halting a few yards away from her. *What a lovely horse!* she thought. *If I can mount it, I can ride it to Silvan.* She approached the animal, but, when she was a few paces from it, she suddenly stopped, for she realized that she had almost walked right into a trap. She was near a lake, and a supernaturally lovely horse had appeared out of nowhere and had unhesitatingly come to her... She backed away from the creature, holding her hands up defensively, for she now understood that she was mere feet away from a dreaded Water-horse.

The creature seemed to sense her fear, for it took a few steps toward her and attempted to nuzzle her outstretched hands as if to say, *Don't worry, I'm simply a horse.* Liliana was not deceived by its behavior, though, and cried, "Get away from me! I know what you are, and I'll not fall victim to your ruse." She searched her brain, trying to remember all she had read about the feared beast, and suddenly recalled a way in which she might subdue it using the fear of iron held by all faerie. She reached into her bag with a trembling hand, felt around until she grasped the desired object, then screamed, "Get back!" as she pulled out an amulet and held it up to the horse.

The animal closed its eyes, and, releasing a piteous neigh, fell to its knees. Liliana ran over to it and pulled off its bridle. "I know you're just a regular horse without this," she said, brandishing it at the creature. "Since you cannot place it back on yourself, you cannot harm me." The Water-horse rose, timidly walked over to her, and bowed its head before her in seeming admission of defeat.

Pleased at having bested the legendary fiend, she boldly addressed it. "I know this isn't your only form. If you'd like you may keep it, and I will hide your bridle somewhere and ride you into Silvan. Once you have helped me complete my errand, I will return it if you promise not to bother me once I have. Or, if you'd like, you can change into your human form and we can discuss what I'm trying to accomplish and how you might best help me. I'm aware you'll need your bridle to transform, so I'll place it back on you but will hold the iron piece next to you whilst I do. If you try to run from or harm me, I will press it into your flesh so your pretty hide will forever be marked. Do I make myself clear?"

The horse nodded, and she asked, "Would you like to change forms?" It nodded once more, so she again held the amulet out. The creature shut its eyes and dropped to its knees, and she placed its bridle halfway over its head. It started to shimmer and, within seconds, had taken on a human form. She snatched off the bridle and placed it into her bag along with the amulet, then told the Water-horse, "You may look now. I have taken the iron away."

It rose, and, when it lifted its head and opened its eyes, she could not help but gasp. The being, clad only in a worn pair of black velvet trousers, a black vest, and large black boots that almost certainly covered hooves, was of indeterminate sex—it had a flat chest but a feminine face and form—and was startlingly gorgeous. It was a head taller than her, and its white, hairless skin glowed. A lustrous black mane fell to its waist, it had large brown eyes ringed with thick charcoal lashes, its soft pink lips peaked in a faultless bow, and the unblemished perfection of its features evoked in her recollections of gods and goddesses that she had seen in books. Without thinking, she exclaimed, "You're beautiful!" then, mortified, turned from the creature, hoping it would not notice how she had blushed.

She heard the Water-horse approach and then found herself face-to-face with it. "You're not so bad to look at yourself," it said, "but you're still an awful person for taking my bridle."

"And I suppose I should have sat upon you, allowed you to drag me into the lake, and silently suffered while you drowned me?"

It smiled, showing perfect white teeth. "Yes! Aren't I enchanting enough to deserve that?"

Liliana glared at it. "How attractive you may be doesn't matter to me, for I'm aware of what you truly are—a disgusting human eater! So, no, your looks have no sway over me, and you had better work with me if you want to get that bridle back."

She marched away toward the path, and it trotted along after her. "Wait, I didn't mean to upset you!" It caught up with her and grasped her by the arm. "Please, tell me what I can do to help you, so that I might have it restored to me."

"How far are we from the town of Silvan?"

"About half an hour's travel when I am trotting."

She groaned. "And the sun is already setting. I do not relish the idea of bedding down for the night in this wood, but I'm afraid of what we might run into should we pass through it in darkness."

The Water-horse appeared contemplative, and it said, "I might know a place where you can sleep safely tonight. If you follow me, I'll take you there."

Wondering if this was an attempt to ensnare her, Liliana asked warily, "How do I know you're not just trying to lead me to my doom so you can devour me?"

"Because you have my bridle. If a mortal takes it from

me, they must replace it; I can only put it on myself if I am the one who has removed it. Without it I'm much like a mere mortal, for, though I do not age, I can fall prey to the same perils you can and only desire the foods you eat. If I led you to your death, I'd be unable to regain my horse form, and so I must keep you safe until it's returned."

She understood that she had no choice but to trust the creature, so, glowering, she said, "Fine, show me where I can spend the night out of harm's way."

The Water-horse beckoned for her to follow, and they walked along the shore until they reached the far side of the lake, then went down an overgrown trail into the forest. After they had gone a short distance, they came to a rocky hillside with a large boulder leaning against it. The creature approached the rock and knocked upon it three times, and it moved aside to reveal the mouth of a cave.

Liliana stared at it incredulously. "Do you honestly expect that I'll feel safe accompanying you into a dwelling where the only exit shall be blocked by a stone?"

"Well, it's either that or spend the night outside," the Water-horse matter-of-factly said, and, admitting that it had a point, Liliana begrudgingly trailed it into the dark opening.

11.

Once both were inside the cave, the Water-horse reached behind a pile of stones and removed a candle, flint and steel, and a wooden splint. Once it had ignited the candle, it had Liliana hold it while it returned the other items to their places, then knocked on the boulder thrice more. As the stone moved over the entrance, sealing them within the cave, Liliana experienced some apprehension about being trapped with such a fearsome creature, but, as she had been assured it did not crave human meat while in its current form, she accepted her lot and determined she would make the best of it.

The Water-horse took the candle from her, and she followed it down a long tunnel to a doorway set at its end. It removed a key from a crevice, unlocked the door, and opened it. Liliana squinted and, as her eyes adjusted to the dimness, grew amazed, for there seemed to be a dwelling beyond the threshold. She could not see much at first, but, once several more candles had been lit, she found herself looking upon a cozy shelter containing a table and two rough-hewn chairs, several shelves filled with books and other objects, and a large bed covered with pillows and quilts. She stepped into the room, and, once she had found her voice, asked, "What is this place?"

"Oh, it's my little hideaway," the Water-horse said proudly. "Sometimes one tires of lurking in a lake's murky depths and would rather relax in a place that's quiet and dry. I suppose I've gotten rather spoiled when it comes to human comforts, for I often travel to and stay in places like Silvan, Lavinia, and Hawthorn whilst searching for my meals."

"How often do you need to eat?" asked Liliana, repulsed yet fascinated.

"When I'm in human form? Regularly, as humans do. When I'm in beast form? Usually a few times a year. I try to eat strong men, as they can tide me over for quite a while, although they don't taste nearly as good as pretty young maidens do." Liliana frowned, and it quickly reassured her that it generally tried to eat blackguards and ruffians. "I mean, since I am what I am, I *have* to eat people, but I try not to consume the good ones—though I'll admit one sometimes has to take advantage of what one comes across, hence my trying to snare you earlier today. I'm sorry about that, for whatever that's worth."

The creature bade her have a seat at the table, and, after she had perched herself on one chair, it sat down on the other and requested her name. "I am Liliana Almwick, and I come from a town a few days' walk from here," she replied. "Do you have a name, or should I just call you Water-horse? Also, I feel ill-mannered asking this, but...are you a woman, or a man?"

"If I was ever given a name, I do not recall it—I may have gotten one many centuries ago, but, if so, I cannot place it. I call myself 'Tancred' whilst visiting the towns, so you may also call me that. And I am neither female nor male, I am something else. I'm sure you've noticed that my appearance is feminine but that I have no breasts, and— how do I put this delicately?—I'm what some might call an 'androgyne'. It's no surprise that my body doesn't fit easily into humankind's categories, really, for I'm not human despite seeming so. Since I'm man and woman combined, you may call me 'they' or 'them,' as you would any two

97

people."

Remembering that she was sitting across from a creature who, in their other form, ate humans, she tentatively asked, "Am I the only mortal you've brought here who hasn't ended up a meal?"

Tancred laughed. "I don't bring meals to this place; the clean-up would be horrendous!" Liliana's face twisted in disgust, and they hastily continued, "Remember, as a Water-horse, my method of feeding is to ride someone into water and drown them before eating them. This cave is the place I bring mortals to who rouse my interest and sometimes satiate...a different hunger. On rare occasions I'll meet folks so captivating that I'll want to spend time with them—I know it seems absurd for a Water-horse to desire human company, but, when you've lived on your own for a thousand years, you get lonely sometimes—so I bring them here for as long as they'll stay. Most pass only a day or so with me, for they know what I am and fear spending too much time with me. A few have stayed with me for weeks, though, and we have spent joyful days riding through the woods and even more joyful nights..."

They trailed off, for they noticed Liliana reddening. "Let's just say I've had many good times in this cave." A trace of melancholy entered their voice. "One man stayed with me for many months. He was a skilled musician, and had bronze skin, dark hair, deep brown eyes, and the kindest face I've ever seen. I cried for days when he left me. I think...that was the closest I'd ever come to falling in love," they finished wistfully.

Liliana, who had listened to them raptly, said, "I didn't think a Water-horse could be tenderhearted, but, whilst hearing you speak of those you've cared for and lost, I sensed a sadness within you. Part of me still views you as something to fear, but a larger part pities you and hopes your emptiness shall one day be filled. Though you're still fundamentally a monster, you have shaped yourself into

98

more than that; despite not being human, you've developed humanity. You are a most interesting creature indeed."

Tancred smiled ruefully. "I wish I'd met you whilst in my human form, rather than in that meadow in my other guise, for I think I would have given you my bridle willingly." Touched by their words, Liliana reached across the table to clasp their hand. Sheepishly withdrawing from her grasp, they said, "I'm afraid I don't have any food stored here. I don't visit regularly and so don't keep it stocked. We may be hungry tonight."

"I suppose we're in luck that I have some, then," declared Liliana, taking out the remainder of the food she and Juliane had filched from the Wrathscalders' larder. She offered some to Tancred, who, whinnying with delight, gobbled a large apple, a piece of bread, and a hunk of cheese. Licking their lips, they thanked her for sharing the repast, and she said, "Well, I don't have to worry about saving any for Juliane, as she's surely being fed by Rhoswen, and so I can afford to part with it."

Tancred peered at her curiously. "Who is Juliane?"

"She's my traveling companion, and why I'm journeying through this forest on my own. I am her guardian, and I'm supposed to help her reach the Darklands, a kingdom some distance from here. The problem is that she throws herself at every woman within spitting distance, and this has placed her in a nasty predicament."

Tancred was intrigued. "Your friend is a maiden who likes other maidens?"

"Yes, a bit too much."

"I have known few women who've liked other women 'too much'," said the Water-horse. "She must be a very unusual creature."

"She is indeed," agreed Liliana, for, to her surprise, she found that Juliane's quirks had grown somewhat endearing to her during their travels, Goddess knew why. "I'll be honest with you: Juliane is actually Julian Stoneshire,

99

prince of this land. Someone I'm close to turned him into a girl due to his horrid behavior toward women—she wanted him to see what it was like to be one so that he might develop an increased understanding of them. I am helping him get what he needs to undo his curse, as I feel somewhat responsible for his plight. I'm sometimes unsure of why I continue to assist him, though, for he—I mean, she—is still frequently an ass."

Tancred raised their eyebrows and encouraged her to go on, and she related how Juliane had gotten ensnared by Rhoswen. "I have until tomorrow night to find someone willing to replace her, someone willing to sacrifice their life to obtain a faerie muse. I am afraid I won't find anyone, though, and that she'll remain in service until she's sucked dry."

"I'll take her place," Tancred said quietly.

Liliana nearly spit out the bit of bread she was chewing. "What did you say?"

"I'll take her place. I'm the perfect substitute, as my life-force cannot be drained due to my being immortal—the only way I can be killed is by being fatally wounded. I could replace your friend and dally with the fairy until she tires of and releases me—or I can try to eat her. I've always wondered how fairies taste."

Liliana understood that they were being serious, and her eyes widened. "You're right, you *are* the perfect replacement. If you offer yourself to her, she may never again have to kill for sustenance!"

"Or, if she decides to release me, perhaps I can eat the bodies of those she kills so that only one need die instead of two?" Tancred suggested playfully, then immediately dodged the apple that went whizzing past their head. "I'll just pretend I didn't say that," they murmured, smirking, as they reached down to pick it up off the floor.

After straightening, wiping the apple on their trousers,

and consuming it in three bites, Tancred said, "I've told you of my inclinations and have heard more than enough regarding your companion's, so I feel at liberty to pry into yours. Do you like women? Do you like men? Or are you, like me, someone who takes advantage of whatever enjoyable affair falls into their lap?"

"I don't rightly know," Liliana admitted. "I know I have found both women and men attractive, but everyone I've been drawn to has been at least as feminine as I am."

"Do you consider me feminine, and therefore attractive?"

"I think you're the most beautiful being I've ever seen. I will let you determine whether I'm attracted to you or not based on that information."

"Impertinent wench," scolded Tancred, unable to hide their grin.

Liliana continued, "I suspect that I prefer women to men and have throughout my life, but, when I was younger, I always assumed that if I liked a girl she would not reciprocate and so didn't try to form any connections. I've found few men I've met attractive; as Juliane in her male form was one of them, I decided to let myself compete for her hand, and... Well, you know how that turned out." She paused, then said, "I'm twenty-six years old, and I've never really *been* with anyone—that is to say, I've never experienced more than a kiss."

Tancred stared at her, open-mouthed. "You're a virgin."

"I am," she admitted. "I suppose you'll now want to eat me due to virgins having a marvelous flavor?"

"No, I still like you too much to eat you. Besides, I recall virgins tasting musty."

"You must be wrong, because, according to Rhoswen, I'm a delicacy."

"Are you *trying* to convince me to eat you?"

Liliana stuck her tongue out at them, and they both burst into laughter. "I'm still having a hard time believing that you've never been with anyone," Tancred remarked once they had settled down, "for you are charming and clever and, though not as gorgeous as I—for few are, after all—nonetheless exceedingly attractive." When Liliana informed them that it was the epitome of vanity to compliment oneself while praising another, they pretended to pout, then the pair dissolved into giggles once more.

After they had calmed Liliana changed the subject, for it made her uncomfortable to discuss her lack of experience in certain areas. Tancred gladly engaged her in fresh conversation, and they proceeded to talk for hours about a variety of things. Liliana eventually wandered over to the shelves to look at the books there and found one with astonishing pictures written in a language she had never seen nor heard of; Tancred told her they could translate it for her, and so the duo sat down upon the bed and read the story together. Liliana kept losing track of the plot, though, for an idea had crept into her mind as she had gotten to know (and to greatly like) the Water-horse and she found she could not stop reflecting upon it. As Tancred read on, oblivious, she came to a decision regarding the matter and determined that she would act upon it forthwith.

Tancred soon finished the book, and they placed it on the floor next to the bed and, sighing contentedly, turned to Liliana. "I'd forgotten how marvelous that one was. It was good of you to bring it to me." She thanked them for sharing it with her, and the pair, noticing just how near to one another they had gotten while reading, exchanged shy glances—and then suddenly they were in each other's arms, mouths pressed together in a kiss. It was enjoyable but brief, for Tancred broke it and said, "I'm sorry, Liliana, you were so close to me and—"

"Don't apologize, for I've wanted to kiss you all night," she interrupted them. "Frankly, I'd like to do more than just kiss you."

"You're not saying you want to..." the Water-horse

trailed off, reddening prettily.

"I most certainly am. I've not dared to take this chance for too long, and I cannot imagine a better opportunity. I'm tired of being the sensible person who always overthinks things. I want to give in to my desires for a change."

"But I've been with so many people—I am, after all, a thousand years old. Believe me, I'm interested, as I'm terribly attracted to you, but I also like you a lot. You're someone I would have gladly handed my bridle to, so I don't want to spend one night with you only to have you regret it. I guess...I'm not as much of a monster as people might believe me to be."

"I will not regret it," she assured them. "I'd expected that the right moment would come during this quest. I had thought I might end up letting Juliane be my first partner, as I believed I might eventually give in to my attractions if her behavior improved, but my being with you is a more perfect circumstance than I could have foreseen. You're not a woman or a man, you're a Water-horse, and I think you're one of the most amazing beings I have ever met. I cannot imagine anyone more fitting to share the occasion with."

Convinced, Tancred lowered their eyes and said softly, "I will do whatever you wish, then. I want this to be everything you've ever hoped it would be."

Liliana climbed across the bed until she was nearly in Tancred's lap, and, placing her hands on their head, lifted their face to hers. "May I kiss you?" she asked coyly, and, when they whinnied in assent, she placed her lips firmly on theirs. They keenly returned the kiss, and she embraced them, stroking their long black mane. Things were growing heated when she suddenly withdrew her mouth from theirs and whispered in their ear, "Tancred, before we continue, I have one thing that I must ask."

"Go ahead."

She hesitated, then said, "Is *all* of you, um, humanly

103

proportioned? I've seen horses, and I don't think I could..."
Her voice trailed off, and she blushed deeply. Tancred let
out a hearty laugh and assured her she had nothing to
worry about, and so she gladly recommenced kissing them
and the pair fell backward onto the bed, happily enfolded
in each other's arms.

12.

Liliana woke in near-darkness the following morning, at first confused as to where she was, but, once she had shaken off sleep, she remembered that she was in the Water-horse's cave, having shared its bed in more ways than one. She initially felt a touch of alarm at being left on her own, but she soon convinced herself there was nothing to fear and let her mind wander to what had happened the night before. Her experience with Tancred had been nothing short of bliss, and she now felt confident she would be able to successfully dally with whomever she might desire to. She knew her rash actions had been more like Juliane's usual behavior than her own, but it had been freeing to act upon her impulses for once. Smiling, she determined that, from now on, she would give in to her impetuous side from time to time, as the results of doing so could be delightful.

The door swung open and she covered herself with a blanket, but, to her relief, it was only Tancred who entered the cave. "I'm sorry if I worried you by leaving you alone, I'd just gone out to fetch us some breakfast." They poured the contents of the bowl they were carrying onto the table, and Liliana discovered that they had picked some blackberries and apples and had spent the morning catching and preparing fish. The Water-horse pulled two plates from a shelf and placed some food on each while

Liliana dressed herself. She joined them at the table, and
the pair ate quietly, for Tancred stared at their food
throughout the meal, seemingly deep in thought. After
finishing their portion, they pushed their plate away and
looked up at her. "Liliana, I have something to say."

"Yes, Tancred, what is it?"

"I would like to ask you to stay with me a while." Noting
her surprise, they quickly continued, "You can ride me into
Silvan this morning. I'm sure it won't take long for us to
find someone so desperate for food and shelter he wouldn't
mind warming the fairy's bed. We can gallop to her home
and make the exchange, then we can take Juliane to the
forest's edge so she can finish her quest and you
can...return here with me."

"You certainly have planned all this out," Liliana said
gently, "but, though I'd love to spend more time with you, I
promised Juliane I would assist her in breaking her curse. I
must keep that promise."

"But it's not your fault she's in that state, so you
shouldn't feel obliged to help her!" Tancred's expression
was piteous. "I'm...beginning to feel things for you, things
I've felt only once before, for the musician I'd spoken of.
It's not because of what we did last night, for I've been with
many others in that way and have rarely developed
romantic intentions—I started feeling this way before then,
after merely conversing with you. I feel as if I've known you
for ages, despite our only meeting yesterday, which leads
me to believe that...there might be something special
between us. I think that, should you allow it...I could grow
to love you. Please, stay with me and let me try."

Liliana rose from her chair and went to them, then
reached down to cradle their face in her hands. "I know
how you feel. Part of me should be frightened of you, but I
find I hold no fear of you, only a deep affection for you.
Regardless of my feelings, though, I cannot stay with you. I
made a vow to help Juliane reach the Darklands, and I

need to keep it. I must be fully honest with you—and with myself, I guess—that I...hold affection for her also, though I often have no idea why. It must be that I can see something beautiful in her despite her flaws, just as I can see so much loveliness in you, a creature many would call a monster."

Tancred pulled their face from her grasp so she would not see their eyes glistening, and she told them, "I'll make you a promise, just as I made one to Juliane: I will ensure that we'll one day meet again. Do not despair, dear Tancred, for those who are destined to return to one another shall always find a way to."

The Water-horse wiped their eyes with the back of one hand and rose from their seat. "We should leave for the fairy's at once, then. We don't have time to waste."

"Are you sure you still want to give yourself over to her? We could always ride to Silvan to find a substitute, like you'd suggested. If we do, we can deliver them to Rhoswen, and you can join Juliane and I on our journey."

"But if we don't, your friend is doomed," said Tancred, "and, though it would please me to no end were you to give up your quest and remain here with me, I know not fulfilling your oath would pain you. If I offer myself as her replacement this morning, you two can make haste and hopefully reach Silvan before sunset. Sometimes...we must make sacrifices for those we care for. You're willing to risk so much for Juliane, who to me seems unworthy of your effort—how could I not do the same for someone as deserving as you?"

They grinned weakly, and Liliana embraced them. "Tancred, you're wonderful! Come, then, let us make haste to Rhoswen's."

They exited the cave and, once the Water-horse had sealed it, walked through the forest and around the lake until they had reached the path. Tancred told Liliana, "You must take my bridle and place it on me. Once I have changed forms, remove it from me and put it in your bag. If you were to leave it on me, you would stick to me when you climbed upon my back. I might react instinctively and jump into the lake with you, and I would never forgive myself if that happened. I'm sorry you'll have nothing to hold on to, but it will be safer that way."

"I will have you to hold on to. That will be enough," Liliana reassured them, and she reached into her bag, pulled out their bridle, and placed it on their head. They started to shimmer, and soon the majestic horse once more stood before her. It knelt and she removed its bridle, then, with some difficulty, pulled herself onto its back. She wrapped her arms around its neck and, after pointing it in the right direction, clung tightly to it as it took off at lightning speed toward the fairy's cottage.

They came to the crossroads about two hours later, and Liliana halted the Water-horse and dismounted. "You must change forms here," she told them, "as Rhoswen's home is but a short walk down that path. If you transform within sight of her, she'll know what you are and will refuse the exchange. We need to make sure she believes you're a perfectly ordinary human."

She placed the bridle on the horse, and before long Tancred's perfect face was smirking at her. "A perfectly ordinary human? As if anyone would ever think someone like me was one."

"Fine, then pretend you're a much-better-than-ordinary human," she playfully scolded, "as long as you also make Rhoswen believe you desire to serve her."

"That I can do."

She gave them the shirt, vest, waistcoat, and hat that she had worn as Landon so they might appear a mortal man, and, once they had put the clothing on, they cut quite a dashing figure. They removed their bridle and placed it in one of the waistcoat pockets, then the pair headed up the path to Rhoswen's home.

When they arrived at the cottage, Liliana knocked on the door several times but received no answer. She turned its handle and, finding it unlocked, pushed it open and then stepped into the home, the Water-horse close behind her. The smell of unclean bodies hit them, and Tancred wrinkled their nose in disgust. "Apparently they've been too busy to wash."

Liliana put her finger to their lips, then pointed to the door at the end of the hallway. "They're probably in there." The duo crept down the passage, and, once they had reached Rhoswen's bedchamber, Liliana cautiously opened the door.

She gasped, for the room was unspeakably dirty: pillows and blankets were strewn everywhere, garments covered the floor, and plates of half-eaten food were piled on every piece of furniture. However, the state of the chamber was only mildly distressing when compared to Juliane's, for he was lying upon the bed in a soiled, tattered chemise, and his hair streamed in limp, greasy tendrils over the pillow he was propped on; worst of all was his face, though, for he looked exhausted, as if he had hardly been allowed sleep since she had left. He said, in barely a whisper, "Liliana, you've returned for me. I can scarcely believe it. Did you find someone to take my place?" She nodded and gestured to where Tancred was standing, and he sighed in relief. "Oh, thank you. I knew you could do it. Now maybe I can rest..."

He dropped off to sleep before finishing his sentence, and Liliana called out, "Rhoswen, are you in there?"

"I am," a voice rang out from behind a folding screen at the back of the room. "I'd heard the door open and presumed you'd returned with Juliane's replacement, and so I'm just making myself presentable. I shall be out shortly."

Rhoswen soon emerged, looking as stunning as ever; her golden hair was plaited into a long braid crowned with a circlet of pearls, and she was wearing a white dress that shimmered like starlight. She glanced around the bedroom. "Oh, what a mess we've made. Let me clean this up." She snapped her fingers, and the chamber was suddenly immaculate—which made the still-filthy Juliane stand out terribly. "There, that's better," she said, then turned to Liliana. "Are you going to present my new lover to me?"

"Yes, of course," replied Liliana, and she beckoned to the Water-horse, who stepped into the room.

Rhoswen scanned them appreciatively. "Ooh, he's a very nice find, for he's almost as pretty as I am! Wherever did you discover him?"

"She didn't discover me, I discovered her," Tancred said proudly.

"What my friend means," Liliana interjected hastily, "is that, when I was making inquiries in Silvan, Tancred overheard me and declared he was in search of a muse and would benefit from dallying with you."

Rhoswen seemed to believe this story, for she cooed, "He's the best kind of lover, one who gives himself of his own accord rather than is tricked into doing so! I am sure he'll create great works, for I've been told I am quite inspiring." She threw her arms around Tancred. "What marvelous things you shall accomplish before all your life-force has been spent!"

Liliana was barely able to stifle a giggle as the Water-horse mouthed, "Little does she know," over the fairy's shoulder.

Rhoswen released Tancred from her grasp and told Liliana, "You have brought a suitable replacement. Juliane is free to go."

Relieved, Liliana went to the bed and shook Juliane awake. He opened his bleary eyes slowly, but, when she informed him that he had been liberated, he nearly jumped out of the bed. "When can we leave?"

"After you've washed, brushed your hair, and changed

your clothing. What you're wearing should be thrown into a fire."

He swiftly disappeared behind the folding screen to have a thorough wash, and, while he did so, Liliana asked Rhoswen if they might have some food for their travels. The fairy blinked her eyes and wiggled her nose, then instructed Liliana to look in the main room. She did so and discovered that the table was now covered with dishes, and so she wrapped as much as she could fit in a linen napkin and placed it into her pack alongside her refilled water vessel.

She returned to the bedroom to find Tancred begrudgingly tolerating the fairy's attentions and Juliane, now fully dressed, brushing tangles out of his clean hair. After reminding him to fill his pack with some food and his belongings and to join her outside once he was ready, she asked Rhoswen if she might bid farewell to her friend before departing; when the fairy begrudgingly allowed this, she led Tancred out of the house into the bright sunshine. She found a tree large enough for both to stand behind so there would be no risk of Rhoswen spying on them, and, once they were sheltered from view, she wrapped her arms around the Water-horse, and they held each other tightly.

When they finally released one another, Liliana asked Tancred which tavern they visited most during their travels to Silvan. They identified "The Whinnying Stallion" as their regular haunt, and, after jesting that it was fitting that they should frequent such a place, she pulled her book from her pack and wrote its name on one of the pages. "I know where you shall be for now, but, if Rhoswen releases you, please leave me a letter at the tavern letting me know your whereabouts. Once Juliane and I have finished our quest, we shall pass through Silvan on our way home. If you have left me something, I will use it to find you; if not, we shall come here to check on you and, if you're still in bondage to Rhoswen, shall find someone else to take your place. Then, if the idea still appeals to you...we can spend some time together and see if what we now feel for each other might develop into something else."

Tancred whinnied sadly, and Liliana once more pulled them into an embrace. Staring into their eyes, she said, "Take heart, dear Tancred—who knows what might happen? You could find love with Rhoswen and forget all about me. Please don't let my leaving cause you pain you needn't suffer."

"It's pain I will gladly bear, for I am grateful that, despite being a monster for a thousand years, I'm still able to feel something for someone." Tancred smiled sadly, and, seized with affection for them, Liliana impetuously pulled their face to hers and kissed them, for she knew that, if their lips ever met again, it would not be for a long while.

Their farewell was interrupted by Juliane, who called out, "Liliana, are you there? Rhoswen won't let me leave until she's assured the new offering will take my place." Releasing each other, they came out from behind the tree to find him standing upon the cottage stairs scowling impatiently. "I thought you'd left without me. Can you send him inside so that the fairy won't come after me?" he asked, gesturing irreverently at Tancred.

The Water-horse ascended to where Juliane stood tapping his foot and, pointing at Liliana, said, "That woman is the greatest I have ever known. You've no idea the sacrifices she's made to help you to achieve your goal, sacrifices you seem undeserving of. Show her respect, and do not allow anything dreadful to happen to her. Should any harm come to her of your accord, if ever I find you, I shall tear you limb from limb." They neighed fiercely, then climbed the remaining steps and entered the house.

Liliana walked away down the path, and Juliane yelled, "Wait for me!" and chased after her. "How dare my replacement speak to me that way?" he said indignantly once he had caught up with her. "He obviously doesn't know he's speaking to a princess, for he wouldn't have the nerve to say such things if he knew I could have him thrown in a dungeon merely for looking at me the wrong way!"

"*They* would have the nerve to say such things, for they are a Water-horse and aren't afraid of such consequences as you might give them."

"A W-Water-horse...you mean, one of those horse creatures that eats people? You've given Rhoswen a Water-horse in my stead?"

"Yes. Hopefully she doesn't find out that I've fixed the exchange in our favor, but, even if she does, we should be many days away by then."

"How wonderful, you've tricked the trickster!" Juliane exclaimed, then he immediately blanched. "Will they really rend me to shreds if something happens to you?"

"I should not like to find out if I were you."

He shuddered, then, curious, asked, "But, why would a monster like that be so protective of you?"

"They aren't a monster, and I guess I just have that effect on some people—erm, beings," said Liliana, then she pulled ahead of him, and they walked in silence to the crossroads.

13.

The travelers soon reached the path leading to Silvan, and Liliana let Juliane know that, if they made haste, they would arrive in the town before sunset; he grumbled about having to travel such a distance after having not been allowed much sleep, but reluctantly trudged along after her. They walked for hours until finally he wailed that he could not go on without a rest, and Liliana told him that they were just a short distance from the clearing she had met the Water-horse in and could stop when they reached it. Upon their arrival Juliane, releasing a squeal of delight, ran over to the lake, dropped onto its bank, and gulped handfuls of the cool, clear water. Suddenly he sat up, coughing and grasping his throat with both hands. A concerned Liliana rushed over to him. "Juliane, what's the matter?"

"Something went down my gullet," he wheezed. "I fear I am choking."

Liliana peered down his throat to see if anything was lodged there, but the object seemed to have vanished. He assured her he was fine and had probably just swallowed an unduly large mouthful of water, but she remained unconvinced, for something about the incident reminded her of a thing she had once read. She retrieved her book from her pack, opened it to the section on faerie woods, and, after scanning the pages awhile, let out a groan.

"What's wrong?" asked Juliane.

"That was no large mouthful of water. You have caught a joint-eater."

"A what?"

"A joint-eater. It's a fairy found in or near bodies of water that takes the form of a newt. It lives in the guts of whoever accidentally swallows it and eats half the food its host does, and, in this way, gradually starves them to death."

Juliane grabbed his belly and shrieked, "I don't want to die! How do I get it out of me?"

"You must eat something salty, then recline near the water with your mouth open until the creature grows thirsty. Only then will it exit from you."

"That's horrible!" said Juliane. "Are you sure you're not just trying to make me do something silly so you can have a laugh at me?"

Vexed, Liliana thrust the tome toward him. "If you don't believe me, read it for yourself."

He perused the page, went white, and quickly closed the book. "Well, I guess I have to get this thing out of me. Do we have anything salty?"

Checking their store, Liliana found some dried beef, and Juliane ate it, then stretched out lakeside and waited for the accursed creature to leave his body. As he was exhausted from his servitude to Rhoswen, he soon fell asleep with his mouth hanging open. Liliana had wanted to stay awake to keep an eye on the proceedings, but despite not intending to she, too, ended up dozing off.

Juliane woke hours later to find that the sun was setting, suffusing the lake and meadow with a soft orange glow. He was fleetingly awed by how beautiful everything looked in the dying light, but then he recalled why he had been lying on the ground in the first place and felt a twinge of despair. He felt unbelievably parched and, exhaling resignedly, decided to have some water even though the joint-eater

115

had not yet emerged, for he was sure he could remove it once they had reached Silvan.

As he leaned over the lake, he felt a strange sensation in his gut and, with a mixture of relief and dread, understood that the creature haunting his stomach had finally chosen to make its exit. He screamed for Liliana, and she woke to find his throat bulging as something moved up through it. Juliane's mouth opened wide, and a large orange newt burst from between his lips, dropping into the lake. He fell backward onto the ground, panting. "Remind me only to drink water I've first examined from this point forward!" he groaned, then he immediately put this new practice in place, filling his drinking vessel and checking the water before downing it.

Liliana had to keep herself from laughing at him, for he looked endearingly pitiful, but then noted, with dismay, that the sun had left the horizon. "Due to your trouble with the joint-eater, we've wasted yet another day in this faerie wood. It seems we would have been better off taking the path to Lavinia after all." Juliane grudgingly conceded that she was right, and they were determining whether they should try to continue to Silvan when they heard a strange sound, like the flapping of many wings, coming from the west. The noise was accompanied by a rank smell like that of a rotting corpse, and Liliana's face contorted in terror as she said, "Oh no, the Sluagh."

"Don't tell me we're going to be troubled by yet another wicked creature!" Juliane moaned.

"Not creature, *creatures*. The Sluagh are said to be the souls of the restless dead, the spirits of people so evil that no god nor goddess would allow them a pleasant afterlife. They come in hordes from the west, and are rumored to steal the souls of the dying by entering through the west windows of their homes and snatching them away—"

"Well, as far as I know neither of us are dying, so we should be fine," Juliane interrupted hopefully.

"They're also said to hunt for victims among those not at imminent risk of death, so that they might snatch them into the air and drop them from great heights."

"Then what shall we do?" wailed Juliane. "We cannot outrun them and are hours from shelter. We are doomed!"

"We are not!" cried Liliana, for a solution had come to her. "I know a place where we can shelter for the night. Stay close to me and take care where you tread!" She ran to the far side of the lake, Juliane close behind her, and led them through the woods until they reached Tancred's cave. When she knocked on the boulder and it moved to reveal the entrance, she almost shouted with joy, and she pushed Juliane inside and stepped in after him. She grabbed Tancred's flint and steel and used them to light a candle, then, hearing the beating of wings drawing nearer, hastily knocked upon the stone. It slid back into place, and she used the candle to guide them to the door at the end of the passageway; finding the key where Tancred had left it, she admitted them into the hidden chamber.

"What is this place?" asked Juliane, awestruck, and Liliana explained that it was where she had taken shelter the night before and that it belonged to the Water-horse. She was sure he would have many questions about what she and Tancred had been up to during their time there together, but, to her surprise, he instead declared that he would like nothing better than to have a good rest for the first time in days and hastily climbed into the bed.

Liliana, for her part, determined that she would try to fall asleep as quickly as possible so as not to dwell on memories of the previous evening, and so she stripped to her chemise and joined Juliane under the covers. His breathing slowed as he dropped into slumber, and, as she huddled next to him, she began to feel better about choosing to journey onward with him. She stared at him awhile and, once she was sure he would not hear her, whispered, "Juliane, please know that I'm making the

117

sacrifices I am not just because I feel responsible for you, but because I sense something wonderful exists within you. I can only hope this journey will help it to emerge." Juliane smiled sweetly in his sleep, and, less miserable than she had anticipated she would be given the circumstances, Liliana soon drifted off as well.

***

When Liliana woke the next day, she checked the time and discovered it was already mid-afternoon. She roused Juliane and explained that they needed to leave immediately if they wanted to make it to Silvan before nightfall, so they quickly ate and readied themselves, then exited the shelter. When Liliana knocked upon the boulder and it blocked the entrance from view, she realized that she would not see the cave's owner for quite some time, and, as the travelers walked through the woods toward the lake, an air of melancholy surrounded her.

Juliane, noticing her solemnity, attempted to draw her out with what he hoped would be pleasant conversation. "Liliana, I was thinking about what Rhoswen revealed the other day—that I desire you and that you're attracted to me but loath to admit it? Well, I know I'm not always selective about whom I give my attentions to, and I know you're still a virgin, but—"

"Who told you I was a virgin?" Liliana interrupted him.

"Rhoswen did. She said she discovered when she kissed you that you're a virgin who would like to be with either a pretty girl or a pretty boy but who hasn't yet been with either. Well, since I'm a pretty girl who used to be a pretty boy, and since we do seem drawn to one another...I thought I might suggest that we act upon our attractions at some point—if you want to, I mean," he hastily assured her.

"Rhoswen is wrong," Liliana said quietly. "I am no longer a virgin."

Juliane was at first confused by her words, but, as their import dawned on him, his eyes went wide. "Did you dally with the Water-horse in that cave we stayed in?"

"Yes, I did, and it was wonderful."

"But they're a beast, a creature who eats humans! How could you have been with them?"

"Tancred may act like a beast when their nature forces them to, but their heart is kind. They had me remove their bridle to ensure my safety, and, once I got to know them, I wanted to be with them."

"But they kill people!"

"And some might say that that you do as well, for you certainly kill their spirits. Think of the string of women you have used and cast aside—how many of them are still aching from the things you've done? There are some who would say you're no better than a beast, but I would disagree with them; there's more to you than that, for there's much good within you that counters the bad. The same can be said for Tancred."

Juliane crossed his arms, unsure of how to respond. He walked this way for a while, grumbling under his breath, then admitted, "Perhaps they aren't so bad after all. But, why did you have to dally with them?"

"Because I wanted to. I developed an attraction toward and a liking for them, and so I decided the time had come for me to be with someone."

"But it isn't fair!" cried Juliane.

Liliana peered at him inquisitively. "What isn't fair?"

Casting his eyes downward, he sulkily said, "I've been drawn to you from the moment we spoke at my party—as if you couldn't tell—and I've known you for longer than that *thing*. If you were going to choose to bed someone, why couldn't you have chosen me?"

Liliana stopped walking and turned to him, face red with anger. "Are you honestly upset that I was with someone who wasn't you when you were literally dallying with

Rhoswen whilst I was? You're incorrigible, do you know that?" She wagged a finger in his face. "If I want to be with someone, I shall be with someone. If I want to be with you, I shall be with you, and if I want to be with another, I shall be with another. You can have congress with whomever you'd like, and I shall do the same. I do not belong to you, and I don't appreciate your treating relations with me as something you deserve to have or a reward you should earn if only you behave!"

Liliana stormed away across the field, leaving a remorseful Juliane, pleading that she wait for him, behind her. Suddenly, she cried out and dropped down onto the grass, clutching her left leg. Juliane, duly concerned, rushed over to her. "Liliana, what's wrong?"

"I've done something unwise. I was cross with you and wasn't watching where I was going, and so I brushed against that."

Liliana pointed to a plant with sharp thorns and bell-shaped purple flowers, then showed Juliane the side of her left leg. Where the top of her boot met the bottom of her dress, the exposed flesh bore a large scratch. "That's a nasty cut," he said. "Let's clean and dress it."

"I don't think you quite understand the graveness of what's happened," she chided him gently. "I ripped my leg open on a thorn—which would not have been so bad—but, unfortunately, the blossoms of this plant are some of the most noxious in existence, and, as I stumbled, one brushed against my wound. If I've only gotten a bit of the flower's poison in my scratch I will live, but my vision will blur, I will lose my balance, and I may become confused, hallucinate, or even grow insensible for a time. If I have gotten much poison in it...I may die."

Juliane grew distressed. "What should I do, then? You can't die, Liliana, I need you."

"Go to the river and wet some cloth, then assist me in

washing and binding the wound. If we clean it well, perhaps we can mitigate the worst effects. Just make sure you don't duplicate my injury, or we shall be in even more trouble."

She dug through her bag until she found "Landon's" trousers to give him, and he ran to the river and soaked them, then returned to her as swiftly as he could. Kneeling beside her, he asked, "Shall you clean it, or shall I?"

"I think you should, as my sight is dimming."

He washed the wound as best he could, then asked what he should do next. "There's a container of salve in my bag," said Liliana. "Take it out and spread some on my injury. There may also be something else to help in my book..." She abruptly stopped speaking, closed her eyes, and dropped into a death-like slumber.

Juliane, terrified at the thought of losing her, rummaged through her pack until he found the salve, which he carefully daubed on the scratch. He feared he might not have done enough to ensure her recovery, though, and so took her book from her bag and flipped through it until he came to the section marked "Faerie Woods." He came upon a picture of the deadly flower, accompanied by a recommendation: *If this plant's poison has entered the body through a cut, a poultice that will significantly reduce its influence can be applied to the affected area.* Though he blanched when he saw that the poultice was comprised of crushed ants and human blood, he nevertheless set off to find an anthill as soon as he had finished reading.

While searching, he considered the interaction that had given rise to the ordeal. He determined that Liliana had developed an affection for the Water-horse during the time she had spent with them, and that the thought of her having such feelings for the creature made him experience something he believed might be jealousy; he also knew that she had left Tancred in order to continue assisting him

121

with his quest, and that this meant she was fond enough of him to at least temporarily forsake her would-be paramour. This gave him hope, for he had been dwelling upon her even while in service to Rhoswen and, though he was loath to admit it, had concluded that his attraction to her was...becoming something more than purely physical.

He had certainly made a blunder while trying to tell her this, though, for he had acted impulsively and had focused on his carnal desires without intending to—he had come off as selfish and entitled and had driven her from him. His behavior was the cause of her needing to fight for her life, and so he vowed he would do everything possible to save her from an untimely death. He hoped that, when she was well, she would give him another chance to express himself, and that he would know the right thing to say when the time came.

Juliane searched along the lake's edge for an anthill and, when he could not find one, crossed the meadow to check alongside the path. Discovering one under the shade of a great tree, he prodded at the hole until a swarm of ants emerged, then chose several large ones and mashed them in his hands. He ran to where Liliana lay sprawled on the ground and was gladdened to find her heart still steadily beating, so he removed the crushed ants with a rag, then took her sword from its scabbard and, gritting his teeth, slashed his left palm. Though he yelped at the pain, he managed to squeeze some blood onto the ant paste and to mix the ingredients together.

After applying the poultice to Liliana's scratch, he set about cleaning, salving, and covering his own wound. Once he had finished, he checked her injury and was delighted to discover that it already seemed to be healing. He hoped he had done enough to save her from a terrible fate but knew he likely would not find out if his ministrations had worked for a while; if she had absorbed much poison she might sleep for hours and they would once more be stuck overnight in the faerie wood, and he did not fancy any further encounters with the foul creatures inhabiting it.

He considered returning to Rhoswen's to beg the Waterhorse's assistance in transporting her out of the woods, bitter feelings toward the interloper be damned, but knew he would need to leave her alone to do this and worried something might happen to her in his absence. Pondering potential solutions, his eyes fell upon his travel pack, and, as a plan to get Liliana out of the forest sprang to mind, he hurriedly put it into action.

14.

Liliana drifted through the mists of oblivion, trapped in deepest slumber, under the influence of the noxious plant. She had expected pain and terror in this in-between state, but, to her surprise, found tranquility and pleasant dreams instead. Strangely, though, Juliane's face, creased with worry and pleading with her to awaken, kept popping up among them. She was uncertain as to why he seemed so uneasy, for she relaxed in a haze of past and present wonders and could not understand why anyone would desire that she quit them.

Visions of him would not abate, though, and she grew curious about what was causing him such distress—then her mind reeled as she understood that she was in a dream-land created not through her own will, but by the poison that coursed through her body. Trapped in the blackness inside her head, she screamed that she wished to be freed, and feared no one had heard her until Juliane's face once more came into view. He begged her to return to him, and, within the darkness, she screamed, "I need to wake up!" She felt herself being drawn into the light that was issuing from him, and, when she next said, "I need to wake up," she found that, to her relief, she had spoken the words aloud.

She opened her eyes and discovered a now-joyful Juliane leaning over her. "Liliana, you've returned to me!

I'm so glad that you have. I had hoped you were merely resting whilst your body dealt with the poison."

"How long did I sleep for?"

"I didn't check your sundial, but I'm guessing for several hours, as it's now growing dark."

Liliana groaned. "Oh no, now we're stuck in the awful faerie wood for yet another night! I'm so sorry, Juliane."

"There's no need to apologize. We've escaped the forest and are now but a short distance from Silvan."

Believing that her ears might be deceiving her, Liliana decided her eyes would not also lie and turned her head to one side. Though she could not see much, what she did see confirmed that they were indeed no longer in the forest, for cottages with candles burning in their windows dotted the fields surrounding them. "I can scarcely believe it; you've gotten us out of the treacherous woods! How did you manage it?"

"Sit up and you'll see."

Liliana slowly lifted herself and found that she was on a large piece of luxurious green fabric. "It's the dress the Wrathscalders gave me," explained Juliane. "I knew I needed something to place you on, so I tore it and laid it out under you, then pulled you out of the forest. I hope you aren't sore, I tried to avoid dragging you over any rocks."

"But it must have taken you hours to get me here!"

"Well, my arms are a bit tired, but it was worth the effort to ensure your safety," he admitted, smiling shyly.

Liliana checked her leg and saw a poultice had been applied to it. With Juliane's assistance she rose carefully to her feet, and, after a minute, felt able to stand and then even to walk on her own. "Juliane, it's incredible—my wound no longer hurts, and it isn't affecting my gait. It seems to have healed already. Thank you—you're amazing!"

"I used your mother's recipe, so it's really her you should be thanking. I merely followed her instructions."

Liliana peered at him curiously. "Are you sure you're Juliane, and not some fairy being who has taken on Juliane's form?" Stammering, he asserted that he was most definitely himself, and she assured him, "I wasn't making an accusation, merely teasing you. It's just that you took such care with my injury and reacted so humbly to my praise, and I've not seen much of this side of you. I have to confess that I rather like it."

Clasping him, she kissed his cheek, thanking him again for saving her life. Juliane eagerly returned her embrace, and, figuring that this might be a good time to share the things that had been on his mind, said, "Liliana, I—"

She released him and spun to face the town that sparkled before them. "Make sure to tell me whatever you meant to once we've arrived in Silvan, Juliane, for we must get there as soon as possible." He reluctantly agreed, and, amazed at how quickly she had recovered after her near-fatal encounter with the deadly plant, followed her as she bolted toward their destination.

***

The travelers reached Silvan in less than an hour's time, and, after having been trapped in the faerie wood for so long, were overwhelmed and captivated by the city's many sights, sounds, and smells. An upside of their being ambushed by the Wrathscalders and spending so many days in the treacherous forest was that they still had seventeen gold coins left, so, when they came upon a marketplace where sellers were hawking their wares and all kinds of delicious foods were being cooked over open fires, they used two coins to buy themselves a roasted chicken, two tankards of ale, a loaf of bread, a block of cheese, and an apple pie.

As they had some coppers left from their shopping, Liliana suggested that they bring their food over to where some musicians were performing. The band consisted of a fiddler, lutist, horn player, and drummer; the music they performed was exceedingly lovely, and the travelers especially enjoyed the frequent singing of the lutist, a bronze-skinned young man with shoulder-length black hair. During a pause between songs he proclaimed, "To love lost and lessons learned," then began to sing the most beautiful song Liliana had ever heard. Something about it touched her deeply, and, when she strained to make out the words—"rode you by the water," "took off your bridle," "sheltered in your secret place"—she gasped as she realized that she might have written this song herself. The man pouring his heart out through song was none other than Tancred's lost musician—she was sure of it—and it was obvious that he still adored the Water-horse and was aggrieved that he could not be with them.

As the thought crossed her mind, a clod of earth flew past her, hitting the lutist in the forehead. He cried out and fell backward onto the ground as more clumps came sailing toward the other musicians, who shrieked and ran off through the marketplace.

Cruel laughter rang out from behind the travelers, and they turned to find a trio of men standing nearby. One was short and stout, one was tall and lean, and one was great in both stature and width, but all wore nasty grins and held lumps of dirt in their hands. The shorter man, who seemed to be leader of the three, jeered at the lutist. "Looks like yer friends 'ave gone off and left ye to fend for yerself. I guess no one will stick around to 'elp ye, for they know ye deserve what ye got comin'." The other men cackled at his words and, raising their clods aloft, prepared to throw them.

Liliana, who had been watching the scene, outraged, decided that she had seen quite enough. She rose to her feet and shouted at the ruffians, "Stop that behavior at once! This man does not deserve to be persecuted. Leave him be!"

127

The men just gaped at her at first, then they began to laugh riotously. Catching his breath, the thin one exclaimed, "Look, Leofrick, 'es so weak 'e needs to 'ave girls defend 'im!"

The squat ringleader, who was apparently Leofrick, sneered at Liliana. "Mind yerself, girlie. Do not get involved in matters that don't concern ye. The man ye defend is a sodomite, a perverse creature who shouldn't be allowed to sing 'is foul ditties in public. Leave and let us finish what we came to do."

"It's of no matter to you whom this man chooses to be with," said Liliana, her face stern. "I've already told you once to cease your unruly behavior. Do *not* make me tell you again."

The taller men retreated a few paces, but Leofrick, reddening, stepped forward. "Are you tryin' to pick a fight with us, girlie?"

"I am not *trying* to do anything, and I'm most certainly no 'girlie,' but, if it's a fight you want, then it's a fight I shall give you. Three against two is fairer than three against one."

"You mean 'three against three'," added Juliane as he stood up beside her.

She glanced at him uncertainly, for she doubted he would be of assistance during a fray, but then pulled her sword from her scabbard and offered it to him. "Use my blade. Do not kill anyone unless you must, for I'm opposed to taking a life without sufficient cause."

He looked down at the sword, then back up at her. "But what will you use to fight?"

"These men seemed to be armed with nothing more than their wits—and those seem quite dulled—so I will just use the hand-to-hand combat skills I know."

Juliane gulped, but nevertheless took the sword and assumed what he hoped was the correct stance. The men had been watching the travelers, faces masks of amusement covering their underlying wariness, and they flinched as Liliana lifted her arms and held her clenched fists before her. "Well, are you going to leave him be?" she asked. "If not, you'd better fight us. We'll teach you not to gang up on a defenseless man—that is, unless you're too cowardly to face us."

The loftier fellows exchanged uncertain glances, but Leofrick, enraged, addressed each in turn. "Gavin, Dorin, don't just stand there, go after 'em! We'll show 'em it's foolish to stand up to us."

The men hesitantly approached the travelers—Gavin, the tall thin one, headed toward Liliana, while the stouter one, Dorin, moved toward Juliane—and, once Gavin was within striking distance, Liliana lifted her skirt, kicked out her leg, and swept his feet out from under him, sending him to the ground. As Dorin neared Juliane, he slashed out with the sword and, to his great surprise, caught the giant man's braces. They snapped with a satisfying twang and the man's trousers fell to his ankles, and he stumbled upon them and fell over, landing on his face in the dirt. Liliana whispered, "That was brilliant! How did you manage it?"

"Through sheer luck, I fancy," said Juliane. "Even a blindfolded mouse finds crumbs on occasion."

Liliana turned to Leofrick. "It looks like we've defeated your friends already. I guess they're not fit to fight against the likes of us." Leaning over the fallen men, she hissed, "You should find a better leader, for yours is willing to sacrifice you in battle whilst he just watches. Now, leave here in haste, or I shall have my friend cut your arms off so that you may never again throw dirt at an innocent person." Taking her at her word, they scrambled to their feet and raced away without even casting a backward glance at the commander they had abandoned. Leofrick had grown to resemble a beet, and Liliana said, "So, are you going to stand against us, or will you also flee? It would be a pity if your friends told all of Silvan that they fought the woman warriors but that you didn't have the nerve to."

A furious Leofrick gritted his teeth, then, releasing a great yell, charged toward them. Juliane cringed and hid behind the sword, praying he would not have to use it, but, when the man was just short of an arm's length away, Liliana stepped forward and caught him squarely on the jaw with her right fist. He stopped and lifted his hand to his face, eyes wide with shock and pain, and she took the opportunity to land a blow on his left cheek. He recoiled from her, and she continued her barrage of punches and slaps until he covered his head and ran away squealing through the marketplace. Several who had witnessed the fight cheered, for they knew Leofrick was a lout who deserved the poor treatment, then, entertainment over, returned to their business.

Juliane was mightily impressed. "You can wield a sword, use magic, read a map and sundial, and conquer men using only your arms and legs—what can't you do?"

"Well, I'm not very good at embroidery," admitted Liliana, feigning sorrow, then she cast him a wink and the pair dissolved into giggles.

The musician had been watching the altercation with amazement, and, once it had ended, wiped the dirt from his forehead and called out, "I hate to interrupt your celebrating, but may I have some assistance getting up?" The travelers rushed over to him and, each taking an arm, hoisted him to his feet. "Thank you," he said, dusting himself off, "not only for helping me to stand, but for all you've just done for me. If not for you, I'm certain those men would have beaten me insensible. I'm not sure who you are and why you chose to defend me, but I'm grateful to you all the same."

"We had to help," said Liliana. "We heard your music and were moved to..."

She trailed off as she locked eyes with him, and he

gasped. "You have known them."

"What?" she said, confused.

"Tancred, the Water-horse—you have known them as I have."

Liliana was taken aback. "How do you—?"

"There is a look about you that I'm familiar with, for I see it reflected in my own mirror daily. Once you've seen into their soul, you're never the same again. I see this change in you."

Juliane, annoyed that yet another person was swooning over the Water-horse, said, "I'm sorry to interrupt this lovely discussion, but you do remember that we just beat up three bullish brutes, right? It's unlikely they'll readily let this affront go."

"You're right," agreed the lutist. "Knowing Leofrick and his gang, they may very well return seeking vengeance. I'm sorry I've gotten you into such a mess. Please, let me make it up to you by providing you with lodgings tonight should you need them. I don't have much, but what I do have I'll happily share. Besides," he gestured at Liliana, "we have more to discuss."

Juliane, surly at the thought of Liliana spending an evening praising the Water-horse with the stranger, tried to convince her that they should procure a room at an inn, but she was curious about what the man had to say and so took him up on his offer. The travelers followed the musician as he wove through the city streets, and they soon left Silvan's center and traveled along the path leading away from the city. Juliane bemoaned all the unnecessary walking and their not finding lodgings in Silvan proper, but, when Liliana assured him that they would be closer to their next destination when they left the following morning and would additionally be saving coins by staying with the lutist, this seemed to finally appease him.

15.

Before long the musician led the travelers onto a stony path that branched off the main one, into a glen of trees. There, situated within the foliage, was a rustic but charming cottage. "This is my simple home," the man said as they approached it. "I inherited it from my parents when they passed about four years ago. As I've said, I cannot offer much, but you're welcome to partake of what I do have."

He unlatched the door and bade his guests enter, then followed them inside. In the center of the hut the embers of a fire softly glowed in a fire pit, and he went to it and stoked it until it roared into a bright blaze. By the glow of the firelight the travelers spied a large mattress in one corner of the room, a table with three chairs in another, a coffer with a mirror and basin in the third, and a smaller mattress in the fourth. A small table near the fire held cookware and utensils, and there was a curtained area against one of the walls that their host informed them could be used for washing and changing. Though the cottage was sparsely furnished it was quite cozy, and beautiful landscapes adorned its walls; the musician attributed the art to his mother, who had been a skilled painter, and shared that his father had also been a musician and had taught him to play several instruments. "I suppose we were a very expressive family overall," he said, a trace of sadness in his voice.

He encouraged the travelers to take a seat at the table, and, once they had, went to the coffer, opened it, and removed a brown bottle. "This is wine my mother fermented. We were saving it for a special occasion, but..." He trailed off, his face wistful, then suddenly smiled. "Well, I can't think of a better reason for celebrating than your saving me from those villains." He grabbed three cups and brought them, along with the vessel, over to the table. He sat in the remaining chair and, uncorking the bottle, poured a generous portion of wine into each glass. "To new friendships!" he proclaimed, tipping his drink into his mouth.

Liliana drank her beverage delicately, savoring each mouthful, while Juliane speedily quaffed his; once he had finished, he slammed the empty cup down on the table and cried, "Let's have some more!" The musician poured them both another cupful but recommended that they imbibe it slowly this time due to its strength, so Juliane tried to sip his daintily. The man took occasional gulps but was generally still and quiet. It was obvious that he was in deep thought about something, but it was uncertain whether he was contemplating the creature he and Liliana had spoken of earlier or was dwelling on something else entirely.

Liliana eventually broke the silence. "I'm sorry, we've been very rude. You have brought us into your home, yet you know nothing of us, and we know nothing of you."

She shared their names with him—though she made up a surname for Juliane, as she did not want the man to recognize him as the prince transformed—then explained the bare bones of their quest. Their host revealed that he was Geoffrey Bauldry, aged twenty-seven, that he made his meager living as a musician, and that he had lived happily with his parents until their deaths four years prior. "And, yes, I'm a sodomite," he said wryly. "Well, that isn't completely true, for I do find women attractive on occasion—and, of course, my greatest romance was with someone neither male nor female—but, as I tend to prefer the company of men, I suppose it's as fitting a designation as any."

"Don't feel bad," Juliane told him, for the wine had taken hold of his tongue. "I prefer women and have been with many, and Liliana likes women better than she does men."

Geoffrey raised an eyebrow and turned to Liliana. "Is this true?"

"I suppose it is. I believe I favor women, but a pretty person of any gender can catch my fancy."

"I'm assuming a pretty non-person like Tancred might also?" Geoffrey said playfully.

Juliane rolled his eyes at yet another mention of the Water-horse, and, seeking to avoid their becoming the topic of conversation, said, "Geoffrey, we've heard much from you about your parents, but naught about why they're no longer with us. What happened to them?"

Geoffrey's face fell, and his eyes grew misty. "You needn't tell us if it's too painful to speak of," Liliana assured him, casting Juliane a stern look.

Geoffrey sipped his wine thoughtfully, gazing at the fire, then said, "Oh, confound it all! I know I must tell someone what's happened, and, if Tancred has taken at least one of you into their confidence, you must be people worth telling. Moreover, I may burst if I don't." He took a swig of wine, claiming, "I'm going to need it," then proceeded to share his story.

"My parents, being skilled artisans, were called upon by the king of a neighboring land for the provision of services. My mother was commissioned to paint a portrait of him, whilst my father was asked to write him a ballad. They toiled many months and, by the end of their labor, had each produced a work fit for royalty. Together they traveled to the king's palace to share their creations, but...only one of them returned home."

"What happened?" asked Juliane.

"My mother's painting was well-received, and, when my father began his song, the monarch seemed to be enjoying it. However, his voice went sharp for just a moment, and the king scowled and..." He paused, growing pale, then soldiered forward. "He grabbed a bow and shot an arrow through my father's heart."

Liliana gasped, horrified, and Juliane nearly spit out the mouthful of wine he had taken. After he had swallowed, he exclaimed, "How awful! What did your mother do?"

"What could she do?" said Geoffrey. "The king is a powerful and frightening man, for it's said he is a necromancer and can speak with and control the dead. After retrieving my father's body, she left the castle and returned home to me, but she was not the same afterward, for she loved my father dearly. She no longer painted, nor sung, nor laughed; she didn't eat much and scarcely slept, and she wasted away before my eyes. Not even three months after the cruel king killed my father she too was put in her grave, taken by cholera—we had an outbreak in Silvan and she was too weak to fight it."

"Hence, my being left on my own, greatly bereaved, and lonely apart from that period when I lived elsewhere with someone I cared for dearly—I think you know the time of which I speak," he jested, gesturing at Liliana.

As she had listened to him a sense of dread had risen within her, and she asked, in barely a whisper, "What is the name of the king who killed your father?"

Geoffrey's face grew stony, and he hissed, "Korben Darkwood."

This time Juliane *did* expel his wine. "Korben Darkwood? But he's the person we're on our way to see!"

Geoffrey pushed his chair back from the table, eyeing

the travelers warily. "You're not friends of his, are you? I wouldn't have thought persons like yourselves would be."

"We aren't his friends," Liliana reassured him. "We have never met him and don't know much about him, other than that his son has something we desperately need—"

Juliane gently interrupted, "If it makes it easier for him to understand, you can tell him my secret, Liliana."

Having received this permission, she explained, "Juliane is, well, not actually Juliane—she's Julian, prince of this kingdom. She's been cursed to remain in female form until we can procure some hair from Prince Arthur Darkwood, as it's what's needed to end the enchantment."

"As far as curses go, it's not a terrible one," Juliane admitted.

Geoffrey looked at him, and his eyes widened. "You *are* the prince! Though some changes have obviously befallen you, your form is much the same overall, only female rather than male. I must confess, I rather fancied you when I was younger."

Juliane, warmed by the compliment, replied, "Thank you, kind sir. If I ever choose to dally with a man once I've returned to my male form, I shall consider you foremost for the role of my consort." He cast the musician a mock-lascivious glance, and they burst into a laughter so infectious that Liliana could not help but join in on it.

Geoffrey, sobering first, asked, "How do you plan on removing the hair from the prince, though? Are you sure you're prepared for the consequences should you be caught?"

"It matters not what the consequences are, it's what needs to be done," said Liliana. "However, we have in our favor that we are, well..."

"We're attractive women, and you know it," Juliane broke in. "In order the end the curse, I must get hair from not just any prince, but from a prince who is in love *with me*. Therefore, I must use my feminine wiles to charm him so that I may procure his hair."

He winked, and Geoffrey laughed once more. "Then I can't see how you could possibly fail! But I hope my story has taught you to be cautious around Darkwood, for you're surely risking your life if you're anything other than guarded whilst near that vicious beast." His face darkened. "I would volunteer my assistance, but I know that, should I ever meet the king, I would take vengeance upon him, and that would be of no help to you."

He sighed, and Liliana, hoping to change the subject to a brighter one, inquired as to how he had met Tancred. The musician's face lit up at the mention of the Water-horse, but Juliane, upon hearing it, theatrically proclaimed himself to be tired. Geoffrey told him that he and Liliana could share the larger mattress, so he flounced over to it and, within minutes, had fallen asleep.

Once Juliane had left them, Geoffrey said, "I believe we can now talk about Tancred. I felt discomfited doing so whilst she was around, for she seemed to bristle at their name."

"I'm not sure why," replied Liliana, "for they saved her from a dreadful fate. She had dallied with a fairy mistress and would have remained in servitude to her until drained had I not found Tancred. They volunteered to take her place, both to assist me and to potentially discover what fairies taste like."

Geoffrey laughed. "That sounds like Tancred! But it seems Juliane may be jealous of the time you spent with them—care to share why that might be?"

Blushing, she bade him first relate his own experience with the Water-horse. "One day, about a year ago, I was playing and singing in the marketplace and they approached me. They listened raptly for over an hour and asked me to come with them after, so I eagerly followed them to the entrance of the faerie wood. There I became afraid, for I knew then that they were no mortal man, but they assured me that they meant me no harm, that they'd been enchanted by my music and wanted to know me better. They changed their form and let me remove their bridle, and I rode them through the forest until we arrived at their cave. I re-bridled them, they returned to their human form, and... Oh, what wonderful months we spent together! It was the best time of my life." He grinned at Liliana. "I assume you have a similar tale to tell?"

She was at first unsure of how much she should share, but, after thinking it over, decided to reveal everything, adding upon finishing her story, "I'm sorry if my telling you of my time with them hurts you, for it's obvious you still hold affection for them."

"I am not hurt—nor jealous, for that matter—regarding the closeness you share with them, for to truly know them is to love them. I feel as if they, being the unique and long-lived being that they are, are capable of having room in their heart for many."

Liliana, feeling emboldened, said, "You know why I left Tancred—I had a promise to keep and a friend to assist—but why did you part with them if you so enjoyed your time together?"

Geoffrey bowed his head and, when he lifted it, his eyes brimmed with tears. "I was a fool. I was afraid of them, of what they are and how they made me feel, and I feared they would tire of a mere mortal like me and leave me heartbroken. I decided to make sure that wouldn't happen by leaving them. That may be the greatest mistake I have ever made."

Liliana was seized with pity for him, and, though a small part of her envied his relationship with the Water-horse, a greater one sensed that he was meant to return to them. "Why don't you go back to them, then?" she said. "They're presently with Rhoswen at her cottage in the forest, but you could bring a replacement to her and could win them back.

It's obvious you still adore them. As someone who cares for them also, I want to see them happy, even if that happiness can be found with another."

Geoffrey smiled sadly. "I would love to rejoin Tancred, but I doubt they'd have me."

"They would gladly have you! I know for a fact that you're still much-beloved by them, and I'm sure they would welcome you with open arms should you return to them— just keep in mind that you might first have to rescue them from a wicked fairy if you do."

"You've given me a lot to think about, Liliana Almwick," said Geoffrey, wiping his eyes. "I will likely spend the night tossing and turning, pondering what my next steps should be. Hopefully I shall have an idea of my path in the morning." Grasping her hand, he thanked her for her encouragement, then they went off to their respective beds. Liliana felt the slightest trace of regret regarding her meddling, but she also somehow knew that she had done the right thing, no matter the consequence, and so fell asleep with conscience untroubled.

16.

The following morning Liliana tried to rouse Juliane early, for she wanted to ensure they reached the next town before nightfall, but the cups of wine he had taken the night before made him slow to stir and she had to shake him several times before he opened his eyes. Geoffrey, awakened by Juliane's groans, went to fetch water from the well so his guests could refill their vessels and have washes before departing, and, after they had dressed and shouldered their packs, led them back to the main road. Once they arrived at the crossroads, they embraced and said their farewells. Geoffrey thanked Liliana for the hope she had given him the night before and let her know he was still considering her recommendation, and, after she had wished him well in determining which course to take, the travelers headed off along the path leading from Silvan.

After they had walked an hour, Liliana pulled out her map to show Juliane that they were but a few hours from the next town, Pultare, and so should easily make it before nightfall if they did not experience any mishaps; after Pultare would come three more days of walking, then they would reach Darkwood's domain, where her map would no longer be of use to them. Juliane shuddered when he heard the king's name. "I'm none too pleased about having to meet that man, even if I must woo his son to regain my rightful form. He shot an arrow through someone's heart for singing the wrong thing! What if I do something to upset him?"

Liliana reassured him, "With your charm and beauty, how could he possibly take umbrage at anything you do?" Juliane seemed to grow less troubled upon hearing this, and she was glad of it, for, though loath to admit it, she, too, worried about Darkwood's foul disposition.

The path to Pultare was well-tended and led through pleasant rolling hills, and they found themselves enjoying their travels for the first time in a while. Juliane considered that this might be the ideal time to share his feelings with Liliana, but, as he wanted to make sure he knew just what to say before saying it—for he had blundered significantly the last time he had tried to do so—he carefully contemplated his words as they marched along, only replying in brief to Liliana's bright chatter. After they had walked awhile, she said, "Juliane, you haven't spoken much this morning. Is something on your mind?"

Hoping he had found the words needed to properly express himself, he began, "Liliana, I..." as they crested a large hill—but, instead of finishing his sentence, cried, "Look!" He pointed ahead of them, and Liliana spied the reason for his amazement: a large swathe of sea that stretched from the sandy shore below them into the distance as far as the eye could see.

Enchanted by the view, he ran down to the water, took off his boots and stockings and left them on the ground along with his pack, then waded ankle-deep into the foam, shrieking with delight. Liliana, amused, followed him leisurely. "Have you never seen the ocean before?"

He confessed he had not. "It's wonderful!"

"It is, isn't it?" she agreed—then she removed her boots and stockings and deposited them on the ground, tied her skirts around her waist, and plunged into the water alongside him. They squealed with laughter as they danced through the waves, and then Liliana mischievously splashed Juliane, he did the same, and they engaged in a battle until both were soaked. The day was fortunately warm, and so, panting and giggling, they sprawled out on the sand to dry. Juliane decided that their frolicking might have created the perfect opportunity for him to reveal his inner workings to her, and he was about to when Liliana squinted and said, "What's that over there?"

He followed her line of sight and spied a brown mass some ways down the coast. He got up off the sand and cautiously approached the object, and, upon reaching it, exclaimed, "It's a dead animal!"

Liliana, coming up behind him, identified that it was a seal and, after explaining what that was to Juliane (for he had never heard of the animal), bent down to examine it. "This is strange," she said. "None of the meat is left, only the skin, and it's been cleaned and sealed in a way I've never seen used on a hide. It's obvious no beast killed it. It might have been killed by a sailor, for I've heard these creatures sometimes interfere with their work, but I'm not sure why one would have preserved the pelt only to leave it behind."

Juliane lifted the skin and wrapped it around himself. "It's lovely and warm. If someone's left it, I'm going to keep it."

Liliana looked at him uncertainly. "I don't know if that's a good idea. It might have been left here for a reason. Also, I think I remember something..." She realized Juliane had already wandered away up the coast, so, sighing, she shrugged her shoulders and trotted after him.

As the path they needed to take ran alongside the ocean, the travelers felt confident they would not lose their way if they kept it in view and so continued their walk along the shoreline. Juliane could hardly pull his gaze from the sand they were treading on, though—he would stop to pick up shells, laugh at crabs as they scuttled along, and poke bits of seaweed with his feet—and Liliana had to keep reminding him that they would not make it to Pultare by nightfall if they lingered for too long. After his third scolding he begrudgingly admitted she was right, and, from that point forward, tried not to let himself get too distracted.

Soon the path curved inland into a wooded area, and the travelers reluctantly re-shod themselves and stepped back upon it; they were heartened to find, though, that it continued adjacent to the sea, so they could still smell the salt air and hear the waves crash as they traveled along. Liliana was uneasy in spite of the pleasant surroundings, though, for she could not shake the impression that they were being followed, but, after they had walked an hour and she had still not heard or seen anything untoward, she determined that she would not let herself grow distressed over what was probably just an off hunch.

Around midday they arrived at a pleasant clearing, and they decided to take a short rest and to have a meal. Juliane plopped down in the shade of a large tree and happily stuffed bread and cheese into his mouth, and Liliana was about to join him when she heard a rustling in the bushes nearby. She spotted a figure lurking in the foliage and, scrambling to her feet and drawing her sword, screamed, "I am armed, so show yourself!"

Juliane, understanding what was happening, shrank back against the tree and began digging through his pack, hoping to locate his dagger in case it was needed. The only thing he had managed to find so far was a wooden comb—and he was praying he would not have to use it to defend himself—when the travelers heard someone say, "Please, put away your weapon, I mean you no harm." The speaker stepped into the clearing and, without thinking, Juliane ran the comb through his disheveled hair, for a lovely woman stood before them.

She had radiant brown skin and dark hair that fell to her

stomach in thick waves, and she wore a piece of sailcloth held closed with a rope belt. Liliana lowered her sword, for she realized that the one who had trailed them was a selkie, a shape-shifting creature capable of living in the water as a seal and then taking its skin off to live as a human on land. Knowing both the habits of selkies and of Juliane's history with pretty maidens, she inwardly groaned and readied herself for what she was sure would be a cringe-worthy interaction.

The woman told Juliane, "You have something that belongs to me, as the pelt you're wearing is my hide. I followed you in hopes of reclaiming it, but, once it grew clear you meant to keep it on, I knew I had no choice but to reveal myself to you. As you have my skin, I will do what you ask of me."

"W-what do you mean?" he sputtered in reply.

"She's a selkie, a magical creature that spends much of its time as a seal in the ocean but may remove its sealskin to walk among humans," said Liliana. "A person who finds a selkie's hide may choose to marry or bed the selkie or to request some form of assistance from it. They may keep the selkie with them for as long as they wish, for it shall stay with them until it can reclaim its skin. I'm guessing we may have a new addition to our traveling party."

Juliane pondered her words for a moment, then told the stranger, "I shall give you back your skin once you've helped us reach Pultare safely."

Liliana goggled at him as she and the selkie, in unison, said, "Truly?"

"Yes, truly. I have learned my lesson about dallying with creatures of lore." Juliane shot Liliana a winning grin which she could not help but return, and she told herself, *He may be changing after all.*

Once the selkie understood Juliane meant what he had said, she expressed her sincerest gratitude. "I left my skin on the shore for just a bit—I had gone to fetch berries from a bush a few minutes' walk inland," she explained, "and I came back to where I'd placed it to find that it was no longer there. I scanned the coast and saw you walking in the distance, so I jumped into the water and swam after you. Upon drawing nearer to you I discovered you had my pelt, and so decided I should trail you to see if I might snatch it back without your noticing. I worried you wouldn't return it to me, but I shouldn't have fretted so, for I find women are often more gracious than men in these matters."

Liliana expected Juliane to take umbrage at this but was once again surprised when he curtsied and said, "Of course, we women must support one another." He shot her a wink that made her start laughing, but she quickly stifled herself when she noticed the look of confusion on the selkie's face.

The party, now consisting of three, continued along the path to Pultare, and the selkie, whose name was Irmene, proved to be an entertaining companion, for, after she had grown comfortable with the travelers, she regaled them with tales of her many adventures. "Many years ago," one account began, "I visited a tavern in Silvan, for I'd heard skilled musicians would be playing there that day. I had my skin with me, rolled into a pack, and left it in a corner like a fool whilst I went to get a pint. I returned to find a shipwright holding it on his lap and, as he had my skin, he asked me to become his wife. I married him—for, as you know, it's the way with selkie women—and was with him for several years, but, though I was happy enough, I missed the sea terribly."

"One day I was going through a trunk and—oh, joy!— came upon my skin, so I put it on and returned to the ocean. I still miss my husband at times, for he was a loving man, and kind apart from the dirty trick he'd played with my hide. I may seek him out one day, but cannot do so for another two years, as we female selkies cannot see the humans who've withheld our skins for seven years after we've reclaimed them of our own accord. I'm not sure why, though. It seems we immortals have a lot of silly rules put upon us—perhaps this is to make things feel fairer to humans, as they don't enjoy the privileges of everlasting life and shape-changing?"

"Of course, male selkies have it easier than female ones, but what else is new in a world ruled by men?" Irmene grumbled. "They needn't marry those who find their skins, and they can come to the lonely who've shed seven tears into the sea and offer themselves to them. They also have strong seductive powers, a siren-like ability to enchant with their words and songs. Selkie males will frequently captivate mortal maidens, then take them to bed or to wife until they tire of them. Beware a beautiful man whose words feel like a lullaby, for he is surely a selkie. If you're not careful, you may awaken upon a beach with a chemise full of sand!"

Irmene's carefree chatter made the journey to Pultare pass swiftly, and the trio became fast friends. When they finally neared the town the selkie let the travelers know she had taken them as far as she could, and Juliane reluctantly handed her skin over. After she had embraced them both she again thanked Juliane for his kindness, then handed him a whistle carved from driftwood. "If you're ever in trouble, blow on this. As you didn't choose to keep my pelt, I'm not forbidden from seeing you again for any length of time, and, because I'm grateful for my freedom, I'll help you to regain yours if ever you need me to." She then ran to the ocean and, reaching it, flung her hide over herself, transforming into a seal. She barked one last farewell before diving into the water, and the travelers watched as she swam farther and farther out to sea, until she disappeared into the horizon.

Juliane waved at her receding form. "She was so nice. It's a shame she cannot come and go as she pleases, for she's always in thrall, either to the sea or to whoever keeps her skin."

"At least we aren't owned by the sea nor by anyone else, and so can choose the company we'd like to," said Liliana.

"That's true. If given a choice, I'd still choose you, though. I couldn't ask for a better traveling companion."

"Oh, stop it, you'll make my head swell to unreasonable proportions," replied Liliana playfully, then she placed an arm around Juliane's shoulder and squeezed him gently.

He was thinking of the perfect response to this gesture when she turned and started down the road to Pultare. Frustrated that he had missed out on yet another opportunity, he sighed, shoved Irmene's whistle into his pack, and ran along after her.

***

Upon reaching Pultare the travelers were delighted to discover that it was a charming seaside village with quaint stone buildings and welcoming citizens. They were thrilled to have reached it well before sunset, and Liliana suggested they reward themselves for their timeliness with a fine room and a fine meal. Juliane agreed wholeheartedly, so they pranced to the village inn, "The Pig's Whistle," and there requested lodgings for the night from the landlord, a cheerful man named Erasmus Gelp. He took the two gold coins they offered and brought them to a room containing a large bed, a coffer, a nightstand topped with a wash basin, and a table with two comfortable chairs. When they asked him where they might find a splendid supper, he recommended the inn's tavern, so, once he left them, they washed, then locked the room and headed downstairs.

They were pleased to find that the innkeeper had been speaking the truth regarding the tavern's agreeableness, for the food looked delicious and the barmaid, an affable woman named Tamela, took a liking to them and gave each a free pint of ale. To show their appreciation for this gesture, they ordered the most lavish dishes the establishment served and, after paying for their meal, let her keep the excess.

They sat down in a quiet corner of the room to enjoy their food, and, midway through their repast, Tamela came to their table and filled their pints with stronger beer; she let them know that the drinks were on the house due to their compensating her so heartily, and proceeded to top their glasses off twice more during the meal. Liliana protested this at first, for she feared they might experience unwanted effects should they imbibe too heartily. However, Juliane assured her that, since they were taking their meal early, they would have ample time to sleep off the alcohol's effects, and so she decided it would not hurt her to have a few flagons with him and let herself drink what the barmaid had given her.

Once she had finished her meal and tipples, she started to act in such a giddy fashion that Juliane began to fear her trepidation had been wise, for it seemed the drinks had affected her more than they had him. He considered bringing her to the room to rest, but then she surprised him by throwing her arms around him and pulling him to her. He let out a squeak, and she released him and apologized. "I'm sorry, that was rash of me—but you're beautiful, and you've been so good recently, and I wanted to embrace you, so I did!"

She let out a cackle, and he decided that he did not want her to go to bed just yet, for he hoped she might show him more affection should she stick around. "I wasn't bothered by it," he assured her. "I'd actually like another, or perhaps even a kiss..."

He leaned forward in hopes she might plant one on him, but he had timed his actions poorly, for she had grown distracted by some musicians who had started playing a lively tune. "I want to dance! Oh, Juliane, come dance with me!" She pulled him to his feet and dragged him toward the center of the room, where several people were dancing a spirited jig. Once they had reached the others, Liliana offered them a cheerful salutation and joined them in their frolicking, and Juliane, getting into the spirit of things, grabbed her hands and spun with her about the room until both were panting and shaking with laughter.

He was once more considering requesting a kiss, opinions of those around them be damned, when Liliana was intercepted by a man in blue. He asked her to dance, and she said, "Why not?" and, flinging her arms over his shoulders, pranced with him along the dance floor. Juliane, surly about this, was about to interrupt them when someone asked if he would care to dance. As Liliana seemed to be having a good time skipping about with her partner, he decided to throw caution to the wind and accepted the proposal, and he soon found himself whirling from one partner to another, feeling like the queen of the room.

Once the song had ended, some men asked him if he would fancy having some mead with them, and, as he was loath to refuse drinks when others were offering them, flirted his way into a free glass. He was so busy basking in the adoration of those around him that he at first did not notice Liliana had disappeared, but, once he did, he excused himself and went looking for her.

He did not have to search long, for he found her seated at a table next to the man in blue who had stolen her away during the dance. He did not like how the stranger had his arm around Liliana's shoulders, and it caused him further annoyance that she was gazing at the man in a manner she had heretofore reserved only for himself (and perhaps, he had to admit, for that blasted Water-horse Tancred), and only for when he was on his best behavior. It did not help that the stranger was godlike; he was exceedingly tall, had brown skin with nary a blemish and dark curls touched

149

with gray that fell to his neck, and his face was the epitome of patrician good looks.

Jealousy worming through his gut, he approached the pair, trying to act casual. "Liliana, dear, there you are! It seems you're enjoying yourself, but it's time for us to retire to our quarters, as we have much ground to cover on the morrow."

Liliana neither turned her head nor acknowledged his greeting, merely continued staring at the man, who told him, "Why don't you go off to bed and leave her to me? I'll ensure no harm comes to her." He punctuated this statement with a knowing look, and Juliane's heart sank. It was unusual for Liliana to behave in this manner—she had such a strong sense of duty that it was unlikely she would forsake him so easily—and he also believed it was not just his vanity that made him feel that she might be beginning to care for him in a way that was more than friendly, so it was hardly fitting she would cast him aside for someone she barely knew.

He sensed there was something wrong, that the stranger was exerting a sinister will over her, and, as if the man had divined his thoughts, he smirked in a way that said, *She is with me now, and there's nothing you can do about it.* Feeling defeated, Juliane marched away from the table. He was certain Liliana was under some sort of enchantment, but he was unsure whether he could help her escape it. Regardless, he decided that the first thing to do would be to talk to the barmaid about the mysterious fellow who had so quickly gained a hold over her.

17.

Juliane made his way through the crowd of revelers and found Tamela, who had just finished serving the mob of young men who had earlier tried winning his affections. "What is it, poppet?" she asked upon seeing Juliane's worried expression. "Ye seem concerned."

"Tamela, the man my friend is with—could you tell me what you know of him?"

The barmaid glanced across the room at Liliana and the stranger. "Oh, 'im? If 'e's what's worrying ye, ye needn't trouble yerself. That's Lord Ichthus. Comes 'ere once a week or so to 'ave a meal and 'ear a tune—'e don't trouble nobody. Sometimes 'e gets 'is eye on a pretty maid and ends up leaving with 'er."

"What happens after he does?"

"I don't rightly know," said Tamela. "Strange, though—now's I think of it, the ladies that go with 'im always end up returnin' 'ere a few days or weeks later, and you know what? They don't remember 'im and don't recall goin' anywhere with 'im. They don't even recognize 'im. Isn't that a lark?" She giggled and started to say more when Juliane abruptly disappeared into the crowd, so, shrugging her shoulders, she returned to serving the bar's other patrons.

Juliane had not intended to be rude, but, upon hearing Tamela's description of Lord Ichthus's behavior, he had realized that he needed to act immediately, for he had recalled Irmene's warnings regarding male selkies and understood Liliana had fallen under one's influence. As he approached her and her would-be suitor, he pondered how he might ensure her release from the creature's clutches, and, after considering his options, decided the best way to defeat the brute would be by using his wits. He knew selkies lost their powers if their hides were destroyed and that, if he obtained this one's, he would hold sway over him. It was just a matter of figuring out how to get it.

Putting on his most charming smile, Juliane stumbled into the table Liliana and the stranger were seated at and feigned drunkenness as best he could. "Ooh, those men were too kind! They told me I'm pretty then bought me three more glasses of mead even though I'd already had one." He flopped down on the bench next to Ichthus and, tilting toward him, shouted, "D'you think I'm pretty?"

Ichthus could barely mask his irritation. "You are indeed pretty, but you're also intoxicated."

"I am not!" said Juliane, slapping the man's arm. "I'm fine. Four cups of mead aren't too many to drink."

He forced out a coughing fit and fell onto the selkie, who was now unable to hide his displeasure. "Please remove yourself from my shoulder, for, in your state of inebriation, you may soil my garment."

Juliane was pleased his illusion had tricked the creature, for it seemed Ichthus believed he was drunk and was therefore unlikely to grow suspicious should he pry for information. He sat up and stuck out his lower lip. "You don't have to be nasty. I was just coming over to be with my friend. She's my *closest* friend, d'you know that?" Leaning toward Ichthus, he muttered conspiratorially, "Sometimes we do things friends aren't supposed to, if you know what I mean."

He bit his lip and giggled, and the selkie brightened, for it seemed he had understood Juliane's insinuation and was now envisioning himself dallying with not just one woman, but two. Using a much kinder tone than he had previously, he said, "Oh, really? Why, then you must tell me all about them."

Juliane exclaimed, "I most certainly will not, for I am a lady! We ladies can get up to things, and you...cannot...know...them." He jabbed his finger into Ichthus's arm to punctuate each of these last words, then rested his chin on the selkie's shoulder and purred, "I see that you like my friend and that she likes you. Well, I like you too. If you're going somewhere together, may I join you?"

Ichthus grinned lasciviously. "Of course. Three can have more fun than two."

"Then where are we going?" asked Juliane, hoping he did not sound too keen to know.

"I've rented a room upstairs for the evening. We could head up together if you wish."

"I need to clean up first! I've spilled drink all over myself!" protested Juliane, getting up from the table. Positioning himself in a way that gave the selkie a choice view down the front of his dress, he said, "I'll join you when I'm done washing up. Which room will you be in and when can I expect you?"

"Room five, end of the passage," said Ichthus. "I'm just finishing up my meal—which shouldn't take more than a quarter of an hour—and then I shall be there."

Juliane simpered, "I'll be waiting by the door for you, so don't take too long," and then walked away from the selkie, swinging his hips as he went. He observed, with some satisfaction, that Ichthus could not stop staring at him as he exited the room, and he admitted to himself that he was not too bad at being an attractive woman after all.

Juliane ran to the entrance of the inn, for he recalled seeing a ring of keys hanging behind the innkeeper's desk.

He hoped to get a key to Ichthus's room without Master Gelp interfering, so that he might get into it before the selkie could, and found that he was in luck, for the landlord had fallen asleep in his chair. Creeping behind the dozing man, he reached above him and removed the ring from its place; he set it on the desk, searched it, and suppressed a squeal of happiness when he discovered a spare key for room five. He carefully removed it and replaced the ring on the nail, then, filled with apprehension, ascended the stairs and made his way to the selkie's room. He fit the key into the lock and turned it, and this time allowed himself a cry of joy, for the door swung smoothly open.

Entering Ichthus's room, he found it was even more lavish than his and Liliana's, for it had a large canopy bed, a roaring fireplace, and a tub large enough for a full-body wash. He was at first amused by the selkie's demanding water to frolic in even while in human form, then sickened as it dawned on him that Ichthus had likely brought several women unable to refuse his advances to this very room. He felt disgusted that this was the way some men chose to treat women, but he also found himself feeling ashamed, for he recognized that, as a man, he had employed his own unsavory practices. Though he had certainly never forced nor tricked someone into a dalliance, he had engaged in countless affairs with servant girls whom, he now realized, might have participated for fear of losing their positions. Knowing this, he vowed to never again take advantage of the hired help and to only seek intimacy with his noble peers—perhaps, if he was being fully honest with himself, with one noblewoman in particular.

Understanding he was wasting his time with ruminations and wishful thinking, he shut the door behind him and locked it, then resumed the task at hand: finding Ichthus's skin. "Now, if I were a selkie, where would I store my pelt?" he asked himself, and, finding he had no particular answer to give, searched the room for the perfect hiding spot. He soon found it, for shoved under the bed was a trunk that had seen better days that almost certainly contained what he was seeking, for it was held closed with a lock. He considered trying to break it open but figured this would be challenging, if not impossible, to do, for it appeared sturdy and might be constructed of magical materials; furthermore, he might damage the pelt in doing so, and, though he was unsure whether this would release Liliana from the selkie's spell, he was certain it would make the creature loath to parley with him.

He scanned the room and noticed a glint of silver on the underside of the tub, so he hurried over to it and ran his hand along its bottom. A key came off it into his palm, and he swiftly unlocked the trunk and tugged the lid open. The hide within was luxurious, remarkably soft and a lovely shade of silvery gray, and Juliane pulled it out and wrapped it around himself, then climbed onto the bed to wait for the selkie and his intended target.

He was not kept in suspense for long, for he soon heard a key turn in the lock. The door opened, and, trembling in anticipation, he positioned himself so that Ichthus would see him immediately upon entering. The selkie stepped into the chamber, a blank-eyed Liliana in tow, and found Juliane laid out before him. "My dear, how did you get into my room? I see you've been waiting for me..." He trailed off when he noticed what Juliane was wearing, and his bronze skin paled. "How did you get that?"

"I found it. 'Twas easy. You know, if I were a selkie I wouldn't leave my skin in a place where it might be so effortlessly discovered, for, should it be destroyed whilst I was seeking maidens to bewitch, the consequences would be most dreadful."

Ichthus glowered at him. "What must I do to get it back?"

"Release my friend from your influence. I know you've enchanted her, as there's no way she'd abandon our quest of her own accord. Free her from your spell, or I shall toss your hide into the fire and you shall never return to your beloved ocean."

Ichthus's face at first grew alarmed, but his expression soon softened into one of bold cunning. He shut the door gently, then approached the bed. "Lovely maiden," he cooed, "why must you threaten me? I know you desire me and do not really wish to harm me. Why don't you hand me my skin?"

Juliane felt his mind cloud and, recognizing that the selkie was attempting to charm him, steeled himself against his advances; he was happy to find this was not difficult to do, likely because his knowledge of Ichthus's identity had decreased any siren-like power the selkie might have otherwise had over him. To ensure the enthrallment would not eventually affect him, he got up from the bed and took off the pelt, then skipped over to the fireplace and dangled it near the blaze. "I'm sorry, Ichthus, but your luck has run out. Your enticements won't work on me, for, as you might have guessed from our earlier conversation, I'm more interested in other ladies than I am in the likes of you."

Ichthus, seeing his hide held so close to the fire, gulped and pleaded, "Please, do not burn my skin! I shall do whatever you wish."

"Then free my companion, now!"

Sighing, the selkie made some gestures before Liliana's face, and her glazed eyes instantly cleared. She shook her head and looked around, confused. "Where am I? How did I get here? I remember dancing in the tavern but recall nothing from afterward."

Juliane informed Liliana of the selkie's behavior and intentions, then ambled over to her and handed her the pelt. "What would you like to do with him?" Liliana, face contorted with rage, stepped forward and slapped Ichthus across the face. The creature shrank from her, fear twisting his features, and, apparently more concerned for the safety of his skin than for that of his personage, begged that she be careful with it so as not to damage it.

She removed her sword from its scabbard and he fell to his knees, beseeching her not to destroy it, but she demanded that he quiet himself, for she did not intend on rendering it unwearable, and proceeded to carve the letters "L" and "J" into the chest. "Now you will always remember the women who bested you," she said, tossing it at him. "Perhaps this will teach you only to bed women who willingly return your advances." She grabbed Juliane's hand and they headed to the door, but, before they reached it, she told the selkie, who was clutching his hide and sobbing. "If you ever come near us again, we shall find that hide of yours and ensure that, after we're through with it, nothing remains of it but ash."

Ichthus let out a wail and buried his head in his skin, and Juliane, barely stifling a giggle, gently tugged at Liliana and reminded her that they should be going. After making a few more vague threats, they departed from the selkie's chamber and hurried back to their own. Entering it, they threw themselves on the bed and burst into laughter— Juliane's fully joyous, for he had saved his companion with skills he had not been aware of possessing; Liliana's somewhat uneasy, for she had come so close to being subdued by the treacherous creature.

***

Sobering, Liliana told Juliane, "I knew I shouldn't have taken so much strong beer. I don't drink it often, so it affected me more than I'd expected it to. I started dancing with that fiend, he looked into my eyes—and the next thing I know, I'm in his bedchamber! I wouldn't have been so vulnerable to his charms had I been in full possession of my wits."

"That may be true," said Juliane, "but don't blame yourself. You had no idea you would run into one of his ilk when you allowed yourself to imbibe so heartily. The things that happened were beyond your control. You can let go and enjoy yourself now and again, you know," he teased. "You don't always have to be the sensible one. I don't mind taking an occasional break from my gadding about to let you have your turn at being reckless."

He beamed at her, but she did not seem to notice, for she had risen and, staring at the floor, suppressed a shudder. "If you hadn't intervened, he might have done all sorts of terrible things and I wouldn't have even remembered them. Thank you for saving me from a truly awful fate...and for saving my life yesterday as well. I feel like I haven't been helping you as much as I should be lately—like I've been...letting you down."

Juliane sat up and gently placed a hand on her shoulder. "You most certainly haven't been! I might have been the hero these past few instances, but you've been my savior on so many occasions I'd have to rescue you several more times before even coming close to considering us even. You got us away from the Sluagh, you alerted me to the stray sod, you threw the charm that helped us escape the Sisters, you helped me outrun the faerie dog..." He folded his hands in his lap, then stared down at them. "And you handed someone you obviously care for over to Rhoswen so I wouldn't be sucked dry by her, even though it was my own foolishness that got me into trouble in the first place. Even if I spent my entire life freeing you from various traps, it still wouldn't feel as if I'd made as much of a sacrifice as you did then."

Liliana turned to him and grasped his hands, and he lifted his head to find her smiling at him. "The sacrifice I made was worth it. Tancred can handle Rhoswen, so I'm not worried for them, and you—why, look at how much you've accomplished in just a few days! You keep growing

throughout this journey, and it's...actually quite attractive."
She noticed she was still holding onto him and, blushing,
let him go. "Thank you for knowing the right things to say
to help me feel better. You really are a wonder—and, as I'm
now clear-headed, I swear it isn't just the drink talking!"

She laughed, and Juliane noted, not for the first time but
perhaps more openly to himself than ever before, that her
unique features, combined with her intellect and character,
granted her a beauty most rare. Momentarily smitten, he
once again hoped they might share a kiss, but she bustled
away from him and over to the wash basin before he could
make this suggestion. He sighed as he watched her splash
water on herself, and as he gazed at her, unthinking, she
looked over her shoulder and caught him admiring her.

He turned his face away and stared at the ground,
silently praying that his behavior would earn him teasing
rather than reprimands. Deciding that it would be best to
deal with any consequences forthwith, he turned back to
her, and was relieved to find that she did not appear cross.
"Were you casting adoring looks at me?" she said coyly. He
started to stammer a response when, to his astonishment,
she approached him, sat down next to him, and, placing
her face inches from his own, asked, "Juliane, would you
like for me to kiss you?"

He pinched himself to make sure he was not dreaming,
and, after determining he was not, said, in a trembling
voice, "Y-yes, I would." He was immediately besieged by
regret for having not responded in a wittier fashion—after
all, this was an occasion he had been waiting for and it
merited a clever response—but then it mattered no longer,
for she pulled him to her, her warm breath tickled his
cheek, and then her lips pressed upon his.

He had to stop himself from groaning when she broke
the kiss, but he received some consolation from his
certainty that she was not planning on releasing him just
yet, for she continued to clasp him tightly. Bringing her

159

mouth to his ear, she whispered, "Juliane, I must tell you—I've wanted to do this for a while. I've been attracted to you ever since we first met but couldn't allow myself to be with you, for, although your appearance enticed me, your behavior repulsed me. But...it's like you've become a brand-new person, one I find myself strongly drawn to, and I feel I need no longer resist my attractions." She gazed into his eyes. "Juliane, you've grown very special to me during our travels, and, since I no longer feel I'd regret our being together, I must ask...would you like to spend the night together?"

He opened his mouth to tell her, "Yes, of course, I'd love to," but, as she stared at him expectantly, it dawned on him that she was viewing him as a woman and wanted to be with him because she was attracted to him as one. This idea inserted itself into his brain and refused to be dislodged, and he grew distressed because the most alarming thing, the thing that caused him such unease, was that a substantial part of him—one that seemed to be growing daily—was fine with her seeing him as a girl and desiring him as such; this was likely a natural consequence of being trapped in a woman's body for so long, but, regardless, it was frightening to feel so comfortable with it. It was as if he was losing his sense of self, or had perhaps already lost it...and, if it could be so easily lost, was it truly his to begin with?

Terrified by the thought, he covered his face and shrieked, "No!" He felt Liliana's grip on him slacken as he shook his head and said, "I'm not a woman, I'm a man. I could never be a woman. I'm a man. I mustn't forget that."

When he removed his hands, he found Liliana staring at him, her features flooded with a heartbreaking array of feelings. Tears welled in her crystalline blue eyes, but she blinked them away and stood up. "Liliana, I'm sorry!" he cried. "Please, wait!" He rose and placed his hand on her shoulder, but she refused to look at him. "Please don't think my response had anything to do with you. I just didn't know how to feel. I don't know why I acted that way—"

"You don't? Well, I do." She turned to him, eyes flashing. "You were upset because I'd forgotten your maleness—I was seeing you as a girl and was drawn to what I saw. Even after all the strength you've seen women display during our journey, you can't bear to be thought of as one of us. It upsets you, because you still feel that we're lesser than men."

Juliane considered her words; though her assessment did not seem to describe his thoughts exactly, he was still too unsure of how he felt to assert this with any conviction. "Perhaps you're right," he said, "but, if I was thinking that way, I wasn't doing so willfully, and I certainly did not mean to hurt you with my foolishness. I would love to kiss you again, as it might help me gain some clarity..."

He reached out to her once more, but she shied away, her spark of anger now a smoldering ember of dismay. "I can't," she murmured, staring at the floor. "I thought you'd changed for the better, but now...I'm having a hard time believing that you won't just return to being the man you were before once you've received your cure." She glanced up and, seeing she had wounded him, said, "I'm sorry, but I cannot lie about how I feel, and I cannot be with someone whose future behavior might cause me to look back in shame upon our time together, no matter how unmistakably drawn to them I might be."

She trudged over to her side of the bed and clambered under the covers. Juliane remained standing, silent, staring at her prone form. There were so many things he wanted to tell her: that he cared greatly about how she felt despite his callous response; that, upon regaining his male form, he would be different from how he had been and that this was largely because he had known her; that he was silly and frightened and did not know who he was anymore and that this had caused him to respond impulsively...but he understood that saying anything more at that moment would only cause further damage. Climbing into bed, he whispered, "I'm so sorry, Liliana, I never meant to hurt you," to her proffered back, then he closed his eyes and, worried that he had ruined any sort of chance he might have had with her, drifted off to fitful sleep.

18.

The travelers woke later than they had intended to the following day and hastily washed, dressed, and packed their bags without a word passing between them. Leaving their room, they descended the stairs to find Master Gelp still snoring near the inn's entrance, so Liliana wrote him a letter alerting him to their departure—which she wrapped around the room key and left on the table next to him—while Juliane stealthily slid the key to Ichthus's chamber back onto the ring. They exited the building, closing the door gently behind them, and Juliane uttered a silent prayer that Ichthus was a late enough sleeper that they wouldn't run into him that morning.

They checked their packs and discovered they were low on food and water, and, as Liliana reported that they were unlikely to reach another town by nightfall, stopped at a morning market to purchase victuals and fill their vessels. The sun was already high in the sky as they bid farewell to Pultare; they were relieved to leave it despite its apparent charm, for it harbored both painful memories and a vengeful selkie and these things had soured their feelings toward it.

As they walked in silence along the coastal path leading away from the village, Juliane gathered his courage and said, "Liliana, we should talk about what happened last night."

"Which part of last night are you referring to, Juliane?" she replied. "As you know, I was quite unsteady due to both the drink I'd taken and Ichthus's enchantment, so much of the evening is foggy for me. I'm not sure if I'll be able to recall what it is that you'd like to discuss."

Juliane stepped in front of her, arms folded across his chest, and straddled the path, blocking her course. "You know which portion of the evening I'm referring to. I refuse to continue onward until we talk about it."

Liliana sighed. "Fine, Juliane, I..." Suddenly, her manner changed; it grew light and carefree. "I don't remember our conversation terribly well, but I do remember being quite giddy at the time. I felt very grateful to you and fond of you for your assistance with the selkie, and I reacted hastily. I threw myself at you without taking your feelings into account. I'm sorry for doing this and can assure you it won't happen again."

She stepped over Juliane's outstretched left leg and resumed her course down the road, but he followed her and, taking her by the hand, drew her to a halt. "Please, don't just walk away and pretend something important didn't happen last night. I know I hurt you and damaged our relationship. I was the one in the wrong—it's why I apologized then and will continue to do so now. I want to make things right between us, but I need you to tell me how."

Liliana's carefree mask quivered, but, though there was sadness in her eyes, she spoke blithely. "You needn't worry! I'm perfectly fine. I understand that my behavior last night was untoward. I took my dreams and placed them on you and almost pushed you into a role you're not comfortable with. I admit that I've been forgetting you're not a woman at times and so have been drawn to you as such, and you made it clear last night that I was wrong to do so—I'll not make the mistake again. I will gladly assist you in completing your quest, and, after you've regained your male form, why, I'm sure we'll remain great friends...but it's probably best if we forget the things that I said last night. I'm sure you'll want to resume your old life and princely duties as soon as we've returned home, and I don't want to stand in your way."

Her voice trembled as she uttered these last few words, but she managed to maintain her jovial expression until she had turned and marched away down the path. "Come along!" she called over her shoulder. "We need to cover as much ground as possible before nightfall!"

Juliane at first lagged behind her, dejected, for he feared he had wounded her irreparably. However, once he had managed to catch up with her, he noticed the pained look upon her face, and seeing it filled him with resolve. He knew that, if he could prove to her that he was devoted to indefinitely remaining the kinder, gentler Juliane he had become, he could rebuild their connection so that she might trust him again and allow him to work his way back into her favor—and perhaps, one day, into her heart. Braced with a renewed sense of purpose, he fell into step alongside her as they continued down the path toward lands unknown.

The road seemed to wind on interminably, and the travelers followed it for many hours until it abruptly ended near a rocky plain. "Wonderful. Now how are we supposed to get to the Darklands?" moaned Juliane, throwing himself down on one of the stones.

"Don't worry, I'm sure I can determine our course," said Liliana, seating herself on the rock nearest his and taking her map from her pack. "We've been walking along this shoreline, so I'm guessing we are now right about here." She placed her finger on a part of the map featuring a coastline that resembled a set of ragged steps. "I think we must go north a little, then east, then north and east again, and so on and so forth, until we come to...here."

Her finger moved to the right edge of the map, and Juliane felt a thrill course through him as he realized they had but a few days more of travel before reaching the Darklands—that is, if they did not experience any problems, for it seemed as if trouble kept finding them along their way. He gulped and, trying to stay positive, said, "Why don't we head north of these stones to see if the path reappears there?"

Liliana agreed with this suggestion, so she repacked her map and they rose and started northward. Juliane experienced a sense of mounting dread when he noticed an expanse of foreboding green growth looming before them. "Oh no, not another sinister wood! You remember all the foul things we went up against the last time we passed through a forest—please tell me we don't have to go in there."

"I'm afraid we do," said Liliana, after taking another look at the map. She pointed at the first jagged piece of coastline. "Do you see where that 'step' is? That must be where we are now—and, as you've likely noticed, there are tree-like shapes covering the stretch of land above it and continuing to the border in the far east. This means a forest almost certainly blankets that entire area and is likely impossible to get around. We're just going to have to look for an entrance into it and hope the road we find takes us to the Darklands...and not to our doom." She rolled the map up and thrust it back into her bag. "I suppose we should get going." Juliane, his stomach turning somersaults, trailed her as they neared the wood, which seemed to grow larger and more menacing with each step they took toward it.

It did not take them long to find the path into the forest, for, after they had walked north a few minutes, they came upon a rough-hewn sign marked "Woods" featuring an arrow pointing into the thicket. "It's a good thing they placed this here, or I might never have known these were woods," Juliane remarked dryly upon seeing it.

This drew a giggle from Liliana, but she stopped laughing as a flock of birds rose up out of the forest, screeching ominously as they flew away. "Perhaps that was an omen?" When Juliane, trying to lighten the tension, suggested that the birds had simply found her laugh so pleasing that they felt moved to take wing, she smiled thinly. "I suppose. Oh well, we must push ahead regardless, as we need to find shelter before nightfall." She adjusted her pack on her shoulder, then set off down the road into the wood, Juliane at her heels.

The path into the forest was not well-maintained, and Liliana had to frequently use her sword to cut back growth blocking their way. She complained about its lack of care-taking, but, when Juliane volunteered that it might be overgrown because no one had taken it in a while, she was unsure whether the idea comforted or unnerved her and so decided not to think about it and simply forged ahead. They walked for hours but, though it was growing dark, still had not discovered suitable shelter. Liliana was beginning to lose hope when, suddenly spying something, she exclaimed, "I have found our overnight spot!"

She pointed at a sizable cave looming ahead of them, and Juliane, incredulous, said, "You want us to stay there tonight? But, it's wide open, there doesn't seem to be anything to block the entrance with, it's—"

"It's either that or sleep outside on the ground, where we're vulnerable to everything," she interrupted. "Which would you prefer?" He gestured sheepishly at the cave, so, grunting, she strode resolutely toward it. He followed her uncertainly, for the place gave him a bad feeling, but, as he was uncertain why it did, he decided it would be best to keep his apprehensions to himself.

***

Upon entering the cavern, the travelers were pleased to discover that it was quite long, enabling them to go far enough back into it to adequately shelter from the elements; less pleasant discoveries, though, were the remains of a fire-ring as well as piles of dried leaves that seemed to serve as makeshift mattresses. "Don't worry, those who've stayed here were likely others traversing the forest. It's doubtful they will return," said Liliana, as she created a fire in the ring. "This may be a known haven in this part of the forest. And the leaves will provide us with more comfortable beds than we could have anticipated!"

Juliane was not reassured by her words, for, to him, the fire-ring appeared to have been recently used, and this suggested someone had been present not long before their arrival. He was well aware of what sort of people might live in a cave inside a menacing forest and of how they might react if they came home to find strangers in their beds, and this made it difficult for him to relax and enjoy the food they had purchased in Pultare. Calming his nerves became an even more difficult task when he went to his leaf pile to rest, for he uncovered a bright green serpent within who hissed and bared fangs at him. Liliana drew her sword and sliced the creature in two, then admitted that, though she had been loath to slay it, it had been of a very poisonous kind that might have killed him had it bitten him. She checked the leaf-beds for further unwanted tenants and, finding none, assured Juliane there would be no additional dangers, but the experience had left him shaken, and it took him a while to fall asleep once they had settled in for the night.

He was eventually able to doze off, but his slumber was fitful and plagued by nightmares. After having several that were merely alarming, he had one that was downright terrifying. In it, he had awakened to a light shining upon his face and, after his eyes adjusted, found a large, hairy, brutish-looking man holding a torch standing before him.

He had turned to wake Liliana but discovered she was no longer by his side, and the man, grinning obscenely, had come toward him with arms outstretched. He was barely able to suppress a scream as he woke gasping and shaking, for it had all seemed so real.

Once his trembling ceased, he checked on Liliana and was overjoyed to find her sleeping peacefully upon her leaf pile, but then his mood soured as he realized that he needed to pass water. He and Liliana had agreed that they would leave the cave to do this, but the harrowing dream had made him loath to go out into the woods, where anything might be lurking. He decided an acceptable compromise would be to relieve himself near the back of the cave far from where she slept—she might give him a hard time about it in the morning, but that was preferable to his squatting vulnerably in the dark forest.

Though the fire was little more than embers, it cast enough of a glow that he was able to guide himself to the rear of the cavern. Reaching it, he turned his back to Liliana, lifted his skirts, and squatted so he would not dirty his boots. He squinted at the wall of the cave as he did his business, and, after a while, noticed that the surface he was mindlessly staring at was covered with artwork.

He dropped his skirts and, fetching a torch Liliana had constructed, lit it in the fire and then carried it over to the marked wall. By the torchlight he was able to discern that the images on it were paintings of beasts that resembled people but were not wholly human; one had wings instead of arms and a beak for a mouth, another a tail and sharp talons upon its reptilian feet, a third a wolf's head and furred paws for hands. Gazing at the images made him uneasy, and he determined that this was because the creatures in the pictures were eating so grotesquely: meat hung from their mouths, blood coated their extremities, and shreds of flesh surrounded them as they enjoyed their vile repast.

He realized that the images reminded him of the gods he had once seen in one of his father's books, and the alarming thought crossed his mind that the cave might be a place where worshipers had come—and perhaps still came—to make sacrifices to the man-beast gods depicted upon its walls. He was considering waking Liliana to let her know of his discovery when he noticed an as-yet-unseen painting down near where the cave wall met the floor. He bent low to shine torchlight on it and, for the second time that night, barely kept himself from shrieking—for the picture was of a torn-apart human body, and he realized, with a flash of horror, that the monsters portrayed in the art were eating human flesh.

Placing the torch against the wall, he stumbled backward from the terrifying image, but he slipped in the puddle he had made and fell onto the floor, landing upon something hard covered in leaves. He reached out to grasp it and finally choked out the scream he had been holding in since waking from his nightmare, for his hand touched something that was undoubtedly a human skull. He thrust the object away and, as the awareness that he had fallen upon a body in what was likely a place where people were sacrificed to beast-gods caused terror to overwhelm him, he dropped into merciful oblivion.

19.

Juliane emerged from his faint to find himself in a state of disarray and confusion. He remembered losing his footing and tumbling into a pile of leaves, but at first could not recall any other details surrounding his circumstances—then, all of a sudden, he was flooded with the recollection that, before he had swooned, he had found images of monstrous beasts eating people on the wall of the cave and, startled, had fallen backward onto...

He squealed as he realized that he was still lying on some poor soul's remains, so, after determining he was uninjured, he rolled out of the leaves, relieved to not have come into contact with any other bones during his time on the floor. He had intended on getting up to rouse Liliana—for he felt it would be best not to tarry in a place that was likely used for human sacrifice—but, as his eyes adjusted to the dimness, he abandoned this plan and instead shrieked her name as loudly as he could, for he had discovered the travelers were no longer alone.

The creatures that had entered the cave could have emerged from the paintings on its walls, for one was unbelievably tall with mottled green skin, protruding golden eyes, and webbed hands and feet; another was covered in coarse brown fur, had a snout and black nose, and bore limbs resembling a bear's; and the third was silvery in color, with scales on its head and arms, and

171

boasted bulging fish eyes and a gaping toothless mouth. Juliane yelled Liliana's name once more, but, noticing that the frog-creature was about to grab her, he turned, seized the torch from the wall, and moved to fend the beasts off.

Liliana, awakened by his screams, let out one of her own that was quickly muffled by a cold, clammy palm. She attempted to bite it but found her teeth could not reach it, so she tried wriggling in hopes of slipping from the grip of the thing grasping her. Another limb encircled her waist and she felt herself being lifted, and, though she struggled and kicked, she could not force her captor to drop her. She reached for her sword, but the monster holding her noticed her behavior and removed its hand from her mouth to pinion her arms to her body. "Juliane, help!" she cried, as the creature hoisted her into the air.

Juliane had been striking out at the fish-being with the torch, but upon hearing her cries rushed to her defense. He unfortunately did not notice the bear-creature creeping up behind him, though, and, as he swung the torch at the beast holding Liliana, it grabbed him and lifted him as easily as it would a feather. Understanding that there was little chance of their escaping the monsters—and remembering the fates of the humans pictured upon the wall—he let out a shriek and fainted once more.

Liliana screamed his name, for she feared he had been harmed, but lost all hope of assisting him as she was flung over the toad-beast's shoulder and carried out of the cave. She saw the fish-creature pick up their packs and the bear-horror throw Juliane over his shoulder like a sack of turnips, then she saw no more, for she had been taken out into the woods where it was too dark to discern much of anything. They were transported through total blackness for what seemed many miles, then Liliana began hearing noises in the distance that grew louder with each step the creatures took; they were obviously bringing their prisoners to an intended destination, for, as they neared it, there was an uproar of whoops and cries.

They soon entered a clearing featuring a platform bordered by burning bonfires at its center, and Liliana was roughly lowered onto a poorly made chair atop it. She once more attempted to free herself, but her captor hissed, in a voice that made her blood cold, "If ye squirm and try to escape, I will knock ye out and let my friends take bites of ye." Terrified, she froze, and the creature bound her to the seat with thick, strong rope. She was vaguely aware that a still-insensible Juliane had been placed on a chair next to hers, but she was too paralyzed by fear to fully comprehend anything, for she could now see that she was surrounded by an array of beasts more hideous than anything she ever could have imagined.

They appeared to be hybrids of persons and animals, for each displayed both human and non-human attributes; there were monsters with dogs' heads and paws, brutes with wings and beaks, horrors with claws and snouts and razor-sharp teeth. The most terrifying thing about this congregation, though, was that so many of its members were looking at her and Juliane as if they were pieces of meat in a shop window. Some were salivating, and a particularly bold one stepped forward and poked Juliane's arm with a talon-tipped finger. "Get away from her!" yelled Liliana, and, though the creature snarled at her, it begrudgingly rejoined the crowd.

The three kidnappers stood on the platform apart from the rabble, and, after basking in its adulation for a while, they called for quiet and began to speak. "We founds these two juicy darlings in the painted cave!" the bear-creature announced. "We saws a firelight, we wents in, and there they was, so we broughts them back to shares with you!"

The crowd cheered, and the bear-thing requested silence once more. Juliane was woken by the clamor just in time to hear it say, "Now we must haves a chat, as we always does when we finds hoo-mans. Does we keep these ones to mates with, or does we eats them?" He started to swoon once more, but Liliana hissed at him, and he reluctantly joined her in listening, appalled, to the monsters' dialogue. "Bufonus, what say ye?" the bear-horror asked the frog-creature who had carried Liliana from the cave.

The hideous beast, yellow eyes blinking, drew so near to the travelers that they could feel its hot, carrion-scented breath wash over them. After it had studied them awhile, it straightened and declared, "I think we should keep them, Ursiden. They're pretty and seem strong. I think they'd be fine breeders, as they might survive birthing our young."

"And, if they doesn't, we can always eats them then!" said the bear-creature, Ursiden, which caused the crowd to burst into applause and Juliane to disgorge his most recent meal.

Ursiden cast him a brief look of disgust, then turned to the fish-creature who had also been part of the raiding party to ask its opinion on the matter. The monster, whom Ursiden called Salmonay, replied, "I think we should speak with Saurenia before we make any decisions." Ursiden and Bufonus scoffed at him and the mob groaned, but Salmonay persisted, scaly limbs trembling, "We all know that, if not for her, we wouldn't be here, and we also know she has the power to sustain or to destroy us. It would be unwise to send these two to the breeding place without her having a say in the matter. It might incur her wrath. I gather we've not forgotten what she did to those who tried to revolt not so long ago?"

The crowd nodded silently, and several of its members visibly quaked. Ursiden wrung its paws and said, "You might bes right, Salmonay. Lets us fetch Saurenia."

Only Bufonus stood firm in its defiance. It swung to face the throng and cried, "Cowards! There's nothing to fear. We can choose our own destinies and needn't run to Saurenia like children whenever we must make decisions. We're monsters, so what have we to fear, even from the likes of Saurenia?"

A voice rang out from the rear of the horde: "Bufonus, did I hear you speak my name?" The crowd parted to let the speaker pass, and the travelers beheld a strange figure advancing through the throng. She was clothed from head to foot in a red silk cloak, her hands were encased in brown leather gloves, and her face was covered with a dragon mask; the only part of her unconcealed were her eyes, which blazed a strange shade of orange-red. She was most certainly the Saurenia the beasts had been speaking of, and, when she reached the front of the mob, she drew gasps of shock as she rose into the air and then softly alighted on the platform.

She confronted the frog-thing, who had noticeably blanched. "Bufonus, did I just catch you speaking ill of me?" When the creature stammered that she must have misheard it, she shook her cloaked head sadly. "Oh, Bufonus, you not only talk badly of me, you also lie to me? How disappointing."

She reached out, placed her hand on Bufonus's forehead, and chanted a few syllables. The crowd shrieked as the frog-monster was enveloped in an orange glow and, within seconds, all that remained of it was a desiccated corpse and a toad that croaked loudly and hopped off the platform. "I knew I shouldn't have resurrected that one," Saurenia said cryptically, then she turned to the travelers. "Who are you, and why are you traveling through this forest?"

Liliana gathered her courage and replied, "I am Liliana Almwick and my friend is called Juliane. We are noblewomen from a faraway town and are passing through these woods to get to the Darklands, as we have business to attend to there."

She held her breath and waited for the masked figure to respond. She was not kept in suspense long, for Saurenia muttered Liliana's name to herself, then told the crowd, "These two are mine. Bring them to my chamber and untie them, then leave us be." She floated off the platform and passed through the mob, then issued a final order, "Don't delay," before disappearing into the woods.

The throng moaned and one of the beasts grumbled, "Why does she get the choicest morsels?" but the creatures nonetheless immediately obeyed Saurenia's request. Ursiden and Salmonay lifted the travelers from their chairs and, pushing them along, led them into the forest and through a tunnel of thorns. Upon exiting the thicket, they spied a small, agreeable-looking stone dwelling, and they were marched to its open doorway, untied, and shoved through it. As the door closed behind them, their hearts sank as they realized that they had been left alone with a very powerful being, for they were still uncertain as to why she had chosen to spare them.

Juliane cowered behind Liliana, who stood with arms crossed and glared uneasily at the cloaked figure before them. Saurenia, who had seated herself in a chair next to a blazing fireplace, noticed their discomfort and laughed heartily. "Unlike the others, I have no interest in eating you, so there's no need to be afraid. Please, have a seat. I would like to speak with you." The travelers cautiously sat down on two chairs they deemed a safe distance from Saurenia, and, once they had, she removed her mask and hood to reveal a thoroughly unexpected countenance. She did not appear to be fully human, and yet was not monstrous like the others they had so far encountered in the forest: her face was classically beautiful and her gleaming hair tumbled in waves to her chest, but her skin was bright green and her locks were of the darkest emerald. She had red-orange oblong eyes, shimmering turquoise scales grew upon her cheeks and forehead, and, when she opened her mouth, she displayed pointed canine teeth and a slightly forked tongue.

"There now, that's better, isn't it?" she said, shaking her

freed head. "I'm not nearly so frightening without my mask on. I keep my appearance hidden around my subjects, for I fear they might otherwise perceive my similarity to humans and might try to take a bite out of me! Then again, they might not, for, as you've witnessed, I have ways of dealing with them should they misbehave. It's always best not to find these things out through experience, though." She paused and looked pointedly at the travelers. "Have you anything to ask me, or have I rendered you speechless?"

Liliana said timidly, "You called those things your 'subjects.' Are you their...queen?"

"I suppose I am, in a way," replied Saurenia. "In case you hadn't already figured it out, I'm what some might call a sorceress. For years I lived alone in these woods, only venturing out of them to obtain supplies, for I was tirelessly working on a new form of magic. You see, I had mastered the basics of necromancy—summoning the dead so I might temporarily return them to life or control their spirits—but I wanted to find a way of giving enduring life to the deceased. Those I resurrected were merely undead or could only remain alive for brief periods, so I immersed myself in my studies, read many aged tomes, and performed many experiments, until I finally lucked into the knowledge I'd been seeking."

"I had mixed certain ingredients together and sprinkled them on a corpse I'd exhumed whilst reciting the appropriate words, and I'd once more resigned myself to failure when, unexpectedly, a mouse ran out of a corner of the chamber and clambered onto the body. The room filled with an orange light, and, once it faded, I found before me a man-sized creature equal parts human and mouse. It was at first frightened and tried to attack me but, after I'd subdued it with a suitable spell, I explained who I was and what role I'd played in its creation, and it was soon able to view me as its master and friend."

"That was Musko. It was my first victory, and provided

177

me with the answer I'd been seeking to the question of how to recreate long-lasting life from human death: bring together the shell of a human with a living animal, and, when the proper items and words are used, they will combine to create a new being that will live out the remaining lifespan of the animal it was formed from. Quite simple, really, but my greatest triumph. Musko passed years ago, but, since mastering the process, I've created many more like it, sometimes using choice human remains in the process, other times using...not so choice ones, like the ones used for Bufonus. As it was comprised of a toad and a murderer who'd been hanged, I should have known it would be trouble. Though my creations don't retain the memories of their former human selves they do tend to retain their temperaments, which can be problematic at times."

Liliana, who had been listening raptly, asked, "But, if you made those creatures, then why have you cultivated in them a taste for human flesh?"

"I didn't teach them to eat humans, they unfortunately developed that inclination on their own," said the sorceress. "My earlier creations, like Musko, were made from human bodies combined with smaller animals and were therefore relatively harmless once brought under control. However, my latter experiments, those blending corpses with animals such as wolves and bears—well, those creatures are highly skilled hunters, and, when their natures combined with human intelligence, it resulted in their seeking out more complex prey. They began to hunt and brought back...meat to share with the others, those who hadn't initially desired human flesh acquired a taste for it, and, well... They don't usually eat people, though— they're generally content with eating animals—and they don't get many chances to hunt that sort of prey..." She trailed off, shrugging.

"Your letting them remain alive is inexcusable," an

outraged Liliana scolded her. "You have the ability to destroy them, yet you continue to allow them to live and to cause harm?"

"Think of me as their mother," said Saurenia matter-of-factly. "I can't kill my children, can I? Besides, I'm something between what they are and what you are and so hold no real allegiance to either side. My loyalty's more based in circumstance and lies with whoever is kindest or of most benefit to me. I know it sounds callous, but that's just the way it is."

"If that's the case, then why save us? How do we know you won't just use us in your experiments or allow your monsters to tear us apart? Can you give us any reason why we should trust you?"

A wry grin spread over the sorceress's face. "Because, Liliana Almwick, I am indebted to her whose witch-loins you sprung from."

Liliana was momentarily stunned, and Juliane, who had been silent up until that point, indignantly asked the sorceress, "What do you mean by saying that?"

"I mean that Liliana's mother, the Lady Satiana Almwick, is an old friend of mine. I've not seen her for ages, but, when I was younger, I spent many years under her instruction. She taught me much of what I know and helped me to cultivate my natural affinity for magic use. When I heard your name and recognized you as her daughter, Liliana, I knew that I must offer you my assistance."

Liliana peered at Saurenia warily. "If this is true, then how is it I have never heard my mother speak of you? How do I not remember you from my childhood?"

"That is simple to explain. You're around twenty-five years old, correct?" Liliana specified that she was twenty-six, and Saurenia continued, "I'm a dozen years your senior and stayed with your family until I was twelve, so left your home shortly after your birth—I remember you as a baby. And it's likely your mother never mentioned me because, when I was fifteen, she and I had a disagreement of sorts. She was never comfortable with my interest in necromancy—it was why I had to leave her tutelage—and, during a meeting of the witches' circle we both belonged to at the time, I...did something that greatly displeased her. This is part of why I feel I must help you with whatever task you're undertaking. If I do, perhaps she will allow me back into her good graces."

A tear slid down her cheek, and she wiped it away and sighed, "Well, there's no benefit in dwelling on the past, only in looking toward the future. Now, if I've proven myself trustworthy enough to be brought into your confidence, would you mind telling me the object of your quest?"

Though she still did not completely trust Saurenia, Liliana tentatively shared the account of their journey with the sorceress—though she left out some bits she felt the sorceress did not need to know, like their carrying magic, for safety's sake. Once she had finished, the travelers sat in uneasy silence, awaiting Saurenia's assessment. Presently she said, "I think I might know how to best help you reach the Darklands. From what you've told me you can hold your own physically against many foes, but neither of you are proficient in magic use, and there are creatures in this wood that may only be felled with powerful spells. I believe it would be of most benefit to you were I to join your traveling party—at least until you've crossed into Darkwood's territory. I've heard he is an extremely powerful necromancer, so I'm unlikely to be able to help you once you've entered his lands."

The travelers were uncertain whether the sorceress had their best intentions in mind, but, as they understood that they had little say in the matter, they begrudgingly permitted Saurenia to join them. To show them her good will, she suggested that they sleep in her bed so they might be well-rested for the next day, reassuring them that she would be perfectly comfortable in her chair by the fire. They hesitantly accepted her charity, but had to admit, upon climbing onto her mattress, that it was one of the most comfortable things either had ever rested on—and, when she informed them that she could produce beds of air nearly as splendid, they more willingly resigned themselves to her company.

They slumbered peacefully for most of the night, the one exception being when Juliane was roused by Saurenia, who was sitting by the fire conversing with a glowing glass ball. He was initially unnerved by this, but, as he knew the sorceress was a necromancer, he decided that she was likely just communicating with spirits to gather information for their journey. He coughed loudly to let her know he was awake—he did not want her to think that he was spying on her—and she said, "I'm sorry if I disturbed you, I'm just readying things for the morrow." She did not seem concerned about being caught out, so, feeling reassured, he quickly returned to sleep. Once she was sure that he had, Saurenia resumed preparations for the things she knew awaited them along the road ahead.

20.

It was nearly noontime the next day when Saurenia woke the travelers and bade them prepare to leave; Liliana was at first cross at their having been allowed to oversleep, but, when the sorceress explained that she knew of a spot a few hours' walk from there that would be a fitting place to spend the night, she grudgingly accepted her reasoning. Saurenia gave each traveler a magical item to help them along their way—Liliana a torch that would light if "flame" was spoken while holding it, Juliane a square of fabric that would become a tent if told to "grow"—and, after they had a sumptuous breakfast at her fireside table, she helped them fill their bags with the remainder of the delicious food. After receiving this bounty from the sorceress, the pair started to believe she was well-intentioned after all and grew more comfortable with her presence in their party.

Once they had finished their preparations, the trio left the cottage, crept past the sleeping human-beasts, and set off eastward into the thick wood. Saurenia was a more useful guide than anticipated, for she seemed to know the forest well enough to navigate it without a map; whenever the path forked, she was able to lead them down what she claimed was the correct route. After several hours they found themselves in a large clearing, in the middle of which stood a wooden hut with a thatched roof and door fastened with a sturdy lock. The sorceress turned to the travelers and proudly said, "My memory has served me well. This building is a known haven in these parts. It's always kept shut so that forest creatures may not enter it—after all, you know how dangerous it is to sleep in a place with an open doorway in this wood." Liliana scowled at her tasteless jest, and she hurriedly continued, "Fortunately, I have a key. We shall bed down safely tonight."

"Wonderful!" exclaimed Juliane. "Perhaps we shall finally go one day of this journey without running into some sort of trouble..." Before he could finish his sentence, something large flew over them, momentarily blocking the sun. "I spoke too soon," he grumbled, digging through his bag in hopes of finding his dagger. The thing could at first only be seen in silhouette, but, once it grew clearly visible, Liliana drew her sword and held it at ready—though she doubted it would be of much use, for the creature circling above them was a large wyvern, a menacing dragon-like beast.

It plunged down from the sky and alighted in front of the hut, blocking any potential escape into it. It dwarfed the building in size, had large wings and two hind limbs tipped with menacing claws, and was covered in thick black scales. Its body was serpentine, with a belly that dragged on the ground and a long tail tipped with a poisonous barb, and its massive head featured piercing red eyes and a snout with protruding nostrils. It had a mouth full of terrifying teeth and, when it spoke, the voice issuing forth was a cross between a growl and a hiss. "What have weee heeere?" it asked, then it promptly answered itself, "It looksss like two humansss, and a...sssomething that'sss not quite human. I wonder which will tassste bessst?"

"Not me!" Juliane squealed impulsively.

Liliana rolled her eyes at him, then brandished her sword. "You shall never find out, serpent!"

"Ohhh, you belieeeve calling meee a ssserpent will

wound meee?" said the wyvern. "How very quaint. Sssince you are ssso unruly, I think I shall gobble you firssst."

Liliana paled visibly but, keeping her resolve, called out, "If you want me, come and get me—but, be forewarned, I shall put up a fight the likes of which you've never dreamed."

The wyvern let out a boisterous laugh and started moving toward her. Juliane, forgetting his desire to self-preserve, flung himself in front of her and shrieked, "No! Please don't eat her!"

She looked down at him, a strained smile upon her lips, and whispered, "I know you're trying to help and it's very sweet, but your efforts are likely to get us both killed."

She stepped over him and stalked toward the wyvern, sword held aloft, as it continued to proceed stealthily forward. "I could charge you if I wanted," it said, "but it isss ssso much more amusssing when I play with my food."

As the gap closed between them Liliana uncertainly readied herself for conflict, but she suddenly felt a hand on her shoulder and turned to find Saurenia beside her. "You will not be able to beat this creature with mere man-made weapons, and it will slay you and feast on your remains if you're fool enough to try and fight it. Only magic will defeat this beast—and, luckily, I know the right incantation to subdue it."

Seeing the reason in the sorceress's statement, Liliana stepped behind her, and Saurenia pulled a small staff topped with a green jewel from her cloak. The wyvern said, "Do you think you can bessst meee with that pieeece of rubbisssh? It looksss like you will be firssst to die, sssorceresss." Saurenia was unmoved, and, raising the staff into the air, cried:

Bind this creature
Lock it away,
So that it may not

Take our lives today.
Hold it fast,
Make it sleep.
Trap it somewhere
I can keep.

The wyvern laughed heartily and gloated, "Isss that all you have to ussse againssst meee, sssorceresss? It doesss not sssseeem effective..." Suddenly the gem started to shine, and a ray of light shot out from it toward the creature. It hit the beast and bathed it in a green glow, and, shrieking, it started to shrink. It was soon no bigger than an egg, and the beam receded into the cane, carrying the diminished wyvern with it and sealing it inside the jewel. Saurenia placed the now-occupied staff back into her cloak, then flourished her hands victoriously.

"Saurenia, you did it! You defeated the wyvern!" cried Liliana, impetuously throwing her arms around the sorceress.

"Had you doubted I would save us? I would never let anything happen to the daughter of Satiana Almwick, even if she wasn't as brave, clever, and resourceful as you are."

Liliana released the sorceress and, blushing fiercely, stammered words of thanks. Juliane, for his part, grumbled to himself that the sorceress had earned Liliana's trust more easily than expected. For some reason, this worried him. It was true she was a useful companion to have along on the journey—after all, she seemed to have just saved them from certain death—but there was something about her he had begun to dislike. Saurenia was suspect, after all—surely a beast as mighty as the wyvern could not have been felled with a simple rhyme? He searched for the root of his unease and found nothing concrete, but his disquiet remained, for he was sure there was something not entirely charitable about Saurenia's volunteering to assist them, though he could not yet identify what it was.

His attitude toward the sorceress softened once she had ushered them into the hut and secured the door, for she instantly created a fire in its fireplace that made the tiny structure feel homelier. She then picked pebbles off the ground, turned each into a parsnip, and roasted them on the fire; they were a delightful accompaniment to the food taken from her table that morning, as well as the ale that flowed from a goblet that she assured them would not empty until each had taken their fill. She also created beds of air as promised, and, when Juliane climbed onto one, it felt almost as if he was upon his mattress at home.

He had started to begrudgingly attribute his negative feelings toward her as resulting from jealousy—which, he had to admit, he did feel sometimes when around someone he perceived as a potential rival for Liliana's affections—when he heard what sounded like nails being dragged across the outside wall nearest him. "What was that?" he cried.

A malicious cackle rang out, and a menacing voice croaked, "Ohhh, dearie, wouldn't ye like ta find out? Come outside and I'll show ye."

Terrified, he looked to Liliana for assistance, and she asked the sorceress, "Is that a wi—"

Saurenia, unperturbed, said, "Yes, that would be a wight. There's a burying ground near here. I should have warned you: some of the bodies I took for my studies didn't work out well, so I replanted them. Damned things just won't stay down, though—"

She was interrupted by Juliane shrieking, for he had noticed a cloudy eye housed in a rotten socket staring in at them through a hole in the wall. "I see ye!" crowed the creature, and the scratching noises grew louder still.

Liliana asked Saurenia if she believed the hut could withstand much of an onslaught by the creature, and, when told "no," she sat down next to Juliane and did not protest when he clung to her arm. "Liliana," he whispered, his eyes wide, "What's a wight?"

"Are you sure you want to know?" she said, and, when he nodded his head uncertainly, she told him, "A wight is a deceased person who has become reanimated and bears malevolent intent—namely, to suck the lifeforces of the living until they also become withered husks."

Horrified, Juliane moaned, "Does everything in this forest want to kill us?"

Liliana was about to respond when she was startled by Saurenia, who had begun laughing raucously. She turned to glare at the woman. "What's so amusing to you?"

The sorceress wiped tears from her eyes. "You are. Do you think I cannot deal with a minor nuisance like this? Compared to the wyvern, it is nothing."

She snapped the fingers of her left hand twice, and a white glow issued from her fingertips. She pointed them at the eye still lurking in the peephole, and, when she snapped once more, a beam shot from her hand, entering it. The wight retreated from the hole, and the travelers heard it scream and felt the building sway. Once the hut had stopped shaking, Juliane, perplexed, asked what had happened. "Why don't you take a look and find out?" said Saurenia, turning the key in the lock.

Juliane gulped, then slowly pulled the massive door open. He cautiously put his head through the gap, looked around, and quickly pulled it back inside. "I think I'm going to be sick. There are pieces of flesh and bone *everywhere*."

Liliana took her own look through the doorway, but her response to the mess was one of wonder rather than revulsion. "Are those scattered remains all that is left of the creature?"

"Indeed," Saurenia said proudly. "Direct pure white magic into the socket of one of those things and, within seconds, you have yourself a once-more-dead wight."

"I don't believe it!" exclaimed Liliana. "First you defeat a wyvern, then you destroy a wight, all within a few hours' time! I must admit, I misjudged you, Saurenia. I had feared you would be an unfaithful ally, but you've certainly proven your worth as a traveling companion. I'm in awe of your skill and can only wish to one day become as proficient a magic user as you are."

"I'm sure you shall," said Saurenia, clasping her by the shoulders. "The blood of Satiana Almwick flows through your veins, so I don't doubt your potential to become a powerful sorceress should you choose such a path, especially as you also have the intellect to succeed as one." Flattered, Liliana thanked the sorceress, and, after having been granted permission, enthusiastically embraced her.

Juliane viewed the interaction with a mix of displeasure and unease—the latter of which grew when Saurenia, catching him glaring at her, cast him a coy wink over Liliana's shoulder. He was unsure whether it had been intended as a jest or had been meant to mock him, but, regardless, it was clear to him something was not right. He and Liliana had wandered the forest for many hours the previous day and had run into nothing in daylight, yet, with Saurenia in tow, they had stumbled upon two life-threatening monsters before the sun had set, both of which she had defeated handily. It seemed too convenient that she should know just the right way to take care of each foe they came across, even if she was a proficient sorceress.

He wondered if she was perhaps leading them to places where she knew trouble lurked so that she might demonstrate her skills to them—but, if so, why? To make them indebted to her? To ensure they believed in her pure intentions? To impress one, or both, of them? Whatever the reason behind her potential treachery, he determined that he should stay on his guard, for Saurenia was someone best kept under close watch.

21.

Once the party had finished their interrupted meal, they lounged on the airbeds, which the sorceress had drawn into a circle, and Saurenia regaled the travelers with stories of her magical escapades and countless affairs. "I am drawn to essence rather than appearance," she explained, "and so have found myself attracted to beings both male and female, as well as to some whose genders I would have difficulty defining. One time I was digging up a body for an experiment, and I turned to see the most beautiful spirit I had ever laid eyes upon..."

Juliane, who would have generally listened enthusiastically to tales of dalliances with ghosts, instead found himself drifting into contemplation regarding Saurenia's behavior. He closed his eyes, ran through some potential reasons why the sorceress might have been showing off earlier that day, and eventually lit upon one he believed fit: she was trying to woo Liliana. All her actions pointed to this, and her admission of harboring attractions toward some women seemed to confirm it. A wave of regret washed over him as he imagined her swooping in to claim Liliana's affections, for he understood that, had he not been so caught up in his own head in Pultare, he might have used the opportunity to forge a secure bond between them that not even one as alluring as Saurenia could have broken.

He was so absorbed in his thoughts that he nearly jumped when he heard the sorceress say, "I wonder what's going through that pretty head of yours—care to share it with me?"

He snapped out of his daze to find things had changed considerably while he had been lost in contemplation, for the fire had dwindled, leaving the hut in shadow, and Liliana now slumbered peacefully on one of the airbeds. The remaining beds had been drawn tightly together so that they merged into a larger one, and Saurenia stretched out next to him upon it. She had removed her cloak for the first time since their meeting, revealing a black and green gown that hugged every curve. Resting her head upon one arm, she purred, "Welcome back! Now, do let me know what's been on your mind. I noticed you weren't listening to my ribald story and so figured you must be having some very distracting thoughts. I was hoping you would share them with me."

Caught off guard, he tried to respond, but no words would come out. Saurenia giggled, "Oh, Juliane, you're even more adorable when you're discomfited!" She leaned toward him, put her mouth to his ear, and whispered, "In case you hadn't noticed, I'm trying to seduce you."

He pulled back from her, startled. "You're trying to seduce *me*? But I thought you were interested in Liliana. You kept saying such flattering things to her—"

"Me, showing that kind of interest in Liliana? How ridiculous," interrupted Saurenia. "I was just trying to make her feel good about herself, that's all. She's the daughter of my mentor, the woman who helped raise me— being with her in *that* way would be like being with my sister! You, on the other hand, are just as attractive as she is, and lack any pesky familial-type connection to me. If we must risk life and limb to successfully deposit you on Darkwood's doorstep, I figured we might enjoy ourselves together along the way."

Juliane relaxed a bit but continued to stare warily at her. He was tempted to accept her offer, for she was powerfully attractive, but knew that his refusing a night with her would increase the chance of Liliana one day allowing him back into her good graces—so, filled with resolve, he said, "I'm sorry, Saurenia, but I cannot be with you. It's true you're quite lovely, but I find my mind is with another. It would be unfair to you both were I to dally with you."

Saurenia glanced knowingly at Liliana's sleeping figure. "Juliane, are you telling me that you're harboring sentiments for that peacefully slumbering copper-haired angel?" He felt his face burn, and she squealed, "Oh, you are! I can tell from the way you've reddened at my question—not to mention the way you gazed at her all day." He merely stammered in reply, and she continued, features twisting slyly, "What would you say if I told you I could arrange it so that you could be with her in a way you've only dreamed of being?"

"I'd say you were offering me false hope so that you might convince me to give in to your wiles," Juliane responded cautiously.

She laughed heartily. "Oh, Juliane, why do you have so little faith in me? Have I not defeated dread beasts, produced food from stones, and raised the dead? Do you honestly believe I cannot find a way to make your fantasy come true in a manner that suits my needs?"

He sat up, scowling indignantly. "I will not allow you to use trickery to make Liliana desire me. That would be dishonorable and unfair, and I'd rather earn her affection than obtain it through dishonest means."

"Why, Juliane, I think the Almwicks' little plot to teach you to be more sensitive to the plight of women has succeeded," said Saurenia, causing him to redden once more. "Besides, you needn't worry about my bending Liliana to your will—why would I do that when it would be of no benefit to me? The solution I have in mind is far more practical."

She walked over to Liliana, stooped over her sleeping form, and carefully plucked a strand of hair from her head, then returned to Juliane, who sat watching her curiously. She held the hair against her forehead and muttered a series of strange words, and he gasped and shielded his eyes as she was engulfed in a brilliant purple light. The glow soon faded, and Juliane gaped when Saurenia—or, more accurately, she who had been Saurenia—grew visible once more.

Standing before him was a perfect copy of Liliana, so like her in appearance that he would have believed it was indeed her had he not been able to spy her sleeping figure out of the corner of his eye. Red-orange hair had replaced the sorceress's shimmering black tresses, greenish-toned skin had been exchanged for pale flesh, and sparkling blue eyes radiated from a face that was now undoubtedly Liliana's. The only noticeable difference between the real Liliana and the false one was that the impostor did not have spectacles and was garbed in the gown Saurenia had been wearing—though it was obvious that Liliana's figure was the one now filling it.

He croaked, "How...did...you...?" but was unable to finish his sentence.

Saurenia—or, more accurately, the faux Liliana—asked, "How do you like my new look?" She glanced down at her changed form. "It *is* a very nice transformation. I mean, I cannot create the non-bodily aspects of her appearance, but her physical body...why, I do believe I've successfully reproduced it." She gave a little twirl, then turned her attention to Juliane, who was radiating a palpable mixture of fear, wonder, and desire. She sultrily swayed over to where he sat and, bending over him, said coyly, "You've not yet told me if you like it."

He was in awe of her, for she looked so much like Liliana that he could almost convince himself that she truly was her—and, though he *knew* that she was not, he found himself less resistant to her charms with each passing moment. "You're enchanting me, aren't you?" he said, and was displeased to find he sounded more intoxicated than he had hoped to.

"I most certainly am not!" the sorceress responded with playful indignation. "You're just so attracted to Liliana that, when you have her before you, when you can feel her against you"—she sat down next to him, flung her arms around him, and pressed herself close to him—"you have a difficult time hiding your interest."

Juliane tried to keep his wits about him, but, as "Liliana" embraced him, his skin began tingling, his heart beat faster, and heat suffused his face and body. Still trying to resist the sorceress, he broke free from her grip. "This isn't right," he moaned. "If Liliana finds out I've dallied with you—especially if she discovers that you took *her* form to entice me—she'll never speak to me again."

"Ohh nooo, I don't think so," cooed the impostor. "I think she'd be flattered to know that you desired me because I looked like her. Also, think of it this way: you may never get to be with the real Liliana, and I'm the next best thing." She leaned in until her face was inches from his, and whispered, "How is she ever going to find out about us? You and I are the only ones who will know about this, as I certainly don't plan on telling her. She doesn't own you; she's not your lover, she never has been and might never be, but I could be...*right...now.*"

The remainder of Juliane's already-weakened willpower slipped away, and he found himself agreeing with her—he was holding out hope for things that might never be rather than taking advantage of available opportunities. He did not owe Liliana anything—like she had said, he was not beholden to her nor she to him. A part of him still doubted whether he should give in, of course, for he knew he might face unwelcome consequences for doing so, but it was speedily silenced as "Liliana" suddenly pressed her mouth to his. He was pleasantly surprised to find Saurenia not only looked like his companion but also smelled and tasted like her, so it was easy to forget that it was not really Liliana kissing him. She broke the kiss to bury her face in his neck, and, without thinking, he sighed, "Oh, Liliana," and he heard her giggle, "Close enough," before once again planting her lips upon his.

What followed was admittedly marvelous, for Saurenia had claimed vast experience in carnal matters and certainly did not disappoint, but Juliane found the dalliance even more enjoyable because, whenever he opened his eyes, he saw Liliana smiling back at him. Once they had finished, they rested together, eyes closed, entwined in each other's arms. Juliane turned to gaze upon "Liliana" one last time only to be disappointed, for he discovered Saurenia had already regained her true form. "Greetings, Juliane," she said. "It seems Liliana returned whence she came—care to waste some time with me now?" He muttered that he was exhausted, and she pouted and replied, "Fine! Go to bed, then." With a gesture of her hand she parted the airbeds, and she moved hers in front of the fire, then grabbed her cloak off the floor, mantled herself, and hopped into bed. She yawned and stretched, then called out, "Oh, Juliane? Before I settle in for the night, I'd like to tell you something."

"Yes, Saurenia, what is it?" he replied, stifling his own yawn.

"It's just...I *might* have been straying from the truth a little when I promised I'd never tell Liliana about what occurred between us tonight."

Juliane's heart sank as he grasped the import of her words, and she continued, "Don't get me wrong, I don't *want* to tell her about our little tryst, but I do like having the information available should I need to use it. I doubt I shall have to—I'm sure you'd never turn on me nor try to turn her against me—but it's very helpful just in case. You know, I didn't seduce you intending to entrap you, but it's definitely an added benefit!" Juliane's face contorted in anger, and Saurenia said, "Oh, come now, don't be cross! I enjoyed our time together, and I gather you did as well. I'm sure you have nothing to worry about, and that she'll hear nary a word from me. Anyway, goodnight," she finished, turning her back to him.

Juliane tried to sleep but found his mind so preoccupied that it was difficult to silence. What if Saurenia did choose to tell Liliana about what had happened between them? What if she had planned to the entire time? If she let Liliana know that Juliane had once again allowed himself to be tempted without regards to the consequences, she might not speak to him again—especially if she found out that, while trying to regain her approval, he had let himself be seduced by someone who had worn her face and form!

He tossed and turned and was so lost in thought that he did not notice Saurenia sit up, pull a handful of powder from her cloak, and blow it in his direction—but he felt its effects immediately, for his worries ceased and he was soon slumbering soundly. Saurenia grinned triumphantly, then resumed reclining on her bed and gazed into the fire, her strangely beautiful face contemplative.

There was a flurry of movement, and the sorceress rose to find Liliana climbing out of bed. "I'm sorry to have woken you," she apologized. "I was hoping to get a drink."

She started toward her pack, but stopped when Saurenia whispered, "Don't waste the water in your vessel. Come to me and I'll give you some."

The sorceress was holding the magic goblet, and Liliana took it from her and drank her fill. She was about to return to her own bed when Saurenia reached out and gently grasped her arm. "Would you sit and chat with me for a while? I have been having a difficult time sleeping and believe I'd benefit from some conversation." Liliana obliged and sat down next to her, and the sorceress said, "I appreciate your honoring my request, for I'd like to discuss something weighing on my mind..."

22.

Juliane woke the next morning to find that Saurenia and Liliana had drawn their beds together by the fire and were muttering to one another conspiratorially. This filled him with dread, and, gulping, he shakily called out, "Good morning!" They exchanged a knowing look before returning his greeting, and his heart sank, for he was certain they had been discussing what had occurred the night before.

He determined that the best course would be for him to be honest with Liliana about what had happened and to express regret for his impetuous behavior, but he found himself foiled in doing this, for, during their morning preparations, Saurenia was constantly nearby. Frustrated, he dressed himself, gathered his things, and headed out of the hut, hoping he might intercept her leaving on her own. He had no such luck, though, for she exited with Saurenia, so, grumbling, he shouldered his pack and trudged along after them.

The party walked for a long while, with the conversation between Liliana and Saurenia scarcely ceasing, and it was only after many torturous hours that an opportunity to speak with her finally presented itself. When the road forked before them, Saurenia informed the others that she must use her powers to assess which path they should continue on and would need complete silence to do so, then she stepped off the road and vanished into the trees. Juliane rehearsed his apology in his head, and, when he felt certain the sorceress would not overhear them and intervene, said, "Liliana, there is something I must speak to you about."

Liliana—who, surprisingly, seemed more cheerful than he had otherwise expected her to be—asked, "What is it, Juliane?" She placed her pack on the ground and sat down next to it, and, after he had done the same, said, "Go on, I'm waiting."

Her expectant stare caused him to grow tongue-tied, and the ideal phrasing he had crafted escaped him. Scrambling, he lit upon what he felt would be a good opener. "What do you think of Saurenia?"

Liliana beamed. "I think she's amazing! Why do you ask?"

Her resoundingly positive reaction unnerved him, and he hesitantly continued, "Well, it's just...I don't know if I trust her. To be honest, all the foes we came upon yesterday seemed too convenient—it was so easy for her to defeat them, it felt almost as if the conflicts were planned. I think she might be trying to lull us into feeling secure with her...perhaps so she can drive us apart?"

Liliana considered his words, and seemed about to reply when, suddenly, her mouth fell open. Juliane, uncertain of what was happening, was taken aback when she said, "Oh, I know why you're voicing 'concerns,' Juliane—you heard Saurenia and I last night, and you're jealous and trying to sway my view of her!" Still confused, he started to stammer a response, but she interrupted, "Don't pretend you don't understand what I'm saying! You must have listened last night when we..." She trailed off, face reddening.

Juliane's eyes widened. "You were *with* Saurenia last night?" Liliana, tight-lipped, nodded, and he exclaimed, "But, I also was with her last night! When I woke this morning and saw you talking with her, I feared she'd told you about our tryst to upset you—it was what I wished to speak to you about. I had no idea you'd also been with her." Further realization dawned on him. "She was with us both last night because she does, indeed, intend on separating us. She was hoping to make each of us grow infatuated with her so she could say or do things to cause us to be at odds with one another, so that she might have power over us both. I'm only glad we had the chance to speak about this and to unravel her plot before it succeeded."

He beamed at Liliana, but, to his dismay, found that his words were not having the desired effect, for her face had grown stony. "Oh, Juliane, this is rotten behavior, even for you," she hissed. "I'd guessed you'd be jealous—after all, I remember the fit you threw about my being with Tancred—but I never dreamed you'd stoop as low as this. To say you were with Saurenia before me—I cannot believe you're capable of such spite!"

Juliane assured her he was speaking the truth, but she growled, "There's no way you could be! When I woke last night, after perhaps an hour of slumber, you were already fast asleep. Saurenia was still up, and she revealed that she'd developed an attraction to me; she admitted that she sees in me all the traits she valued in my mother, and that these attributes, coupled with my physical form, have resulted in her desiring me. We spoke for a while, and, well, one thing led to another..." She sighed contentedly, then went on, "She suggested that, once we finish helping you with your quest, we visit my mother so she can beg her forgiveness. Afterward I shall come live with her, and she will help me become a sorceress of her caliber." She glared at Juliane. "The only reason you'd claim to have been with her before me and would say she has foul intentions would be to drive me from her. Well, I know your tactics, Juliane! I think it's despicable that you care so little for my feelings that you'd try to keep me from being with her just to suit your own needs."

Juliane, aghast, at first merely gaped at her, then, shaking off his daze, he reached out and grasped her shoulders. Bringing his face near to hers, he stared into her eyes. "Liliana, what's happened to you? Have you been placed under some kind of enchantment?"

Pushing him away, she got up off the ground. "I am not enchanted, nor suffering from any affliction, nor being swayed by an outside will," she snarled. "I've developed a fondness for someone I've deemed worthy, and I'd appreciate your not challenging my sentiments."

Juliane, scrambling to his feet, cried, "Liliana, I promise I'm not acting this way out of jealousy nor desire, but out of true concern! Think on this a moment: you appear even more enamored of Saurenia than you were of Tancred, and I believe that what you felt for them was real. I know that you also...at least, at one point...seemed to feel something genuine for me. Could all these other feelings really have been so easily eclipsed by affections for someone you scarcely know without a bewitchment having occurred?"

Liliana's expression grew uncertain, and, encouraged, he continued. "Please, consider what I'm saying: why would I lie about being with Saurenia? Don't you believe I care enough for you not to harm you for my own gain?" He approached her, and, voice breaking, said, "I may be boorish and impulsive, and I know I've made countless poor decisions whilst thinking only of my carnal needs or reacting impetuously to my emotions, but I know that I have never shown actual malice toward you, and my trying to persuade you to scorn someone for my benefit would be a malicious act. I would never purposefully do anything to injure you, and I think that, deep down, you know that." Liliana's face softened, and he reached out and clasped her hands. "I was a fool not to say anything before, and especially to push you away in Pultare, but I must tell you that I—"

"And what is going on here?"

Juliane released Liliana and turned to find the sorceress standing behind him. "Well met, Saurenia," he said weakly.

She smirked at him. "Well met yourself, Juliane. Now, what were you two up to? You seemed to be having quite a spirited dialogue."

Juliane spun back to Liliana and was disheartened to find her gazing at the sorceress as if she was indeed enthralled. "Saurenia, it's so good you've returned to us," she said. "Juliane and I were actually discussing you; more specifically, we were arguing, because she made the ridiculous assertion that the two of you had been together last night." She glanced at him coolly, then turned back to the enchantress. "What say you about this?"

Saurenia let out a tinkling laugh. "I'd say she has a wondrous imagination." Ignoring Juliane's outraged cry, she strolled over to Liliana and carelessly flung an arm over her shoulder. "Or, more accurately, marvelous fantasies. It may be that, whilst she was slumbering, she dreamed of being with me." Making sure her words were loud enough for Juliane to hear them, she murmured, "She knows about us, does she not?" Liliana nodded. "Well then, perhaps she overheard us whilst she slept, and her mind created a picture for her enjoyment? This seems the likeliest explanation. Don't be cross with her. I'm sure she didn't intend on wounding you by telling you what she thought had happened, and that she just wanted to be honest with you."

She guided Liliana toward the left-hand fork. "I've determined that this is the correct path. Come along, Juliane, we don't want to lose you!" she called over her shoulder. As they made eye contact Saurenia shot him a triumphant grin, then she and Liliana proceeded along the path.

Juliane trailed after them, feeling numb, for he knew his tryst with Saurenia had not been a dream, and he was unsure of why the sorceress had been with both travelers and had then betrayed one and lied to the other. Perhaps she had desired to know both and, discovering she preferred Liliana, wished to pretend her affair with Juliane had not occurred? He hoped this was the case but doubted it. There was something more going on here, and he decided to prepare himself for a potential skirmish or snare. Believing the pair ahead of him were too busy fawning over one another to notice what he was up to, he dug through his bag, plucked out what he felt might prove useful in dire straits, and placed it where he might easily access it should his suspicions prove correct.

***

The party traveled for many hours, with neither Liliana nor Saurenia acknowledging Juliane as they walked along—not even the sky's darkening caused their chattering to cease. Not wanting a bad state of affairs to grow worse, Juliane interrupted them to ask Saurenia whether they were nearing an overnight destination, adding scornfully, "I ask because I doubt it is safe to spend the night out in the open due to the creatures that haunt this forest—you know, half-animal, half-reanimated-corpse monsters that eat people. Then again, I'm said to have ridiculous, troublesome dreams whilst sleeping on comfortable beds within shelter, so perhaps slumbering out of doors might be of benefit to me."

The sorceress did not take the bait as hoped for and instead responded in perfectly civil tones, "Have no fear, Juliane, I have a place in mind for us to bed down for the night that should be mere minutes from here." She turned to Liliana. "I am delighted to inform you that I'm bringing us to the abode of none other than the venerable Lavinia Moonshade." Noticing Liliana's confusion, she explained, "Lavinia Moonshade is the mother of all sorceresses, the leader of our coven. She's as old as dirt, as powerful as the sun, as cunning as a serpent, and, fortunately for her fellow enchantresses, as generous with her time and knowledge as the day is long. It was she who taught your mother most of what she knows! Perhaps she'll impart some of her wisdom to you." Liliana, hearing this, grew pleased at the prospect, while Juliane groaned at the thought of their being around yet another potentially treacherous woman.

They soon entered a clearing, where they spied, in the near distance, a manse of glowing purple stone surrounded by majestic elder trees. They approached its entrance, a massive wooden door adorned with an elaborate brass knocker, and Saurenia banged the ring down twice, then stepped back and listened. Slow, shuffling steps sounded within the house, and presently the great door crept open and a figure stepped into the deepening twilight.

Standing before them was the oldest woman Juliane had ever laid eyes on. She was remarkably short, reaching to only the shoulder of the towering Saurenia, and her skin, which was a strange shade of purplish-gray, sagged off her angular features. A mass of coarse gray hair was piled into a crown-like peak atop her head, and she wore a black robe that engulfed her tiny frame. Most notable were her eyes, though; they were small and dark, and shone with a wisdom that signified many years of learning. They reminded Juliane of a hawk's, and he understood that this was a woman who could be exceedingly gentle with those she cared for, but who would not hesitate to unleash her talons on those who crossed her. She was dangerous, and he determined that he would take care not to upset her during his time in her home.

"Saurenia!" the wizened woman squealed gleefully, throwing her arms around the younger sorceress. "How are you, my dearest pupil?"

"I am well, Mater," replied Saurenia, releasing the aged lady. "My studies have been fruitful, and my creations, whilst trying at times, have turned out to be an asset overall." Juliane snorted at this, and she quickly changed the subject. "How have you been?"

"As well as can be expected, given my age," the crone, who was undoubtedly Lavinia Moonshade, said with a weary smile. "I suppose I cannot complain, for I find I still learn new things every day. Now, tell me, why have you come to see me, my dear? The witches' circle is not until the next Blood Moon."

"I have come to beg favor of you, Mater, that my companions and I might shelter in your home until morning. I am helping them navigate through the forest, so that they may reach the Darklands safely."

"The Darklands?" shrieked Mater Moonshade. "Why would you want to go to that terrible place lorded over by that terrible man?"

Liliana, voice trembling, said, "Mater, we must see King Korben Darkwood. He has something we need to complete a quest, so, although he's a dreaded figure, we must still chance an interaction with him."

Lavinia Moonshade squinted at her as she spoke, and, once she had finished, stepped closer to her. Liliana had to keep herself from flinching as the crone raised a knotted hand to her face. "I feel as if I know you, though I'm sure I've never met you. Why do I feel this way? Who are you, young lady?"

Saurenia came up behind the elder sorceress and laid a hand on her shoulder. "She is the seed of one of our own, flesh and blood of a sister who hasn't graced our circle for some time. I believe you know of whom I speak, Mater."

Mater Moonshade gasped, and, withdrawing her hand, whispered, "Satiana Almwick." A faraway look crossed her face, but she quickly shook it off. "Of course. I should have known you were her kin, for you have the same glow she had at your age—I knew her then, you see, for I've been the Mater of this witches' circle for many centuries. Your mother was one of my most skilled students. It's a shame she chose to forsake her powers after losing your father and siblings."

"Not entirely, much to my chagrin," Juliane muttered carelessly, then he let out a squeak as he realized he had spoken ill of Lady Almwick in company that obviously held her in high esteem.

Fortunately, no one seemed to heed his remark, for Mater Moonshade, eyes shining, embraced Liliana and declared, "The daughter of Satiana Almwick shall always have a place in my household." She requested an introduction to Juliane and, once she had been given it, assured him he was also welcome in her home. He began to feel that, despite her intimidating reputation and immense power, Mater Moonshade really was just the kindly old lady she seemed to be—and his certainty only increased when she brought them inside, for she led them through an entrance hall and down a passageway to a dining room featuring a fireplace and a huge table covered with delicious dishes. They seated themselves, and, as they consumed the meal—which Mater Moonshade identified as having been produced with magic, "so eat as much as you'd like, dears"—Juliane contemplated asking if they might stay with the Mater a few days more. He changed his mind, though, when he noticed how Liliana gazed at Saurenia throughout the meal, and determined that it would be best to get to the Darklands as soon as possible, for, once they reached it, the sorceress might leave them after all and he might have the opportunity to bring Liliana to her senses.

The Mater, though gracious to Juliane, spoke little to him, instead focusing most of her attention on Liliana, for she seemed very curious regarding Satiana Almwick and her recent activities. Liliana was polite but guarded at first, as, though Saurenia seemed to trust the woman wholeheartedly, there was something unnerving about her interest. However, it eventually occurred to her that the crone might be trying to ascertain if the Lady had deemed her daughter worthy of her magical knowledge and if, consequently, she was deserving of potential apprenticeship. Thrilled by the thought, she began to respond openly to the elder sorceress's queries, and before long the two were chatting like old friends.

After a lengthy meal, Saurenia rose from her chair and declared that it would be best if the travelers were shown to a bedchamber, for their journey on the morrow required their being well-rested. The Mater got up from her seat and beckoned that the party follow her; taking a lantern off the mantelpiece, she lit it and, holding it in her left hand, brought her guests to a door at the rear of the room. She opened it, and the group entered a dark hallway lined with doorways. The aged sorceress led them to the last one on the left, pulled a large ring of keys from her pocket and selected one, then opened the door. She held the lantern aloft, its rays revealing the contents of the room—two large beds, a table and chair, a folding screen, and a fireplace— and, when she gestured with her right hand, an eerie glow filled the chamber as an unearthly green fire appeared in the hearth. "I hope you find this room suitable, and that you sleep well whilst in my home," she told the travelers, then she retreated down the passage to the dining room.

When Saurenia poked her head into the chamber to wish them a peaceful rest Liliana asked if she might stay awhile, but she shook her head, claiming that she needed to catch up with her esteemed teacher, whom she had not seen for many weeks. "Besides, it would be disrespectful if we engaged in, erm, last night's activities whilst staying in her home. You will just have to enjoy Juliane's company in my stead." She briefly embraced Liliana, then hurried down the hallway after the Mater.

Disappointed, Liliana huffily closed the chamber door and threw herself onto one of the beds. "She could have at least given me a farewell kiss."

Juliane, hoping to capitalize on her displeasure, said,

"It's possible she doesn't want her superior to know that she's interested in someone who isn't also a powerful sorceress. Or—and just consider this, please—maybe she's using your infatuation with her as a means of bending you to her will and she doesn't really want to spend time with you?"

Liliana glowered at him, then went behind the screen to wash. Once she had returned to her bedside, she told him, "I don't need you to give me a hard time right now, Juliane. I know you're saying these things because you're envious of Saurenia, so I'm paying them no mind."

Juliane got out of his bed and crossed the room to hers, then stood over her, hands on hips. "Maybe your affection for Saurenia isn't real, and is the product of some sort of enchantment, as I have suggested. Or maybe," he continued, leaning in until his face was near hers, "you don't really feel the way you claim to regarding her. Perhaps you dallied with her out of curiosity and a desire to make me jealous, and are acting enamored with her to teach me a lesson after what happened in Pultare?"

Liliana grew red and sputtered, "I am not...I did not...I would not..." She rose to her feet, shaking her finger at him. "It just goes to show how vain you are, believing something like that. You think so highly of yourself that you cannot possibly understand how someone could desire another. Well, let me tell you something, Juliane Stoneshire: you're not as pretty as you think you are, not as charming as you wish you were, and certainly not as clever as you believe yourself to be!"

Anger spent, she fell back onto the bed and, pulling the blanket over her head, turned her back to him. Juliane was frustrated with himself for wounding her further—he apparently could not stop saying the wrong thing—and he crouched down next to her and whispered, "I'm sorry, Liliana. You're right, I do think only of myself much of the time. I've hurt you yet again, but I want you to know that, no matter how inconsiderate I've been in the past, I honestly meant well this time. I really do want you to be safe and happy." He took his turn at washing, then climbed into his bed. "Goodnight, Liliana," he called out softly. "I hope that, if it's what you truly desire, you shall find contentment with Saurenia once our journey is over."

He turned toward the wall and soon fell asleep, but, unbeknownst to him, Liliana remained awake, gazing at the ceiling, thinking. She knew she had been overly harsh with him, and yet he had not acted defensively and had even apologized for his behavior. Perhaps he *was* truly concerned regarding Saurenia? She was unsure of why, for it seemed to her that the sorceress had been nothing but forthright and helpful during their travels, but she admitted to herself that he might have noticed something she had not—maybe she *was* captivated by Saurenia and couldn't see it. She promised herself that she would be more observant the following day and would not allow herself to be so easily wooed; having frivolous times with the sorceress was one thing, making future plans with her without knowing her very well was quite another.

Satisfied that she was behaving more like her usual rational self, she rolled onto her side and tried to rest, but Juliane's accusation that she had chosen to dally with Saurenia just to bother him gnawed at her. She had not consciously done so, and yet...

She burned with shame as she recalled how, during her tryst with Saurenia, she had accidentally called out his name, and how the sorceress had gone to him and, removing an eyelash from his face, used it to assume his appearance. Liliana would never have revealed this to anyone, but she was glad it had happened and she had enjoyed the dalliance more because of it—for, although Juliane had hurt her and she was loath to trust him again, she was still drawn to the bumbler, Goddess knew why. Blushing, she swore to herself that she would never share what had transpired with him, and, with some effort, she was able to still her thoughts and fall asleep.

23.

Liliana had anticipated a restful slumber, but instead found herself plagued by distressing dreams. In the one she could recall best, she had returned home and, overjoyed, searched for her mother only to find her in her bedchamber sobbing upon her bed. "Mother, I'm back!" she cried, then, noticing the Lady's piteous state, asked, "Why are you weeping?"

Satiana Almwick lifted her head and, seeing Liliana before her, moaned, "Oh, my dearest daughter, I wish you were truly with me, but I know you're merely a fancy of my mind, for there is no way you could be here in the flesh."

Confused, Liliana approached her mother and wrapped her arms around her. "Mother, I have indeed returned to you—why wouldn't I have?"

Lady Almwick pulled away from her daughter, her expression heartbroken. "Oh, my sweet child, don't you understand that I am in mourning for *you*? You're dead, dear Liliana, killed during your quest to the Darklands."

Wailing, she buried her face in her pillow, and Liliana, feeling cold, noticed a strange mirror sitting in the corner of the room. She feared what she might find reflected within but knew she had to look no matter the consequence, so she advanced forward, head lowered so as not to spoil herself. When she reached the glass, she gingerly lifted her face to peer into it—and staggered backward, for it showed her Saurenia and Mater Moonshade, sneering and cackling hatefully. Suddenly the Mater's arms burst through its surface, and they were not human arms, but rather twisted birds' limbs adorned with sharp talons. They latched onto her, and she screamed as they tore into her flesh and the sorceress, shrieking triumphantly, pulled her into the mirror.

She woke from the dream with a cry and at first thought she might be caught in yet another, for she found she was lying upon the floor of a large brass cage. As she gathered her senses fear stole over her, for she realized that this was not another nightmare—while she had slumbered, someone had trapped her in this enclosure. Did the Mater have enemies who had laid siege to her home? Had Saurenia's monsters found the manse and, breaking into it, captured her for use in a future meal? She tried to keep calm by seeking out Juliane, whom she hoped might still be nearby. She called out his name and was relieved when he responded from somewhere off to her right, "Liliana, is that you? Where are you?"

"Yes, it's me. I'm over here, to your left." Peering through the gloom, she was eventually able to pick him out: they were in some sort of room dedicated to alchemical research, and he was tied with a thick cord to a plush chair in the shape of the Mother Goddess. "I'm in some kind of cage," she told him, and, after checking her prison, reported, "It has a rather solid lock, one I don't think I can break. It looks as if we're trapped. Who could have done this?"

"We could have, dear," said a voice to her left. Filled with dread, she turned to find Mater Moonshade standing next to the cage, a wicked grin wrinkling her aged face. A smirking Saurenia stood behind her, holding a candle. "Surprise!"

"B-but, why?" Liliana stammered.

"Because," said Mater Moonshade, stepping closer to the

cage, "you're Satiana Almwick's child, and we hate your mother."

"What do you mean?" Liliana cried in disbelief. "You were both extolling her virtues mere hours ago, and you were asking about her throughout our meal!"

"I was gathering information under false pretenses, foolish girl," said the Mater. "One cannot strike at an enemy if one doesn't know how to best wound them."

A painful truth dawned on Liliana, and she turned to Saurenia. "And I suppose you were also just gathering information when you said all the things you said, and we..." She trailed off, lowering her head so the sorceress could not see how red she had become.

"Oh, Liliana," cooed Saurenia, leaning toward the cage, "you shouldn't take my actions too personally. I would have done the same to any relation of Satiana's." She brought her face near the bars. "I *did* enjoy our time together, if that dulls the sting at all—but, then again, I must tell you some things that will likely worsen your pain. To start with, I arranged all the conflicts we faced during our travels, so you would feel more secure with me once I'd bested our foes. I also never had any true romantic interest in you, I was merely softening you so you would be more agreeable...and your infatuation with me wasn't a fully natural one. A short incantation helped magnify the attraction you were already feeling...well, let's just say I caused your feelings for me to grow more swiftly than they would have otherwise."

"Oh, and Juliane was speaking the truth—I *did* dally with you both during our night in the hut. I just lied and said I hadn't in hopes you would disbelieve her should she discover my intentions weren't noble and try to impart this to you. You know, despite your being a very bright girl you certainly discarded your friend's word and put your faith in me readily enough. I guess my magic and charms are more effective than I'd thought—I mean, I suppose they must be, or I wouldn't have been able to seduce you both so easily!"

She laughed heartily, and, seething with anger, Liliana threw herself against the cage wall, hoping to strike her. Saurenia reared back and rebuked her, "Now, Liliana, that's no way to react to being bested!" A sinister expression replaced her mirthful one. "Do you want to know why I've brought you here, and why I abhor Satiana Almwick? I'm sure you do."

When Liliana did not respond, she continued, "After your father and siblings died, your mother came to what would be her last witches' circle. I was still just a girl then, and I worshiped her, for she had treated me as a daughter for many years—until I began exploring necromancy and she turned me out of her home, informing me that I needed to explore that kind of thing on my own. My heart grieved when I heard of her tragedy, and I hoped to help her in whatever way I could to possibly earn back her favor. I knew she didn't approve of my dark magic, but I thought she might tolerate it if I could use it to..."

She sighed. "I had made such great plans—or so I thought. When she arrived for the circle, I brought her into the dining hall where the other sisters were waiting and seated her at the table, then I placed my crystal before her, and I...summoned your father and siblings."

Liliana gasped, and Saurenia cried, "I was so young! How was I to know that, when their spirits came to us, they would appear as they had been during their final moments alive—torn and mangled—and would be crying for help? Your mother screamed and pushed my crystal from the table, and their images swiftly faded. She turned to me and said, 'How could you do this to me, when I raised you as my own? You are no sister of mine.' She then stood and addressed the circle. 'How could you let this happen? Truly, none of you are my sisters. You're wicked and have used our magic for dark gains. If I must, I shall spend the rest of my life keeping you from ever hurting another as you've hurt me.' Sobbing, she ran from the room—"

"And she has kept her word ever since," the Mater concluded. "It may seem as if she has largely ceased her sorcery, but she's really spent the past score of years quietly undoing any magic a sister has done that she has deemed harmful. That, my child, is why we all loathe her—and why, when Saurenia discovered you were her offspring, she delivered you to me so that I might orchestrate a retaliation."

"I was only a child, and she could not find it within herself to forgive me," hissed Saurenia, tears welling in her eyes. "I loved her, and she cast me aside due to a misunderstanding!" She struck her fist against the cage and lowered her head; when she raised it, Liliana couldn't help but shudder, so fierce was the expression upon her face. "But now I shall have my revenge! I have used and tricked her daughter and will now leave her to a fate worse than any pain Satiana Almwick could ever have inflicted upon me!"

Sneering, she turned and skulked off toward the doorway, but, before exiting through it, she peered over her shoulder, righteous indignation twisting her features. "Oh, did I say, 'leave *her*'? I meant 'leave *him*'—I shall leave *her son* to a dreadful fate!" Liliana shrieked and fell to her knees, and Saurenia said, "Enjoy explaining that." With an exultant flip of her hair, she left the building to return to her monsters—of whom she truly was the greatest one of all.

***

Several minutes of unbearable silence passed, then Juliane hesitantly asked, "Liliana, what's going on? What did she mean when she called you your mother's son?"

He regretted the words as soon as they had left his

mouth, for Liliana offered no reply. Instead, Mater Moonshade said, "Yes, do explain why Saurenia referred to you as that." When she received no response her face darkened, and she threatened, "I may have to do something horrible to your friend if you choose not to."

Juliane squealed and begged mercy, but the Mater laughed at his pleas and advanced toward him menacingly, only stopping when Liliana cried, "Leave her alone! I will speak—just, please, do not harm her."

"Well then, time to come out with it, or I might change my mind about leaving her be. What did Saurenia mean when she spoke of you in that way?"

Liliana had been staring at the floor and, when she lifted her head, Juliane could see her eyes were moist and that pain strained her features. "Liliana, you don't have to say anything if you don't want to," he told her. "It's likely she'll just kill us both anyway. If my dying sooner keeps you from having to speak of things that bother you, it's a fate I'm willing to deal with."

The Mater glared at him, but Liliana wiped her eyes and said, "It's fine, Juliane. I can share my story, no matter how it might upset me to do so, if it will ensure your safety for at least a little while longer." The sorceress stared at her, an expectant smile playing at the corners of her mouth, and Liliana, casting her eyes down, whispered, "I used to be known as my mother's son."

"What was that, child? You must speak louder, for I could not hear you. If I cannot understand your words, I cannot be sure of what you're saying, and therefore cannot promise Juliane's safety."

Liliana, meeting the sorceress's gaze this time, said more forcefully, "I used to be known as my mother's son."

The sorceress cackled, then strode over to the cage and hissed, "Oh, child, I think you're avoiding the point. What you aren't stating outright is that you...used...to be...*a boy!*"

Liliana's face contorted in anger, and she screamed, "I

was never a boy! *Never!*"

The Mater, caught off guard, reared back from her captive, then erupted into laughter. "I've upset you, haven't I? Well, if you weren't a boy, then what were you?"

Liliana looked the sorceress boldly in the eye and coolly stated, "Though the world might have seen me as a boy at one time I did not feel like one, and so believe I never truly was one. Is that a sufficient explanation?"

The Mater laughed once more. "Oh, child, you've done a fine job beginning your tale, and it seems your friend wants to hear more, as do I. Go on, then."

Liliana asked Juliane, who was staring at her open-mouthed, "Do you recall how, early on in our journey, you questioned why my mother hadn't just transformed me into a man, so that I might guide you without your knowing my true identity?" He nodded. "Well, the reason she couldn't was because she would have required the same materials needed to return you to your male form, for I am...under the same enchantment."

Juliane's eyes went wide, and Liliana continued, "When I was a small child, I was miserable, for I understood that I wasn't the person others thought me to be. I knew in my heart and mind that I was a girl but was told by those around me that I was a boy, and this filled me with deep sadness. I didn't understand why I couldn't be a girl, and I was at one point filled with such despair that I contemplated flinging myself from a window. When I told my mother how I was feeling, she determined that, if I was to be happy, she would have to do something to help me, to...change me. She cast the Spell of Transmutation on me to make me as I am now, and I've celebrated each day of my life—even the difficult ones—since becoming my true self."

She searched his face beseechingly. "Juliane, I know I've been harsh with you at times regarding your mistreatment of and disdain for women, and I think this is because...I had to go through so much in order to *be* one. I hope you now understand why I'm very sensitive regarding these matters, and why it was so important for me to help you see the error of your ways. I...suppose I don't have anything more to say."

Juliane was stunned by her revelation, but, after taking a moment to consider things, he cleared his throat and said, "Liliana, who you were at one time doesn't matter to me, who you are now does—and who you are is the greatest person I've ever had the pleasure of knowing. I believe I would feel that way no matter who you were, for I was drawn to you even as Landon—and, though it may not mean much coming from the likes of me, I would likely desire you no matter your gender, for I hold you in that high of esteem."

Reddening, he ducked his head. When he lifted it, he found Liliana was looking at him in a way that made his heart leap, for there was most certainly adoration in her gaze. She mouthed a "thank you," and seemed as if she might say more when, to his chagrin, Mater Moonshade broke in. "How very sweet and sentimental—and how perfectly poignant under these circumstances. It looks like the dilemma that I shall present to you will be more of a difficulty than I could ever have anticipated!"

When he saw how wickedly she grinned Juliane gulped, and he stammered, "W-what do you mean? What sort of a dilemma?"

"Oh, a very simple, yet quite consequential, one," the sorceress replied. "And your response to the quandary I shall pose will determine whether you shall leave my home a free man—and I do mean a free *man*."

"What? What exactly are you saying?" he yelped.

"I'm saying that I have the means to change you back into the prince you once were, but that my doing so is contingent upon whether you behave in the way that I want you to."

"But, how can you possibly do that? From what I've heard, reversing the transformation requires my getting the hair of a prince, but I must make him fall in love with me and—"

The Mater stayed him with a harsh burst of laughter. "Silly child, do you not believe that I have the wherewithal to undo the spell should I choose to?" She strode over to him and leaned forward until he could feel her fetid-smelling breath upon his face. "I have the power to transport a prince from anywhere in the world into this room in the blink of an eye. I can make this selfsame prince fall in love with you through the administration of a single potion, and I know what must be done to break the curse. Satiana Almwick's belief that the person who placed it must be the one to remedy it is incorrect, for, as long as one knows the proper phrases to be spoken and patterns to be painted on the skin, they can release someone from it." Her voice grew persuasive. "Just think, Juliane, you could leave here today as Prince Julian, and go back to the life of trysts and pleasure-seeking you've so greatly enjoyed."

Knowing the Mater's assistance was likely to come at a terrible price, he said, "But what must I do for you to help me?"

"Ah, I was hoping you'd ask," the sorceress replied. "You must pledge your allegiance to me and aid me in accomplishing a very important task: my revenge against Satiana Almwick through the destruction of the thing she cares for most...her daughter."

Juliane sputtered, "I can't, I won't, I couldn't possibly. I care about Liliana, I—"

"Nothing you say will change my mind," Mater Moonshade interrupted him. "Do not waste your breath or my time, or I may choose her fate without any input from you."

Paling visibly, he ceased his protests, and the Mater

explained, "I'm not a cruel person, and so don't want to destroy Liliana completely—after all, she's done nothing to pain me other than exist as the child of my enemy—but I *do* plan on destroying the essence of who she is, so I suppose it's somewhat the same...but there I go, prattling on. Just as you've been transformed, so too will she be, but her alteration shall be decidedly less pleasant. You see, with your help I can change her into whatever she most dreads becoming—which, to me, seems to be an old man on death's doorstep. For someone who feared becoming a man as they aged this is a most undesirable fate, and I shall enjoy the transformation immensely."

Juliane gaped in horror, Liliana groaned within her cage, and the sorceress, pleased by their reactions, continued, "I know an incantation that, when recited by two in unison, will cause the target of their words to undergo the change I have spoken of. If you aid me in casting this spell, I will do what's necessary to return you to your masculine form and will ensure you get home safely. I will then transport the transformed Liliana to her mother, and will enjoy the look of despair upon Satiana Almwick's face when she opens her door to find the thing her beloved daughter has become, the sadness that will fill her eyes as she understands that she will watch that thing wither and die—"

"No!" Juliane screamed, causing the Mater to stumble backward. She cast him a look that chilled his blood, but this did not stop him from timidly asking, "And what happens if I choose not to do what you request of me?"

"Then I will make the decision as to what I shall do with her on my own and will erase your memory. I never intended on harming you, my threats were only meant to bring your friend to speak. You've done nothing to wound me, and, as I've mentioned, I'm not a cruel person, but I cannot have you running off to seek help. If you refuse to assist me, I will perform a ritual that will leave your mind blank, then will deposit you in a nearby town. There's a chance you could remember who you are if someone recognizes you or something triggers your recall, but you'd most likely end up spending the rest of your days where I left you. I'm sure you could still lead a wonderful life—just, not as a prince." She cackled. "Let no one claim I am unkind when I offer dooms as pleasant as this...well, at least to some people." She craned her neck to leer at Liliana, who put on a brave face despite being thoroughly terrified.

She turned back to Juliane, who had bowed his head in deep thought, and expectantly awaited his response. He soon lifted his face and said, "You've given me a lot to think about, Mater, and I do not believe it would be wise for me to make a hasty decision regarding the matter. Therefore, I humbly request I be given three days' time to consider all you've said, so that I might choose the best option."

He cast Mater Moonshade a pleading look, and she said begrudgingly, "I will give you the time you've requested to mull things over—as I'd mentioned, no one can accuse me of being unkind to those who haven't duly garnered my wrath—but keep in mind, child, that, if your choice hasn't been made by the end of it, I'll keep my promise to wipe your memory and bring you elsewhere. And remember that, no matter what you decide, your friend's fate is in my hands, and what will be done with her shall be of my choosing!"

"Of course, Mater," Juliane agreed.

The sorceress eyed him warily, then shouted, "Mark my words!" She rushed from the room, cloak flapping behind her, leaving the travelers alone and staring at each other—one's eyes filled with despair, the other's shining with a secret hope.

24.

Once she was sure the Mater was no longer within earshot, Liliana said softly, "Juliane, you needn't have done that. If you're hoping she changes her mind given some time, you'll be sorely disappointed—you might even decrease your own chances of escape by putting off your decision, as someone capable of holding that strong a grudge isn't likely to look kindly upon those she sees as spoiling her plans."

She sighed, then, voice trembling, continued, "You should call her back in and let her know you'll help her. I suppose I should count myself as fortunate, for she doesn't plan on killing me, merely transforming me...and I'm sure my mother can undo whatever curse she places on me. If I just get the ordeal over with, you'll be able to leave this place returned to your original form. At least I'll have helped you complete your quest after all, even if it wasn't in the way we'd intended."

Juliane was seized with affection for her, for she had sacrificed so much to assist him and continued giving of herself even in her hour of need, and his heart filled with joy, for he knew he would finally be able to repay her kindness. "But we *are* going to be able to finish our journey as we'd intended to," he told her, "because I'm going to get us out of here!"

Liliana smiled wearily. "It's nice of you to promise such

things, but it's probably better that you don't. Holding on to false hope may make any suffering I face seem worse in the end."

Rather than protesting, Juliane raised his left hand, which he had managed to free from its bindings, and waved it at her as best he could. He stuck it into his neckline and, with a flourish, removed an object dangling from a cord around his neck from underneath his clothing. Liliana squinted at it and, when she realized it was a wooden whistle, clapped her hands with glee. "The gift from Irmene! I'd forgotten all about it. I had no idea you even remembered having it, let alone that you were wearing it. What a stroke of luck!"

"Well, actually, I put it on right after you and I argued on the way here," Juliane said. "I thought there was just...*something* not right about Saurenia's behavior, so I decided to prepare myself in case anything was amiss. I'm glad now that I did."

Liliana grimaced. "Juliane, I'm so sorry that I didn't believe what you told me and didn't heed your warnings. If I had, perhaps we wouldn't be in this mess right now. I—"

"Now is not the time to chastise yourself," he interrupted. "Once we've gotten out of here, you may rebuke yourself as much as you'd like." He waggled a finger at her, and, stifling a giggle, she asked what he planned on doing. "I'm going to summon the help Irmene promised. I don't know if there's a body of water linked to the sea near here; if there is, she may get to us quickly. If not, she'll have to traverse the forest to reach us, so I asked the Mater for a three-day contemplation period in case she must travel by foot. All I need to do now is toot on the whistle to request her assistance. Here's hoping she can hear me." He lifted it to his mouth, and, after a brief hesitation, pursed his lips and blew.

He was dismayed to discover the whistle emitted no sound, so tried blowing it once more and was once more disappointed. Liliana offered encouragement, reminding him that magical items frequently worked differently from non-magical ones, but still he wondered if his gesture would produce any result—and understood he might have to wait three days to find out. He had never been a patient person, even during the best of times (which these certainly were not), so he hoped for success, prepared for failure, and tried to think of the things he would say to Liliana—the ones he kept wanting to say but had not yet expressed the right way—once they were out of danger.

Hours passed, and, though the circumstances were highly distressing, the chair Juliane was confined to was very comfortable, so, despite his best intentions, he found himself dozing off; after stirring himself for the fifth time, he decided it was not worth fighting off sleep and let himself rest. Liliana managed to stay awake awhile longer, but she eventually curled up on the floor of her cage and drifted into fitful sleep.

***

Juliane woke to find that the fire in the fireplace had dwindled to embers, darkening the room, and he found that the shadows disquieted him. He gave a loud sigh of discontent, as his bottom and legs were sore from staying in one position for so long, and he was unpleasantly surprised to hear another from elsewhere in the room. He glanced around frantically, trying to identify where the noise had come from, then relaxed as he understood it had likely just been an echo. His relief did not last long, though, for he noticed the chamber door, which the sorceress had closed upon leaving, was now standing open.

He detected breathing in the room beyond the doorway and, hoping the lurker was merely the selkie being cautious, called out, "Irmene, is that you?" The breathing quickened, he heard movement in his direction, and his heart sickened as he understood that what was coming toward him couldn't possibly be Irmene, for, even in her seal form, she had never...slithered.

Trembling, he stared at the doorway, and, when what was making the noise moved into view, he had to keep himself from screaming. Filling up almost the entirety of the door frame was a being so monstrous it pained his mind to look at it. The creature resembled a woman bedraggled and risen from the grave from the waist up— her hair hung in limp tendrils, her skin was chalk-white and flaky, and there was a gaping socket where her left eye should have been—but from the waist down it was a mass of twists and loops resembling thick lengths of dark rope...but rope that oozed and squirmed and left trails of slime upon the floor.

Juliane hoped that if he remained perfectly still the thing might not notice him, so he slowed his breathing, closed his eyes, and sat, frozen, listening. His stomach tightened as the thing started to move again, and he discerned, with increasing dread, that it seemed to be headed in his direction. He opened his eyes and instantly wished he had not, for he saw the monster making its way across the room, and he let out a screech when it halted mere inches from his trussed body. It raised several hideous tendrils toward him and slurred, "What have we heeeeeere? It looks like a delicious morsel waiting to be unwrapped and devoured."

He struggled to break free but was stuck to the chair, and he shrieked in terror as the thing used its coils to loosen the ropes binding him. For a moment he believed he might escape its clutches once the ties were undone, but one look at the many wriggling limbs ready to snare him dashed his hopes to pieces. Wishing to avoid a gruesome fate by any means possible, he yelled, "Liliana! Mater Moonshade! Anyone! I'm going to be eaten! I beg of you, please save me!"

The thing did not stop fumbling at his bonds, but, though its hungry expression remained unchanged, a voice emanated from its unmoving lips: "Hey, you need to be quiet and stop squirming, or someone might hear you! You're no help to me moving around like that."

Confusion cut through Juliane's fright, for the voice was unlike the creature's gruff one—it sounded musical, lilting, much like that of... "Irmene!" he cried, relief washing over him. "Irmene, is that you? Are you inside that loathsome body?"

"I beg your pardon!" the Irmene voice responded, disgruntled. "My body's certainly not loathsome! I... Ohhhh, I see. Juliane, you must be half-asleep. I think you're dreaming, which is probably why you're screaming. Wake up, silly girl."

Juliane opened his eyes, and almost sobbed with joy when he discovered that he had been having a nightmare and that it was no monster who was untying him. "Irmene! You've come! The whistle worked after all!" The selkie scowled at him and gestured that he should be quiet, and he continued in a whisper, "Words cannot express how delighted I am to see you. When did you receive my summons?"

"I got it this morning and came as fast as I could. I was able to swim here, fortunately, as there's a river that runs to the ocean nearby. Crossing the woods would have taken me much longer."

"But, how did you find us?"

"I looked for the light—or, in your case, lights. You must have whistled twice," Irmene said. "When the whistle's blown, it creates a noise I can hear no matter where I am and produces an undetectable orb that rises into the sky. It emits a glow once reaching a certain height, so I can see it shining over wherever the person who's summoned me is calling from. It's lucky the person holding you here didn't

225

notice the lights over their home."

The Mater's so stooped she probably isn't capable of noticing them, thought Juliane, and he was about to voice this observation when he felt his bonds loosen. He shook himself, and the ropes fell to the floor. "I'm free!" he squealed. "Thank you, Irmene!"

He rose from his seat to gratefully embrace her, but found he was unable to stand and fell back onto his chair. Irmene, giggling, reminded him that he would have to take some time to get the feeling back into his limbs before getting up, so he stretched his legs and, once he felt able, gingerly rose to his feet and grasped her hands, thanking her. "Twas nothing for a swimmer as strong as I," said the selkie, "but I remember there being two of you. Where's Liliana, and does she also need my help?"

"She's over there," he replied, pointing across the room, "and she needs it even more than I did." Irmene rushed over to the cage while Juliane, still not quite steady on his feet, gingerly followed her; once they had reached it, Juliane hissed, "Liliana, wake up, Irmene is here to help." He repeated the phrase a few times and, when she did not awaken, jabbed a finger into her back.

Bleary-eyed and grumpy, she rolled over to face him. "Why are you prodding me, Juliane?" she grumbled, then, remembering where she was and what had happened, quickly sat up. She was about to ask how he had escaped from his chair when she noticed the selkie. "Irmene, it's so good to see you!"

Irmene did not respond to her greeting, for she was staring at the lock on the cage door. After turning it over several times, she said, "I'm sorry, but I can't help with this."

"B-but, why?" sputtered Juliane.

"Because it's enchanted. I might be able to pick it if it was an ordinary key-lock, but this one's held shut with magic. We'd have better luck trying to saw through the cage bars than trying to open it by force."

"Whatever can we do, then?" wailed Juliane. "We can't just leave Liliana here to face the fate Mater Moonshade's planned for her."

"I'm sure you won't have to," Liliana said confidently. "I'm comfortable enough with spells that I can likely do whatever is required to lift the one on this lock. I just need the right incantation or materials."

She had the others check the room for a spell book that contained a fitting conjuration, but, after a fruitless search, they collapsed near her cage. "It's hopeless!" Juliane moaned. "There are so many books in here, we'll never find the right one!"

"That's because what we need cannot be found in this room!" cried Liliana, realization dawning on her. "When Mater Moonshade was tormenting me, I noticed a star-shaped charm hanging from a chain around her neck. I would bet my head that it opens that lock."

"Don't bet your head, for we need all the assistance you can offer us!" said Irmene. "But I think you're right. The lock has a star-shaped hole, so inserting the thing you've mentioned is likely to open it."

"Liliana, you've discovered the solution to our problem!" declared Juliane. He started to dance a victorious jig, then abruptly stopped, blanching. "If what we need is on that old hag's neck, how are we going to get it from her?"

Liliana asked if he and Irmene had come across their packs while checking the room and frowned when he replied that they had not. "That's unfortunate, because my pack contains something that could help you obtain what we need."

Juliane, realizing what she was referring to, squealed, "The Pulvis Lapsus Memoriae!" Irmene asked him why he was uttering such strange words, and he explained that they meant "memory loss powder" and that, when used properly, the powder in question was capable of putting

227

people to sleep and wiping away their memories. "If we can get it and sprinkle some on that nasty sorceress, she shall fall asleep, and we can steal her necklace and then make her forget we were ever in her home! Isn't it wonderful to think of Saurenia coming here for the Blood Moon witches' circle, asking what became of us, and receiving only a blank stare in reply? It almost makes the trials I shall undoubtedly face whilst trying to recover that thing from the Mater worthwhile!"

He smiled weakly, and, seeing how frightened he was, Liliana suggested that Irmene accompany him on his errand; once she had agreed to this, he seemed to brighten a little. She flew to the room's doorway and disappeared through it, and he ran after her yelling, "Wait for me!" Liliana watched them go, then sat down on the floor of her prison and prayed to the Mother Goddess that she would, on this day, show favor to those who would use her magic for light rather than those who would use it for darkness.

25.

Juliane trailed Irmene to an open doorway in the adjacent room. "This staircase will take us to the ground floor," she said. "Now, to head up it." She proceeded cautiously, as the stairwell was dark and neither in the party carried a light, and Juliane fell into step behind her, at times grabbing onto her sailcloth dress for fear of losing her in the near blackness. He exhaled in relief once they had reached the top step, then his stomach clenched once more as she opened the door before them.

He discovered that they were at the end of a familiar hallway, and he whispered confidently, "I know this place. Follow me." He tiptoed down the passage, Irmene trailing behind him, to the first door on the right. He cautiously turned the handle, the door swung open, and, when he stuck his head through the doorway, he was pleased to find his and Liliana's bedchamber unoccupied. He stepped inside and beckoned that the selkie follow him, and she entered, closing the door behind her.

Juliane searched for Liliana's bag and found it easily, for she had stuck it deep beneath her bed in a place where others might not look but where he, knowing her well, had expected it to be. Irmene lit a candle and handed it to him, and, rummaging through the sack, he soon found the packet of Pulvis Lapsus Memoriae, wrapped in the gloves he had given Liliana. Once he had the powder, however, he realized that, although he had cast the dust before, he had not uttered the incantation that created the memory loss—Liliana had done that part. He guessed it was written somewhere in her book, and so he reached into her pack and retrieved the tome. Flipping through its pages, he came upon one marked "Powders," and, scanning it, softly cheered, for he had found what he had been seeking. *Luck has been on my side so far*, he told himself. *Perhaps this is a sign that I am meant to save Liliana.*

He committed the words, "Let memory fade, in sleep be lost," to memory but folded the page in case he should he forget them, then closed the book and stuffed it, and the powder packet, back into Liliana's pack. Knowing the easiest part of the mission had been completed and that a difficult, dangerous, and potentially fatal portion of it still lay ahead, he shouldered Liliana's bag and handed Irmene his own. "I guess it's time to find the lair of the serpent," he said, smiling wanly. "Here's hoping the Mater doesn't know we're coming."

Leaving the room, they proceeded down the corridor, using the candle to illuminate their surroundings. Juliane, trying to act braver than he felt, said, "I suppose our next step is to find the Mater and use the powder on her. At least we're lucky that it seems to be nighttime, for it means she's likely asleep. Now, if I were a centuries-old witch, where would I choose to bed down?"

They tried to answer that question by checking each room off of the hallway as well as every other chamber on that floor, but they discovered only empty beds, shelves of books and potions, dusty furniture, and boxes covered with strange runes that Juliane would not have opened for all the gold in his kingdom. He was starting to despair when the selkie, remembering that the house had an upper story, suggested that the sorceress would likely be found up there. They searched for a stairwell leading to it and found one hidden behind a large tapestry in the dining hall. "This

Mater you speak of is a wise old crone indeed," said Irmene, "for she's done much to ensure she remains undisturbed whilst slumbering. We must be wary, for there may be traps in place to prevent her enemies from reaching her." Juliane, who had not considered this possibility, gulped and started to tremble, but nonetheless followed her as she swiftly mounted the stairs.

Upon reaching the top step they grew certain they had finally located the witch, for loud snores emanated from beyond the thick door before them. They opened it and found themselves in a stone hallway with three doorways. The deafening snores came from behind the door at the end of the hall, and Juliane ran to it, gripped its handle, and, praying the Mater would not awaken, tried to pull it open.

Juliane was surprised and disappointed (and, to be honest, slightly relieved) when his efforts produced no result; no matter which way he tried opening the door, it remained firmly shut. After much pushing and pulling he stepped aside to let Irmene take a turn, but she also could not budge it. Dropping to her knees to examine it, she said, "It seems to be held closed with an incantation. I suppose this shouldn't shock us—I mean, this Mater Moonshade is the queen of witches, after all."

Juliane bemoaned their plight, then his mouth suddenly fell open. "I've got it!"

"What have you got?" asked Irmene, confused.

"The answer to our problem." He grabbed the book from Liliana's bag. "If this door's locked with magic, then what we need is a spell to 'unlock' it."

"Ooh, good idea, clever girl!"

He thumbed through the tome until he came to a section marked "Locks," and he crowed, "I've found it! This spell is for 'universal magic lock-picking,' so it's sure to work on this one pitiful door!"

Holding the book before him, he read:

Let me unlock any door ahead,
Let no barrier keep me at bay.
Let nothing stand between me and my course,
On this or any other day.
Let my path be clear and well-marked,
Let my mind be skilled at hoping.
As long as purpose lights my way,
Then every door shall open.

To his astonishment, once he had uttered the last word every door in the hallway flew open. He hurriedly closed the one to the Mater's room, for he was not yet ready to enter it, and was about to prepare the memory loss powder when Irmene said, "Why don't you check the other rooms first? They might contain items that could help you on your journey." While Irmene stood watch in the hallway he entered and explored each chamber, and, though he found nothing of note in the first one, he came upon a tightly wrapped parcel with the word "invisibilia" printed on it inside a chest in the second.

He opened it carefully to reveal a worn leather cloak, and, once he realized what the object might be, he ran back to the selkie. "Irmene, would you do me the favor of watching me as I put this on?" he asked. She agreed to, and he raised the cloak into the air and threw it over his shoulders.

He asked if she noticed any change in him, and was disheartened when she replied, "No. Am I supposed to? What are you up to, Juliane?" He was about to remove the garment when he noticed a curious clasp at its neckline, a piece of brass shaped like a pair of spectacles. He secured the fastening, and Irmene gasped. "Juliane, where are you?" she hissed, looking frantically around the room.

"I'm right in front of you," he replied, scanning his body

232

and determining that, although she could not see him, he remained visible to his own eyes.

"But you can't be! I can hear your voice, but you're not there!"

Giggling, he unfastened the clasp, then lifted his head to find Irmene gaping at him. "What happened, Juliane? Where did you go just then?"

"I didn't go anywhere," he replied playfully. "Whatever makes you think that?"

Her face darkened and he knew she was growing cross, so he ceased his teasing and told her that the cloak had rendered him invisible. She smirked triumphantly. "And I'm the one to thank for your discovery! If you hadn't searched the rooms, you wouldn't have found it."

"You're right," he said. "I'm sure this will be very useful in the future..." His eyes widened. "And also, right now! I can wear it whilst casting the powder on the Mater! Even if she wakes, she won't be able to see me, and so cannot harm me...or stop me!"

Feeling more self-assured than before, he pulled the gloves on, poured a handful of memory loss powder into his right palm, and, after placing the packet into his bag, had Irmene help him fasten the cloak. After she assured him that he was most certainly invisible, he cautiously pulled the door to the Mater's bedchamber open with his unencumbered left hand. He found himself peering into a room shrouded in darkness, and he timidly whispered, "Here I go," then stepped through the doorway.

***

At first Juliane could not see anything, but, as his eyes adjusted to the dimness, he was able to see that the chamber was much larger than he had anticipated; it had three small windows that allowed moonlight to filter in, and it contained a curtained bed, several chests, a table and

233

wooden chair covered with papers and objects, and a smaller bedside table. After committing his surroundings to memory, he gingerly closed the door behind him, then he crept toward the bed, for the snores emanating from it assured him the Mater slept therein.

He shuffled along, taking care not to bump into anything, and was only a few strides from his target when he stepped on something he had not noticed during his survey of the room. There was a screech as a black blur dashed across the floor and under the largest table, and, when he saw its green eyes glaring out at him, he cursed himself for not considering that of course the mother of all witches would own a cat and for (just his luck) stepping on its tail.

After some time had passed, he felt sure the beast's noise had not wakened the Mater, and he was about to continue advancing toward the bed when he heard something that made his blood run cold: "Carman, was that you? Why did you howl, my dear?" Mater Moonshade had risen in bed and was sitting perfectly still, listening. She pulled back the bed-curtain, and Juliane saw her eyes, looking very much like the cat's, shining out at him. He knew she was almost certainly unable to see him, but it still made him uneasy to be so near to her, and he was grateful he had possessed the foresight to close the chamber door behind him.

She took a candle from the bedside table and, snapping her fingers, produced a flame upon its wick; holding it before her, she scanned the room carefully, then placed it back on the table. Juliane hoped she would return to sleep, but, to his dismay, she instead called to the disgruntled cat, "Carman, come to Mother, Mother wants to see you." It came out from its hiding place and jumped onto the sorceress's bed, and Mater Moonshade bent down and crooned into its ear, "Now, my dear, you must tell Mother what you saw, or heard, or felt. Mother must know everything, my pet."

Juliane shuddered in horror, for, to his astonishment, the cat responded to the Mater's query with a series of high-pitched screeches and yowls. Once it had quieted, the Mater raised her head and looked around the room. "Hmmm, this is very interesting. Carman says there was someone in this room before, for they trod upon her tail, but, in spite of this, the room appears to be empty. I thought that whoever had been in here might have already left, but Carman says she did not see the door open. Perhaps the intruder opened a window and flew out?" She squinted her eyes, smiling craftily. "Or, perhaps you're still in the room, trespasser? If I listen closely, I may hear you breathing."

She held her palm to her ear, and Juliane, holding back the shriek that was so close to escaping, stood perfectly still and slowed his breathing until it was barely discernible even to himself. The room was as silent as a tomb, and, after what seemed an eternity, the crone pulled her hand away and shrugged. "Well, I guess there's no one here after all. Perhaps no one ever was in the room? Perhaps something fell from a table onto you, Carman? Why don't you come and sleep with Mother, won't that help you feel better?" The cat meowed in assent, then curled up at the foot of its mistress's bed. The Mater cast a sly glance around the room, then closed the bed curtain, fell back on the bed, and was soon snoring away once more.

Juliane noticed that his outstretched right hand was shaking, and, as he feared he might drop the powder, he held it close to himself as he advanced toward the sorceress's bed. Reaching the bedside, he grasped the bed curtain with his left hand and carefully pulled it back. He leaned over the Mater's prone form, and, as he peered down at her, a gasp escaped his lips, for the witch's eyes popped open and she sprang up in bed.

He retreated a few paces, cowering, for Mater

Moonshade had pulled back the curtain and was staring around the room wildly. "I knew it! I sensed someone was still lurking! Who are you? Why are you in my chamber?" An unfamiliar look twisted her features, and he understood, with a sense of satisfaction, that she was frightened. "Are you another magic user? Do you dare try and take what's mine? You should know that I won't give it up easily!"

Juliane stood motionless, fervently wishing that she would calm herself and go back to sleep, but he understood that this would not happen, for she had seen the curtain move and was aware that she was not alone in the room. He knew he needed to throw the powder on her to end the nightmare but worried he might not be successful if he tried to, for she kept bobbing her head in all directions.

Her movements suddenly ceased, and he stole forward, hoping to dust her—but she abruptly tilted her head upward and, sticking her nose in the air, sniffed ardently. An evil grin spread over her face, and he experienced terror for what seemed the hundredth time that night when she said, "I know who you are. You're one of the travelers I locked in my dungeon. I can tell by your smell. As I've sealed Liliana in her cage with a charm, you must be her companion...I know it's you, Juliane!" Despite his best intentions he could not keep from yelping, and the Mater leered triumphantly into the darkness. "You may hide from me now, but I will tear this room apart searching for you— and, when I find you, I will tear *you* apart!"

She poised as if to spring from the bed, and, fearing that this would be his only chance to strike before she pounced on him, Juliane prayed to every deity he could think of as he threw the handful of Pulvis Lapsus Memoriae into her face.

The powder's effect was immediate and powerful, for the witch put her hands to her face and cried out once, then tumbled back onto the bed, fast asleep. Juliane was at first stunned that the enchantment had worked, but, once he was certain it had, he began to dance around the room, crowing, "I have bested Mater Moonshade! I, Juliane Stoneshire, whom some might consider the most helpless prince ever to walk the earth, have defeated the mother of all sorceresses!" His revelry was interrupted, however, by the cat, Carman, who had gotten up from the bed and stood near the edge of it, hissing in his direction. He had the sobering thought that, as the cat had "spoken" to its mistress earlier, it might tell the sorceress what had happened once she woke, and so he placed the hand coated with memory dust on its head and it was soon slumbering as soundly as its owner.

Irmene, hearing his triumphant shouting, charged into the room and, spying the prone Mater, exclaimed, "Oh, Juliane, you've done it, you've bested that horrible witch! Now, take that magic cloak off, for your lurking about unseen unsettles me." Juliane removed the powdery gloves, then undid the clasp and shook off the cloak; visible once more, he embraced his friend, and the two jigged madly across the floor. "I hate to interrupt our merriment," Irmene said breathlessly, "but shouldn't we save the celebrating for *after* we use the spell? I mean, aren't they only sleeping right now?"

Juliane had forgotten the need for the incantation during his revelries, and he ran into the hallway and snatched up Liliana's pack. He carried it into the Mater's bedchamber, pulled the book from it and opened it to the folded page, then yelled, "Let memory fade, in sleep be lost" several times. "That's certain to work. Now, to retrieve the charm from the Mater and return to Liliana."

"One step ahead of you," said Irmene, who had already clambered onto the mattress. Reaching a hand behind the slumbering sorceress's head, she unclasped the necklace, then, grabbing the item with one hand, she climbed off the bed and curtsied at him. "Lead the way, oh mighty Witch-tamer."

"Certainly," he replied, grinning as he placed the tome and cloak into Liliana's pack and pulled it onto his shoulder. They exited the room and Irmene grabbed Juliane's pack off the hallway floor, then they raced down the stairs and through the castle, deliriously happy that they would soon free their friend from her prison.

26.

L iliana paced the cage, anxiously awaiting her companions' return. She had tried to rest but found that her nerves prevented her from sleeping, and so had decided she would instead occupy herself with travel preparations in case of escape—and, ever the pragmatist, also considered what she might tell Juliane to aid him in his quest should she be unable to leave with him.

What seemed like hours passed, and her mind shifted from planning to worrying, for her friends still had not come back. She grew concerned that they had run into Mater Moonshade, for she knew that, if this had occurred, death was the fate the sorceress had likely bestowed upon them. The idea of the witch harming the selkie, who had shown the travelers such kindness, caused her great sadness, but this paled in comparison to the sorrow she felt at the thought of the Mater killing Juliane.

She realized that she cared for him in a way she would not have deemed possible at the outset of their journey, and that she would be devastated if she lost him before getting a chance to apologize for favoring Saurenia. Burning with shame, she recalled how he had tried to warn her of the sorceress's treacherous designs, how she had disregarded his concerns and had even accused him of expressing them for his own benefit. She now understood that his intentions had been pure, and considered that maybe, just maybe, he did view her as more than just another conquest to bed and then brag about. She fervently hoped he would return so she could tell him she was sorry, let him know she treasured their friendship, and...perhaps share with him how she wondered what might come of their connection once their journey had ended.

She waited and waited, and eventually found herself nodding off despite her worries. She curled up on the cage floor and was starting to doze off when she was startled by a loud thud. Her eyes popped open, for she knew the noise had been the stairwell door slamming, which likely meant one of two things: either her friends had come to save her, or the Mater had discovered them and, having dispensed justice, had come to dole out her fate.

Trembling, she stared at the doorway, for she could hear footsteps tapping along the floor, but, even as they drew nearer, she could not see anyone approaching. Suddenly, the terrible thought crossed her mind that whatever was coming *could not be seen,* for the footsteps had now entered the chamber and the one making them still was not visible.

She wondered what awful new experience she might be subjected to—for, whatever the thing was, it seemed to have four legs rather than two—but tried to appear unafraid by standing up and shouting, "Who are you? Why are you hiding from view?" The invader uttered what sounded like a laugh, and, furious that it found her feigned bravery humorous, she yelled, "Show yourself, you coward!" The creature made no reply, and her anger drained away, leaving only dread. Hearing its steps still forthcoming, she retreated to the rear of her prison, placed her back against the wall, and prepared herself for conflict, for she hoped she could strike at the thing even if she could not see it.

She heard the invisible intruder approach the cage and fumble with the lock, and she stifled a scream when it fell to the floor and the cage door swung open. For all her good intentions she could not move; she instead cowered at the rear of the cage, for she knew she was trapped. Prepared for her potential death, she closed her eyes and said, "Whatever you are, if you must take me, at least do so quickly."

To which she received the reply, "Though I'm sure I'd enjoy that, we don't really have the time for it right now. Let's just focus on getting out of here instead."

Liliana opened her eyes and, to her relief, found Juliane's face just inches from her own. She was tempted to throw her arms around him, but she stopped herself when she remembered someone else was likely still in the cage with them—and not just Irmene, who stood next to him. Lowering her voice, she said, "I hate to bear bad news, but I'm afraid the creature who unlocked the cage door—you know, the one who left it open so you could enter—might still be lurking in this room. It isn't visible, so we must be careful to avoid it as we make our escape."

Though she spoke quite solemnly her words did not seem to distress her companions, for they instead started to giggle. She at first did not understand why, for she felt the hidden creature posed a substantial threat, but, as first Juliane and then the selkie dissolved into full-on laughter, she realized that they knew something she did not. She noticed that a sizable cloak was draped over both of their shoulders, and that it was not fastened, and that it had a clasp shaped like a pair of spectacles... "An Inuisibilitas Pallium," she gasped, for the garment they were wearing was a powerful invisibility cloak, one of only a handful in existence. Once her wonder at their discovery had passed, it dawned on her who the frightening hidden entity—or, more accurately, entities—had been. "*You* were the invisible thing menacing me?" she said, disbelieving. "I was terrified! I thought something was coming to kill me. How could you do such a thing?"

Juliane tried to stammer a response, but Irmene glided in front of him and placed her hand on Liliana's shoulder. "It was my idea to play the trick. I thought it would be amusing to give you a little scare, but I should have listened to Juliane. She had suggested that the prank might not be a wise idea, but I insisted we carry on with it, and now we've made you upset. I am so sorry and can only hope you'll forgive us for the pain we have caused you."

Liliana's anger subsided, and she gently clasped the selkie's shoulders. "I forgive you. You didn't know your behavior would hurt me, so I won't hold it against you."

She embraced Irmene, and Juliane, who had been watching the proceedings with astonishment, experienced yet another shock when the selkie winked at him over her shoulder. Once Liliana, ever resolute, had grabbed her pack from Juliane and had exited the cage, Irmene handed him his bag and whispered, "I've saved you twice tonight, so I think you might now be as indebted to me as I once was to you."

She winked once more before following Liliana, and Juliane stood dazed a moment before hurrying after her. He understood that Irmene had taken the blame for his behavior—as he had really been the one to suggest the trick—and wondered why she had drawn Liliana's ire onto herself rather than allow him to suffer the consequences of his decision. He felt he still had much to learn about women and might never figure everything out but determined that he would try his best to as he caught up with his friends, who had already gained the stairwell.

Once they had exited the Mater's home the travelers identified which way they had come from earlier on in the journey, and the three went swiftly in the opposite direction and did not stop until they were well-concealed behind a thick barrier of trees. Liliana rummaged through her pack and found the torch Saurenia had given her, and, when she instructed it to "flame" and it lit itself, she grumbled, "At least she was speaking the truth about something."

She moved to grab her map, but Irmene stayed her. "You don't need that now, you have me! We selkies are excellent navigators, and, as I've traversed this forest many times, I know exactly where each path will take us. So, where do you want to go?" When they told her that they were headed to the Darklands, she grimaced. "You want to go there? I've heard naught but bad about that place, but as you wish. Follow me." She grabbed the torch and, holding it in front of her, led the way as the trio advanced into the woods.

***

The party walked along in darkness, the travelers staying close behind Irmene as she effortlessly navigated the forest. Juliane tried to focus on his feet and the uneven ground sprawling beneath them, but he could not help darting his head up to glance around him every so often. He felt uneasy, for, though they were far from the place where Saurenia and her monsters held dominion, there was always a chance one (or more) of the creatures might be lurking nearby. He recognized that this line of thinking was unhelpful and that he was likely scaring himself for no reason but also could not stop dwelling on it, so he was relieved when Irmene led them into a large clearing and said, "This is a good place to stop, as it's far enough from that sorceress's dwelling that we're unlikely to cross her path. Also, this part of the forest is under the protection of a wood nymph, so we should be free from the torments of beasties should we stay here overnight."

Though wary of the "protection" of any creature remotely resembling a fairy after his encounter with Rhoswen, Juliane decided to trust his friend's judgment and so started to set up camp. While the selkie made a fire, he took out the tent Saurenia had given him and ordered it to "grow," and it was soon sizable enough to easily fit three underneath. Liliana had been gathering branches, and she came back with an armload to use in propping and fastening it. Once they had finished, Juliane stepped back and surveyed their handiwork. "It's not bad at all, I think, especially for someone who's never set up a tent before."

"I believe I can make it even better—or, at least, more comfortable to spend the night in," said Liliana. She climbed inside it and sat upon the ground, then opened her pack and retrieved her book. "I recall seeing a spell to produce air-beds like those Saurenia created among the many my mother gave me, and I think I can manage it." She flipped through the pages until she found the incantation, then chanted, "Da mi lecto, ut est mollis ad mane." She squealed with delight as a lovely blue bed appeared, and she repeated the phrase twice more to create additional ones. "I did it, and I'd never even tried the spell before!" she crowed. "Perhaps I have my mother's natural affinity for magic after all."

She stood and found that Juliane had entered the tent. "I knew you could do it," he said shyly. "You always accomplish the things you set out to."

She reached out and embraced him. "I wanted to do this at the Mater's when you'd safely returned, but I was too upset to at the time."

"I understand," he said, face burning. "I'm sorry we frightened you, it wasn't our intention to. We were just being foolish and—"

"I know," she interrupted. "I'm not angry anymore, I'm just glad you're both all right. I was worried the witch had caught you sneaking about, as you'd been gone for so long." Releasing him, she sat down on an air-bed and, raising her eyes to meet his, said, "You've not yet told me what happened during your foray into her lair."

Joining her, he shared his adventure in the Mater's

chamber, and she blanched when he told her how the witch had woken and nearly caught him. "If I'd not been wearing the invisibility cloak, she most certainly would have killed me."

"I'm relieved nothing happened to you, for then I would never have been able to apologize," said Liliana, her expression rueful. "I allowed a contrived infatuation with Saurenia to come between us. I didn't listen to your concerns about her and even accused you of having wicked designs, and my doubt resulted in our being captured and nearly destroyed. I am so sorry, Juliane—can you ever forgive me?"

Without hesitation, he replied amicably, "I already have. I've hurt you many times and you've always forgiven me— why wouldn't I give you the same courtesy? Besides, I *do* have a history of inconsiderate behavior, so you can be excused for incorrectly assuming my actions to be uncharitable on this occasion."

Liliana grinned. "You really are a marvel! Whenever I think I've figured you out, you prove me wrong." Her smile softened, and she said quietly, "I have been wondering if I behaved unjustly after the...incident in Pultare. I think I might have misjudged you that night. At the time I believed you held malicious intent, but I now see that you no longer seem capable of malice—at least, not toward me. Perhaps I presumed the wrong motives for your actions then, as I did during the affair with Saurenia, and responded in an overly harsh manner?"

Juliane's heart started to beat faster, for he knew his chance to tell her all that had been on his mind had finally come. "Liliana, I—"

Without warning, Irmene popped her head into the tent. "Oh, doesn't it look cozy in here! Are you two busy? I've just finished preparing food and was wondering if you'd like some."

Juliane stifled a groan as Liliana replied, "A meal would

be wonderful! I'm famished." She turned to him. "Juliane, you're likely as hungry as I am—would you like to eat with us?"

"I guess so," he grumbled, sore that his attempts to speak with Liliana had once more been thwarted. He decided that, as he *was* quite ravenous, a meal would not be the worst thing to endure, so he reluctantly rose from the airbed and followed the others out of the tent. To his surprise, a veritable feast awaited them: Irmene was roasting fish and turnips over a fire she had made on skewers fashioned from branches. "Where did you get all this?" he asked, astonished.

"I'm a selkie," she replied matter-of-factly, "so, if there are fish anywhere, I can find them." She removed the food from the skewers and gave each traveler a fish and handful of vegetables before serving herself, then they all sat around the fire and, Juliane had to begrudgingly admit, thoroughly enjoyed their repast.

After they had finished their meal they chatted awhile, until Liliana expressed that she was tired and, bidding the others farewell, withdrew to the tent. Juliane knew he should join her and rest, but he did not feel ready to lie down just yet, as he was still energized from defeating the Mater. He decided to continue sitting near the fire, and to use his time alone with Irmene to ask her why she had covered for him earlier that day. Clearing his throat, he began, "Irmene, I was wondering if there was a reason why you—"

She lifted her hand to stay him. "I know what you're going to ask, so you need not finish your question. You want to know why I took the blame for our blunder earlier, is that right?" He nodded sheepishly. "Well, I could see how upset Liliana was, and I figured that, if I could shift her feelings onto me, you two would get along better during your travels ahead. After all, you'll be spending much more time together in the coming days, whilst I'll be leaving you once you've reached the border of the Darklands—"

"You'll be leaving us?" he interrupted, visibly dismayed. "But you've been so helpful thus far, and we'll likely need you then more than ever!"

"I understand that," she said gently, "but I mentioned before that I've heard no good comes of going to the Darklands, and I will reinforce my position by letting you know that all the selkies I've known who've gone there...have never returned." Juliane's face whitened, and she hastily continued, "Don't worry, you're unlikely to experience the harm Korben Darkwood inflicts upon my kind—unfortunately, selkie hides are quite valuable to those who practice the Dark Arts. But, back to my point, I cannot risk my skin, for without it I could never return to the sea, so I'm afraid I cannot come with you."

Juliane sighed, but admitted it would be callous to ask her to accompany them to a place where she would be at risk. His face had grown so forlorn, though, that she pitied him and tried to lighten the mood. "Oh, I wanted to let you know that I also did what I did because I feared that Liliana believing you orchestrated the prank would damage your bond with her. I didn't want that to happen, because I know you like her."

Juliane turned crimson and sputtered, "I, um, don't know what you mean, Irmene. I..." The selkie gave him a knowing look, which vexed him, so, composing himself, he calmly replied, "Of course I like her, Irmene. She's a very likable person. Everyone we've met during our travels has liked her—well, except for those she's had to defeat, but it's to be expected that they wouldn't—"

"You, my friend, are speaking hogwash," Irmene said matter-of-factly. "You know very well what I'm insinuating, and you're trying to talk your way around it. Fine, I will restate things plainly: I know you like Liliana in a way that

I do not, that you are *attracted* to her, and so I made sure your connection with her wasn't harmed by our silly stunt. Now, what have you to say about that?"

He tried to think of a response that would make him seem blameless of the charge but could not come up with one, so, shrugging his shoulders in defeat, he admitted in a tiny voice, "You're right. I *am* attracted to Liliana."

"I knew it!" Irmene roared triumphantly. "Some ignorant folks might not acknowledge it for what it is, but I recognize desire when I see it." She reached out to pat him on the arm. "Thank you for your honesty. I'm honored that you've entrusted me with this knowledge."

He paused for a moment, then said, "Since I've been truthful with you about some things, I suppose should also be about some others." She encouraged him to go on, and so he told her of the circumstances that had led to his curse and of what he needed to do to break it.

Once he had finished, Irmene thoughtfully murmured, "That explains why you must go to the Darklands. I wish you didn't have to, though, for I've heard it's a terrible place." She shook her head, then continued brightly, "So, have you told Liliana how you feel about her? Oh, I'm getting ahead of myself—how *do* you feel about her? I mean, you've confessed you're attracted to her, but is your interest, erm, purely physical?"

Juliane blushed. "Well, it was when I first met her—when I was still a man—but I don't feel that way anymore. I've discovered that she is intelligent, strong, brave, resourceful, and determined...and I now find myself not only desiring her physically, but also...hoping something more might come of our friendship."

Irmene's eyes widened. "Your attraction has become romantic?" Juliane stammered that he thought so but needed time to be certain, and she said, "It's all right, Juliane, your secret's safe with me should you choose not to tell her—but, you really should tell her! Nothing ever comes of feelings one keeps hidden."

"I know," he admitted. "I keep planning on revealing my feelings to her, but never seem to find the right opportunity to do so." *Especially since I keep getting interrupted whenever I try to*, he mentally added.

She drew near to him, then whispered conspiratorially, "Since I plan on leaving you two once we've reached the Darklands, why don't you tell her how you feel whilst you're alone with her? You'll be walking together with little chance of disturbance—it seems to me like the perfect time to have that conversation!" Her hope was infectious, and Juliane found himself thanking her for the suggestion. "Not to worry, I'm always willing to help a friend," she said. "Besides, to be honest, I think she may return your sentiments." He expressed gratitude for her support, and she beamed at him. "Think nothing of it. You were kind enough to give me my freedom when you had my skin, so you're more than deserving of my help and friendship." She embraced him, and, though he was sad at the thought of losing her the next day, he tried to remain positive by acknowledging that their friendship was the first he had ever had where he desired nothing more than passionless companionship from an attractive woman—which, he had to admit, was a major accomplishment for the likes of him.

Feeling good about this—and, he had to admit, strangely comfortable with his female form and the effect that it, and his quest, had been having on his worldview—he bid Irmene good night and retired to the tent, where he curled up on the air-bed nearest Liliana's and pondered what might lay ahead until sleep found him.

27.

Irmene awakened first the next morning and busied herself with preparations awhile before waking her friends, for she knew they were exhausted after their trying experience at the Mater's. When she eventually determined that they could sleep no longer, she stuck her head into the tent and trilled, "Good morrow! Are you aware that it's now well past noontime? If you want to get to where the wood meets the Darklands by nightfall, you had better get up and get ready!"

Juliane groaned and covered his head, for he regretted staying up later than he should have the night before, but Liliana sprang from her bed and grabbed her book from her pack. She thumbed through it until she found an incantation to dispel the airbeds, and, reading it aloud, watched as hers shrank to a dot of color and vanished. She repeated the process with Irmene's, then, after determining that Juliane would not get up unless forced to, recited the spell once more and giggled as his bed disappeared, spilling him onto the ground.

"Why did you do that?" he asked crossly. "I was having a fantastic dream."

"About Rhoswen, I'd wager," she said, then ducked as a piece of bread flew past her head. "Well, at least you're awake now. Prepare yourself for travel, we haven't a moment to spare if we want to reach the Darklands by sunset. You don't want to stay in this forest another night, do you?"

Juliane shuddered. "Given the choice, I'd skip it. In fact, I think I'd rather sleep in a bees' hive than spend one more evening in this place."

"Then it's good you're getting up and getting ready now," said Liliana, turning from him to remove the sticks from the tent.

"I know I should be getting ready, so you could be less condescending whilst telling me to do so," he grumbled, and, sticking her tongue out at him, she snatched up her pack, shoved her book into it, and ran out of the tent. He wistfully watched her go, then gathered his own things and hurried to join his friends. Once he had packed the tent in his bag—he discovered that shouting, "Shrink!" at it caused it to return to its smaller size—the party checked the clearing for any items they might have missed and, after ensuring that everything was accounted for, set off into the woods.

The sky was a cloudless blue, the sun so brilliant that its rays filtered through the trees to illuminate the path. When Juliane remarked on how safe and tranquil this part of the forest seemed, Irmene stopped and looked around. "It is nice here, isn't it? It's because Cornemusa holds sway and ensures that those who walk within are free from the threats lurking elsewhere in the forest." Juliane, confused, asked who she was referring to, and she explained that Cornemusa was the wood nymph she had mentioned the night before. "I wonder if we'll run into her today. It would be nice to see Musa—that's what her friends call her, for her name is lengthy but she hates being called 'Corny'—as it's been many moons since I last did."

She requested that her friends continue following her along the path, and the party soon entered a glade filled with trees and flowering bushes. Irmene and Liliana sat at the foot of a large oak and ate some food from Liliana's pack, while Juliane, after grabbing his portion and devouring it, decided to explore the clearing a little. As there were so many beautiful flowers growing there, he determined he would find one to give to Liliana, and so he looked over each blossom until he found the perfect one, a red bloom flecked with purple and gold. He reached out to pluck it, but, as he did, he heard someone say, "I wouldn't do that if I were you. That plant is very particular about its appearance, and it will certainly grow upset should you remove one of its flowers."

Startled, he turned to face whoever had made the recommendation, but found no one beside him. He wondered if Liliana or Irmene had spoken, but they were deep in conversation and were not paying attention to him. Though he searched inside the bushes and behind the trees, he could not find a trace of the one who had spoken to him, so he decided that he had imagined the voice and would try to forget about it. However, when he turned back to the flower, he was disheartened to once more hear the unseen speaker. "If you'd like something pretty, perhaps you'll settle for a colorful leaf that's fallen from a tree? It's almost as beautiful as a blossom, and you won't cause harm to a plant should you choose it instead."

He backed away from the bush and cried, "Who said that? Where are you?"

His friends, noticing his distress, hurriedly joined him, and Liliana asked, "What's the matter, Juliane? Why are you yelling?"

"*Someone* keeps talking to me, but I cannot see them. Some bodiless *thing* keeps telling me that I shouldn't pick flowers."

Liliana started to laugh, for she thought he was jesting, but Irmene, eyes sparkling, said, "Oh, invisible one, take pity on some lowly travelers. We beg of you, show yourself and ease our minds."

"If you insist," replied the voice. "I will reveal myself to you, but, before I do, I shall offer a clue as to my nature: I am fine with being called many things, but you must not, under any circumstances, call me 'Corny'."

"Musa!" shrieked Irmene. "Oh, Cornemusa, you're such a rascal! Now that you've played your trick, come out from wherever you're hiding."

"I just may," the voice replied.

Liliana whispered to Juliane, "Look at that tree! It's...changing." A sizable elm near the bush Juliane had been surveying had started moving, and the travelers watched in amazement as first legs, then arms, then finally a neck and head became visible. A tall, broad, awe-inspiring woman now stood where the tree had been; her skin was the color of bark, her "hair" was a mass of twigs and vines, she was clothed from shoulder to ankle in a garment composed entirely of leaves, and antlers grew from her forehead. She moved toward them and, halting before Juliane, glared down at him from her imposing height. "It's not nice to pluck blossoms from my bushes. It hurts them and makes them upset—and when *they* get upset, *I* get upset."

Juliane stammered, "I'm s-sorry, Cornemusa, I d-didn't know bushes could get upset. I—"

"Do you know what the consequence is for trying to pick flowers in my domain?" she interrupted sternly.

Growing pale, he squeaked, "No."

Cornemusa leaned over him, and he closed his eyes and prayed the punishment she planned on dispensing would not be too severe. She reached out, grabbed hold of his nose, and...proceeded to squeeze it while making a long, loud rude noise.

He opened his eyes to find her smirking at him, and, while Liliana tried stifling her giggles, Irmene howled with laughter. "I told you she was a rascal, didn't I?"

Juliane turned from white to red, and grumbled, "That wasn't very nice."

Cornemusa leaned toward him and, in a voice that might have been meant as a whisper but did not come out as such, said, "If it would help you to feel better, I could take you to the nearest bower and we could dally there awhile." Juliane's eyes widened, and he tried to respond but found no words would come out—he had never been propositioned so boldly. As he gulped like a fish out of water, Cornemusa turned to Irmene. "She's not familiar with what we wood nymphs are like, is she?"

Liliana, feeling brave, said, "I don't believe she is, but I am." Cornemusa trained an appraising eye on her, and, directing her speech at Juliane so that she would not have to look at the formidable being, she explained, "Wood nymphs are minor deities, protectors of forests and the plants and animals that dwell within them. They are known for their love of singing, dancing, and generally making merry, as well as their tendency to mate with those of any gender casually and without care."

"I've changed my mind," said Cornemusa, gazing at her admiringly. "I no longer desire the pop-eyed one, I'd prefer the clever one."

"We don't have time for dalliances now!" exclaimed Irmene. "I need to help these fine folks get to where they're going."

"Oh, Irmene, you're always in such a rush," moaned the wood nymph. "Why don't you all stay with me for a while? It would be such wonderful entertainment."

"Not everyone wants that kind of entertainment, and you know it. Some of us have places to go and things to do."

Cornemusa pouted briefly, then smiled brightly. "Well, if you're set on continuing onward, I suppose I could accompany you to your destination. And, no, I don't have any underlying motives, if that's what you're thinking. Frankly, I'm bored. This patch I take care of is *too* peaceful sometimes, and it would be good to explore other parts of the forest. It would also give me the benefit of spending time with my favorite selkie, which is a grand one indeed."

Grinning, Irmene embraced the wood nymph. "It is wonderful to see you, Musa. It's been too long since last we met." The pair held each other until the selkie remembered the others were still with them and, blushing, said, "I guess it's time for us to be on our way, then."

She grasped the wood nymph's hand, and the reunited immortals, walking together and talking incessantly, moved along the path and into the forest so swiftly that their mortal companions struggled to keep up with them. Eventually Cornemusa glanced back at the stragglers. "Irmene, we are being uncivil to your friends. We've been chatting away and have forgotten all about them!"

She apologized to the travelers, then insisted that the selkie make introductions. "Cornemusa, this is Liliana, and this is Juliane," said Irmene, pointing at each in turn. "They are completing a quest. Along their way they discovered my skin and, rather than keeping it, gave it back to me. They have therefore earned my loyalty and friendship, and I've chosen to assist them in reaching their intended destination."

"And where are you two off to?" asked the wood nymph.

"The Darklands," Liliana replied solemnly.

"The Darklands!" shrieked Cornemusa. "Oh, my dear girls, why would you ever step foot in that place? If I may give a word of advice: you should complete your mission by visiting, well, anywhere else, because, when it comes to the Darklands... Let's just say that it's unwise to go there."

"Your report is only the latest of several unflattering ones that we've received," said Liliana. "Unfortunately, we must travel there regardless, for there's nowhere else we could go and still successfully complete our quest."

"Oh, well, that's too bad. You poor things." Cornemusa clucked her tongue. "There are many reasons why everyone will warn you away from the Darklands, you know."

"We've heard that its king, Korben Darkwood, isn't the most benevolent ruler," Liliana admitted.

"That is indeed the truth," said the wood nymph, "though I remember a time when he was a kindly and charming man. Those days are now, sadly, far in the past."

"What happened to make him as he is now?" asked a curious Juliane, so, as they walked along, Cornemusa told them the king's story.

"Many years ago," began the wood nymph, "King Korben Darkwood ruled the Darklands alongside his wife, the charitable and much-beloved Queen Aliallah. The pair were deeply in love and were very good to their people, and all in the kingdom were happy and content until the queen tragically perished whilst giving birth to the prince, Arthur, twenty-three years ago. The king grieved mightily for his wife, and, try as they might, the citizens of his kingdom could not comfort him. After many years of mourning, he decided he could not spend the rest of his days without her, and so started to search for a means of restoring her to life. Of course, the only effective option of those he had considered was necromancy."

"So that's why he became a necromancer!" Juliane said. "It all makes sense now."

"Don't interrupt," Cornemusa demanded testily, then she continued, "Darkwood tried using many forms of the Dark Arts to bring her back to life, but all his efforts were fruitless. He could revive her, it's true, *but* only in a manner that left her *changed*. Necromancers are quite capable of raising the dead to use as slaves or to control like puppets—that is, they can return them to a sort of half-life—but, though some undead can remember their former lives and retain their personalities, they are not fully *alive*. Korben Darkwood wanted his wife returned to him as a living person, and the means of accomplishing this eluded him."

"As the years passed and his endeavors remained unsuccessful, he became increasingly obsessed with the acquisition of arcane knowledge and began to neglect his kingdom and subjects. The prince, Arthur, tried bringing his father to his senses, but the stubborn man refused to quit his studies and even demanded his son assist him with them. The denizens of his land grew concerned, for he was not maintaining the kingdom properly, but nothing could sway him from his course. Though the people of the Darklands thought this worrisome, they suffered patiently because, at the time, Darkwood was still a benevolent ruler who would reluctantly suspend his investigations to fix problems when hounded to. About five years ago, though, things greatly changed—many say, for the worse."

"What happened?" Juliane asked breathlessly, for he was so caught up in the wood nymph's narrative that he had forgotten her order not to distract her.

Cornemusa cast him a withering glance but went on. "Around that time, King Darkwood once more became involved in the goings-on of his kingdom and began restoring it to its formerly glorious condition. However, the citizens of the Darklands found that the man who had returned to governing more fitly was different from the one they'd once known; he appeared concerned only with the state of his lands and not with that of its people, and he behaved cruelly to those who expressed complaints or spoke out against him. His subjects grew afraid of him, for, though he continued to grow as a sorcerer, he seemed to have ceased searching for a means of reviving his wife and to have instead decided to use his acquired knowledge for evil purposes."

"It is said that, once Darkwood understood that his efforts to return Aliallah to who she once was would forever remain a failure, his heart hardened, and he determined that, if he was to be miserable without her, then all those around him should be miserable as well. Now the Darklands are a feared place, ruled by a tyrant who cares for no one and lives only to obtain power by any means."

She shook her head and, having finished her tale, fell silent. For a moment no one spoke, then Liliana said softly, "What a tragic story. The poor residents of the Darklands— they must live in constant dread of their king."

"Indeed," agreed Juliane, "and yet I cannot help but feel sorry for Darkwood, as his meanness seems borne of great pain. It's a sad state of affairs for all those involved." Recalling that the prince had been mentioned, he asked Cornemusa, "But, what of Arthur Darkwood? Is he as terrible as his father?"

To his relief, she replied, "I don't believe so. He's a quiet young man and appears to serve as a representative of the king. From what I've heard, he's the one who goes out into the kingdom to fix things whilst his father stays locked inside the palace with his experiments. He is said to be civil to those he interacts with. Why do you ask?"

"Well, because, if we *have* to go there, which we unfortunately do, it's good to know that at least one person in the royal family might be kind to us," he replied, trying to sound carefree.

"Are you planning on seeking an audience with the Darkwoods?" Cornemusa asked incredulously. "If you are, you may be sorely disappointed, for not just anyone can demand the king's attention. Besides, even if you do get it, you may not like having it."

Juliane gulped, for he had not considered this, and was grateful when Liliana intervened. "We appreciate your words of warning, Cornemusa, but we must go to the Darklands and make the acquaintance of King Darkwood regardless of what may happen."

"I see," the wood nymph said softly. "Then I hope, for your sake, that all goes well and that you leave the

Darklands unscathed." She seemed uncertain for a moment—as uncertain as anyone of her bearing and godlike standing could seem—then added, "Just make sure not to cross Korben Darkwood, for I've heard he controls an army of the undead and uses them to do his bidding. It would not be a good idea to anger him."

Hearing this, Juliane couldn't help but tremble, and it crossed his mind that having to spend the rest of his life as a woman might not be so bad after all if it meant he could avoid interacting with the fallen king. He was about to voice this when he felt Liliana grasp his hand. "Do not allow yourself to be consumed by fear," she whispered, "for things are often not as they seem. Besides, we know Darkwood's secret: his cruelty and anger stem from his grief. If we keep this in mind, things may turn out better for us than they have for others."

She smiled warmly at him, and he saw no hint of fear in her eyes. *If she can be brave about this, then I can be as well*, he reassured himself, and, squeezing her hand, he jested, "Well, then, I suppose we should continue onward to our doom now." Cornemusa, casting him yet another disdainful look, returned to walking beside Irmene, who had pulled ahead of the others. Juliane sighed, for he hoped that he and Liliana were not being foolhardy, and he took advantage of the opportunity presented to continue holding Liliana's hand as they proceeded down the road toward the Darklands.

28.

The party trudged on for hours, and Juliane started to worry that they might have to spend yet another night in the wood before reaching the Darklands; though he was still frightened of the place he was eager to leave the forest, and so fervently wished to reach their destination, regardless of what a rotten turnip its ruler might be. To his delight, they suddenly stepped out of the forest into a field spotted with flowers, and Irmene crowed, "We're almost there! I've successfully led you to the westernmost border of the Darklands. After we've crossed this patch, you'll be right where you want to be."

She grinned at Juliane, and he couldn't help but return it. Despite all the terrible things he had heard about Darkwood, he was glad to finally be reaching his kingdom, for it meant he would soon be facing the object of his quest. He even whistled a little as they walked along, for he was cheerful at the thought of returning home to his parents and, hopefully, introducing them to someone who had grown very dear to him. He looked over at Liliana, who seemed to be deep in her own thoughts, and resolved to tell her all that was on his mind once they had crossed the border. Others might fear the Darklands, but he found himself looking forward to reaching it due to the good things he hoped would happen while he was there.

The path they were on climbed upward as the field

turned into a gently sloping hill, and before long the band had reached its summit. Juliane peered downward, and his whistling abruptly ceased when he saw what awaited them in the valley below. The path wound down the hill and across another field, but, beyond that, a great abyss scarred the land; it seemed to be miles across, and, try as he might, he could not spy a means of getting over or around it. "We have to get past *that*?" he asked, and, when Irmene responded in the affirmative, he paled. "How? There doesn't seem to be a way across."

"You're right, it's a curious thing," the selkie replied. "There should be a bridge there. I wonder why we cannot see it."

The party ran down the hill and across the field to the divide, and, upon arriving at it, discovered the reason for the bridge's absence—the structure that had once spanned the rift now rested at its bottom. "What do we do?" moaned Juliane. "That was our only means of crossing."

Liliana retreated from the edge of the ravine, sat upon the ground, and closed her eyes. "I could create a bridge using magic, but I'm worried that, should I make a mistake or the spell not very last long, we'd be plunged into the pit." Opening them, she feebly admitted, "I'm not afraid of many things, but I've never been very good with heights."

Cornemusa had been watching the others, amused, and decided it was time to intervene. "Why are you distressing yourselves? I mean, you do remember that you have a wood nymph in your company, right?" The others turned to goggle at her, and she continued, "I can request help from plants and animals alike should I require it. I'll make sure you can cross."

She placed her hands together and closed her eyes, and her companions gasped as her body began to issue a brilliant green light. Her eyelids flew open, revealing glowing green orbs, and, releasing a cry, she ran to the brink of the abyss and pounded her fists upon the ground.

Two thick vines shot up out of the earth, flew across the rift, and landed on the other side, where they burrowed into the ground and up out of it and then tied themselves into a terrific knot. Next, thinner tendrils sprang from the dirt, winding themselves over the larger vines until they formed a lattice full across their lengths. Finally, countless smaller vines twisted upward over the structure, surrounding it with a protective cage. A sturdy-looking bridge composed entirely of greenery now covered the rift, and Cornemusa, exiting her trance, surveyed the results of her labor. "That's not too bad, if I may be so bold as to say so."

"Oh, Musa, it's wonderful! It's just what they need!" said Irmene, beaming, then she turned to the travelers, and her smile softened. "Now that you have a safe means of crossing, I guess it's time for you to head to the other side, and for us to say our farewells. I will miss you both greatly, for you've shown me a kindness I'd never received from other humans. I'll always be thankful for the time we've spent together." Her eyes glistened with tears, and Juliane and Liliana both rushed to her and clasped her.

Irmene withdrew from the hug first, leaving Liliana and Juliane still holding each other; they parted hastily, and stood staring awkwardly at the ground until the selkie said, "Juliane, do you still have my whistle?" He pulled it from his neckline in response to her query, and she asked him to remove it and return it to her. Though reluctant to do so he did as she requested, but his spirits lifted when she placed a curved shell in his hand. "I cannot allow you to keep my whistle, as it will only summon me once," she explained. "This shell, however, can be used to call to me from the beach near Pultare. I will hear it if I'm nearby and, if so, will join you so that we may once more revel in our friendship."

Juliane, eyes misting, threw his arms around her, and she pulled him close to her. "Make sure you take care of yourself, and that you let Liliana know how you feel," she whispered. "I see the beauty in you, Juliane, and I think she does too. Keep showing it to her every day and she's sure to one day be fond of you...like I am fond of Cornemusa. She may be a rascal, and I may not see her as often as I'd like, but she nonetheless holds a special place in my heart. Remember when I told you that I know desire when I see it? Well, it's because I know from personal experience."

She released him, leaving him wide-eyed and speechless, and, when she began to laugh heartily, he couldn't help but join her. Cornemusa curtailed their merriment by reminding them that the travelers needed to make haste across the bridge, as she did not want the plants strained for too long, so, after each had once more embraced Irmene and had thanked the wood nymph for her assistance, they made their way to the intricate mass of greenery that they hoped would bring them safely across the rift.

Once they had stepped on the bridge and had walked a few paces, Liliana found herself frozen to the spot. "I cannot move, I'm so afraid of taking a false step and plunging through the vines into the void below. I'm not sure how to make myself go forward. I'm sorry, Juliane, I—"

"You needn't worry about your fear keeping you from crossing," he gently interrupted, "for you needn't look where you're going to cross. Will you...allow me to help you?"

He held his hands out to her, and she took hold of them and closed her eyes. He turned and, pulling her close to him, placed her arms around his waist. "I promise I'm not trying to be overly friendly. I just want to keep you near me to ensure your safety."

"I know," she said, giving him a squeeze. "I trust you,

Juliane."

He trudged forward, making sure that both her feet and his own landed squarely on slats of greenery with each step they took. It was a treacherous course, and he several times feared the bridge was really a nightmare they would be forced to cross for all eternity. To his relief, after what seemed like ages they finally came to its end, and they rushed off it and collapsed onto the soft grass on the other side.

As they lay panting on the ground, they felt a great rumbling, and they watched in amazement as the plants disentangled themselves and withdrew to the other side of the chasm. The bridge was unmade as swiftly as it had been constructed, and soon no trace of it remained. Her role in the proceedings finished, Cornemusa waved once before heading back toward the forest, and, after yelling some words of encouragement to them, Irmene followed her into the woods.

The travelers at first just sat and stared at one another, for each scarcely believed they had finally reached their intended destination, then Liliana got up to check the sign posted near the path behind them: *You have reached the formal border of the Darklands. Enter at your own peril.* Suppressing a shudder, she turned to Juliane. "We've arrived at the place we've been hoping to reach, so I suppose we must now cross into it."

She went to him and, reaching down, offered him her hands; he grasped them, and she helped him to his feet. He walked over to the sign and, once he had read it, said, "I guess I'm as ready to enter it as I'll ever be." He started off down the path, Liliana falling into step beside him. "I've got a prince to beguile, and I might as well get it over with."

***

The travelers found that, to their relief, the route into

the Darklands was easy to follow, for the road was well-maintained and each path that branched from it was marked with a destination. Juliane had no doubt that the main road would eventually bring them to Darkwood's castle, and, though the sky had changed from a cloudless blue to a soft violet, he was not afraid of being stuck on the path overnight, for he knew they were likely to find lodgings should they require them.

After walking for several minutes, they came upon a landscape of rolling hills dotted with neat cottages and, for the first time, encountered residents of the land, who greeted them in a cordial but hesitant manner. Juliane was unsure whether he felt comforted or annoyed by the number of people they were meeting along their way, for, on the one hand, it was unlikely they would come across any monsters in such a populated area, but, on the other, their frequently running into the citizenry was denying him the opportunity to speak with Liliana privately.

Luck was on his side, though, for the path soon entered a secluded wooded region. Believing that this might be the only time alone they would share before reaching Darkwood, he decided to seize the moment. "Liliana, now that it's just the two of us, I have something I would like to talk with you about. I wanted to let you know I—"

"I know what you're going to say, Juliane. You're going to tell me you've begun developing desires for me that aren't purely physical, feelings of a romantic nature that could grow into love should they be properly cultivated. I can guess this is the case because, well...because I'm harboring similar feelings for you."

"Why can't I ever tell you things without being interrupt—" He stopped speaking and, as the meaning of her words sunk in, he turned to her, gaping, but she would not look at him and continued striding along purposefully. "Don't walk away, Liliana. Please, talk to me," he implored her, but she would not stop and reminded him that they must keep going if they were to reach their destination before nightfall. Frustrated, he picked up his pace and, stepping in front of her, planted himself in her path. "I know trying to halt you like this hasn't worked in the past, but, now that you've admitted that you feel for me as I do for you, you might be more willing to yield to this intervention!"

He was surprised and discouraged to find that, though she finally stopped to speak with him, she seemed hesitant to do so. "Here I am, Juliane. I'm not sure what else you would like to happen, but I think it would be unwise for us to tarry here long."

"You're not sure what else I would like to happen? Why, I'd like to embrace you and dance joyfully with you through these woods! I've waited many days to tell you how I feel—how I desire you not just in the way I did before, but in a way that I believe could become something much more. I'm overjoyed that you may feel the same." Blushing, he went on, "I've been considering what I hope might happen after we've returned to my kingdom once my curse is broken, and I think that...if you're open to it...I would like for us to continue spending time together so that we might determine if the attraction we share is...one suitable for marriage."

Cheeks burning, he searched her face, and was relieved when her expression softened. "Oh, Juliane, you truly have changed so much. I don't think the old Prince Julian would ever have been able to admit he was growing enamored with someone. It's true that I care deeply for you...but I cannot make any promises about our having a future together once this journey has come to an end."

His face fell, and she hurriedly assured him, "It's not that I fear you'll return to your old ways once we've reached home, it's just that—well, you *will* be different from how you are now in at least one way, and I'm not sure if the feelings I have for you are only for the person you are currently. I was attracted to you as Prince Julian, but was unsure if I could ever feel something more than physical for you...and, though I *do* feel something more for you as you are now, I don't know if I still will once you've regained your male form. I wonder if I might be developing an adoration only for the woman you've become, a woman who'll no longer exist once you've completed your quest, rather than for the man you have been and will be again. If that's the case, it would be unfair of me to commit to anything beyond our just spending time together and seeing how things transpire. I apologize if this isn't what you wanted to hear from me."

Juliane's face crumpled, and Liliana took hold of his hands. "Dear Juliane, do not let this pain you. I'm not claiming that I could never love you as Prince Julian, I'm just telling you that I still need to figure out whether I'm capable of—"

"Please, don't say anything else," he softly interrupted. "I do not need for you to further explain why you feel as you do, I do not want you to offer me reassurances that could prove false, and I certainly do not wish for you to pity me. I'd planned on telling you about my feelings for quite some time and knew I must speak my mind regardless of how you might react, so do not trouble yourself—I was aware you might respond in this manner and took the risk. I understand you have your doubts, and I respect your dealing with them in the way you see fit." He wiped his eyes with the back of his hand, shifted his pack, and, trying to sound merry, said, "You're right, by the way. We really should keep moving if we want to reach Darkwood's castle by nightfall."

He stalked forward on the path, and, as she watched him go, she questioned if she had done the right thing, for she knew that fear of her burgeoning affection for him had fueled her disclosure. A part of her wondered if her concerns were baseless, if she was allowing them to control her and to curb the development of a meaningful connection, but another part worried that, if she offered him unblemished hope despite her misgivings, she might cause him greater pain should she end up turning from him. When she realized that letting the conversation end on this note would likely wound him most of all, she called out his name and ran after him. Startled, he turned to find her rushing toward him; reaching him, she threw her arms around him. "I'm so sorry, Juliane," she said. "I shouldn't have spoken so rashly."

"It's all right. I understand you might not feel the way that I do, and that's fine."

"But you *don't* understand. I think I *do* feel the way that you do, but...I'm afraid." She let him go, and his heart started racing as she looked into his eyes. "I have never experienced an attraction quite like this, one that seems so much more than just purely physical. I'd believed something like it might blossom between Tancred and I—and, I must confess, I still hold fondness for them and wonder what might have been—but I find that I've certainly developed it for you, and it frightens me. I need time to figure out my feelings, to grow comfortable with them. Can you...give me that time?"

He paused for a moment, then, smiling shyly, replied, "Of course I can. I'm still a bit afraid of all this myself—it's strange to desire more than just an affair!" He lowered his head, for her gaze discomfited him. "But, although I'm unnerved by my feelings for you sometimes, I believe that they're real, and could grow into a lasting romance if properly cared for. I will gladly give you the time you need to search your soul, because I know that, once you do, you'll discover that your feelings are surely as authentic as mine."

He lifted his face and was thrilled to find her grinning at him in a way that made his heart sing. "Oh, Juliane, thank you for listening and taking the time to understand me, even though what I meant to say came out all wrong at first. You make it so much easier to believe in the truth of my feelings...and in what they could become." She clasped him and leaned forward, and he understood, with a thrill, that she intended to kiss him. Deciding that it would be worth waiting for her verdict on her emotions should she still deign to give him attention of this sort on occasion, he closed his eyes and waited for the moment their lips would meet.

His delicious anticipation was rudely curtailed by the sound of approaching feet, and he heard someone say, "You there! Who are you, and what brings you to the Darklands?"

Liliana released him, and, feeling surly that yet another pleasant moment with her had been foiled, he opened his eyes and yelled at the interlopers, "Confound it all, why are you disturbing us?" He immediately regretted his actions, though, for he found he had scolded four men wearing leather armor and bronze helmets; two of them carried pikes, the others had bows, and all wore swords on belts around their waists. They appeared to be a band of well-trained guardsmen—and all were pointing their weapons at the travelers.

Juliane gulped as he understood that this was not just another vexatious interruption, and, trying to think of something helpful to say, he blurted the first thing that came to mind: "We're merely travelers to your land and mean you no harm. In fact, we were just about to leave, so we'll be on our way."

He started back down the path but only managed a few steps before Liliana grabbed him and pulled him back toward her. "What are you doing?" she hissed. He tried telling her that he had a plan, that they could pretend they were departing the kingdom and camp somewhere along a side path until the threat had passed, but, despite his best intentions, his response came out as incoherent babbling.

269

She rolled her eyes and, continuing to keep ahold of him, addressed the guardsmen. "My friend and I have traveled from afar to seek an audience with Korben Darkwood. We wish to be brought to him, so that we might explain the cause for our visit and hold congress with him."

"What exactly *are* we going to claim is the cause for our visit?" whispered Juliane, but, when Liliana cast him a stern look, he understood it would be best to discuss the details when they were not being menaced.

The men talked among themselves awhile, and, after they seemed to have reached a verdict, the elder of the pike-wielding guardsmen approached the travelers and asked, "You're hoping to meet with King Darkwood?" When they acknowledged that they were, he said, "Then you'd better come with us. You can join us of your own volition, or we can use force to make you. It's your choice."

Juliane murmured, "I think we should go with them willingly. I'd like to get to Darkwood's castle in one piece." Liliana agreed, and she let the man know that they would accompany the guards of their own accord. He rejoined his companions and ordered the travelers to enter their midst; once they had, the unit proceeded forward along the path. The prisoners hurried to keep pace with their captors, and Juliane, trying to remain hopeful, told Liliana, "Well, we can at least be positive about one thing: we will certainly reach King Darkwood, for these fellows surely know where he is."

29.

The party walked along in silence, until Juliane broke it to ask if they would be taken to Darkwood as requested. The elder pike-wielder, who appeared to be the leader of the unit, sneered at him. "If I were you, I wouldn't be so eager to make the acquaintance of King Darkwood. In my experience and the experience of my fellows, he is not a pleasant person to be around."

"We've heard much of his stern nature, but still must meet with him," said Juliane. "Hopefully he isn't as disagreeable as he's rumored to be."

"'Stern?' 'Disagreeable?' Oh, these are but mild words to use when describing Korben Darkwood," spat the guardsman. "I myself would use ones like 'terrifying,' 'loathsome,' and 'abominable,' as they all fit him quite well. Wouldn't you agree, men?" he asked his comrades, who all nodded hastily.

"But, if you feel that way, then why work for him? It surprises me that you'd do the bidding of someone you dislike so intensely."

"My dear girl, we have no choice," replied the man. "Korben Darkwood isn't someone you say 'no' to—not unless you desire losing your life or sanity." He hesitated, then said, "I'm not sure whether I should tell you more, for I'm afraid of Darkwood and therefore try not to speak ill of him, but I think you should know what you're heading into.

Does anyone else want to speak, or shall I?" He turned to his companions, and, with their encouragement, went on.

"My name is Richard Ward, and I've been Darkwood's Captain of the Watch for many years; I served of my own accord for most of them, but for the past few have done so begrudgingly. I once considered the king both my ruler and friend, but now..." He shrugged his shoulders. "Korben Darkwood has been obsessed with necromancy for more than a score of years, ever since his wife died whilst giving birth to their son. For a while he sought a means of fully restoring her to life, but he appeared to give up on this mission around the time he became the tyrant he presently is, about five years ago. It seems that, once he'd determined that it was futile to try and bring her back 'whole,' he decided to instead use his arcane knowledge to create fear and pain, so that he might bend his subjects to his will."

He sighed. "We have all functioned as his slaves ever since. We do as he tells us, for we're afraid of what might happen should we not. Those who've crossed him have either disappeared or have been found raving in the streets, claiming they'd been tormented by unspeakable nightmares. Only those who have been targeted know for certain—and they aren't available to speak with or are no longer capable of speaking sensibly—but it's suspected that Darkwood controls a horde of creatures he has resurrected from the grave and that he uses them to intimidate, madden, or kill people he dislikes. Because of this we live our lives in fear, and dream of the day when he passes and his son, who seems a decent man, takes over his throne. Until then, we must follow his orders to keep ourselves safe—which is why, when we arrive in Darkton, where the castle is located, we must bring you to the dungeon."

"The dungeon?" Juliane said incredulously. "But we've demanded a meeting with Darkwood! We're distinguished visitors—we shouldn't be imprisoned like common ruffians!"

"Weren't you listening to a word I spoke?" Ward asked harshly. "Refusing the king's commands means risking life and limb! I'm sure you're just as important as you claim to be, but we must treat you as we would anyone else to ensure our safety, and that means you must be confined until Darkwood determines what he'd like done with you. It's the law, and we must follow it."

Juliane moved to utter additional protests, but Liliana stayed him. "Your pleas won't sway these men, for it's obvious they're terrified of their ruler. I think it'd be best if you saved your energy. Once we're imprisoned, we can try to figure out a means of escape." Understanding that she had a point, Juliane reluctantly ceased his objections, but still mumbled under his breath as the party continued onward to Darkton.

Darkness fell, and the guardsmen lit torches and held them aloft so the party could see the road before them. Soon the travelers noticed a light shining through the trees and, exiting the forest, found themselves in front of an immense wooden gate flanked by blazing torches and set into a seemingly endless stone wall. When the Captain strode up to it and knocked upon it, an opening appeared in its surface and a pair of eyes glared out at them suspiciously. "Who goes there, and what business have ye?" demanded the gatekeeper.

"It's Richard Ward, Captain of the Watch. We've returned from our inspection of the main thoroughfare earlier than expected, for we've discovered intruders who desire a meeting with the king." The eyes disappeared from the window, and the massive portal slowly creaked open. The guardsmen ushered their captives through the gateway, and the apprehensive travelers looked first at each other, then at what lay ahead of them. Before them was the most coldly beautiful city either had ever set eyes on, comprised of elaborate shops, houses, and passageways constructed of a strange blue stone that seemed to glow softly in the moonlight.

At the center of this metropolis stood a tall, twisted palace topped with tapering towers that loomed over the other buildings. "The dungeon can be found within the cellar of that castle—which is, if you yet hadn't guessed it, the dwelling of King Darkwood," Richard Ward said. "We shall take you there forthwith." The party proceeded along the winding streets, each step bringing them closer to the foreboding structure. Juliane noticed many of the town's citizens peering at them as they passed by; several shook their heads sadly, and he felt a knot tighten in his stomach as he realized that they likely believed he and Liliana might never return from the place they were being led to.

After countless turns they came to a weathered door set in stone, and, pulling a key from his pocket, the Captain of the Watch unlocked and opened it. Once the travelers had been pushed through the doorway, the party proceeded down an interminably long corridor until they came to yet another door. Richard Ward knocked on it, and it was opened by a plump, lofty man wearing a brown smock and carrying a sizable ring of keys. "Ah, Master Ward!" he said. "I wasn't expecting you, but it's nonetheless a pleasure to see you. For what reason am I honored with your visit?"

"The Watch found these strangers wandering the main path to the city," replied the Captain. "I have brought them to you so that you might keep them here until I've asked King Darkwood what he would like done with them. I'm loath to do this, but it's what the king has requested and, as you know—"

"We don't go against the king's orders," the jailer finished his sentence. "Believe me, I'm quite aware of what might happen if we do. Oh well, I suppose they'd better come with me."

He bade the travelers enter and, once they had, Ward told them, "I shall speak to the King right away and return once I have been given an answer." He rejoined the other guards, and the band swiftly retreated down the passageway.

The jailer closed the door, then turned to the travelers. "I'm sorry, my dears, but I'm going to put you in a cell now. I'll try to find the best I have, but, as it's a dungeon, there are none too fancy, I'm afraid. Darkwood's rules must be followed, unfortunately. I do hope you aren't too cross."

Liliana had considered taking the man by force, but, as he seemed as downtrodden as the guardsmen, instead took pity upon him. "We understand, Master, um..."

"Henry, my name's Henry," said the jailer. "You don't have to call me 'Master' anything, just call me 'Henry'. I used to be a baker, now I'm keeper of this dungeon because we no longer need many sweets, as we don't have much to celebrate these days." He grimaced, then apologized. "I'm sorry, I talk too much. I'm guessing you've already gathered we're none too happy in Darkton, so I needn't say more and make your lot seem even worse." He led them down a hallway surrounded on both sides by empty cells. "Most of these aren't occupied, for I don't get many prisoners to mind nowadays," he explained. "King Darkwood has his own way of dealing with those who upset him, I'm afraid. It's said he uses monsters to—" He stopped himself, shaking his head. "There I go talking too much again."

He halted before a sizable cell containing two mattresses and some sconces that filled it with a soft light. "I think I'll put you here. It's large and clean, and it's also right near the old man—it'll be good for him to have company, for he often seems sad and lonely. Hopefully you won't have to stay in here long, though." He opened the barred gate and ushered them into the cell, then locked the door behind them. "I'll go see if I can fetch some victuals for you. I'll return as quickly as I can." He offered them an apologetic smile, then headed off down the hallway, disappearing from view.

Juliane threw himself onto the cell floor, groaning. "What rotten luck! It seems Darkwood's as much of a brute as he's been made out to be. I wouldn't be surprised if he keeps us here until we've gone mad."

Liliana sat down next to him and tried to offer him some encouragement. "Don't despair just yet, for at least our dungeon keeper seems kind and will likely take proper care of us. I suppose it could be worse."

"Oh, it most definitely could be worse," a voice interjected. "Being in the dungeon is no great pleasure, but I believe it's a better option than being anywhere near that vicious Korben Darkwood. If I were you, I'd pray he decides to keep you down here, because then at least you're safe from the likes of him."

"Who said that?" asked Liliana, standing up and looking around.

"I did. I'm the old man the jailer mentioned. I'm in the cell across from yours."

Juliane rose to his feet to join her, and the pair squinted out into the dimly lit passage. Once their eyes had adjusted to the gloom, they discovered a short, rotund, mustachioed man with gray hair sitting in the cell opposite theirs. He was surrounded by piles of material, and a large loom stood at the rear of his chamber. "Greetings to you two," he called, waving at them. "I'm sorry you're in the same predicament I am, but I'm pleased to inform you that, though you may be stuck here a while, it's not all bad. The mattresses are comfortable enough, the food is passable, and our gracious jailer Henry is willing to smuggle in nice things whenever he can manage to. It's not much, but I hope it's some sort of a consolation."

"You mentioned we may be stuck here a while," said Liliana. "Have you yourself been here long?"

"Aye, for quite some time now," the old fellow replied

276

glumly. "I cannot be sure exactly how many days have passed, for it's difficult to mark time here, but I believe it has been years since I last saw the sun. When Darkwood himself places you in this dungeon, it's because he intends to keep you available to him for as long as he wants you."

"You've been trapped in this place for years? How awful!" cried Juliane. "For what reason does he keep you here?"

"He desires something from me, and I haven't yet given him it," the man replied. His eyes twinkled, and a mischievous grin spread over his kindly face. "He thinks I am unable to make it for him, but the truth is that I choose not to."

"But, why? If you give him what he wants, won't he release you? Why not give in to his demands if doing so might grant you your freedom?"

"Because I'm unsure that giving him what he wants would result in his letting me leave. I'm afraid that, once he has it, he might just destroy me like he has so many others." The old man paled. "He has been known to make people disappear, and I fear he might do the same to me once I've provided him with what he's seeking. So, I keep pretending that I cannot fulfill his request, and, though doing so leaves me stuck in this dungeon, his still requiring something from me keeps me safe."

"What is it that he needs from you?" asked Liliana, for she was curious as to what a sorcerer as powerful as Korben Darkwood might require of this unassuming aged fellow.

"He wants me to make him a special carpet. He says he needs it for some rituals, and I fear that, were I to give it to him, he would use it to do dreadful things. So, each time the guards check on me, I tell them I've not yet gotten the design quite right, and they report this to him, and he leaves me be a few more weeks. It's not the most pleasant existence, but at least I'm out of harm's way for now."

The travelers gaped at each other, for both had suddenly recognized the man, and they cried out in unison, "You're Wilbur Crestshorn!"

"I am, indeed," he admitted, perplexed. He asked for their names and, once he had been given them, said, "Since you're both strangers to me, how do you know who I am?"

"We've met your wife Rose!" said Juliane. "We stopped at her inn one night on our way here. Once she'd grown comfortable with us, she told us how you'd disappeared after leaving for a meeting with Darkwood. She still misses you terribly and hopes you'll soon come home."

"Oh, Rosie, my Rose, my adored wife." Wilbur Crestshorn's eyes filled with tears. "I'd feared my lovely Rose would have given up on waiting for me after all these years, and hearing that she still dreams of my homecoming brings me both joy and sorrow. My greatest wish is that I might return to her, but I fear it will never be granted. I'm afraid the only fate in store for me is to spend the rest of my days rotting in this cell whilst the king awaits the creation of a rug that shall never be."

"Don't give up just yet, Master Crestshorn," Liliana said gently. "We're hoping to have an audience with King Darkwood and, if we do manage to speak with him, will advocate for your release. Perhaps we can convince him to let you accompany us when we leave the Darklands?"

"That's a marvelous notion, but not a very probable one." The man sighed. "The king won't just let me go after all my years of disappointing him because some pretty girls have asked him to; this may work with others but is unlikely to work with him. Also, you must remember that he may decide not to meet with you and may leave you down here like he has me. It's not good to allow oneself to be too hopeful regarding dealings with Korben Darkwood."

Liliana was about to respond when they heard footsteps approaching; they waited for the jailer to appear and were surprised when instead Richard Ward came into view. "You two are in luck," he told the travelers. "I have told King Darkwood of you and he's very interested in meeting you. I shall have Henry release you and you'll come with me straight away."

Before long the jailer returned with some bread and cheese, and, once he had heard the Captain's news, he unlocked the cell, freeing the travelers. He handed them the food, which they gobbled gratefully, then Master Ward grasped each firmly by an arm and led them through a doorway to an ascending flight of stairs. "We'll be sure to discuss your plight with the king!" Juliane called out to Wilbur Crestshorn, and he prayed the old man had heard him as he and Liliana were dragged up the staircase.

After climbing countless steps, the exhausted travelers came to a door, and the Captain opened it and ushered them into a hallway lined with doors and decorated with tapestries bearing arcane symbols. He brought them to the end of the corridor, where a set of large double doors stood before them. "This is the entrance to the throne room," said Richard Ward. "King Darkwood wishes to speak with you alone."

He released them, then stepped back and, arms crossed, waited for them to enter the chamber. Liliana glanced over at Juliane, who was white with fear, and whispered, "Allow me to do the talking." He nodded, and, taking a deep breath, she grasped the right door's handle and pushed it open.

30.

Juliane grabbed Liliana's free hand as the massive door swung inward, and she gave him a squeeze as they stepped through the doorway into a sizable chamber featuring statues of menacing gods they did not recognize: a horned monstrosity with jagged teeth and cloven hooves; a viscous mass with a dozen eyes; a winged marine creature with a mass of feelers upon its face. The room contained no other furnishings except a fireplace and two thrones carved from the same glowing stone that comprised most of Darkton's buildings. One was unoccupied, but upon the other was seated a person so imposing that the travelers could not help but quake under his gaze.

He was clothed from neck to foot in robes of red and black velvet that engulfed his gaunt frame, and had a thin angular face, a head of dark hair, a coarse black beard that fell to his chest, and pale grayish skin. His hands were bony and spider-like, each finger tipped with a nail that could only be described as a talon, and his green eyes glowed with malign power. The thought crossed Juliane's mind that, if this man's son was anything like him, it would be difficult to pretend to fall in love with him, for the menacing figure before them was surely the king they had been seeking, the dread Korben Darkwood.

They cowered before him, and a knowing smile played over his lips. "Why are you so frightened, young ladies?" he asked, his voice reminiscent of grating hinges. "I'm sure you've heard much about me, but, though it's true I can be a stern ruler, I am not unreasonable and will not smite you without cause. Of course, I do wish to know who you are and why you've come to my domain, and not providing me with an answer could be seen as a slight..."

He trailed off, chuckling mirthlessly, and Liliana, gathering her courage, said, "My Lord, my name is Liliana Alm...shire, and my friend is Juliane Stone...wick. We are noblewomen from the kingdom bordering your own and have traveled for nigh on two weeks to get here."

She paused, unsure of what else to say, and King Darkwood told her, "While I'm flattered that you've gone to such great lengths to reach my realm, I'm still uncertain as to why you've come. You will now enlighten me as to the cause for your visit—that is, unless you'd rather spend some more time in the dungeon, perhaps each in your own cell? I've heard one can sometimes more adequately gather one's thoughts when kept in darkness and solitude."

Liliana frantically searched her brain for a reasonable-sounding explanation and, catching on one, said, "My Lord, we had heard that you have a son of marriageable age. As Juliane has been seeking a husband, and as there are so few eligible men where we live, when she found out about the prince she decided to travel to your land in hopes of making his acquaintance. As she and I have been friends since girlhood and I'm more versed in the ways of the world than she, I accompanied her to ensure she did not meet with harm along her way."

She cast a stern look at Juliane, who had opened his mouth to protest, and he instead managed a weak smile and simpered, "I do so look forward to getting to know him."

Korben Darkwood stared at the pair, then burst into thunderous laughter. Confused, Liliana asked, "My Lord, what causes you such amusement?"

The king ceased his roaring and replied, "I'm entertained by the idea that you would embark upon such a treacherous journey just to meet my son! It seems you know nothing of him, and, though you may know something of me, it's likely none of it is good. Your traveling here could have resulted in your being felled by any one of several dreadful creatures along the way, and you faced the possibility of being thrown into my dungeon even if you did arrive safely. You are either very brave or incredibly foolish to have taken the risk."

He continued, a thoughtful expression upon his ashen face, "It's true there are few maidens near Arthur's age within our domain, and fewer still of noble blood. I hadn't thought about whether he desired to marry—after all, I am his father, and I think that, in some ways, I still view him as a child—but, now that you've presented the idea to me, I see it's only right that he be given the opportunity to make the acquaintance of suitable prospective wives. He helps me with my business in myriad ways, allowing me to focus on my researches whilst he cares for my subjects, and...I suppose I've been selfish these many years, for I've never before considered that he might desire a love similar to the one his mother and I once shared."

Rising in his seat, he pulled on a cord dangling near his left hand. A tone sounded in the hallway, and Richard Ward entered the throne room and, bowing before the king, asked how he might be of service. "Go tell my son that we have visitors who request an audience with him, and that he should come to the throne room forthwith," said King Darkwood. "Before you leave the palace—for you're free to return to your watch after this—let the steward know we have two guests who will be staying with us for an indeterminate amount of time, and that he should prepare suitable quarters for them." The Captain of the Watch assured the king that his requests would be carried out immediately, then swiftly left the room.

While the men were speaking, Juliane slunk over to Liliana and hissed, "Why did you say that I'm looking to marry the prince? You know I'm merely trying to get him smitten enough with me that a lock of his hair will end my curse. What if he starts pressing me to wed him before he's developed romantic feelings for me? You know my parents were going to force me to marry someone I didn't love—what if his father expects the same of him?"

"You'll just have to tell him that you're not yet ready if he asks for your hand earlier than expected. Say you must be sure he truly cares about you before you pledge yourself to him. Blame your behavior on the fickle whims of women—goddess knows they've been blamed for everything else," she whispered back, a smirk lifting the corner of her mouth. "Besides, how else did you think you might get close to the prince? You're going to have to woo him if you want him to fall in love with you, there's no way around that."

He shrugged, admitted she was right, and was about to say more when the pair were startled by the sound of the door slamming shut. They turned to find the king staring at them, and, when he was sure he had their attention, he announced that his son would be with them shortly and that they might talk among themselves while waiting for him. Having Darkwood's eyes upon them made them reluctant to continue their discussion, though, so they stood in silence until one of the doors swung open, and the man they had been waiting for entered the room.

When Arthur Darkwood stepped into view Juliane almost sighed in relief, for the man was so different from his father in both appearance and demeanor that, had he not known they were related, he would never have guessed so. The prince was pale and thin like the king, but his skin was milky rather than ashen, his build willowy instead of bony. He wore a dark green tunic, black trousers, leather boots, and a black and green silk cloak. His dark brown hair fell thick and lustrous to his shoulders, his features were noble but displayed no trace of haughtiness, and his face was youthful and free of blemish. His deep brown eyes seemed to sparkle, and his face conveyed a warmth that put Juliane at ease. *He's almost as pretty a man as I was. Having to pretend to be enamored with him shan't be as much of a chore as I'd expected*, he told himself, then was immediately ashamed at having had the thought.

Prince Darkwood bypassed the travelers to clamber onto the empty throne. "Well, Father, why have you summoned me?" he said blithely. "I gather it has something to do with the pair standing before me."

Korben Darkwood seemed to have been resting, and he fluttered his eyes open to glare at his son, who was leaning back in his chair and grinning. "You don't have to be so frivolous," he scolded. "I've called you to me so that you might meet some guests who will be staying with us a while. The tall red-haired one is Liliana and the one with brown hair is Juliane. They are noblewomen from the neighboring kingdom, and they've come to make your acquaintance in hopes of your finding one of them a suitable marriage prospect."

Liliana moved to clarify that only Juliane was seeking to wed the prince, but the king cast her a withering look that made her mouth dry up and her lips snap shut. Prince Arthur stared at the travelers, then rose from his seat to make his way over to them. "Is my father speaking the truth? Have you both come to court me? If so, then I'm truly a very lucky man."

Finding her voice, Liliana said, "My Lord, to be honest, only Juliane came with the intent to create an alliance with you. I merely accompanied her on her journey to ensure her safety, as my family isn't wealthy enough that I would consider vying for the hand of a prince."

"That's a terrible shame," he replied, "for you're both so

lovely. At least I shan't have the burden of choosing between you, then! Although," he added, "if I wanted, I could pick whomever I liked best, as I shall inherit enough wealth that it would be of no concern to me even if my intended were but a pauper. I'm one of those fools who seeks to marry for love rather than money, you see, and so might easily fall for either of you."

Liliana blushed and started to stammer, so Juliane, hoping to come to her rescue, stepped in front of her. "My Lord, will you also give me a chance to speak? You may find that, if you do, I shall prove myself a more than capable conversationalist."

It was Arthur Darkwood's turn to flush. "I'm dreadfully sorry—as I'd mentioned, I am hopeless when it comes to romance, and I can scarcely believe that such accomplished women have traveled so far in hopes of wooing me! I am truly honored, and promise you that, in the days to come, I will allot you all the attention you deserve."

He turned to address King Darkwood, but, as the elder man appeared to be dozing, he turned back to the travelers and whispered, "My silly old father has fallen asleep! I pray you don't take offense at his behavior—he's a stubborn old goat who spends more nights than he should attempting unfeasible feats of magic, so he frequently slumbers at inopportune times." He went over to the king and leaned toward his ear. "Goodnight, Father. Please go to your bedchamber, for you know sleeping in your chair always makes your bones ache on the morrow."

Returning to the travelers, he said, "I guess it's up to me to guide you to your quarters, then. I think I shall give you something of a grand tour along the way! Please, follow me." He headed toward the double doors and his guests hastily followed him, for neither desired to spend a minute more in the discomfiting presence of Korben Darkwood.

Prince Arthur led them into the corridor, where he spent

time explaining what lay beyond each of the six other doorways therein. "This hall is the center of the castle, and behind each of these portals is a 'spoke' of rooms that branches from it. This stairway leads to the kitchen and scullery." He opened the left-hand door nearest the chamber they had just left. "If you need anything to eat during your stay with us, feel free to visit downstairs and our kitchen help will provide you with sustenance." He closed this door and opened the one next to it, and the travelers gasped in delight, for before them lay a cheerful dining room featuring a large table bedecked with delightful dishes. "Are you hungry? Would you care to eat something whilst we finish our tour?" the prince asked, and both eagerly nodded, then invaded the room and piled plates high with tarts, cheeses, and other delicacies.

They carried their spoils back into the hallway, and happily consumed them while Prince Darkwood provided them with additional information. He crossed to the right side of the hall and, after informing them that these three doorways led to passageways lined with bedchambers, opened the door furthest from the throne room. He requested that they follow him down the corridor, and Liliana asked, "But what is beyond the sixth door, my Lord, that last door on the left?"

"Clever girl," said the prince, beaming, "you've noticed the room I regularly forget about! That is my father's study. He always keeps it locked, and I'm only allowed to enter it when he requires my assistance—which isn't very often. It's full of old books, strange bottles of liquids, and all sorts of other interesting items...but my father can be very testy about things in general, and about his researches in particular, so, though I welcome you to explore all the other rooms in the castle, I'd advise you avoid entering that one, lest you desire incurring Father's wrath."

The travelers, fearing the consequences of angering Korben Darkwood, hurriedly assured him that they would never dream of entering the chamber without the king's permission. "Good," replied the prince. "Despite what you might think you know of him, you'll find my father agreeable enough if you avoid crossing him—and you're fortunate that you have me to instruct you on how to do so, as I've become a master at it due to necessity!"

He let out a strained laugh, then headed off down the torch-lit passage so speedily that his guests had to jog to keep up with him. Eventually he stopped before a door and, flinging it open, declared, "Here we are!"

The travelers stepped into the room and found that it was well-furnished yet cozy, and contained a table topped with a water jug and bowl, several plush chairs, a chest with a mirror, a blazing fireplace, and a bed with the covers turned down. "What a lovely room," said Juliane, dropping his pack onto the table. "We shall certainly be comfortable here."

"We?" the prince said with a giggle. "Surely you don't think the both of you will be sharing this chamber? This is a castle, Juliane; there are dozens of rooms, there's no need for you to crowd into one. Liliana will have her own bedchamber near yours. Come along, Liliana, I'll show you to it."

Juliane considered protesting, for he had hoped that sharing yet another bed with Liliana might bring them closer still and might allow her to more readily admit the feelings she seemed to be developing for him, but, as he did not wish to challenge the man he had to woo, decided not to. He watched as Liliana followed Arthur Darkwood down the hallway to another door. For a while the prince stood before her and chattered brightly at her, then he grasped her hand and kissed it, opened the door, and ushered her into the room.

Juliane viewed the interaction with concern, for he had begun to worry that Prince Darkwood was already smitten with Liliana and that, if this was the case, it would make his

plans of seduction difficult to pull off, but he grew relieved
when the man noticed him lingering in the doorway and
came over to him. "Dearest maiden, I hope you didn't think
that I'd forgotten to bid you farewell! I did not intend to
slight you—I had planned on settling your friend into her
quarters and then returning to you. Will you accept my
apology?" he asked, taking hold of Juliane's hand and
kissing it.

Simpering—only somewhat deliberately, for Arthur
Darkwood was disarmingly charming—Juliane assured
him no harm had been done. "That is," he continued coyly,
"if you promise to take me on a private tour of the
passageways that we've not yet had a chance to investigate.
I know you said we were free to explore all the rooms but
the king's study on our own, but I fear I might get lost in
such a maze-like building. I'm hoping someone who knows
this castle well might show me around and ensure I return
safely to my room." He placed his hand on the prince's
shoulder, and, blushing, the man vowed to take Juliane on
the requested excursion as soon as he could manage the
time to do so. As Arthur Darkwood gamboled away down
the hallway, waving fondly as he went, Juliane
begrudgingly acknowledged to himself that he might enjoy
ensnaring the prince more than he had expected to.

31.

Juliane had planned on visiting Liliana once the prince had left him, but, as he was very tired, he determined he would put off the call until the morrow and would go to bed forthwith. His mattress was quite comfortable, and, after stripping to his chemise, he climbed into bed and quickly fell fast asleep. He stayed that way until the following morning, when he was awakened by a knock at his bedchamber door.

Assuming Liliana had come to see him, he sleepily stumbled over to it and swung it open, but, to his surprise, it was Arthur Darkwood who stood before him. "Good morning, fair maiden!" he said. "I don't mean to disturb your slumber, but I wanted to know if you'd like to take the tour you requested last night."

Painfully aware that he was standing before the prince in only his undergarment, Juliane replied, "My Lord, I would love to join you, but I should dress myself first."

Red-faced, he shut the door and began fumbling through his pack in hopes of finding something suitable to wear. "If you're searching for a garment, may I make a suggestion?" the prince called from the hallway. "The trunk in your room contains some of my mother's old dresses. Perhaps you can find something fitting within?"

Grumbling, Juliane plodded over to the chest, but when he lifted its lid his complaints ceased, for it was filled with the most beautiful gowns he had ever seen. He chose one of golden silk decorated with gold beading, and, once he had pulled it on and checked his appearance in the mirror, he could not help feeling pleased. *There's no way Prince Darkwood will be able to resist me now*, he thought. *His hair is mine for the taking!*

After running a brush through his locks and pulling on his stockings and boots, he exited the room to find the prince waiting for him. When the man saw Juliane, he grinned broadly. "I'm so glad I recommended you check the chest, for you've found something that suits you perfectly. I believe my mother would be pleased with your wearing her gown." His smile saddened, and Juliane, feeling sorry for him (for it seemed he still felt the absence of the parent he had never known), changed the subject by asking if they would next fetch Liliana. "I hadn't planned on requesting that she come with us," said Arthur Darkwood, seemingly confused, "for you'd displayed interest in a private excursion last night and I wanted to respect your wishes. We could wake her if you'd like, though."

After a brief consideration, Juliane decided that he could speak with Liliana later, as it might be best if he used the presented opportunity to advance his cause. "I suppose you're right, it will be nice for us to spend some time alone together," he cooed, linking his arm with the prince's. "Lead the way, my Lord." Arthur Darkwood did not have to be told twice, and practically dragged Juliane down the passageway in the direction they had come from the night before.

When they arrived at the main hall, the prince led Juliane through one of the doorways they had not entered the previous evening and down an unfamiliar passageway. He took pride in opening several of the doors therein to reveal the splendid rooms beyond them, and even brought Juliane to his own quarters, a series of chambers filled with ornate furniture and fine tapestries. "My father tends to prefer simpler surroundings, but I like for things to be a bit more comfortable," he said. "I hope you'll not think me vain for this."

"Of course not," fawned Juliane. "And where are your father's rooms? Are they located in the hallway we've not yet visited?"

"No, his quarters are off of his study," Prince Arthur replied, "which allows him to leave his bedchamber to work on his researches without having to interact with anyone—myself included." He cast his face down, his expression rueful. "He doesn't have much time for anything other than his magic, you know. For a while he focused purely on necromancy, because he wanted to bring my mother back, but it seems he's given up on that now. I have no idea what he's up to most of the time. He's branched into other forms of sorcery, I'm sure, but he so infrequently allows me to help that I don't know what exactly. I guess he just sees me as an impediment to his work, as he does everyone else." Lifting his head, he sheepishly apologized. "I'm sorry to bore you with complaints regarding my father's lack of sociability."

"You're not boring me at all!" Juliane promised him, for he had spent enough time with Prince Darkwood to note the sadness that crept into his voice whenever he spoke of the king. "I am fortunate to have a family that has always made time for me, so I can only imagine how it must hurt you that your father does not." He recalled his parents fondly, but, strangely, though thinking of them made him wistful, he was having a hard time remembering their faces. *I'd better get my mission over with and return home as soon as possible,* he thought, *or I might not recognize them upon my return!*

He noticed that the prince was staring at him expectantly and understood his mind had wandered. "I'm sorry, I was dwelling on my family. What did you just say?"

"I said I was done moping, and would like to continue

showing you around, if I may?"

Juliane assured him that he would like nothing better, so Arthur Darkwood took his hand and led him down the passageway to a solid-looking door. He opened it, then escorted his guest up a long flight of stairs until they eventually reached a trapdoor. "We've come to one of my favorite places in the castle," said the prince, swinging it open. "Welcome to the Keep."

Prince Darkwood stepped through the opening into the bright sunlight, then extended his hands to help his guest up through it. Once Juliane's eyes adjusted to the glare, he discovered that he was standing on a stone surface surrounded by a waist-high barrier. Moving to one of its edges, he caught his breath when he saw how high off the ground he was—a full hundred feet in the air. The land for miles around was visible from his lofty vantage point; he spied Darkton spread out below him, a thick forest to his right, and the shining sea off in the distance to his left. He was so amazed by the vista before him that he did not notice Arthur Darkwood standing beside him, and he almost yelped when the prince suddenly spoke. "It's a remarkable view, isn't it?"

Recovering himself, he replied, "It is, indeed, beautiful."

"It's all mine, you know, as far as the eye can see—well, it will be when my father passes, which hopefully won't be anytime soon... Nevertheless, as it belongs to my family, I do get to enjoy it even now, and I shall one day be king of it all. It would be wonderful to become queen of a kingdom like this, would it not?"

Juliane started to answer in the affirmative, but, as it abruptly dawned on him what the prince might be hinting at, he spun to face him, indignant. "Are you insinuating something, my Lord? Are you suggesting I might be trying to marry you for your inheritance? Though not as affluent as yours, my family is one of the most prosperous in our realm, so I do not need your money. If you believe I'm courting you only for my own gain, I would appreciate your leading me back to my quarters so that I may pack my things and leave."

He pivoted to stare sullenly out at the vast landscape, and heard the prince come up behind him. "Juliane, I'm so sorry, I didn't mean to upset you. Please, look at me. I want to make things right between us." Peering over his shoulder, he was pleased to find Arthur Darkwood standing near to him, his face the picture of remorse, and he turned to face the prince, who said, "Thank you. I should never have forgiven myself if I had wounded you so greatly that you'd never again look upon me." He grasped both of Juliane's hands. "I did not mean for my comment to seem accusatory and am mortified that it struck you as such. I'm sorry for any hurt I may have caused. Will you accept my apology?"

Charmed by the man's behavior, Juliane blurted, "I had no idea rulers of such considerable realms were capable of showing contrition. Are you this skillful at soothing all whom you wound?"

The prince laughed heartily. "I can be haughty sometimes, to be sure, but I'm more likely to temper my behavior when trying to regain the favor of someone I hold in high esteem. You know, I asked you if you might enjoy being queen of a kingdom like mine not because I wished to insinuate that you might desire my riches, but rather...because I think you could very well become queen of this kingdom someday."

Juliane felt his cheeks burning. "Truly? My Lord, you do honor me."

"It is an honor that you, in my current estimation, deserve. And please, you don't have to call me 'my Lord'— you can reserve that sort of reverence for my father. Just call me 'Arthur'."

"C-certainly, Arthur," he stammered. "By the way, thank

you for bringing me here. I did enjoy the view, and our disagreement did not sway my opinion of the place."

"I am delighted to hear it," said Arthur, "for I anticipate that, though this is the first time we've visited it together, it shan't be the last. Come, let us go back inside. You must be hungry, and I'm sure a sumptuous meal awaits us in the dining hall."

Prince Arthur was not mistaken, for, when they arrived in the dining room, they found an array of delicious foods upon the table—as well as Korben Darkwood, who sat at its head and glared sullenly while they took their fill. His morose air and the occasional withering remarks he directed at his son at first unnerved Juliane, but, as the prince seemed to pay the king little mind, he grew less unsettled as the meal progressed. By the end of it, he found that he was thoroughly enjoying himself despite King Darkwood polluting the surroundings. He realized that this was due to how comfortable Arthur made him feel, for they chatted without ceasing and it seemed as if he had known the man for a year rather than a day. *He's making it so easy for me to pretend I'm falling in love with him, one would almost think that I truly am*, he said to himself— then he burned with shame for having had yet another tender thought about the prince, something that had been happening with more frequency than he had expected.

After the meal the pair spent hours meandering around the rest of the castle, and he felt a pang of disappointment when the prince told him that he would be bringing him to his room shortly, as he unfortunately had duties to attend to. As they approached Juliane's bedchamber, Arthur said, "Oh, I wanted to let you know that I sent a maidservant to your quarters earlier today to take your soiled clothing to be washed. I believe she left you some underclothes but has taken your outer garments. I would be honored if you'd continue to wear my mother's dresses from the trunk until your items are returned to you."

Juliane promised that he would and thanked the man for his thoughtfulness, and then they were at his bedroom door and he found himself reluctant to enter it and take leave of the prince. His reticence was somewhat tempered by their farewell, though, for Arthur bowed to him, kissed his hand, and trilled, "Good night, fair lady. " Juliane found himself so flustered by the man's genteel behavior that he was barely able to mumble a response before dashing into his room.

Closing the door, he leaned against the wall, basking in the glow of all he had accomplished that day, for he felt sure the prince was growing enamored with him and that his cure was well within his reach. As he stripped to his chemise and climbed into bed—for he suddenly felt dreadfully tired—it occurred to him that he had not gone to see Liliana as planned. He determined that he would make sure to visit her the next morning and would not allow himself to once more be derailed by enjoyable distractions, then he drifted off into a pleasant slumber filled with dreams recounting his delightful day with the prince.

***

Liliana woke to find sunlight streaming onto her face through the panes of a small glass window. It took her a minute to remember where she was, but, when she did, she could scarcely believe it—she and Juliane had finally reached Darkwood's castle! She took a moment to relish their success—though not too lengthy of one, for Juliane still needed to complete his task. She admitted to herself that a part of her hoped he would decide it was too difficult a feat and would give up on it, for it would simplify deciphering her feelings for him if he remained as he was; she knew this was a selfish desire, though, for the right thing to do, if she did truly care for him, would be to help him obtain what he needed to feel like himself again.

Sighing, she cursed the complicated circumstances, but resigned herself to assisting him in whatever way she could.

She was startled from her musings by a rap at her bedchamber door, and, though she assumed it was Juliane visiting her, decided it would be best to determine the knocker's identity before opening it. She called out, "Who is it?" and, to her surprise, Arthur Darkwood responded that he had come to give her the tour of the castle he had promised her the evening before.

She told him that she would join him once she had readied herself, and, after climbing out of bed, hastily washed herself and combed her hair. She was about to choose a garment from her pack when Prince Darkwood's voice rang out from the other side of the door. "I beg your pardon, but might I suggest something? The trunk in your room contains beautiful dresses that belonged to my mother. As your clothing's surely filthy from your travels, it may behoove you to wear one of them for our walk today so that a maid might wash your dirty things."

Liliana crossed the room and, opening the trunk, confirmed the prince was telling the truth, for it was filled with the loveliest frocks she had ever laid eyes on. She chose one of blue velvet and tried it on tentatively—for she feared any item in the castle might be tainted by Korben Darkwood's influence—and experienced a mixture of disappointment and relief when it did not fit her. "I cannot wear these," she called out. "They're made for a woman much daintier than I. I shall have to wear my own clothing, though soiled it may be."

She grabbed the first dress she could find, pulled it on, and quickly exited the room. "I apologize," she said to Arthur Darkwood, who stood before her looking undeniably handsome in a brown leather jerkin, black doublet, and black velvet breeches. "I'm guessing the Queen was a slight woman, as there's no way someone of my build could squeeze into her garments. I hope I haven't upset you."

"You certainly haven't! Who would take offense at someone not fitting into a dress?" The prince tried to come off as indifferent, but Liliana noticed a stronger emotion flash in his eyes, though she could not determine whether it was disappointment, irritation, or another feeling altogether. "Come, let us make our circuit around the palace." He ambled away down the corridor but turned when he noticed she was not following him. "Is anything wrong?"

"Nothing, my Lord, it's just—isn't Juliane going to join us?"

"I'm afraid not," Prince Darkwood said contritely. "I went to wake her before coming to get you, and she reported that she's exhausted and requires rest. She did, however, wish us a pleasant excursion. Do you mind our going on without her?"

"I suppose not," she replied, but, as she headed down the passageway, she could not help casting a worried glance at Juliane's bedchamber door. "I shall have to check in on her when I return," she muttered under her breath. "I know she wants to make this man fall in love with her, so it seems strange that she should pass up an opportunity to spend more time with him." She was so focused on her concerns that she did not notice Prince Darkwood had been speaking to her. "What did you just say, my Lord?"

"I said that we shall do part of our tour first and then head to the dining hall for a hearty meal, so we shouldn't linger here much longer. Also, feel free to call me 'Arthur.' You can reserve the whole 'my Lord' business for stuffy old men like my father."

"Certainly, my Lo-Arthur," she corrected herself, giggling. She figured that Arthur Darkwood seemed harmless enough and that his showing her around the castle would help her should she need to navigate its halls in the future, so, promising herself that she would go and see Juliane as soon as she was able, she fell into step alongside him. "Please, lead the way."

For the next few hours Arthur Darkwood led her on a tour of the palace, beginning with one of the hallways they had not gone down the evening before then following with the other. He also took her inside several rooms within the corridors, led her into the kitchen and scullery, and even showed her his own quarters. Right before their meal he brought her to the Keep tower, where his behavior, in addition to her fear of heights, made her uneasy, for he proclaimed that it might be enjoyable to be queen of such a realm and then looked at her as if he hoped she might agree. Liliana knew that being at all inviting toward the prince might render Juliane's quest a failure, so she tried to dodge his insinuation by flippantly responding, "I suppose many would enjoy it, but I think I'd find ruling a kingdom of this size taxing."

She was unnerved by the prince's reaction to her reply, for his face seemed to momentarily darken, and her discomfort only increased when they headed to the dining hall, where they were joined for their meal by Korben Darkwood. Though the food was delicious she noticed, as she ate, that King Darkwood seemed to stare at her almost constantly, and that, during the times he did not, he appeared to drop off into a sort of meditative state, mouth twisted into a cruel grin. During these periods Arthur Darkwood would talk incessantly and would ask her probing questions about the journey she had undertaken and her romantic prospects in her homeland. As the meal dragged on a nasty notion took root in her mind: that Korben Darkwood was using his substantial magical powers to exert an influence over his son.

Her conviction only grew stronger when she and the prince continued their outing post-repast, for she noticed that, though Arthur seemed authentic and friendly most of the time, he at times behaved like a different person. She was relieved when he finally escorted her back to her room, but, as she reached for the bedchamber door, he stayed her. "I have something I'd like to give you before we part ways."

Liliana turned to find he had retrieved a necklace from his pocket and was holding it out to her. "It used to be my mother's. As you didn't fit into her gowns, I thought it might be nice to let you have this instead." A tear-shaped pendant dangled from a chain before her, shining an unusual bluish-green. As she stared at it, she felt a chill rise within her, for she was certain the item was magical and that her wearing it would allow the king to exert power over her.

Prince Darkwood asked if he might place it on her neck, but she grabbed it from his hand. "Thank you so much for the beautiful jewelry, I shall be sure to wear it often—and, once again, thank you for the tour! I had such a lovely time." Before he had the chance say anything else, she rushed into her bedroom, slamming the door behind her. She turned the key in the lock then placed her back against the wall and stood utterly still, relaxing only after the prince's footsteps had echoed away down the corridor.

Exhaling, she dropped to the floor and examined the necklace. Closing her hand around it, she shuddered as she felt a strange sensation pass through her palm, and she threw it across the room and then sat warily watching it, as if it might attack her. She determined that it would be best if she placed it somewhere it could not possibly exert an influence over her, and so she stuck it in the bottom of the chest underneath all the fancy dresses—which, to her disgust, made her feel the same way the amulet had when she brushed against them.

She now firmly believed Arthur Darkwood was in thrall to his father and was being used for some purpose, but she was still uncertain as to what. Perhaps the king was in league with Saurenia and the Mater and had been alerted to their visit? Or maybe he was attempting to enchant them, so he could make use of them in some way? Though she was unsure of the reasons behind his plotting, she knew the most pressing thing to do was to share her concerns with Juliane so they might obtain the prince's hair without falling into Darkwood's snares.

She rose, unlocked the door, and pushed it slightly open. Peeking out through the crack, she determined that the passage was clear, and she hurried down the hallway to Juliane's bedchamber. She rapped softly and, when she received no response, knocked louder. She tried the handle and found the door was locked, and she was considering forcing her way into the room when a voice coldly asked, "What are you doing?"

Filled with dread, she turned to find Korben Darkwood standing behind her, a smirk playing upon his thin lips. "Why are you pounding on your friend's door? Hasn't my son told you that she requires rest? It would be best not to disturb her."

Mute with terror, Liliana merely nodded in reply, and, when the king suggested she return to her quarters, she fled. After locking herself in her room, she threw herself on the bed, distraught; she knew she must alert Juliane of the danger at hand but was not sure how she possibly could, for it was clear they were being monitored by the king and that she would be in danger should she again try to communicate with her companion. She tried thinking of other ways she might share her concerns with him, but, to her frustration, found her thoughts drifting. She did not notice how tired she had become—for this was what was causing her mind to wander—and she fell asleep atop her bed covers, still fully clothed, an uneasy expression twisting her features even in slumber.

32.

The following days—if days they were, for time had a strange way of slipping and blurring in Castle Darkwood—only brought Liliana more woe, for she found herself unbearably tired much of the time and, when she was not sleeping, she was kept so busy with activities that she scarcely had a minute to herself. On top of this, the king often lurked in the hallway outside her room, so she rarely felt comfortable leaving it to try and talk to Juliane— and, whenever she managed to, he never answered her knocks.

She saw him infrequently, only during certain mealtimes in the dining hall, and, on these occasions, he was never free to speak with her, for Arthur Darkwood was always at his side. He seemed to barely notice her despite his past professions of adoration, and, though she was loath to admit it, the way he looked past her to instead gaze fondly at the prince caused her undeniable pain. She fell into despair, for it seemed as if she and Juliane might never leave the palace, and she wondered what her fate might be if this did indeed occur.

Juliane, for his part, was enjoying an experience vastly different from Liliana's. Although he also slept often, his waking hours were filled with pleasant excursions with Arthur, and he delighted in getting to know the prince and in spending time with him whenever possible. As their relationship progressed, he began admitting to himself that a part of him desired to remain female so that he might stay with Arthur Darkwood indefinitely; this idea, which he would have deemed repugnant mere weeks before, now seemed so natural that he found himself dreaming of the life they might share without any qualms. He still held a vague recollection of his one-time fondness for Liliana, but she, like all other things connected to his former self and old life, now seemed so inconsequential and so far-removed from the person he had become. He might start to wonder, when he had a spare moment, how the passion he had felt for her could have cooled so quickly—but these moments were rare, and he spent far more time preening before his mirror than worrying about his change in affections.

One day he stood before that mirror and chose a most lavish gown to wear, for Arthur had hinted that they would be going on a special outing and he wanted his appearance to suit the occasion. He was fairly bursting with excitement, wondering what the prince had planned, and he almost shrieked when he heard a knock at his door. Flinging it open, he found Prince Darkwood before him, clothed in a splendid cloak and holding out a nosegay of flowers. "I picked these for you," he confessed timidly.

Juliane placed the blooms in his room, then returned to the hallway. "So, are you going to tell me where we're off to or continue to keep me waiting?" he asked, pouting.

"I'm not going to say anything, for you shall see soon enough," replied Prince Arthur, smirking, then his expression grew serious. "Juliane, do you trust me?"

"Do I trust you? Why ask a silly question like that?" said Juliane, but, when he saw his careless response had wounded the man, he added, "Of course I trust you, dear Arthur. I trust you more than anyone else in the world."

The prince beamed. "I am glad to hear it, for it would

cause me great pain if you didn't." He removed a blindfold from his cloak. "Since you profess to have faith in me, I'm going to ask that you put this on and allow me to guide you. Will you do this?"

Juliane was apprehensive at the thought of being led sightless, but he agreed and, with assistance, covered his eyes. Arthur took his hand and ushered him forward, and they walked for what seemed an hour, only stopping for the prince to open doors, until they came to a staircase. Prince Darkwood helped him up each step, and, after a lengthy climb, they seemed to have reached their destination. Juliane could feel a cool breeze against his skin, and asked, "Are we out on the Keep?"

"Why don't you remove your blindfold, so that you may see for yourself?"

Juliane did as he requested and discovered that they were standing atop a tower he had never visited, one slightly taller than the Keep and capped with a spire. Staring at the land below made him dizzy, so he stepped backward, and found himself clasped in Prince Darkwood's arms. Arthur whispered in his ear, "This is the turret. It's the highest point of this castle and somewhere only I go; none of the servants have keys to it, and my father is too busy with his studies to visit. As far as I know I'm the only person who has been here in years...and that's why I wanted to bring you here. I wanted to share this special place with you, because you've become very special to me."

Juliane could not resist throwing his arms around Prince Darkwood to return his embrace. "Oh, thank you, dear Arthur. I'm honored that you've showed me this part of your world, and I shall treasure this memory always."

"That's not the only reason why I've brought you here, though." Arthur released Juliane, then reached into his cloak and pulled a small box from it. He opened it to reveal the most stunning ring Juliane had ever seen, a band of pure gold topped with a large jewel that glowed with blue-green fire. He gasped as he understood what was happening, and Arthur Darkwood took his hand and said, "Juliane, since the day we met my life has been filled with happiness. I've been drawn to you from the start, and you have only grown more compelling as I've gotten to know you. You came to the Darklands to find a suitable match, and I hope you feel you've found one, for I believe you have. I would like to ask you to marry me and to spend the rest of your days with me as first princess and then queen of this kingdom." He cast his face down bashfully. "I can only hope that you'll say yes."

Juliane froze, uncertain of how to respond. Though he cared greatly for the prince, a part of him wondered if he actually wanted to wed him, for, in doing so, he would be forsaking his old identity, his old life and all it had held for him...including Liliana, whom he knew had been very dear to him during a time not so far in his past. He worried he might merely be infatuated, spellbound by the novel circumstances and Arthur Darkwood's kind manner—or, perhaps, purely spellbound... The notion unnerved him, and he was about to give it additional consideration when he looked at Prince Darkwood and felt his doubts melt away. It was written all over the man's face just how much he cared for him, and this—as well as the ring, for gazing upon the luminous green stone gave him a pleasant sense of calm—convinced him that he was making the right decision, however greatly his lot might change. He took a deep breath, then said, "Of course I'll marry you, Arthur."

He had thought Prince Darkwood's smile could not grow any brighter but found he had been mistaken. "Oh, Juliane, do you mean it? If so, you'll make me the happiest man in the world." After being offered further assurance, the prince hastily placed the ring on Juliane's left hand, and the pair stood staring shyly at each other until Arthur broke the silence. "Would you mind if we...seal our engagement with a kiss?"

Juliane had been dreading this moment, for he knew it was the true test of whether he really could marry the prince—he had never willingly kissed a man and was not sure he would enjoy it—but he gave his assent nonetheless, and suddenly the prince's mouth was upon his and all worries ceased. As he eagerly returned the kiss and, admittedly, entertained impure thoughts regarding Arthur Darkwood, it occurred to him just how unexpectedly things had turned out: he had been hoping to make the prince fall in love with him so that he might end his curse, but, though it seemed that the prince had indeed fallen, he surprisingly had as well!

He could not help but giggle at this, and Arthur stopped kissing him to ask why he was laughing. He gave the excuse that it was due to his feeling merry regarding the engagement, and the prince seemed to believe him, for he said, "Let us return inside. I shall take you to your room so that you may have a rest, then will fetch you later so we can have a celebratory feast!" He grabbed Juliane's hand and, whooping, the pair flew joyously down the stairs and back into the castle.

***

The newly betrothed couple raced through the corridors to Juliane's quarters and, once they had arrived, bid each other a lengthy farewell. Juliane was tempted to invite the prince into his bedchamber for a bit of celebratory dallying, but, upon further consideration, determined that another kiss would be a more appropriate parting gesture. This one was no less pleasant than the first had been, and he was so caught up in the moment that he did not notice the face, filled with a tentative hope for the first time in days, that spied upon them from a doorway further along the passage.

He reluctantly released Arthur and, after they had

305

exchanged some fond parting words, entered his room, where he stood before his mirror, admiring his ring. He was about to climb into bed for a nap when, suddenly, he heard a rap at his doorway. The pleasant notion that Prince Darkwood had sensed his carnal longings and had returned so they might make them manifest crossed his mind, and, giggling, he threw the door open—but it was not the prince, but rather Liliana, whom he found standing on his doorstep.

He stared at her at first, uncertain of what to say—as, he guiltily acknowledged to himself, he had not spoken to her much since their arrival at the castle—but, once he found his voice, bade her come in. "Why, Liliana, it's such a pleasure to see you, as we haven't spent much time together lately," he squeaked, voice betraying his discomfort, as he closed the door behind her. "For what reason have you called upon me this afternoon?"

Liliana had been glancing around the room uneasily, and, when she focused her gaze on him, the concern in her features made his heart sink. "I came to speak with you about something that's been worrying me," she said. "I have reason to believe that King Darkwood has enchanted his son and holds sway over him. I think he has been possessing Arthur at times and that, during those times, he has been using him as a pawn to try and exert influence over you and I— though I'm currently uncertain as to why. At the very least he's doing something to tire us, for I know I feel drained whenever I've just left his presence... What I'm trying to say is that we must tread carefully. You seem to be making great advances toward getting the prince to develop feelings for you, and so are well on your way to getting what you need to break the spell, but we must be wary and work together to avoid any snares."

She waited for him to agree with her and was surprised and horrified when he grew red-faced and spluttered, "B-but that cannot be true! Arthur is his own man, and everything he's done has been of his own accord. I know this because he asked me to marry him today, and I cannot conceive of any reason why King Darkwood might force him to do that. Arthur is kind, and good, and honest, and I..."

He trailed off, hesitant to admit he had accepted the man's proposal, but Liliana nonetheless understood what had happened. "You agreed to marry him? Why, Juliane? I thought you were hoping to make him fall for you so you might claim his hair to undo your curse. I didn't think you'd go so far as to say you'd wed him to accomplish this."

"Well...I didn't say 'yes' just to influence his feelings toward me."

The import of his words swiftly struck her. "Are you saying that you want to marry him and forsake the quest we've so valiantly struggled to accomplish, that you desire to instead spend the rest of your days as Mistress Darkwood? I can't believe it, I—"

"It would be 'Queen Darkwood'," he interrupted haughtily, "and, yes, that's exactly what I'm saying."

She gaped at him, aghast. "But, when we were in the woods together, just before we were brought to Darkton, you said so many beautiful things, things that seemed so real. Are you telling me the strong affection you professed for me then could have dissipated so easily, that you could have so effortlessly fallen for another?"

He nodded curtly, and, filled with despair, Liliana turned to leave the room, for she felt she could help him no longer—but then she suddenly stopped. "Old romantic feelings being abruptly replaced by new ones," she murmured to herself, furrowing her brow. "This has happened before." Her eyes widened, and she spun to face him. "This happened to *me*, with Saurenia! I developed an infatuation with her because I was affected by a spell! Juliane, don't you see? You, too, must be ensorcelled! Darkwood isn't just using his son to try and influence us, he's also using magic to influence you! Please, consider my words and then tell me that I'm wrong!"

Juliane felt a twinge of fear as he recalled briefly worrying that he might be spellbound during Arthur's proposal, and he allowed his face to momentarily betray him. This was all the encouragement Liliana needed, and she strode over to him and grasped him by the shoulders. "Juliane, I'm certain you're under some sort of enchantment. *Something* must be causing you to lose sight of who you are and what you truly care about. Now, to find out what..."

Spying the ring on his finger, she grabbed his hand. "What's this? The stone in this band is familiar...wait a second... It's like the one in the necklace Prince Darkwood gave me!" Juliane glared at her, confused, and she explained, "He gifted me a necklace and asked me to 'wear it often.' It gave me a strange feeling, so I haven't touched it since. I have no doubt that the ring you wear holds power and that it has assisted the king in ensnaring you. Take it off."

"I will not!" cried Juliane indignantly. "Arthur gave this to me because he cares for me, he wants to marry me, he—"

"He gave it to you because his father made him, either by forcing him to or by directly controlling his actions. You must remove it. If you don't, I will pull it from your finger, and I cannot promise to be gentle."

He understood she was being serious, and, as he knew she could easily overpower him, he reluctantly took off the band. "See? I've removed the ring, and nothing has changed. I still wish to become Queen Darkwood."

Liliana's face fell briefly, but soon filled with resolve once more. "Of course, that can't be the cause of the enchantment—at least, not the bulk of it—as you were only given it today. Something else is the main root of your enthrallment, the chief influence..." She paced the room in deep thought, then cried out in triumph and fell onto the bed. "The dresses!"

"What about dresses?" Juliane asked crossly.

"During our first day in the castle, Prince Darkwood asked me to put on a dress from a trunk in my room and to give him all my clothing so that it might be washed. I avoided doing this because the frocks wouldn't fit me, and, when I touched them later that day, they gave me the same uneasy feeling the necklace did. I think King Darkwood was attempting to ensnare me using those garments...and it seems he was able to entrap you with kindred ones, for the gowns you've been wearing aren't your own. I'll bet he promised to return your clean clothing to you—did he ever do this?" When Juliane, tight-lipped, shook his head, she said matter-of-factly, "Then we've found our solution. You must remove that dress and make sure not to wear any others from the trunk to break the king's hold upon you."

Juliane scoffed, "Oh, you're being ridiculous! There's no way some silly frocks could make me want to marry someone! You just want me to take the dress off so you can mock me for standing in my undergarment..." He ceased his arguing when he saw how his words had wounded her, and, softening, he crossed the room, took a seat next to her, and placed an arm around her shoulders. "I apologize for my unkindness, but I still cannot believe that—"

"You can, and you should!" she interrupted. "If a lesser sorceress like Saurenia could cause me to develop feelings for her with a simple gesture of her hand, it's entirely possible that someone as skilled in the dark arts as Korben Darkwood could cause you to grow infatuated with his son by literally enrobing you in magic. In fact, it's likely that he directed his son to propose to you so he could ensure your complete ensnarement by having you wear the ring."

She turned to him. "Please, dear Juliane, listen to me. What I'm going to say will sound familiar, as it's similar to what you said to me when I was a stubborn girl enthralled by a heartless enchantress: do you not believe that I care enough for you that I would wish you all the happiness in the world were it *true* happiness? And do you not think it strange and unwholesome that 'falling in love' with the prince should cause you to reject your old life and leave all those who care for you behind?"

Casting her face down, she confessed, "Do you know how many times I have wished you would desire to stay as you are so that my own feelings for you might be easier to reckon with?" She lifted her head, and her eyes were blazing. "But I would never force something upon you that you do not desire, even if it would be of benefit to me, as that isn't what one does when one truly cares for another! I would rather be honest with you, and take the pain that comes with it, than mold you into someone you'd rather not be, for the only ones who wish to do this to others are those who view them only as instruments. That is what King Darkwood views both you and his son as, and he would have you exactly as he wants with no concern for either of you. You cannot truly love Arthur Darkwood, for what you feel is borne of deception and calculation, and that isn't what love is!"

She turned from him, but not before he had noticed her eyes glistening. He sat speechless for a moment, then sighed. "You're right. I should take this dress off. If what Arthur and I have is real it will exist regardless, so what have I to fear?"

He rose from the bed, started to unlace his bodice, and noticed immediately that his fingers felt clumsy and that he had to focus all his attention on the task to complete it. Once this was done, he removed the dress from his shoulders, and each sleeve seemed an immense weight as it came off. It crossed his mind that perhaps Liliana was speaking the truth, that the gown did have some sort of power over him, and then he was struggling fiercely to disrobe himself until, finally, he stood before Liliana clothed in only his chemise.

She peered at him, face filled with tentative hope, and could not resist leaping from the bed when, with a clarity in his eyes she had not seen in them for days, Juliane spoke her name.

33.

Liliana rushed to Juliane and threw her arms around him, and he laid his head on her shoulder and cried, "I'm so sorry, dear Liliana! I wasn't careful; I didn't reckon that Darkwood might ill-use us whilst we were in his home. I let myself be ensnared and almost ruined all that we'd accomplished. I don't know how you'll ever forgive me."

"I already have," she said, and he lifted his face to find her smiling at him. "Why would I remain upset with you when you were affected by forces beyond your control? Besides," she continued sheepishly, "I'm just exceedingly glad to have you back. The thought that I might lose you to Prince Darkwood after all we've been through together was...intolerable."

He released her and, grinning roguishly, asked, "Liliana, were you jealous of the prince?"

"I don't believe 'jealous' is the best word to describe my feelings, for I wouldn't have minded as much had you cared for us both. I was more afraid, I think—scared that you would marry him, stay here, and become a stranger to me. I couldn't bear the thought of never seeing you again."

"So, it might be that you do feel for me as I do for you, despite your doubts?"

"Well, I cannot be sure we are feeling the same thing, dear Juliane, as you were telling me only moments ago that you'd fallen for Prince Darkwood," Liliana responded coyly.

"How are we supposed to be feeling, again?"

He took her hands in his and stared into her eyes. "Liliana Almwick, I, Juliane Stoneshire, promise that the adoration I expressed for Arthur Darkwood was mere infatuation resulting from my being under the influence of enchanted garments. I've been strongly attracted to you since first we met, and this attraction has only grown as I've gotten to know you. Nothing would make me happier than our continuing to grow our connection after our quest is completed...for I believe you and I may one day have the kind of romance bards write songs about."

He blushed, and she gazed at him affectionately. "We very well might, Juliane," she said, then, feigning doubt, added, "though I do believe I need proof of your feelings to be absolutely certain of them."

He did not initially realize what she was hinting at, but, as the import of her words hit him, he gasped in mock innocence. "Why, Liliana, are you proposing that we affirm our fondness for each other through some sort of...physical act?"

"I might be," she said, then, dropping all pretense, reached out and clasped him to her. "I think now might be a good time for you to kiss me." Before he could do anything more than fervently nod in agreement, she mischievously continued, "Oh, you've taken too long. I guess I'll just have to kiss you instead. I've never been skilled at waiting patiently."

She pressed her lips to his and he melted into the kiss, but, just as he was beginning to enjoy himself, a knock sounded at the door. "Juliane, it is I, your Prince Arthur! I have come to bring you to a feast in honor of our impending marriage."

Juliane groaned at the interruption, then suddenly went pale. "How can I go with him?" he whispered, worry creasing his brow. "Now that I know his father enchanted me to get me to like him and that he's likely under the king's control, how can I possibly pretend to still desire him? And, more importantly, how can I avoid being snared once more?"

"I believe in you, dear Juliane," said Liliana, releasing him. "I know you're capable of many things, and that your pretending to still be enamored with him is just one more that you shall easily master. Now, tell him you've just risen and need some time to ready yourself."

"Arthur, is that you?" Juliane called out sleepily, proud that his voice did not betray him. "I've just woken from a rest, so am not yet prepared to leave my bedchamber. Would you mind coming back for me later? I'll meet you outside my room in a quarter of an hour."

He held his breath, awaiting the prince's response, and exhaled in relief when the man said, "Of course, my darling. I shall return shortly."

He went to the door and put his ear to it, then listened until he was certain Prince Darkwood had retreated down the passageway. He turned to find Liliana removing her dress. "I'm giving you this. I shall go to my room and put on another once you've left, and you can avoid being re-enchanted by not wearing the things in the trunk. You certainly can't go to dinner in just a chemise," she giggled.

"But what about the ring? I cannot wear it, for it will surely affect me, but I'm certain he'll notice it missing from my finger."

Liliana had not considered this, but, though her features momentarily clouded, they soon brightened. "I am sure there's a spell in the book my mother gave me for disenchanting objects—we could use it to make the ring wearable!" Her face grew uneasy. "That is, if I can fetch it from my room. King Darkwood has been patrolling this hallway regularly, and I'm concerned that, should he catch me coming from your bedchamber, he might discover we've unraveled his plans." She headed toward the door, calling over her shoulder, "I suppose I must try regardless.

Wish me well!"

He cried, "Wait!" and, stopping, she looked at him expectantly. "I just remembered—I have an item that might render the well-wishing less necessary." He ran to his pack, grabbed something from it, and brought it over to her.

Liliana was delighted. "The Inuisibilitas Pallium! I had forgotten you still had it. My job shall be easier than expected." She threw the invisibility cloak over her shoulders and, fastening the clasp, instantly disappeared. She opened the door and whispered, "I shall be back," then he heard her pad off down the corridor.

After a short while Liliana returned, throwing off the cloak as she entered the room. "I'm relieved I didn't run into the king," she said, "for, though the Pallium concealed me from view, it certainly did not render me silent. My footsteps have never seemed louder!" She carried the book under one arm, and she thumbed through it until she found what she had been seeking. "Just as I'd hoped! An incantation to dispel the influence of bewitched objects. You know, I can also use it to remove the magic from the gowns in your trunk. Then you can continue to wear them, and the king shall be none the wiser."

She took back her dress and pulled it on, then gathered the enchanted items into a pile. She placed the book atop them, then spun in a circle while chanting, "Purgo magia nunc!" After removing the tome from the heap, she gingerly placed her hand on the pile. "All clean! These things are fine to use now. We are lucky indeed to have this book with us."

Juliane put on the dress he had been wearing earlier and reluctantly slid the ring onto his finger. He checked himself in the mirror and determined that he was presentable enough to join the Darkwoods for dinner, but he still did not feel confident of his ability to feign liking the prince. "What if I can't maintain the farce? I shudder to think of what might happen if Darkwood finds out we've dispelled his hold over me."

"You'll do just fine," said Liliana. "I seem to recall how you convinced a certain Lord Ichthus that you were not only attracted to him but also intoxicated, and I have no doubt your acting skills shall serve you equally well in this case. Besides, you can always just pretend the prince is me, then looking at him dreamily may come quite naturally."

Smirking, she reached out and pulled him to her, and he had to admit that her words were more than half-truth. "But, what will you do whilst I'm entertaining them?"

"I shall do some investigating now that I have the invisibility cloak. I would like to figure out what's going on: is Arthur under his father's direct influence at times, or is he being pressed into doing his bidding? Could he be working with the king rather than being used as a pawn? And for what reason would Korben Darkwood be trying to exert control over us? I aim to discover these things whilst you are keeping the sorcerer and his son busy."

As the last word left her lips, a sharp rap sounded at the door. "Juliane, are you ready?"

He looked at Liliana helplessly, and she whispered, "I believe in you, Juliane. You've accomplished many things you never thought possible during our journey, and I know you can do this." She kissed his cheek, then released him and ushered him to the doorway. "I shall see you soon, my dearest Juliane."

She appeared as hesitant to bid him farewell as he was to leave her, and this filled him with a gladness he was grateful of for myriad reasons—not the least because, when he exited the room, he found himself in the arms of Arthur Darkwood, who misinterpreted the happiness as being meant for himself. "It seems you've missed me as much as I've missed you, my darling! Are you ready for the feast?" Grinning weakly, Juliane nodded, and, trying to keep from shaking, he linked his arm in the prince's and reluctantly accompanied him to the betrothal celebration.

***

When Juliane entered the dining hall, he found that three chairs had been set up at one end of the table and that King Darkwood was already seated in the one at its head. "Come in, come in!" he thundered, gesturing at the other seats. "I am overjoyed to hear my son has found a suitable match, and that I shall soon have a daughter. Sit, and let us honor your impending union!"

Arthur led Juliane to the chair on the king's right, then seated himself in the left-hand one. As the castle steward and a maidservant entered the room and began serving the meal, Juliane glanced at King Darkwood from the corner of his eye and was dismayed to find the man looking at him, a smirk turning up the corners of his thin mouth. He bowed his head until his food was placed before him, then tried to focus solely on eating; he was unsuccessful in this venture, though, for he could not help but notice things that made him uneasy. Korben Darkwood stared at him throughout the meal and seemed to fall into a sort of trance whenever he was not doing so, a wicked smile playing upon his lips, and it was during these periods that Prince Arthur would speak more profusely and say things that seemed out of character. The king would also ask discomfiting questions, and his laughter at Juliane's tentative answers was far from mirthful.

The dinner dragged on, and Juliane nearly leaped from his chair once it had finished. Prince Darkwood walked him back to his bedchamber and there stood before him expectantly, and, although the idea of being physical with the man repulsed him, Juliane braced himself and kissed the prince in what he hoped was a duly convincing manner. He then moved to enter his room, but felt his stomach drop when Arthur grasped his left hand and said, "Don't leave just yet. I'd like to admire your ring." He squinted at it, and

Juliane felt fear course through him as he saw a darkness come over the man's features—for he worried the king had taken possession of his son and, through him, had discerned the ring no longer held any power—but the prince merely commented on the beauty of the bauble before trotting away down the passage.

Sighing in relief, Juliane entered the bedchamber and, closing the door behind him, whispered, "Liliana, are you in here?" He spoke her name twice more and received no response, and he was about to check her room for her when he froze, for something had grabbed him by the shoulders. It hissed at him, and he had started to cry out when the thing began to giggle. He felt it release him, and, when he turned to find no one behind him, he testily said, "Liliana, is that you? You shouldn't do things like that in this castle—you nearly scared me to death!"

Liliana threw off the invisibility cloak and stood smirking before him, hands on hips. "I'm sorry, but I couldn't resist giving you a turn like the one you'd given me at the Mater's."

He begrudgingly admitted fair was fair, then related his mealtime experience to her; listening intently, she nodded at each observation. "You noticed the same behavior I did. It seems King Darkwood has been using his son in an attempt to influence us, but I'm still uncertain as to why."

"Didn't you find anything out during your investigations?"

"Not really. I walked all over the castle and went into every room I had access to, but, though I gave each a full examination, I discovered nothing untoward. I even searched Prince Darkwood's quarters but found nothing there indicating either his cooperation in the king's machinations or his being aware of them. My guess is that he doesn't know he's being used by his father, which is good news for you, as his feelings for you may be authentic. As for more good news, I found your clean clothing in a trunk in the scullery."

She handed him the garments, which he shoved into his pack. "What do we do now, then?" he said. "I still need Arthur's hair, but I'm loath to spend another moment in this awful place."

"I think I might have an idea regarding what to do next, but I must first ask—is there any of the Pulvis Lapsus Memoriae left?"

"There is!"

"And do you believe that enough remains that it could be used on several people—the king, the prince, the steward, and various servants?"

"There's a little more than half a packet left. Though it may not go far when divided among that many, it could probably erase a few weeks from each," admitted Juliane.

"Good!" said Liliana. "Then here is my plan: we shall first enchant King Darkwood, as he's the most dangerous to reckon with, and shall next dust his son and procure a lock of his hair before taking his memory. After that, we will go around the house and use the powder on each servant—we can even break Wilbur Crestshorn out of prison if we put the jailer to sleep! Once we've done this, we can leave the castle, for none dwelling within shall recall us and the unaffected aware of our arrival will assume we've met our fate at Darkwood's hands. We can thus escape from the Darklands and return home without risking the king coming after us."

"Wonderful!" exclaimed Juliane. "I don't know how you come up with plans so quickly, but I'm certainly glad you do. The only thing is, how do we gain access to King Darkwood? He rarely leaves his chambers, and, when he does, he's almost always accompanied by his son or his servants."

"I'm aware of that," said Liliana, face grim. "We'll have to make sure we catch him when he's busy, preferably with his back turned. To do that, well, we'll need to..."

She trailed off, and he noticed she had whitened. "Oh no. Liliana, don't tell me we'll need to break into his chambers? Arthur warned us that doing so could lead to our doom."

"It's either that potential doom or our almost certain doom should we stay here and do nothing," she said firmly. "It's not ideal, but it's our only recourse."

"Well, at least we have the cloak to keep us out of sight...and I know an unlocking spell! I found it in your mother's book when I vanquished the Mater. We could try it on the door to the king's quarters."

"Juliane, you're marvelous!" said Liliana. "This may end up being less difficult than I'd expected." She placed the cloak over her shoulders and had him join her underneath it, and he felt a bit better about things once he had looked in the mirror and determined that they were indeed invisible. "Make sure all your belongings are in your pack, and that you're wearing it under the cloak, for then it will remain unseen," she told him. "We must leave now, for there shall unfortunately be no better opportunity to complete the task. It's time to enter the serpent's lair."

34.

The travelers fetched Liliana's things from her room, then, crowded together under the cloak, they crept down the hallway. At one point they had to press themselves against the wall as a chambermaid rushed by, but, once she had gone, they continued along the corridor until they reached the door to the main hall.

Liliana pulled it open, then poked her head through the doorway. "I think we're alone," she whispered. "We should probably check the rooms off of this one before beginning our task, though, to ensure no one will interrupt us." They squeezed over the threshold, then, hastily surveying the dining and throne rooms, determined both were empty. "We're safe to try opening the door to the king's quarters," said Liliana. "I'll stand watch whilst you recite the incantation."

She stepped out of the cloak, and Juliane grew worried. "But, you're visible now. What if the king catches you?"

"Then he catches me. I can always tell him I'm hungry and came to fetch some victuals. In fact..." She rushed into the dining hall, then emerged with a plate piled high with food. "I actually am hungry, so my excuse is valid. Now, go ahead and cast that spell."

She removed the book from her bag and held it out to him, and he took it with trembling hands and thumbed through it until he came to the right page. He was about to begin his recitation when, suddenly, the door to one of the hallways opened and Prince Darkwood emerged from it. Juliane flattened himself against the doorway as the man came striding toward Liliana, and he had to keep himself from yelping when the prince came within inches of the spot where he cowered.

Liliana, for her part, tried keeping her voice steady as she greeted the prince. "Good evening, Arthur! I came to get some food, for I awakened hungry not long ago. Is there a reason why I wasn't invited to dinner tonight?"

Prince Darkwood was shamefaced. "I'm sorry to have left you out of the proceedings, but I was hasty in planning them. It's just that...the feast held this evening was in honor of my impending marriage to Juliane, for today I proposed to her and she accepted."

"How wonderful!" Liliana trilled in as convincing a manner as she could muster. "It seems you've both found your match after all."

"Indeed," replied the prince, beaming. "In fact, I plan on going to her room right now, for, when I left her after dinner, I received the impression that she would have liked to tarry with me longer. Enjoy your repast!"

Liliana watched him walk toward the corridor that led to the travelers' rooms and, once he had disappeared through its doorway, hissed, "Juliane, you must cast the spell now! If he goes to your chamber and finds it empty, he'll likely come here to inquire of your whereabouts. We must get into the king's quarters before he returns."

"I know, I know," Juliane grumbled. Placing his finger on the page, he found the lines he was seeking and read aloud:

Let me unlock any door ahead,
Let no barrier keep me at bay.
Let nothing stand between me and my course,
On this or any other day.

Let my path be clear and well-marked,
Let my mind be skilled at hoping.
As long as purpose lights my way,
Then every door shall open.

He nearly shrieked when every door in the hall flew open, and Liliana rushed to close each in turn until only the one to Darkwood's chamber remained unsecured; Juliane peered into it, shuddering, for it was as black as a tomb within. "We'll need one of these," said Liliana, grabbing a torch from the wall and then returning to Juliane. She nearly bumped into him, and he unfastened the cloak in hopes of welcoming her underneath it—but, as soon as he had grown visible, she stuck the torch in his hand and bade him re-secure the clasp. "I knew it," she sighed. "The light isn't made invisible by the cloak, as it cannot be held beneath it. Since we'll need it to see, we'll have to enter the room without cover."

Groaning, Juliane reluctantly removed the garment and handed it to Liliana, who placed it in her bag. He looked at the gaping doorway, then back at her, and, seeing she had paled, he grabbed her hand and said, "Let's go together." She smiled and squeezed his fingers gently, then, holding the torch aloft, they stepped into the darkness.

The king's quarters were much larger than they had expected, for the chamber they entered was massive and they could see another beyond an open archway at its rear. Large bookcases covered the first room's walls from floor to ceiling, their shelves filled with some of the rarest and most obscure tomes Liliana had ever heard of as well as several she was not familiar with. In the center of the chamber stood a table covered with papers marked with arcane symbols, and, though neither traveler could decipher them, they shuddered as they looked upon them, for some felt unspeakably old and evil.

They crossed this room and went into the next, which held several tables and benches; some were topped with glass bottles filled with strange liquids and vessels containing loathsome ingredients—Juliane thought he saw human teeth in one and did his best to forget that he had— while others were layered with maps and figures. Liliana stifled a cry when her eyes lit upon a certain parchment, for it was a drawing of a human body accompanied by instructions on how to anatomize and resurrect it. "It looks like the rumors about Darkwood's undead army may indeed be true," she said quietly, then noticed she was speaking to no one in particular, for Juliane was no longer nearby.

He had wandered to the other side of the room, and, seeing he had her attention, whispered, "There's something over here, come look." She joined him and found several large barrels clustered in a corner, radiating so strong a smell that she clutched her nose as she approached them. "What do you think they contain?" asked Juliane.

Liliana pretended she did not know but in truth was barely keeping herself from growing ill, for she had smelled rotting meat before and knew this was what the containers held. Turning away from the awful things, she spied a trapdoor in the floor. It was open, and a set of steps led down from it into a darkness so complete that it made the king's quarters appear brightly lit. The smell of putrid flesh emanated from it, and she could not stop herself from shivering. "Let us take care of Darkwood and leave this charnel house," she said, and Juliane, grasping the import of her words, fervently nodded in agreement.

Having not yet found the king, they navigated the length of the chamber until they came to a door set in its back wall. They trembled in anticipation of what they might find behind it, and Juliane asked shakily, "What if Korben Darkwood isn't in there? What if he's elsewhere, and that room harbors some of the ghastly creatures we've been hearing so many whispers about?"

"We fight them as best we can, then continue our search for the king," Liliana said resolutely. "But he must be in there—there's nowhere else left to look." She reached out and grasped the handle and, finding the door unlocked, slowly pushed it open.

Juliane crept through the doorway first on this occasion, for he wanted to show Liliana he could demonstrate a bravery equal to hers, and he held the torch in front of himself to reveal the confines of the room. The chamber was much smaller than the others and contained only a bed surrounded by a translucent curtain. There was a shape huddled on the mattress, and he whispered over his shoulder, "I think we're in luck. It seems we've caught the king resting." Feeling less frightened than he had been—for he had already bested one slumbering magician—he stepped into the room, went to the corner furthest from Darkwood, and began digging through his bag for the memory loss powder.

Liliana followed him in, and, when she realized she would need to be the one to lift the bed-curtain, she took the torch from him and tiptoed over to the bed, hearkening for any signs of movement. As she drew near to it, though, she sensed that something was not quite right; she could not work out what was bothering her at first, but, as she stood still and listened, it came to her. She crept over to Juliane, who had finally found the packet, and stayed him from pouring the powder into a gloved hand. "Why are you stopping me?" he hissed. "I almost had it ready."

"I think," whispered Liliana, "that King Darkwood may not be in that bed."

"What do you mean?" Juliane's face twisted in disbelief. "Who else could it possibly be?"

"Not 'who else,' what else," she replied. "Whatever is in that bed isn't breathing nor moving, which means it's likely a decoy. Maybe the king has put a figure of himself here to keep others from finding him where he truly sleeps?"

"Or perhaps it is one of the undead he's rumored to control, ready to pounce upon the unwary souls who enter its master's chambers?" Juliane said uneasily.

Liliana frowned. "I hadn't thought of that. I hope that isn't the case." She handed him the torch and then walked back toward the bed, Juliane trailing behind her. "Regardless of what it is, we must uncover it." She reached into her pack and, removing her sword, unsheathed it. Juliane stood beside her, shining torchlight on the bedside, as she used her free hand to grasp the curtain; she took a deep breath and, holding her sword aloft, flung it aside. When nothing emerged from the bed, she asked Juliane to hold the torch nearer, for the body within was still hidden in shadow. He did so, and both could not help but gasp when they saw who was lying there, for it appeared to be none other than Korben Darkwood.

Juliane suggested that the figure might be a dummy of the king, but, when Liliana reached out and poked it, she immediately recoiled. "It feels like an actual body." She stretched her arm out once more and this time shook the figure gently. "I think it's an actual body." Dazed, she looked up at Juliane. "I think that it's Korben Darkwood, and that he's...dead."

"He's dead?" Juliane said. "I can't believe it. I didn't think a sorcerer that powerful was capable of dying." He checked the king and, finding that Liliana's assessment seemed accurate, exclaimed, "This is good news! We can tell the prince his father has passed and can share our suspicions regarding King Darkwood's enchanting us all with him. He seems so kind when he appears to be himself, I'm sure he'd be willing to give me some of his hair should I graciously explain my circumstances to him. We should probably go tell Arthur—"

"You needn't tell me anything, for I already know what you're going to say—that my father is no longer among the living." They turned to find Arthur Darkwood standing in the doorway, a smirk upon his handsome face. "In fact, I'm not only aware that he's deceased, I can tell you exactly how long he's been dead for: five years, three months, and twenty-three days."

35·

The travelers at first stood speechless, gaping at Prince Darkwood. Once Juliane had shaken off his stupor, he stammered, "B-but there's no way the king could have been dead for that long! I was speaking to him just a few hours ago, and I've seen him walking and talking many times over the past few days—"

"Well, it turns out Father dearest wasn't the only person in our family with an aptitude for necromancy," the prince interrupted. "When I grew old enough to assist him, he forced me to join him in his researches, and, well, the student soon surpassed the teacher in skill."

Liliana found her voice. "And you used this...skill...to control your father's body once he'd passed?"

"Precisely. My father was hoping to bring my mother back as a fully functioning person, which is impossible to achieve, but manipulating someone's dead body through sorcery—even using them as a puppet to interact with others—isn't very difficult for a proficient necromancer. Didn't you ever wonder why the king and I never spoke at the same time, why we never walked together, why he seemed to drowse whenever I talked animatedly? You probably assumed it was because he was exerting an influence over me—and, believe me, I wanted you to—but it was really I who was controlling him."

"That means...you're the one who's been tormenting

your subjects the past few years!" Liliana said incredulously. "We heard many tales of your father's cruelty during our travels—you were the one behind his monstrous behavior all along?"

"Guilty as charged, I'm afraid. I have spent the past five years cultivating a fear of my father in his citizenry whilst restoring his kingdom to its former glory, for he neglected it severely due to focusing on his work. I planned on announcing that the king had died after I'd finished remaking things to my specifications. I figured the people of the Darklands would be in such terror of him by then that they'd rejoice at my ascending to his throne and would fulfill my every whim." The prince grinned and shook his head. "I hadn't considered the possibility that someone— or, more accurately, 'someones'—might prove an impediment to my plan."

A terrible idea had taken root in Liliana's mind as she had listened to him speak, and, when she sensed he had nothing more to say, she asked, "Arthur, how is it that you're aware of exactly how long your father has been dead for?"

He gazed at her with unconcealed admiration. "I should have known you would bring that up, Liliana, given how brazen and clever you are. I'm aware of the precise date and time of his passing because I was there when he expired."

She paled. "And...how did he die?"

"In quite a tragic manner, really. He ate something that disagreed with him and passed away suddenly, writhing in agony, during his birthday celebration. He'd asked the cook to prepare his favorite meal, and, once he'd received it, gobbled it greedily. A pity for him, really, as, even with all his arcane knowledge, he didn't foresee my adding an ingredient to it that would cause...undesirable effects."

Juliane, who had been listening to the exchange with mounting horror, cried, "Do you mean to say that you

329

poisoned the king?" The prince did not respond, but the corners of his mouth turned up slightly, and this gave Juliane all the answer he needed. "How could you do that? How could you murder your own father?"

"He was a father to me in name only," Arthur said contemptuously. "That man never once considered how I might feel; from the moment of my birth onward, all he could ever think of was bringing my mother back. He spent barely any time with me throughout my childhood—I had countless nursemaids and servants function as my parents in his stead—and he only really started speaking to me when I became old enough to assist him in his studies."

His lower lip quivered, and he seemed to be trying to keep himself from crying. "I tried to love him, but by the time I'd reached adolescence it dawned on me that he would never truly care about me—to him, I would always just be the awful baby who had killed his beloved wife." His expression grew fierce. "So, I learned as much as I could from him about magic and governance, waited until I was old enough to run the kingdom on my own, then ended his life and took his throne. He's of more use to me dead than he ever was alive."

He fell silent, and stood glowering at the travelers until Juliane asked, "Arthur, where do we fit into all of this? It's obvious you were attempting to exert an influence over us, to manipulate us and to separate us, but we're still uncertain as to why."

Prince Darkwood cast a pitying glance at him. "Oh, Juliane, I had so many great intentions regarding the two of you, but I didn't fully think things through—hence our being where we are now." Juliane's face wrinkled in confusion, and the prince explained, "Your arrival was foretold by one of my familiar spirits. I place them in locations where they might discern threats to me, and so have a few that keep watch over the home of a certain Mater Moonshade—I gather you know her? Imagine my surprise when my informant let me know that two young women had escaped her clutches and were making their way to me—and that one of them was really the transformed prince of the neighboring kingdom."

Juliane's eyes went wide, and Arthur Darkwood laughed. "Yes, I'm fully aware that you used to be Julian Stoneshire, heir to one of the most powerful dominions in this part of the world. It doesn't bother me that you once were a boy—frankly, I would likely have tried to woo you even if you still were one, for you're of great use to me and I recall your having been as handsome a man as I...but I suppose that's beside the point. I must confess that, when you two arrived, I decided to let myself be greedy. You're both very attractive in vastly different ways and living in as secretive a manner as I have been can be very lonely, so I determined that I'd enthrall you so that I might more easily woo each of you. I even held out hope that one or both of you might develop true feelings for me, beyond the magic's influence." He frowned. "But that was not to be. My first mistake was assuming that the dresses I'd enchanted would fit your larger frame, Liliana. They did not, and, as a result, not only were you not swayed by me, but you also uncovered my designs and alerted Juliane to them."

"How do you know this?" she asked, astonished.

"Familiars, remember? I try to make sure they keep me abreast of things."

She pursed her lips, and he continued, "I then tried to make it seem as if my father was controlling me, as if I was under his influence. I had hoped that, if you believed this, you might come to me with your concerns and I could 'assist' you in 'defeating' him—and could thereby gain your trust and perhaps still bring my plans to fruition." He scowled at them. "But you had to go meddling in things you shouldn't have. How was I to know that you'd break into 'the king's quarters'—or, more accurately, my research chambers—and discover my father's state? Now I shall

331

have to reach my utmost aim through other, perhaps less pleasant, means."

Liliana's forehead creased with worry. "Arthur, what is this aim you speak of?"

Prince Darkwood turned to her. "To have Juliane wed me, and to have you either stay on as our companion or return to her kingdom with tidings of our impending marriage. If she and I are joined, I shall eventually become ruler of not only my own realm, but of hers as well."

Juliane's face reddened in outrage. "How dare you plot to marry me so that you might seize my family's kingdom? Even after Liliana had released me from your power I still held out hope that you weren't fully corrupted—that you were also under the king's influence and might be amenable to assisting us—but I now know you're so much worse than I'd ever imagined your father to be. I'm appalled that I ever experienced even the slightest attraction toward you."

The prince's voice grew dangerously quiet. "Juliane, are you saying you won't wed me of your own accord, even if I make the transaction beneficial to you?"

"I am saying," Juliane retorted, "that I wouldn't marry you even if you were the last person on earth and the fate of humanity depended upon our union."

Prince Darkwood's face initially grew slack, eyes filled with hurt, then twisted in indignation. "Is that so?" he said, his tone sharp enough to make Juliane cringe. "Do you truly think so little of me?" He shook his head, clucking his tongue. "It's a pity you feel that way, for, if that's the case, you leave me with no choice but to use harsher measures to secure your hand."

Juliane stammered, "W-what do you mean, Arthur?"

The man said nothing, merely reached into a pocket of his cloak, removed a small bell, and struck it once with the flat of his hand. It let out a resounding tone that caused both Liliana and Juliane to cover their ears, but, once they had uncovered them, they discovered the bell had served a purpose greater than just making an awful din. A multitude of horrible sounds bubbled up from the trapdoor in the room behind the prince, and the travelers understood that the noise had served as a sort of summons, and that whatever lurked in the lightless depths below would soon be making an appearance.

Liliana unsheathed her sword and Juliane dug desperately through his pack until he found his dagger, then they stood back-to-back facing the trapdoor as a gloating Prince Darkwood stepped aside to let through what was coming from belowground. Something clattered up the steps; it was at first an indistinct gray and white figure, but, as it climbed out of the hole, Juliane had to stifle a cry of horror, for the creature was clearly a member of the "undead army" Darkwood (though, as it turned out, the son rather than the father) was rumored to control. The thing's face had rotted away in several places, its white skull showed through the skin of its head, and its limbs dangled perilously from joints worn and exposed. It lumbered toward the travelers, gait unsteady, and lifted its bony arms toward them.

Liliana told Juliane, "Leave it to me. An unstable thing like that shall be easy to destroy." He heeded her words and stepped behind her, clutching his dagger in case he needed it, but she was as good as her word: she slashed at the creature and, in one swift movement, severed its head from its body. The skull lay on the ground—jaws still moving, much to Juliane's chagrin—until Liliana cleaved it in two with a heavy blow. She scoffed, "My, that was easy! Is there no greater challenge in store?"

She immediately regretted her impulsive boasting, for the prince said, "Oh, don't worry, there will be more. That bell tends to wake...everything."

Two undead similar to the first soon came through the

333

trapdoor, and Liliana successfully dispatched each of these, as well as three others that followed. She was starting to feel confident that she and Juliane might make it out of the predicament unscathed, for she had needed to use little of her skill to best these enemies, when she noticed that a new noise, a slithering sound, had replaced the familiar din of skeletal feet rattling up the sunken stairway.

When what was making it emerged from the trapdoor, she let out a startled gasp, for the creature was the most horrifying thing she had ever seen—which was certainly saying something after all she had witnessed during their journey. From the waist up it resembled a long-dead woman—its skin was rotting away, its hair hung limply about its head, and it was missing its left eye—but, from the waist down, it was a collection of slimy coils reminiscent of the bodies of decaying snakes. She felt like shrieking, but was beaten to the act by her companion, who let out such a terrified scream that she felt compelled to turn to him. "Juliane, what's the matter—I mean, apart from the obvious trouble we're facing?"

"That beast!" he screeched, pointing at the monster. "I know it! I saw it in a nightmare I had whilst we were captive at the Mater's—I could never forget something like that. How could I have foreseen it? What does it mean?"

"It may mean," said Prince Darkwood, "that you are in some way receptive to images of the future, that you may be able to sense things before they occur. Or perhaps you 'picked something up' from my familiar whilst in its presence? Regardless, it's a fine ability to have," he conceded admiringly. "Allow me to introduce my most formidable creation. You might notice a family resemblance. I guess you could say that she's the *queen* of my undead."

334

36.

Appalled, Juliane turned to gape at the prince. "You made your own mother into that *thing*?"

"I held no sentiment for her—she never mothered me, after all—and my father had used magic to keep her well-preserved in hopes of restoring her to life, so the most practical thing to do was to make use of her body after his, erm, unfortunate demise," Arthur Darkwood replied. "I decided to give her a special role in my undead army, as befits her, in his honor."

"You are a monster," growled Juliane.

"Oh, Juliane, it hurts me to hear you speak that way about someone you once cared for," said Prince Arthur, feigning sorrow.

"I never cared for you! The only reason I'd even considered marrying you is because you'd enchanted me into doing so."

"And since you're no longer under the influence of that enchantment and are now unwilling to wed me, I suppose I must force your hand in the matter."

Juliane glared at him, then turned to find the nightmare creature nearly upon them. He spun back to the prince, who laughed wickedly. "I suppose you've noticed my threat isn't an idle one?" Juliane grumbled uneasily, and Prince Arthur continued, "I am now going to give you a choice of two fates. The first—which, in my opinion, is the better one—involves you marrying me of your own accord so that together we may rule my kingdom and eventually also yours. The second isn't nearly as pleasant—shall I describe it nonetheless?"

He did not wait for an answer. "If you refuse to wed me, I shall order the queen to attack Liliana. Once it has torn her to pieces, I shall have it come after you, and, when it catches you, it shall hold you in its loathsome embrace whilst I perform a ritual that shall rekindle your affection for me. Which fate do you pick?"

When he saw the man would not be swayed, Juliane sighed and said, "I'm open to discussing the first option, but only if you call off your undead. I cannot think clearly with that *thing* menacing us."

"That's not very kind way to speak of my mother," Prince Arthur scolded playfully, then he struck the bell twice. Its peals rang out, and, though the monstrous queen glared at him, it nonetheless retreated to the hole in the floor and slithered down the steps into the darkness.

Liliana waited until she was certain the creature had descended deep belowground, then ran to the trapdoor and slammed it shut. Returning to Juliane, she said, "You needn't have done that. I could have vanquished that thing."

"You might very well have died trying, and I wouldn't have been able to bear that. Besides, it's better to marry him of my own accord than to be forced to do so." He lowered his voice. "I promise we shall find a way out of this. I'm just trying to gain us time."

Juliane faced the prince. "I am willing to speak with you regarding my fate now. I'm open to choosing your first alternative if you'll provide me some allowances."

"Why should I negotiate with you when I could just follow through on my threats?"

"Because, if you kill Liliana, I shall take my own life before you can place me in thrall—I know you don't want me to do this, as it would ruin your chances of gaining my family's kingdom—and you wouldn't be able to use my body as you did your father's, for I would maim myself terribly to ensure your ruse wouldn't be a success."

Prince Darkwood scowled. "Well then, what are your terms?"

"You must promise that both Liliana and the man imprisoned in your dungeon, Wilbur Crestshorn, shall be permitted to leave the Darklands following our wedding. Master Crestshorn has been your captive for years, and, as he's incapable of providing what you seek, should be allowed to resume his life outside these walls. I would also like for him and Liliana to bear witness to our wedding—only these two, and no others."

"I can promise this," said the prince, "but, I shall only let them go after I have erased their recent memories. I don't wish for them to return with an army desirous of my overthrow due to their recalling wrongs I'd done them."

Juliane quickly agreed to the prince's conditions despite Liliana's protests, then he inhaled, preparing himself for a performance, and continued, "I also need some reassurance, Arthur, that, if you don't already love me, you might one day. The thought of being forced to wed someone who doesn't truly care for me is unbearable, so, if I must marry against my will, I would at least like to know that I might one day be viewed as a beloved partner."

"I can assure you that I feel as much for you as I deem myself capable of feeling for another," said Arthur Darkwood, in as kindly a tone as he could muster. "I'm not sure if I would call it 'love,' but, with time, I could perhaps be convinced otherwise."

Juliane was uncertain if "something like love" would be as effective as actual love in breaking his curse but decided he must chance it. "All right, Arthur. If you can assure me that you'll allow my friends at our wedding and will release them immediately afterward, and that you'll try to cherish me as a wife rather than just view me as a means of obtaining my kingdom...then I will marry you."

"Wonderful! I shall make preparations so that we may wed in the morning."

"In the morning—you mean, you want to get married *tomorrow*?" Juliane squeaked. "Don't you feel that's a little hasty? Perhaps we should wait before we—"

"No," the prince interrupted. "As I've pressed you into this union, I want to make sure the ceremony is held as soon as possible, so that you have little time to try and avoid it. If it weren't so late I would have it today, but, as it's long after dark, I'll hold things off until the morrow." He waved an arm at the travelers. "You're dismissed and may return to your rooms. I will send a maid to fetch you early tomorrow." He turned to leave, but paused to call over his shoulder, "Oh, and, if I were you, I wouldn't try escaping tonight, for I shall have some special members of my 'army' on watch and bumping into them would be...highly unpleasant." He smirked coldly, then sauntered out of the room, leaving his stunned guests behind him.

***

Dejected, the travelers trudged out of the prince's quarters, through the main hall, and down the passageway to their rooms. "Why did you tell him you'd marry him, Juliane?" asked Liliana, who had been silently stewing, as they neared Juliane's bedchamber. "You should have known he would rush you into things. He'd apparently do anything to rule your kingdom." She frowned and shook her head. "I wish you hadn't responded so impulsively. How are we going to get out of this?"

"I have a lot on my mind but don't feel comfortable discussing it here," said Juliane. "Will you come into my room so we can talk privately?"

Liliana nodded, and, once they had locked themselves in

the chamber, she flopped onto the bed. "Well, what is it you wanted to share with me? I hope it's a plan regarding how we might escape from here."

"I may have an idea," he said as he sat down beside her, "but I cannot share it with you."

"Why not?" she asked crossly.

He lowered his voice to a whisper. "Because something may be listening to us. Remember how the prince discovered you'd alerted me to his machinations? He used familiars, and one might be in the room at this very minute."

"Well then, what should we do?"

"We should make the time we have together count by using it to clear the air between us—to be fully honest about anything we feel we haven't been."

She briefly considered his words. "I suppose you're right. Is there anything you feel you need share with me?"

He cast his face down. "Actually, yes, I have something I must tell you." He took a deep breath. "I was speaking the truth when I said I'd been with Saurenia on the same night you had, but I haven't yet shared exactly what happened, and I should."

"You don't have to, Juliane. I was enchanted by her, and there's a chance you might also have been. You needn't feel bad for not resisting her charms."

"But the thing is, I *did* resist *her* charms," he admitted softly. Liliana appeared confused, so, staring at his hands, he continued, "When Saurenia tried to seduce me using her normal guise, she was unsuccessful—I was brooding about how I'd wounded you in Pultare and didn't want to do yet another thing to hurt you. But then she changed her appearance, and, well..."

He could not bring himself to finish his confession but did not need to for Liliana to realize what he was saying. "Are you telling me that you dallied with her because she took my form?"

339

Juliane lifted his face, his expression anguished. "I'm so sorry, Liliana! She looked just like you, and I'd lost all hope of us ever being together due to the incident in Pultare, and I was curious about what it would be like to be with you, and...I'm so ashamed. I was foolish and rash. I completely understand if this changes the way you feel about me."

He turned from her, not wanting to meet her eyes. She regarded him a moment, then said quietly, "You aren't the only one who made use of Saurenia's abilities that night."

Gaping, he jerked his head to stare at her. "Liliana, are you telling me you had Saurenia—"

"Yes, Juliane," she gently interrupted, "I also had her change her appearance during our dalliance. At one point early on during our time together I...accidentally called her your name. She went over to where you slept and plucked a hair from your head, there was a flash of brilliant light, and then...she was you. And, I must be honest, although I tried to deny it...I knew I enjoyed our time together more *because* she was you."

It was her turn to look away, for she did not want him to see how red she had become, but she felt a gentle hand upon her shoulder, and she turned to find him gazing at her with unabashed adoration. "Oh, Liliana," he said, "I'm relieved I wasn't the only one who employed Saurenia's power to that effect. Hearing that you did, even though you were upset with me at the time, gives me hope that you might feel for me as I do for you despite your misgivings."

"Juliane, we've been through so much together, and, as you have grown as a person, I have grown to care ever more deeply for you. I think that, no matter who you are or might become, I...will still feel for you as I do now," said Liliana, then, voice barely audible, she admitted, "I believe I am falling in love with you."

"And I *know* that I'm falling in love with you, Liliana Almwick!" yelled Juliane, almost leaping from the bed. "In fact, I'm so proud of how I feel, I shall tell the world!"

"You shall do no such thing," she scolded. "What if Darkwood's familiars hear?"

"I care not, for he knows I wed him not out of love, but out of necessity."

"True," she said. "Speaking of which, can you really not share your escape plan with me? If you say it very softly in a way that's clear only to me, even if a familiar is present it may not hear you or may not understand."

Juliane furrowed his brow and glanced around the room, then he murmured, "The Pulvis Lapsus Memoriae."

Liliana's mouth dropped open. "Of course! You have some left, as we didn't use it on Darkwood. I—"

He placed his finger to his lips. "The more we speak, the more likely it is that Arthur shall discover our designs."

"Of course," she whispered. "I gather you plan on using it during the wedding?"

"I do."

Her face grew worried. "But what if the prince discovers your plot and intervenes? What if he avoids the dusting or, worse, turns the powder back on you?"

"Then he does. I cannot fret about it, for I have no control over it."

She considered challenging this, but instead sighed. "Of course, now that we've shared our true feelings with one another, we face the likelihood that one or both of us will forget them before the end of the morrow."

Her face grew forlorn but then abruptly filled with resolve, and she rummaged through her pack until she found a small velvet bag. Opening it, she removed a gold chain from which hung a pendant of blood red stone. "My mother gifted me this when I was a child and told me it would bring me good luck. Though I don't believe it's been entirely successful, it may have played a role in bringing you and I together and in keeping us safe from harm during our travels. If so, I suppose it's lucky after all." She took his hand and placed it into his palm. "I'm giving it to

341

you. Even if we're parted, even if you no longer remember me after tomorrow, you will still have it to treasure. Maybe you'll retain its significance somewhere deep within you, and it might one day spark your recollection and...bring us together again."

Juliane, his eyes misty, stared at the necklace. "I cannot accept this. Your mother gave it to you, she wanted you to have it—"

"And now I'm giving it to you. You've grown to mean so much more to me than any bauble ever could."

"Oh, Liliana, I shall treasure it forever!" he exclaimed. After placing the gift into his pack for safekeeping, he timidly said, "I have something to ask of you, but don't want for you to misinterpret my request." She raised a questioning eyebrow, and he continued, "It's just that—I'd like to ask you to stay here with me tonight." He added hastily, "I'm not suggesting we do anything, mind you, I just want to be near to you. There's a chance I won't see you again after tomorrow, so..."

He trailed off, for she had started to laugh. "I shall gladly stay with you! There's nowhere else I'd rather be—wait, that's wrong—there are so many *places* I would rather be, but no one else I'd prefer to be stuck here with."

"Then why are you laughing?" he asked, confused.

"Because you felt the need to clarify that you weren't expecting for us to be together tonight. You've spent such a large portion of this journey trying to dally with me, and after we've both finally admitted how we feel for one another is when you choose to be chaste?"

She giggled, and he stammered, "No—I mean, yes—I mean, I'm still thoroughly interested in being with you in that way, I just didn't know if you desired that. I wanted to make sure you knew that my wanting you to sleep here wasn't due to purely carnal reasons. I—"

"You know, you're quite endearing when you're flustered," she interrupted playfully, then she placed her lips to his ear. "This may be our last night together. I want to make it count."

"Do you mean you want to…"

He squealed as she flung her arms around him and pulled him to her so that their faces were mere inches apart. "Juliane, I think you should kiss me now," she said.

He did not have to be told twice on this occasion, and eagerly obliged.

37.

The following morning, Juliane awoke entwined in Liliana's embrace and gazed upon her slumbering face, for he still scarcely believed that, after weeks of romantic tension, they had finally acted upon their passions. This filled him with a fiery resolve that they should not be sundered, so he left her arms despite being loath to do so, for he needed to ensure that the things he required to carry out his plan were readied before Darkwood sent for him.

He climbed out of bed, went to the pile of disenchanted dresses, and chose an extravagant white one to wear due to its lengthy sleeves. He giggled as he pulled it on—he found it humorous that he, of all people, should wear the color of purity for his wedding—then suddenly paled, for it dawned on him that he was, indeed, expected to marry Arthur Darkwood that very day

He determined that he would do whatever possible to prevent this exchange of vows, and so fumbled through his pack until he found the Pulvis Lapsus Memoriae. He was about to hide it on his personage when he heard a movement behind him, and he turned to find that Liliana had woken and was sitting up in bed, smiling fondly at him. "Good morning, you," she said. "Whatever are you up to?"

"I'm just preparing for my impending marriage," he replied, waving the powder packet at her before sticking it

344

up his left sleeve.

She nodded knowingly and seemed about to say more when a rap sounded at the door. The knocker was the chambermaid Darkwood had promised to send, and Juliane asked if she might fetch him some white gloves to complete his wedding ensemble. After sending her away he shut the door, then turned to find Liliana standing behind him, grinning. "How very crafty! The prince will be less likely to suspect you're plotting something if your gloves match your gown. You know, you may very well be as clever as me despite some believing otherwise."

"Do you think I am?"

"I think you're a more than fitting match for me in many ways." She wrapped her arms around him, and she was about to kiss him when the maid hammered upon the door. Exasperated, he let the woman into the room and took the gloves from her. Pulling them on, he surveyed himself in the mirror. "How do I look?"

"Absolutely beautiful," declared Liliana.

He was tempted to throw his arms around her, but, as the servant was still present, refrained from doing so and instead let the maid know they would need additional time to ready themselves before leaving. She told him that this would be fine, but that she must wait for them in the passageway so she could escort them to the throne room. "Prince Darkwood said I must ensure you make it to him safely, as he doesn't want you getting lost along the way."

"He would say that," Juliane muttered under his breath.

He walked her out of the chamber, then returned to find Liliana already half-dressed; pulling her frock onto her shoulders, she said mischievously, "I wouldn't want to distract you on your wedding day." He stuck his tongue out at her, but nevertheless patiently waited as she finished her preparations and grabbed her pack.

They exited the room to find the maid lurking near the doorway, and they followed her down the passageway,

345

keeping their distance so they could talk without her hearing. "I must admit, I'm very worried," confessed Juliane. "I just hope I can dust the prince without his interfering in some way."

"I have been thinking about your plan since you revealed it to me, and I believe I've determined a way in which I might help you succeed," said Liliana, eyes shining. "I obviously cannot share it with you in case something is listening, so you'll just have to trust me." She grabbed his hand and squeezed it, and he thanked her for the reassurance. Savoring what they knew might be the last tender moment they would ever share, the pair walked hand in hand toward the throne room, only letting each other go upon entering the chamber.

Prince Darkwood stood at its rear, clothed in a white shirt and jacket and cream-colored breeches, and expectantly surveyed the travelers as they advanced toward him. Wilbur Crestshorn stood next to him in his regular shabby garments, a look of confused fright upon his face, but his fear dissipated when he saw who had come through the doorway. "Dear young ladies!" he cried, running to them and clasping each in turn. "I didn't know why I'd been pulled from my prison and assumed I was to finally meet my fate at King Darkwood's hands, but seeing you fills me with hope. Have you managed to convince him to release me?"

"Well, yes," Juliane said, "but things aren't so simple."

The old man seemed perplexed, so the travelers explained the circumstances to him, and he shook his head ruefully. "I had no idea that the king had passed years ago and that his son has been the one tyrannizing this land. While I'm pleased that I shall be able to return to my Rosie, I wish it wasn't at your expense, Juliane."

"I'm just happy to help you in whatever way I can," replied Juliane, then he lowered his voice. "Don't worry, Liliana and I have plans that will hopefully ensure the three of us shall leave here together."

Master Crestshorn was asked to maintain secrecy and vigorously bobbed his head up and down, then the reunited friends turned to face Arthur Darkwood, for he had started clapping. "What a scene, what a lovely show!" he said wryly. He dismissed the chambermaid, then continued, "Now that the servant's left us and you're done telling the aged fellow just how awful I am, I'd appreciate it if everyone could get into their appropriate places. After all, we do have a wedding to get over with."

He ordered Liliana and Master Crestshorn to sit upon the thrones, then asked Juliane to come stand next to him. "I've created vows for us and have drawn up a marriage contract for you to sign that shall make our union official. This will be a short ceremony—after all, we wouldn't want to give you time to change your mind, would we?"

His haughtiness perturbed Juliane, who hissed, "Don't forget that I am only doing this because you've made me. I won't pretend I'm enjoying it, and if I don't like something that you're trying to make me agree to I will say so."

Prince Darkwood shrugged his shoulders. "As you wish. It is, after all, your special day." He turned from the still-fuming Juliane to address the seated witnesses. "Are you ready?" Liliana and Master Crestshorn nodded weakly. "Good! Then, let us begin." He grasped Juliane's hands roughly and said, "I, Prince Arthur Darkwood, take thee, Princess Juliane Stoneshire, as my wife, to have and to hold, for fairer and for fouler, until death parts us. Now, repeat after me: I, Princess Juliane Stoneshire, take thee, Prince Arthur Darkwood..."

Juliane froze, for the prince had said his vows more quickly than anticipated and now expected him to do the same—and he had not yet gotten a chance to prepare the Pulvis. He gulped and silently prayed Liliana would intervene, then, after a second's hesitation, feebly echoed, "I, Princess Juliane Stoneshire, take thee, Prince Arthur

Darkwood..."

"As my wedded husband, to have and to hold..."

"As my wedded husband, to have and to—"

"No!" screamed Liliana, and she leaped from her chair and rushed over to them. "I cannot allow this." Taking the prince's hands from Juliane, she said, "Arthur, you cannot marry her, because...I've fallen in love with you."

"What?" croaked Juliane, eyes bulging and mouth gaping. "What do you mean, Liliana? I thought—" She spun toward him, winking her left eye furiously, and he realized, *This is how she means to help me escape. She plans on sacrificing herself to ensure my freedom. Of all the ways...I wish she hadn't chosen this one.* He couldn't help but say, "Oh, Liliana," and she smiled at him warmly before turning back to the prince.

"Well, what say you, Arthur? I know that I cannot provide you with a kingdom in addition to your own, but I can give you the honest romance you once professed to desire. Will you choose me, despite my not being a princess?"

She stared at Prince Darkwood, her face expectant, and, after some deliberation, he said, "I've considered your words, and, though I'm sorely tempted to take you as my bride in Juliane's stead...I cannot. I must admit that I don't believe I will ever love another as much as I love the power that comes with ruling."

"Scoundrel!" Liliana shrieked. "You may look fancy, Arthur Darkwood, but underneath your finery you're nothing but a common rogue. All your talk of wishing to find true love—you were only lying! You're a monster! More monstrous than any of your undead!" She buried her face in her hands and wailed, and Juliane stared at her in amazement, uncertain why she was pretending to be so upset—until it dawned on him that she was providing a distraction so that he might prepare the powder without the prince noticing. Her subsequent behavior confirmed his suspicions, for she cast him yet another wink from between her fingers before running to hide behind one of the room's statues.

The prince, scowling in displeasure, declared that he must quiet her if they were to continue the ceremony, then joined her behind the hideous figure. Juliane could overhear their heated exchange, and he wasted no time in pulling the Pulvis packet from his sleeve, opening it, and shaking its contents into his left hand.

He wiped off the empty package and stuck it down the front of his gown, and was glad he had done so quickly, for Prince Darkwood soon emerged and returned to him. "Liliana and I have come to a most pleasant agreement. She has decided that, if I am to marry you, she will stay on with us and, erm, tend to our needs, as she cares greatly for each of us. You know, I'm a very lucky man indeed—I wished to have you both when first we met, and it seems my wish shall come true after all!"

The smug expression upon the prince's face caused a burning hatred for the man to flare up inside of Juliane, and, trying to keep his voice steady—for he did not want to spoil his plans—he asked, "Arthur, don't you ever tire of acting this way?"

"Acting which way?" said the prince, feigning ignorance.

"You know which way. You use and mistreat people, you've caused your citizens to live in fear, you have no real friends. You must see that your behavior makes it difficult for anyone to truly care for you. Why don't you just try being a better person?"

Prince Darkwood sneered at him. "What good did being a better person ever get anyone? I'll tell you what it got me: a father who never loved me and a kingdom of subjects who never wanted to get to know me. I have learned that it's best to just do as you please, for then you shall never be disappointed by the failings of another."

Juliane's loathing toward the man dulled, for he found

himself pitying the prince, as his becoming a beast had not been entirely of his own doing. "I'm sorry life dealt you the lot it did, Arthur," he said softly, "but you should have tired of being like this by now."

"Well, I haven't, and you cannot convince me otherwise."

"But I really do think you should be getting tired, Arthur."

"What are you going on about, Juliane?"

"Grow tired, Arthur!" cried Juliane, and, swinging his arm, he hurled the handful of powder into the prince's face. The man scarcely had time to blink before tumbling to the ground, and Juliane, standing over his sleeping form, impetuously shouted, "Let memory fade, in sleep be lost!"

He repeated the phrase several times to ensure its effectiveness, then turned to Master Crestshorn. "I've done it, Wilbur! I've cast a spell over the prince that shall cause him not to remember anything from, oh, perhaps the last ten years! You, Liliana, and I shall be leaving this wretched place in no time."

The old man's face wore a curious expression, and he said uncertainly, "Juliane, I'm indeed delighted that I shall soon return to Wareston, but I must ask...what is *that*?"

Juliane, looking over his shoulder at what his friend was pointing at, felt his heart sink. Something he could not see sprawled on the ground near Prince Arthur; he could hear it breathing, and could see its outline lightly traced in white powder... He ran to the invisible figure and, finding the clasp he knew would be near its neckline, unfastened it—and his most dreaded suspicion was confirmed, for the invisibility cloak fell away to reveal Liliana, whose face still bore traces of the Pulvis.

As he held her sleeping body in his arms, all grew clear to him: she had not only meant to provide a distraction so that he might prepare the powder, she had also put on the Inuisibilitas Pallium in hopes of assisting him—and he had unwittingly dusted her while coating the prince. He groaned, for he knew he had used the incantation rashly and that it had almost certainly affected her as it had Arthur Darkwood. He understood that he would need to wait until she woke to find out just how much of her had been lost to the spell...but he despaired that she would even remember who he was, let alone how she had felt for him before its casting.

***

Though he wished he could continue cradling Liliana, Juliane knew he had little time to spare and so could not waste it grieving the consequences of his actions. He lowered her gently to the floor and rose from his crouch, then asked Master Crestshorn to pull the cord hanging next to the thrones. The bell sounded in the main hall, and the maid who had accompanied the travelers that morning entered the room. She gasped when she saw the prince stretched out on the floor, and, when Juliane instructed her to fetch help as speedily as she could, she rushed from the chamber. Within minutes she was back with the castle steward, Jonathan, who, upon viewing the prince's condition, bade her summon the Captain of the Watch. Once she had left the room, he eyed Juliane curiously. "Begging your pardon, milady, but what, exactly, has happened to Prince Darkwood?"

Juliane was at first unsure of how much he should tell the man, but he finally decided to share all and, as he did, the steward paled. "Milady, are you suggesting that the king has been dead for ages and that we've been providing service to a...living corpse?" Juliane nodded, and he swayed for a moment, then caught himself and sheepishly admitted, "I nearly had a faint just then." The color slowly returned to his cheeks, and he said, "Though it's a shock to hear this it's good to, for the people of the Darklands have been greatly tormented these past five years. Now that we know it was the son's doing rather than the father's, we can handle things properly and throw him into the dungeon."

"That won't be necessary," said Juliane. "Arthur is now affected by a spell that will have resulted in his forgetting a good deal of his life. Since he won't remember the evil man he was—only the good boy he had been before his father's carelessness hardened his heart—the people of the Darklands can provide him with new memories when he awakens. They can make him the benevolent ruler the kingdom feels it needs, the kind of ruler his father once was. The prince was molded into what he was through a lack of love and compassion. I believe his path will be very different should he no longer tread it alone."

"Methinks the lady may be right," a voice rang out, and they turned to find Richard Ward striding through the doorway. "I didn't hear all that was said, but I believe we should give second chances to those deserving of them."

Once he joined the others Juliane begged favor of both men, that they might bring the prince to his quarters and place him on his bed. "He will wake in a while, confused and uncertain of who he is, and Liliana and I cannot be present then, for we may prompt his memory to return to him. Someone else must bring him to his room and must ensure he comes to believe he is a good man and gracious ruler."

Jonathan accepted the duty but begged assistance from the Captain of the Watch in creating a narrative to share with Prince Darkwood, and the Captain agreed on the condition that the steward would relate all that had happened to him. The men lifted the sleeping Arthur, and they were about to leave the chamber when Juliane asked if Richard Ward might cut some hair from the prince before moving him. Though baffled by the request the man did as asked, and Juliane took the lock, put it in the empty Pulvis packet, and placed it into his gown. He watched Arthur

Darkwood get carried out of the room, and hoped that, for both his sake and the sake of the Darklands' subjects, their paths would never cross again.

He heard a sigh and turned to find Liliana stirring, and, hurrying over to her, he crouched down and wrapped his arms around her. She opened her eyes sluggishly and gazed up at him. "Juliane, is that you?"

He was ecstatic that she knew him, for it meant her mind had not been completely erased. "Yes, it's me, dear Liliana. I'm here with you."

"Where am I? This place is unfamiliar."

His spirits sank. "We are in the Darkwoods' throne room. We've just completed our quest. I now have the item I require."

"But, how?" she asked, wriggling from his grasp and sitting up. "The last thing I can recall is our arrival in Darkton."

"That's because I accidentally used the Pulvis on you."

He hastily explained the bare bones of what had happened, and she grew crestfallen. "You mean to tell me that you and I went through so much and yet still prevailed, but that I shall likely never be able to revel in our victory? How disheartening."

"That's not all," said Juliane quietly. "Last night, you and I...were together...and you told me you were falling in love with me."

Liliana, blushing scarlet, was about to question the truthfulness of his words when she noticed how downtrodden he seemed and, realizing that he was being honest, was seized with pity for him. "Oh, Juliane, I'm so sorry that I cannot remember what happened between us. It must be painful to share a moment like that with someone only to have it disappear."

"But...you could once more develop those feelings for me, couldn't you?"

"Yes, of course I could," she said tentatively. "But it may

take me a while to get there. Remember, you now have numerous experiences in your head that I do not. You are here, in the present, but I'm still just exiting that Darklands wood."

Her words encouraged him. "But, when we were in the forest, you told me you were starting to develop romantic feelings toward me. Do you still feel now as you did then?"

"I do, Juliane, but I'm also still uncertain as to whether I shall feel the same way when you're male again," she gently reminded him. "I've said it before, and I shall say it again: I just need some more time to think."

Juliane experienced the urge to cry out that she had already had time enough to figure out what he meant to her, but he recognized how foolish and harmful it would be to do so, as it was due to his rash behavior that she had lost her passion for him. He wanted to tell her many things—foremost of all that he still felt for her as he had the night before and that no change in his form would lessen those feelings—but, before he was able to, Richard Ward rushed into the room. They rose to speak with him, and, breathing hard from his dash to the chamber, he told them, "I have heard all from the steward. You've saved this kingdom, for you have caused our prince to forget his wicked ways—he is, even as we speak, sobbing over the passing of his father and promising to rule the land nobly in his stead. You've miraculously improved the lives of all who dwell in the Darklands. Whatever can we do to repay you?"

Juliane replied, "We would appreciate it if you could arrange transport to bring us and the gentleman Darkwood has kept imprisoned"—he gestured toward Master Crestshorn, who had been trying to keep out of the way—"to Pultare. We'll be able to reach our homes from there, but our having to traverse the treacherous forest that separates it from the Darklands by foot would surely place us in danger."

"I can provide you with what you have requested—in

354

fact, I can do one better," said the Captain. "There's a ship that carries goods from Darkton to Pultare and back that comes here once weekly, arriving in the afternoon and departing in the evening. I'm sure I can secure you passage on it, and you're in luck, for it leaves today! As for your land transport from Pultare, I have a brother there who owns a carriage-making business. I shall give you a letter for him; seek out Charles Ward once you reach the town and, when you find him, hand him my correspondence. I will ensure he provides you with a means of returning home."

"Thank you, Master Ward! We are truly grateful," said Juliane, grasping his hand.

"There's no need to thank me. You've made my life, and the lives of those I care for, once more worth living. It's the least I can do."

Ward bade the three hurry to fetch their things, for the boat would be leaving in a few hours. Master Crestshorn identified that his possessions were still locked in his cell, so, after Juliane had retrieved his pack from his room, the Captain led them into the dungeon. When Richard Ward told Henry the tale he had concocted of the king's death and his son's succeeding him as ruler, the jailer, weeping with joy, swiftly unlocked Crestshorn's cell and returned all his items to him.

Master Ward repeated his story to countless townsfolk as he led the band through Darkton, and the streets were soon filled with singing and cheering the likes of which Juliane had never heard. It struck him that he and Liliana really had saved the Darklands—that, through accomplishing their mission, they had unintentionally rid the land of its tyrannical ruler and had bettered the lives of its citizens—and he knew that, no matter what else happened, he would always have that victory to hold on to. This gave him a pleasant feeling, which helped dispel some of the sadness that threatened to take hold of him each time he looked at Liliana—for, when he did, he thought of what he had unwittingly lost through successfully completing his quest.

The party soon arrived at the wharf, where the boat they had been told of stood before them. Richard Ward had an animated conversation with its captain, and, after coins had changed hands, the man welcomed the trio aboard. The Captain of the Guard borrowed some paper and quickly wrote the letter he had promised them, then they bid him farewell and clambered onto the boat. As Juliane took a seat in its stern, he felt a thrill as it dawned on him that he had, indeed, completed his journey and was finally homeward bound. Liliana came to sit beside him; he smiled shyly at her, she smiled back, and, when he reached out to take her hand, she did not protest. Together they stared out at the vast ocean, and, by the time the ship left the harbor, he had grown hopeful that, during their trip home, Liliana would rediscover what had been stolen from her—and he knew he would be there for her whenever she did.

38.

Though the travelers' journey to the Darklands had been very eventful their return trip to Pultare was much less so—but the little that did occur made Juliane cross, for it prevented him from speaking with Liliana. During their three days' trip by boat Liliana, who apparently had no stomach for ocean travel just as she had no head for heights, was ill most of the time. Though Juliane spent hours caring for her little conversation passed between them, and he knew there was a chance of her not remembering his kindness once her condition improved; he had decided that it would not help things were he to press her regarding her feelings, though, and so he tried to avoid speaking of how he cared for her and hoped that his actions would speak for him.

When they docked in Pultare happier times were in store, for Juliane blew on the shell Irmene had given him and within minutes she had come ashore. The selkie was thrilled to see her friends and listened raptly as they told of how they had defeated *a* Darkwood, though not the one they had expected to. She labeled their victory a cause for celebration and invited the travelers and Master Crestshorn to join her at the Pig's Whistle. They were pleased to return to the establishment, for Tamela welcomed them heartily, and they spent the evening eating and chatting before retiring to one of Master Gelp's finest

357

rooms.

When Irmene left the following morning, the travelers asked Gelp where they might find Charles Ward, and, following the directions he gave, arrived at the shop of the carriage-maker. This Master Ward much resembled his brother, and, after reading the letter they gave him, he clasped each in turn, thanking them profusely. He provided them with a sturdy cart and two strong horses, and the trio climbed into the wagon and sped away from Pultare.

The party stopped in Silvan to check on Geoffrey, but found only a home that, from the looks of it, had not been occupied in many days. They were at first worried, but then Liliana's eyes lit up and her mouth broke into a broad grin. She hurried the others back into the cart, then drove them into the heart of the city, to a tavern called the Whinnying Stallion. She rushed inside while the others waited, confused, and returned to them with a piece of paper. "I knew it!" she cried. "He is with Tancred!" She held the letter out to Juliane, who read:

My beloved friend Liliana,

I'm sorry my handwriting isn't terribly neat, but I am writing this in haste! I want to share the most wonderful news: my musician, Geoffrey, has returned to me. He brought an eager replacement to Rhoswen's home and secured my release, then told me that he had left me for a foolish reason and had sought me out again because he loves me. I believe that I love him too, and I'm elated he's come back to me. He told me you were the one who convinced him to return, because you care for me also. If I'd never met you my life might not be as it is now, and I shall forever treasure you for all that you've done for me.

Geoffrey and I are traveling the world together! We plan on going to many places, so perhaps we shall find out where you live and pay you a visit? I believe we shall.

Again, thank you for everything. I cannot wait to see you when our paths cross once more.

Affectionately yours,
Tancred

He returned the missive to a misty-eyed Liliana. "I feel many things right now," she said, "but foremost among them is joy that my encouragement brought two wonderful beings together. I can only hope that they shall find every happiness with each other and that we shall see them again."

Juliane had expected to feel some discomfort regarding Liliana's emotional response to the Water-horse's letter but was pleasantly surprised to find that he only wished the reunited pair felicity. He pondered this, and realized that it was because he knew that, even if Liliana held affection for the Water-Horse, it would not negate her feelings for him if exist they did. He felt no bitterness toward Tancred for what had occurred between them and Liliana, and admitted to himself that he, too, might one day like to know the creature who had made such an impression upon her. *You're no longer so jealous,* he said to himself. *No matter what happens, this is yet one more benefit of the journey that you shall walk away with.* He told Liliana about this, and she hugged him tightly before spurring the horses forward onto the thoroughfare leading from Silvan.

Just outside the city, where the road split in three, Liliana halted the cart. She suggested they take the path to Hawthorn, for, if they did, they were likely to reach Wareston by the following evening. Hearing the town's name, Wilbur Crestshorn began to weep, so Juliane, giggling, agreed that taking the shortest way would be best. Liliana guided the wagon onto the path, and within a few hours they had reached their destination, where they rented a room at the village's only inn and had themselves a fine rest.

The trio made sure to leave Hawthorn early the following morning, for they knew the day would find them crossing through both Thrallwood, where they would be at risk of being recognized by the Wrathscalders, and the forest where the Sisters dwelt. They were in luck, though, for their travel went smoothly; Master Crestshorn took rein of the horses while they passed through Thrallwood so the others could crouch unseen, and, though they flew through the Sisters' wood so recklessly that they feared the wagon's wheels might come off, they experienced no mishaps. As they neared Wareston Wilbur grew excited, and started to sing, "Wareston, you're the place to be! Wareston, you're the home for me!" His ardor was contagious, so, though they did not know the tune, Liliana and Juliane soon joined him, and all were crooning merrily as they rolled up to the door of the Homely Cottage.

Liliana halted the cart, and she and Juliane jumped down from it. They knocked upon the inn door, and Rose soon answered their summons. "How may I help—" she began, but, when she saw Juliane, she squealed in delight and threw her arms around him. "Oh, Juliane, you've made it back safely! How lovely to see you!" Releasing him, she peered curiously at Liliana. "My dear, you look familiar, but I don't believe we've ever met. Where do I know you from?"

Liliana's face grew bashful. "I, uh, was Landon."

"It's a long story," added Juliane.

Rose's mouth dropped open, but, recovering herself, she said, "Well, then I suppose I must hear it from you. Why don't you come inside...?" She trailed off as she at last noticed who was sitting in the cart. "Wilbur?" she shrieked. "Wilbur, is that you?"

Wilbur climbed from the wagon as fast as his weary bones would carry him. "It is I, my love. I've dreamed of rejoining you for many years, and, now that the time has finally come, I can scarcely believe that I've truly come home."

"We promised we'd return him to you safely," Juliane said softly.

"Oh, Wilbur!" cried Rose, and the long-parted pair rushed into each other's arms. They embraced and kissed and sobbed while the travelers watched them affectionately, and, once they had their fill of crying and hugging, they ushered their friends into the inn, where Rose provided all with a splendid meal that they enjoyed before a roaring fire. The travelers took turns relating their adventures and mission, and an amazed Rose asked, "Juliane, are you tellin' us that you're the prince? That the prince has stayed at our humble inn?"

"Well, I *was* the prince—and, if all goes according to plan, may be yet again—but for now I'm the princess. So, yes, you have been spending time with royalty. Now, don't just start bowing, for it vexes me." He cast Rose a wink, and the room filled with laughter as the merry party finished their repast.

After dinner Wilbur went straight to bed, for the journey had exhausted him, and Rose brought the travelers to the room they had taken when they had last visited her. Liliana tumbled onto the mattress, but instead of joining her Juliane stayed the old woman at the door, for something had been bothering him. "Rose, what would you say if I, being a girl now, told you that I...liked Liliana in a romantic way? Would you and Wilbur still be our friends if you knew this?"

The innkeeper cast him a kindly smile. "It wouldn't matter a whit to me, for you've brought my Wilbur home. You both have my friendship for the rest of my days. I'm sure my husband feels the same way." Juliane embraced her, thanking her for the kind words, then retired to bed. He fell asleep feeling secure that, no matter who he might be or whom he might care for, he would always have a place among the people who truly cared for him.

***

The travelers woke the following morning eager to leave, for, though they enjoyed the Crestshorns' company, the knowledge that they would be seeing their families by the end of the day spurred them onward. They hurriedly washed, dressed, and ate, then bid farewell to their hosts; after many hugs and fond parting words they exited the Homely Cottage, and, after feeding and watering the horses, climbed into the wagon and continued on their way.

They soon passed through the town where they had gotten into the altercation with the two ruffians early on in their journey and knew they were nearing Falsa. "We should go to my house first, though," said Liliana, "for my mother must cure you before I can take you to the palace. I don't think I'd get a very pleasant reception from your parents if I brought you to them as you are now."

Although Juliane had wanted to let Liliana take the lead regarding her feelings for him, he worried that time was running out and that he could no longer wait on her verdict. "Liliana, now that we're close to home, I—"

"I know what you're going to ask, Juliane," she interrupted, and he was heartened by her warm tone. "You want to know how I feel about you, is that right?"

"Well, yes. I don't mean to bother you, but..."

She glanced at him before returning her eyes to the road, and the fondness in that glance gave him hope. "I've been seriously considering the matter and have concluded that...I'm willing to give us a chance. As I've grown quite fond of the female you, I'm...open to seeing what might grow between us once you've regained your male form."

He was slightly disappointed that she could not give him more than a "maybe," but was more so relieved that she

362

had not given him an outright "no." He gently placed a hand on her shoulder. "Thank you, Liliana, I truly appreciate that. I want you to know that, no matter what happens, I shall forever cherish the moments we've shared during our journey."

A smile slowly spread over Liliana's face. "Oh, Juliane, you've become so different from when we first met. Back then I couldn't have imagined feeling for you as I do now."

"I was a bit of an ass," he admitted, shaking his head. "You're right, I am different. For the first time in my life I feel comfortable with myself and...truly happy. And it's all because of the curse upon me and my quest for its cure." He fell silent, then confessed, "I guess it was more of a blessing than a curse, really, if it's enabled me to grow into the person I am now."

"Why, Juliane, are you saying that you've learned the lesson my mother was trying to impart to you?"

"I suppose I am—and don't worry, I won't get cross with you about it on this occasion."

"I have to ask—are you sure you're Prince Julian?" Liliana inquired playfully.

"Well, properly speaking, no, I'm actually Princess Juliane."

"I've said it before and will say it again: you are a wonder. Whenever I think I've figured you out, you surprise me."

"Well, it's a good thing that you shall have many more years to learn all you can about me. You may yet acquire an understanding of the perplexing creature I am."

Liliana briefly let the reins go to squeeze his hand. "I look forward to it," she told him, then they spent the remainder of their ride basking in a contented silence.

Before long they came to the gates of Falsa, and Liliana had Juliane put on the Inuisibilitas Pallium before spurring them forward. She stated her name and reason for entering to the guards on duty, and they exchanged knowing looks, which struck her as odd, but allowed her to proceed without further questioning.

Juliane stayed invisible as they rolled along the city's main thoroughfare, and he could barely curtail a squeal of joy when his family's castle came into view. After passing it they soon found themselves on the outskirts of the city, and Liliana turned the cart onto a dusty path. They rode along until they came to her home, an aging but well-kept manor; Juliane removed the cloak as the wagon came to a halt, and both travelers quickly clambered down from it. Liliana ran up the house's steps, for she was eager to see her mother after so many weeks away from her—but, upon reaching the door, she gasped and, covering her face with her hands, sank to the ground. Juliane trotted up behind her, and, when he spied the parchment affixed to the door, also could not help but gasp, for it read:

Let it be known that, on this day,
The Lady Satiana Almwick has been arrested
For a treasonous act against the royal family
And has been taken into custody by the royal guard
And brought to the palace to be tried for her crime.
Potential sentence: imprisonment in the royal dungeon
for a yet-undetermined period.
Anyone with information about this crime is requested
to report it to the royal guard.

"But how could they have found out my mother is responsible for your state?" Liliana moaned. "You and I are the only ones besides her who are aware that—"

"Saurenia also knows," Juliane interrupted.

She stood up, wiping her eyes, and he went on, "You told her your mother placed the spell on me. All the others who know that I'm cursed don't know *who* cursed me. When was the most recent Blood Moon?"

"Two nights ago. I saw it from the window of the inn in Hawthorn."

Juliane pulled the parchment from the door and examined it. "The ink's still wet, which means this was written not too long ago. I think that, when Saurenia attended the witches' circle, she discovered that we had not only escaped from the Mater but had also erased her memory—and, knowing this, decided to take revenge of a different sort against your mother."

Liliana was livid. "That foul hag! She used us and almost got us killed, and she has now placed my mother in danger. Whatever shall we do?"

"We shall save her. Since this announcement was delivered recently, I'm guessing that your mother was taken today. If we hurry to the palace, we may be able to intervene before they sentence her and throw her into the dungeon."

He turned to head down the steps, but Liliana stayed him. "Thank you," she said. "I know you've not always held a high opinion of my mother, but she has always been my greatest friend and ally. I cannot let her rot in prison."

"Of course," he replied. "I would never let that happen. I know how much she means to you, and, frankly, since I now know that she quite literally helped you become the amazing woman you are today, there's no way I couldn't hold her in esteem. Besides," he continued, smirking, "I'm stuck in this form without her help. Come, let us make haste to the castle. I only hope that we arrive there in time."

39.

Once the travelers had jumped back into the cart Liliana urged the horses forward, and they shot down the path, then turned onto the thoroughfare and sped toward the center of Falsa. Once they had reached the castle, they jumped from the wagon, ran to the building's large double doors, and pounded on them. When a guard answered their summons, Juliane demanded that they be taken to see the royal family. The man refused the request at first, but, when the young lady who strangely resembled the prince called him by name and told him things about himself that she could not possibly know, he relented and let them come inside.

He led them down the entry hall and into the corridor, past the dining room and great hall, to the doorway to the throne room. "I shall allow you to enter but will not accompany you," he told them, "for the king and queen are currently passing judgment and might grow cross should I interrupt them. You may take the risk if you'd like." He pushed the door open and ushered them over its threshold, then retreated down the hallway.

Stepping into the chamber, they were met with an unsettling sight: Juliane's parents were seated on their thrones, King Stoneshire wearing an expression of righteous anger, and before them stood Lady Almwick, fettered in shackles, head bowed. When she raised her head to see who had entered her face was drained of color, and Liliana rushed to her and gathered her in her arms. "Oh, Mother, I'm so glad you're unharmed!"

The Lady managed a faint grin. "My child, it's so good to see you. I had such dreams...I worried you'd never return to me." She returned her daughter's embrace. "I only wish we could have reunited under more agreeable circumstances."

Juliane stormed over to his parents, who were pleased to see him, and they were taken aback when he started to scold them. "Mother, Father, why are you punishing Lady Almwick? I did not desire for this to happen."

The king, finding his voice, said sternly, "Julian, this woman is responsible for your enchantment. Your mother and I were informed by a reliable source—"

"I know the source you speak of," Juliane interrupted. "She is a powerful sorceress with a grudge against the Lady, and, when I crossed paths with her, she manipulated me, placed me in danger, and nearly caused my death. She is no one you should trust."

"But, darling," said his mother, "it's still true that Satiana Almwick is responsible for your predicament."

"That may be, but her actions weren't malicious, and so she shouldn't be punished! She meant to teach me a lesson, not to harm me, and she even had her daughter accompany me to ensure my safety." He beckoned to Liliana, who timidly approached the king and queen, bowing before them. "This is Liliana Almwick. She risked her life on countless occasions to help me get what I needed." He reached into the front of his dress and pulled out the packet containing Arthur Darkwood's hair. "Here it is. Lady Almwick can use it to cure me. Since no harm has been done, she should be released after doing so."

He stood with arms crossed and glared defiantly at his parents, who at first merely gaped at him, but then King Stoneshire turned red and said scornfully, "Julian, this woman cursed you, and you believe she bears you no ill will just because she sent her child to keep an eye on you? How foolish."

Juliane also reddened, and he looked as if he might start yelling when the king continued, "I was told you were under the impression that you needed the hair of a prince who'd fallen in love with you for the spell to be broken, is that correct?" Juliane nodded begrudgingly. "Well, the individual I spoke to informed me that the hair of *anyone* in love with you would suffice to restore you to your 'true form.' Though I'm not quite sure what that means, it is clear to me that the Lady sent you on a dangerous mission for no other reason than to make you suffer, and that she risked the life of her own daughter in doing so."

"That's not true!" cried Lady Almwick. "If the cure you speak of is an actual one, I wasn't aware of it—I haven't participated in magic circles for some time, so my methods may be out of date. I swear I truly did think that a lock of hair from a prince in love was needed to break the curse. I only cast the spell I did because..."

She trailed off, uncertain whether she should continue, and Liliana said gently, "Mother, I can explain." She took a deep breath, then told the king and queen, "My mother used this particular enchantment because she'd previously experienced success with it...with me. I am under the same curse as Juliane, though to me it's no curse, for I wanted to be a girl. I'm sure she's being sincere when she says that she thought the solution she suggested was the right one. I know she would never deliberately place anyone in harm's way, and I beg you to believe this." Casting her face down, she added, "I must confess that I assisted her in casting the spell, so, if she is at fault, then I must share in her guilt."

She fell silent, and King Stoneshire stroked his beard, pondering her words. At length, he addressed Juliane. "My child, what have you to say about this?"

"Father, Liliana and her mother are honest and just

people, and I know they merely wanted to make an example of me and acted without forethought. I've learned much from my journey and feel it was worth going through to end up the person I've become. I beseech you—once the Lady has performed the required rituals, please allow her to return home."

The king grew thoughtful, and he got up and paced the room while the others uneasily awaited his verdict. Finally, he halted in front of Juliane. "I've taken your pleas into consideration, and I have determined that the Lady and her daughter may leave once they have restored you to your rightful form—but, only on the condition that, once they've gone, they shall never again darken our doorstep. Though they meant you no harm their actions still endangered you, so I do not wish to see them again."

Juliane frowned. "But, Father, Liliana and I have grown so close during our travels! I was hoping that, once I'd returned to being prince, we might discuss possible marriage arrange—"

"No!" barked the king. "The woman who helped place a curse on you shall be no daughter of mine. Now, do you accept my terms? Answer me, before I change my mind about showing them mercy."

Juliane hung his head, defeated. "I accept the terms, Father, though it breaks my heart to do so." He turned to Liliana, who looked as discouraged as he felt, and tears filled his eyes. "I'm so sorry, Liliana. My father might soften as time passes, but he's a very stubborn man..." He sighed. "Perhaps we shall meet again in the future, but, until then, please remember how greatly I care for you. No matter what life brings you, I want you to be happy...even if that happiness can be found with someone who isn't me."

He reached into his pack and retrieved a velvet pouch, then handed it to Liliana, who recognized it immediately. "My necklace! How did you come to have it?"

"You gave it to me on one of the nights you no longer

369

recall, the night we…" He paused, flustered, for he did not wish to discuss what they had done that evening front of their parents. Once he had composed himself, he continued, "You told me you wanted me to keep it as a token of your affection, in case I ended up stuck with Prince Darkwood. I know it means a lot to you, so it doesn't feel right for me to keep it."

"Juliane, if I bestowed it upon you then you needn't return it, for I'm sure I intended that you have it for a reason. I…"

She opened the bag and peered into it, then suddenly stopped speaking and removed the necklace from it. As she stared at the item her mouth fell open, and she dropped it on the floor.

"Liliana, what's going on? Are you all right?" asked Juliane, concerned.

"I…remember," she said. "Though I don't recall much of the time the Pulvis took from me, seeing the necklace made me remember the night I gave it to you—what happened, and how I felt. I've been hesitant to say this, but, now that I know what you've truly meant—and still do mean—to me, and knowing that this may be my only chance to share my feelings, I must tell you…" She grasped his hands, smiling through her sadness. "Juliane, I love you. I have loved you for some time but am only now able to clearly see it. If I can leave you with nothing else, at least I can leave you with that." Letting him go, she bent down and plucked the chain from the ground, then placed it in his hand. "Keep this in case we never meet again. Whenever you miss me, look upon it and know that I will always care for you."

Juliane started to respond in kind but was cut off by his father. "There's no time for tenderness now, especially between those who will soon be parted. We want our son returned to us. Stop dawdling so the Lady can do what she needs to."

Juliane glanced at Liliana helplessly. "But I have so

much I want to say—"

"You needn't say it and anger your father. I know what's in your heart," she replied softly. She turned to King Stoneshire. "My Lord, I humbly petition that I be allowed to draw my sword and remove some hair from my head, so that my mother might use it to cure Juliane."

"But, Liliana, I already have the prince's, you needn't do that—"

"Do you honestly believe Arthur Darkwood was truly capable of loving anyone but himself? Besides, you cast the Pulvis spell on him *before* taking his hair, remember? Even if he had been in love with you up until that moment, he would have forgotten you afterward."

Juliane acknowledged that she had a point, and thus the king permitted her to do as she had requested. She cut off a lock and handed it to Lady Almwick, who asked for a candle; she was given one and proceeded to burn the hair to ash and mix it with her spittle. She summoned Juliane before her and had him strip to his chemise, then used the mixture to create a variety of designs upon his arms, shoulders, and back, which she rubbed into his skin. "Whilst you sleep tonight, you shall gain your 'true form'," she told him. "Upon the morrow, you'll awaken as whatever it is you truly desire to be." He thanked the Lady, and she hugged him and let him know she was proud of how he had grown during the journey.

He and Liliana held each other while his father unlocked the Lady's fetters, only releasing one another when King Stoneshire said coldly, "That's quite enough. Lady Almwick, you and your daughter must leave now and must never again cross this threshold." He grabbed Juliane by the shoulder and dragged him out of the chamber toward the dining hall. "As for you, you shall first eat something and then shall go straight to bed. When you rise tomorrow, you'll be your old self again." The last Juliane saw of Liliana was her waving forlornly as the guards

371

pushed her and her mother out of the door.

**

Juliane reluctantly seated himself at the dining table and would do no more than pick at the food given him; the queen watched him with growing concern and even tried engaging him in conversation, but he would not respond to her and instead poked sullenly at his plate. Eventually his father demanded that he speak with his mother, and Juliane, casting the king the most defiant look anyone had ever directed at him, said, "Father, you may be able to control my actions, but you cannot control my feelings, no matter how much you'd like to." Stung by these words, King Stoneshire buried his face in his dinner, and the trio sat in unbearable silence until Juliane finished his meal, excused himself, and exited the room.

He trudged up the stairs to his comfortable, familiar bedchamber, but, although he had dreamed of returning there, he did not feel the satisfaction he had expected to upon entering. He scanned all the artifacts of his former life and admitted to himself that nothing seemed the same, nor ever would be the same, because his experience as a woman had forever changed his worldview. He stared into the mirror at the face and body he had grown so accustomed to and understood, with a touch of sadness, that this would be the last time he would ever see them.

He washed, changed into his night shirt, and climbed into bed, but, though he knew he must sleep for the spell to take effect, he could not keep his mind from wandering to his quest and all he had gained from it—and, of course, to the time he had spent with Liliana. Tears filled his eyes as he realized that he might never see her again, and he found himself longing to relive even the unpleasant bits of their journey if doing so would allow him to share those moments with her once more. A part of him wished he could turn back time to the day they had first met, for if he had behaved differently then he might have saved himself a lot of trouble, but a greater part knew that his journey had been a necessary evil, for he had learned invaluable lessons during it that would help him to be a wiser ruler and better person overall.

He was eventually able to drift off into a slumber filled with strange dreams not unlike the one he had experienced during the night he had been enchanted; these were pleasant rather than distressing, however, for in each he found himself adventuring with Liliana, and, once he had fallen soundly asleep, he did not stir once.

40.

Juliane woke the following morning feeling unexpectedly good, and, figuring that this was due to the spell having worked its magic, hastily checked to see what change in form it had wrought. He at first thought he might still be dreaming, for his chest seemed as ample as it had been the previous night, but, once he had determined he was not, he figured his eyes were playing tricks on him and decided to take a look in the mirror. He climbed out of bed and shuffled toward it, and, upon reaching it, found that...he was the same person he had been the night before.

Surprised and confused, he stumbled backward, landing on his bed. He searched his mind for a reason why he had not resumed being his princely self and initially could not find one; he did not doubt that Liliana truly loved him, he believed Lady Almwick had recited the incantation correctly, he had gone to sleep almost immediately after the ritual as instructed—why had he not regained his true form? He thought about this for several minutes, then, suddenly, a realization struck him.

This was his true form—or, more accurately, *her* true form.

The more Juliane considered it, the more it made perfect sense. She had never felt fully comfortable as a man—she had always prided herself on being "prettier" than other men, had shuddered at the thought of

developing traditionally masculine attributes, and had
never really desired the company of other men—and she
now understood that her many affairs had been her way of
trying to "prove her manliness"; it had taken her enjoying
the company of women as a woman to realize that her
dalliances did not make her "more of a man." She took a
hard look at her past and admitted that manhood had
never felt quite right to her—she had just always assumed
she must be male because it was what she had been told
she was, and that, since others deemed it desirable, it was
something she should be content with. She had been happy
as a woman, not just due to the time spent with Liliana and
the adventures they had shared, but because...she had been
happy to *be* a woman.

She had journeyed for weeks, risking life and limb to
obtain a cure that would return her to her "true form," only
to discover that the one she had been trying to escape from
was the one she had really desired all along.

Juliane found this terribly amusing and could not keep
herself from giggling, and her giggles turned first to cackles
and then to howls as she fully comprehended the absurdity
of the whole matter. Her laughter grew so loud that it
roused the manservant George from slumber, and he
became so concerned about the strange sounds emanating
from her bedroom that he ran to fetch her parents. He
burst into their quarters claiming that "chilling noises"
were coming from a chamber he had thought to be empty,
and the queen, who had been worrying about her child,
rushed to Juliane's bedroom. She knocked gingerly, and,
when told she could enter, opened the door to find a still-
female Juliane rolling on the bed, face red, mouth gasping
for air. "Darling, what's going on?" cried Queen Stoneshire.
"You were supposed to transform whilst you slept, but
you've stayed the same!"

"I have indeed, Mother. I woke up to find that not a
thing had changed during the night and understood that

this is my 'true form'—and it only took me weeks of facing unnecessary hardship to grow sure of it!"

She started giggling again, and the queen asked, "But what will you do now, love? The kingdom knows you as the prince, and, though your father and I can certainly try to explain your change to our subjects, some may not be very accepting of it."

Juliane immediately sobered, and, head bowed, contemplated her mother's words. When she lifted her face once more, it shone with revelation. "I don't care about ruling this kingdom," she said. "My journey, though arduous and frightening at times, provided me with more fulfillment than anything I'd ever done as a prince. I don't want to reign; I want to continue having adventures...and I want to share them with Liliana."

The queen gazed at Juliane fondly. "You really do love her, don't you?"

Though she was hesitant to admit this, as she had not yet shared the depth of her feelings with Liliana, Juliane finally said, "Yes, I believe I do."

"Then you must go to her and tell her how you feel. Your father and I will always be here for you. If you change your mind you're most certainly welcome to rejoin us and inherit the throne that's rightfully yours, but, even if you choose not to, you shall have a place in our family regardless, for you will always be...our daughter."

Juliane threw her arms around her mother and, thanking her, hugged her tightly. "You needn't thank me," said Queen Stoneshire. "Some of us know firsthand what it means to make sacrifices to be with the ones we love and do the things we long to do."

Startled, Juliane released her. "Mother, do you mean you—"

"I met your father whilst he was traveling through the woods that I dwelt in. He was a handsome young prince at the time, but he was not only beautiful, he was also kind and gracious," the queen said. "Though I greatly cared for him, I knew I could not remain...as I was and still be with him, for he would eventually grow old and die, and I would not. For five years he visited me in my forest, and, though I fell more deeply in love with him with each day that passed, I could not bring myself to forsake the life I'd always known."

"When he turned twenty-five, he came to me, forlorn, and told me his parents would force him to marry another if he couldn't wed me, so I visited an enchantress not unlike your Lady Almwick, who changed me into the human I am today. I know that I shall one day die, though I could have perhaps gone on forever had I so chosen, but I've never regretted my decision, for I've shared my life with a wonderful man and have a child whom I love dearly. Sometimes, to gain the fate we truly desire, we must give up what we've grown comfortable with and venture into the unknown. Though this may cause us to lose some things, we tend to gain so many more."

Juliane looked at her mother and, truly seeing her for the first time, felt ashamed that she had for many years considered the queen a simpleton, for she now realized that the woman was wiser than she had ever imagined. "I shall remember your words, Mother, and treasure them always," she said, then, curiosity piqued, asked, "You told me a sorceress helped you become human—what were you before?"

"I shall give you a clue: it's why I have the fair face you've been fortunate enough to inherit from me."

Juliane's eyes went wide. "Mother, do you mean to say that you were...a fairy?"

"Yes, I was one of the fair folk but chose to become mortal. Living forever isn't as splendid a thing as many believe it to be."

"You never knew anyone called Rhoswen, did you?"

"Why, no, darling, I can't say that I did. Why do you

ask?"

"Oh, for no particular reason," Juliane replied, and she embraced her mother once more—mostly to keep her from noticing how she had blushed when posing the question.

King Stoneshire charged into the room at that instant, his face expectant. "Good morning, my boy!" he crowed. "I cannot wait to see..." He trailed off when he noticed Juliane was still female, and he was at first perplexed, then outraged. "That Lady Almwick didn't do what was asked of her! She hasn't transformed you! I shall ensure she receives harsh consequences—"

"Father, stop yelling," Juliane interrupted sternly, and the king stopped his ranting to gape at her. "The Lady did cast the spell as requested, it just didn't work as expected."

"She must have done something incorrectly, then—"

"Remember when she said it would restore me to my 'true form'? Father, this *is* mine."

The king sputtered, "B-but it can't be. You can't remain like this. You'll be a laughingstock. Our subjects won't accept you like this, they—"

"I don't need to be accepted by them, Father. I don't plan on staying to rule the kingdom, I plan on leaving to happily live my life as a woman...by Liliana Almwick's side."

King Stoneshire once more grew incensed. "I told you that you're not to see that woman again! She and her mother endangered you! They humiliated you! They—"

"Their folly helped me find my true self. I have strong feelings for Liliana, Father. I'm going to go tell her of them and see what comes of it."

"Now, listen here, Julian, no son of mine—"

"My name is Juliane, Father, and I am not your *son*."

Her words stunned him, and he stood speechless while she dressed and gathered her most valued possessions into a large sack; she then pulled this bag, as well as the pack she had taken on her journey, onto her back. "Mother,

Father, I'm leaving now. If you need me, you know where to find me, and I promise to visit you frequently. I care for you both greatly, but I must follow my heart and see where it leads me."

She kissed the queen, who whispered in her ear, "Don't worry, I'll bring him around," then hugged her father, who remained silently astonished.

Her parents followed her as she proceeded down the stairs and to the front doorway. She pushed a door open, then turned to them. "I love you, Mother."

"I love you too, my darling."

"And I also love you, my child," croaked King Stoneshire, finding his voice. "Though I may not understand who you are or what you desire right now, I hope I might one day."

"I'm sure you shall," Juliane said affectionately. "I love you, Father—and, though I know I'm not the prince you expected me to be, I believe I shall make you proud nonetheless."

She embraced both her parents, then, having said her farewells, left the castle and walked down the long drive leading from it. When she passed through the palace gates into the city, she recalled the day she had first trod upon this path, and she marveled at who she had been then and at how much she had changed since. As she tried to determine the quickest way to get to the Almwicks' by foot, she felt joy well up inside her, for she realized that, for the first time in her life, she knew *exactly* who she was, what she wanted, and where she belonged.

***

Lady Almwick had expected that Liliana would go immediately to bed upon their return from the palace, for she had traveled far and seemed exhausted, but, to her surprise, her daughter instead bolted from the cart, raced into the house, and ran up the stairs to the study. Upon her arrival she scanned the shelves, then removed one of the books and went through it at length before returning it to its place. The Lady followed her into the room, and, perplexed, asked her what she was doing.

"I'm trying to regain my memories, Mother!" Liliana said, pulling another book from its shelf. "I'm searching for a spell to undo the effects of the Pulvis Lapsus Memoriae, so that I may recall my time in the Darklands!" She explained that Juliane had accidentally used the powder on her when vanquishing Prince Darkwood, and that, due to this, there were gaps in her memory she desperately wanted to fill. "We accomplished so much whilst we were there, I must find a way to remember it all!"

"Is that the only reason why you'd like your memories returned to you?" asked Lady Almwick, and, though her tone was teasing, her smile was kind. "Do you wish only to recall past victories?"

Liliana sighed. "No, Mother, that isn't the only reason. I'm also doing it because I need to remember the time I spent with Juliane." She cast her face down, and her voice quavered. "I'm in love with her, and I shall likely never see her again. I must find a way of reliving the moments we shared in case we cannot create new ones together." She lifted her head and, wiping tears from her eyes, returned to the task at hand. The Lady regarded her daughter affectionately, and, after kissing her cheek, left her on her own.

She spent all night looking for the correct incantation, but by the morning was still none the wiser regarding a cure. She found herself nodding off despite her best intentions, and she ended up falling asleep at the table she had been working at. Suddenly, she was woken by a rap at the chamber door. When she bade the knocker enter, Lady Almwick came into the room, her face full mischievous delight. Strolling over to her daughter, she asked, "How goes your search?" When Liliana responded that she had unfortunately made little progress, her mother said, "Well, it's lucky for you that I've come up with a means of solving your problem."

"You have?" Liliana perked. "Then please, do tell me it, Mother!"

Lady Almwick bent down to whisper in her daughter's ear. "I know the perfect way for you to regain your memories: by having them related by the one who experienced them alongside you."

"What are you going on about, Mother? You know I cannot..." Liliana trailed off as she noticed who stood in the doorway. "Juliane? Is it truly you?"

"I think so," said Juliane. "Then again, I've learned one can never be too sure about these things."

They stared at each other for a moment, then rushed forward and threw their arms around one another. "I'll give you some privacy," said Lady Almwick, winking, and she stepped out of the room, closing the door softly behind her.

Liliana tilted her head back to peer at Juliane. "I cannot believe you're here! Why haven't you changed like you were expected to?"

Juliane said shyly, "Remember how your mother told me the spell would cause me to take on my 'true form'? Well, I guess this is mine. I've discovered I'm meant to be a woman, Liliana."

"Oh, Juliane, it doesn't matter who you are, I'm just so glad to see you. But, does your father know you're here?"

"He does. He wasn't happy about it, but he's accepted that I'm in control of my own destiny. Speaking of which— I've decided that I do not wish to remain a princess, because I'd rather spend the rest of my life exploring the world...with you. How do you feel about this? Are you...open to it?"

Liliana grinned. "I suppose we *could* give it a try, Juliane. There are many lands neither of us has seen yet—

perhaps you might accompany me in visiting them?"

"It would be my pleasure," said Juliane, then she looked into Liliana's eyes. "Liliana Almwick, I love you. I'm hopelessly in love with you. I think you already know that, but I wanted to tell you nonetheless."

"You're right, Juliane, I do know it, but it feels good to hear it nonetheless," Liliana replied affectionately. "I love you as well, Juliane Stoneshire, and I'm looking forward to seeing how our love grows as the years pass."

Their lips came together in a kiss that both had been anticipating, but Liliana soon broke it, for a roguish look had crossed her face. "Juliane, this is your first time inside my home, so I suppose I should give you a tour. Shall we start with...my bedroom?"

"I should like nothing better. Please lead the way!" declared Juliane, and so the pair clasped hands and, giggling, absconded to the aforementioned chamber.